How to Kill your Husband

How to Kill your Husband

(and other handy household hints)

Kathy Lette

W F HOWES LTD

This large print edition published in 2009 by
W F Howes Ltd
Unit 4, Rearsby Business Park, Gaddesby Lane,
Rearsby, Leicester LE7 4YH

1 3 5 7 9 10 8 6 4 2

First published in the United Kingdom in 2006
by Simon & Schuster

A CIP catalogue record for this book is available
from the British Library

ISBN 978 1 40743 172 7

Typeset by Palimpsest Book Production Limited,
Grangemouth, Stirlingshire
Printed and bound in Great Britain
by MPG Books Ltd, Bodmin, Cornwall

To my mum and dad who are celebrating their 50th wedding anniversary this year, proving that a good marriage lasts forever, while a bad one just seems to.

CONTENTS

PART I

CHAPTER 1

THE MERRY WIDOW

I was a forty-three-year-old mother of two when I lost my orgasm. How can you lose an orgasm, you may ask. What is it, a *sock*? Is it in some sexual laundry basket waiting to be paired so it can become a multiple orgasm? People often lose things. Their tempers. Their sense of humour. Their figures. (Do the words 'control top panty hose' mean anything to you?) Their minds. (Post babies, *definitely*.) But not their orgasm. I just couldn't find it. It was more elusive than Peter Pan's shadow. Believe me, I looked for it harder than they looked for the Bermuda Triangle, Amelia Earhart, the Yeti, the *Marie Celeste*, the Loch Ness Monster and the scruples of George Bush.

Perhaps you think that I, Cassie O'Carroll, am the kind of idiot who always misplaces things? It is true to say that I can't find the square root of the hypotenuse either, but that doesn't make me gnaw holes in my pillow and cry myself to sleep at night.

No. My poor muff's in a huff. My pussy left high and dry: positively Miss Havishamed. And

3

there doesn't seem to be a goddamn thing I can do about it.

Mind you, my best friend, Jazz, has lost something much more serious – her husband, the internationally famous surgeon, humanitarian and World Health Organisation expert, Dr David Studlands. And under rather suspicious circumstances too. In fact, as I write this, Jazz is being held on suspicion of murder. Which is where this story begins really, in the visiting room of Holloway Prison for women in North London.

'I've been arrested for killing my husband,' were not words I'd ever expected to hear from the mouth of Jasmine Jardine. 'I'm having George Clooney's lovechild,' perhaps, or, 'What if PMT is a myth and I'm just a bitch?' But definitely not this.

When I can finally talk, I feel I'm dubbing a film. '*What*?'

'Murder . . . Those moronic cops think I've killed Studz. I've been denied bail!'

'MURDER?' I dub again. And there is a made-for-TV movie melodrama to it all. I'm sitting bolt upright in a straight-backed chair in a prison visiting room, staring in a state of gormless astonishment at my best friend. I must have shrieked the last word because the eyes of the prison officer dart over at me, alert but neutral, like the eyes of an over-fed predator, too lazy to pounce. The screw remains slumped in her swivel chair, flicking her newspaper, surly but apathetic.

Fright licks like flames all over me. 'Fuck-a-duck, Jazz.' I'm whispering now, but it still sounds piercing. 'You . . . didn't do anything stupid, did you?'

Jazz gives me the kind of look you'd give a sewage truck which has just backed over your groom on your wedding day. 'You may not have noticed in all the years you've known me, Cassandra, but I seem to be lacking many of the key talents necessary for success as a criminal mastermind.' There's an edge of hysteria in her voice which attracts the prison officer once more. The chair wheezes as she shifts her bulk to pivot our way. 'How could you even think that?'

'Well, excuse *me*,' I reply in a scalding whisper. 'How many times have I heard you make cracks along those lines? That 'marriage is a fun-packed, frivolous hobby, only occasionally resulting in death,' or 'Where there's a will, I intend being in it,' or that 'Not all men are bastards – some of them are dead.' And what about the time you 'accidentally' picked up the wrong malaria tablets for Studz's Amnesty trip to Malawi? You started cooking with full cream to induce a heart attack, for God's sake! I mean, Jeez . . .'

'I was just letting off steam! All women want to kill their husbands some of the time. But joking around doesn't mean I have a licence to kill . . . Good God, I don't even have a learner's permit.'

5

The prison officer snorts. 'Not what the papers say, chuck.' She tosses a pile of tatty rags down between us and, despite the No Smoking sign, lights up a fag.

'The papers? You're in the newspapers?' It's eight in the morning and I have pillow creases on my face, having jumped up from bed and rung a cab the second I got Jasmine's call. I'm still reeling at hearing from my oldest friend. It's been over two months since we've spoken – since she detonated a grenade in my life, to be precise. We'd all read, of course, of Dr David Studlands's disappearance three weeks earlier in South Australia from a place called, ominously, Termination Beach, Cape Catastrophe. (Now *that's* the place to book a holiday.) We'd seen Jazz in tears on television. I'd tried desperately to reach her, but she hadn't answered any of my calls. Until the frantic summons this morning, her disappearance from my life had been as abrupt and bewildering as her husband's.

She flicks the newspapers across the scratched laminate table as though they're radioactive. *Widow Too Merry?* questions yesterday's tabloid above an old photo of Jazz quaffing champagne, to illustrate a report that she was helping police with their enquiries.

'That was taken years ago.' Jazz sighs so loudly I mistake it for an asthma attack. 'Truth is, David and I were trying to get our marriage back together. That's why we went on holiday to

Australia – for the sun, surf, sand, sex. But you know what a tremendous risk-taker Studz is – night scuba-diving, helicopter skiing, driving too fast, going into war zones for Médecins Sans Frontieres . . . Late that afternoon, we were skin-diving. I got tired and swam in, but David snorkelled out beyond the headland. When it started to get dark, I went to look for him. I found his clothes and watch on the beach, where he'd left them. Then I knew something was really wrong.' She wipes away a tear and takes a moment to compose herself.

'We got boats and searched all night,' she goes on. 'People tried to be kind. They kept saying, "You mustn't give up hope." So I clung on, which was worse in a way, because I imagined him like a lost child, hurt and alone. For days I grabbed at theories – that he was working for the CIA and had gone undercover; an insurance scam; kidnap by submarine even! I went around in a daze, completely empty inside. Josh says the truth's staring us in the face – that his dad was swept out to sea. Or worse.' She shudders. 'But I refuse to believe it. I won't believe it.' She slumps forward.

As I wait for her to recover, I take in my friend's thick, straight eyebrows framing sea-green eyes with lashes long enough to hike through, her ripe lips, chiselled cheekbones and golden hair – and marvel for the millionth time how her profile, so delicate it belongs in a Botticelli painting, could be so at odds with her smile, which suggests the possibility of anonymous sex in a dark doorway. And then there's her chin, which juts forward slightly as if to say, 'You and whose army?'

'Jazz . . .' At the sound of my voice she glances up at me with no recognition at all. 'Then why have they arrested you?'

She snaps back to life with alacrity. 'Remember Billy – that prison playwright I had a fling with? Well, he's claiming to the police that I hired him as a hitman. *Moi*! Can you believe that?'

'What the hell else did you expect, dating a criminal? Men like that write ransom notes, not thank you notes. What on earth did you see in him anyway?'

She looks at me sadly. 'Oh, Cass. How long had it been since my husband had made love to me? You know what it's like when you're on a diet and even a rice cake looks delicious? Well, Billy and the other men, that's what they were like. Sexual rice cakes.'

'Your boyfriend's gone an' got 'imself banged up,' the eavesdropping prison officer puts in, uninvited, 'for welfare fraud. An' he's plea-bargainin'. Which is why the beak's refusin' bail.'

'Is that true, Jazz?'

'Basically, yes,' she concedes. 'The man's an evil, lying, Olympic-standard scumbag . . . but of course I wish him only the best.'

The enormity of the situation punches into me hard. I've been following Jazz's escapades at a nervous distance for decades, but this latest scenario has me terrified. We are middle-class women in our forties. We wax our bikini lines and shave our Parmesan. We leave notes under the windscreens of cars we've bumped. Our record collections are classical not criminal. Jazz has the sort of face which you instantly associate with the comment, 'I'd like to travel, meet interesting people and help bring about world peace.' Not the sort of face you'd see on a mug shot.

'Bloody hell, Jazz,' I say. 'What are you going to do?'

'Oh, fake my own death, take a new identity and go and live in a tree with Lord Lucan *obviously*.' Rage bubbles up out of her. 'Life begins at forty, not Life Imprisonment for Killing Your Hubby. What I'm going to do is fight. And until Studz turns up, *you* are my best weapon, Cassandra O'Carroll.'

'Meee?' Jazz's clipped English vowels make my own Antipodean accent ring coarse and trailer-trashy by comparison.

'This,' she gestures indignantly at the papers, 'is character assassination. Now, who knows me best? You, that's who. We've been bosom buddies ever since college. Literally. We bought our first naughty bras together – lacy and racy, with tassels, do you remember? I want you to talk to my solicitor, Cass. I want you to tell her every-thing. Okay, Studz betrayed me. He drove me insane. And yes, at times I felt like killing him . . . But he's the father of my only child. How could

9

anyone think I would want Josh to be fatherless? What kind of a woman would do that?'

A betrayed, broken-hearted, sexually famished woman, I want to say, but don't. In fact, looking at her, all dishevelled, her silken blonde hair tangled and fly away, her cashmere jumper coming unstitched on the shoulder, I feel a knot in my heart. A knot of affection, despite all the things she's done to me this last year. The prison smells of old cigarette smoke and the worn intimacy of cloth too long against flesh. The odour is only made worse by the overlay of antiseptic, seeping up from the linoleum floors. There are no windows. The room sets me on edge, like a dentist's waiting room, or the room where you wait before a job interview – for a job you don't want.

I lean across the rickety table and take her hand. 'What do you want me to do, love?'

There's a shrill shriek of an electric bell. I jump. The prison officer ignores it at first, too enthralled in counting her own dandruff flakes, then she begrudgingly stubs out her cigarette before heaving her grey bulk upwards.

'But,' I look at my watch, scandalized, 'I'm supposed to have another half an hour.'

'Welcome to the wonderful world of Law Enforcement,' Jazz utters sarcastically, passing me my coat. I think she's going to help me on with it, but she seizes my arm instead. 'Cassie.' Her voice is small and terrified. 'I'm being framed.

10

You have got to help me. My solicitor rejoices in the name of Quincy Joy.' She crumples a scrawled address into my hand. 'Her euphoria comes no doubt from the fact that she is not the one up before the Judge like the thousands of poor saps she represents . . . You must tell her everything. Explain things to her. You know – why I behaved the way I did. How things got so Kafka-esque.'

Wake up and smell the Kafka, I would have said in days gone by, but now just stand there numbly as my best friend of twenty-five years is led to her cell. The last thing I hear her say to the prison wardress is, 'You can't stripsearch me on a first date, sweetie. I definitely need dinner and a movie first.'

Dazed, I trudge out into the wintry light. The chill January air nips at my face, and the brick walls of the prison cast long shadows which fall over me like a trap. Free from Persephone's Holloway underworld, I gulp fresh oxygen and dart over Camden Road to hail a taxi as though fleeing back across the River Styx.

By the time the cab pulls up at the Inner Temple, a cobbled Dickensian lawyers' enclave by the River Thames, my fine legal brain is saying, Fucking hell! Jazz may have trained as a chef, but only lobster should be in water this hot.

Quincy Joy's office is furnished with ornate, bow-legged antiques which give the room a

11

ponderous feel. She is blowing on a cup of scalding tea as I enter and introduce myself.

'I've applied for a bail re-hearing.' Her two-pack-a-day voice is languid with tiredness. 'The first magistrate weighed up your friend Jasmine's propensity for sarcasm in one hand and his loathing of me in the other, exactly like a man who is holding your tits. Then he squeezed both. Hard.'

Quincy has red hair, a face constellationed with freckles, and not just bags but baggage beneath her eyes.

'Can they try someone for murder,' I ask, bewildered, 'without a body?'

'Yep, if there's reasonable doubt. Corpus Christi, it's called. There is some rather nasty circumstantial evidence against her. How on earth did a classy woman like Jasmine Jardine ever get involved with a convicted murderer? And what was he doing in Australia? She assures me that you can tell the whole story objectively.' The woman drums her fingers on the desk impatiently.

'Me?' I sit down on the edge of a wrinkled leather chair, facing a painting of two dead ducks and an Irish setter. How to tell the tale in all its complexity? The story of a tripartite friendship: Jazz, the stay-at-home domestic goddess. (To me, any woman who says she gets high on house-work has inhaled way too much cleaning fluid.) Hannah, the childless career woman with a couple of venture capital portfolios tucked up each sleeve and her own art gallery, and me, the primary-school-teaching kid-and-career juggler, who keeps dropping everything.

'Three is a difficult number, don't you think, Quincy? And three women friends is a particularly difficult equation. Especially when you throw love, sex, kids and toy boys into the mix . . . Crikey. I don't know where to start.'

'Just give me a verbal mug shot of you all,' Quincy says hastily, flinching from her scorching cuppa.

Yes, and then she can wrap us up in Crime Scene Tape and bring on forensic teams to piece together the evidence of our felony – which was to fall out as friends.

'Since teacher-training college, Jazz, Hannah and I have been part of a kind of girl minestrone, sharing secrets, reporting arguments with our husbands . . . and then arguing about why we argued with them – and about why the secret of a happy marriage *is* such a well-kept bloody secret! That's how we would have gone on for ever, if it hadn't been for a party we all attended at Jasmine's a year ago. That's when each of our worlds began to fall apart.'

Quincy glances at her watch, then jerks to her feet. 'Look, I've got an urgent submission to get in,' she rasps, in a voice that is one pack short of lung cancer. 'Why don't you write it all down?' She prods a yellow notepad across the blotting-papered desktop. 'And phone me when you're done. That might be easier.'

Easier? I don't think she realizes the emotional roller-coaster I'm about to take her on. The woman needs an official warning not to strap herself in if she has neck problems or is pregnant. What I want to say is, 'This is a bumpy ride. For safety reasons, please keep all arms and legs within the speeding vehicle.'

Instead, I pick up the yellow paper.

I'm supposed to spend the day correcting Year 6 exercises on grammar.

Question: What comes at the end of a sentence?

Answer: Life imprisonment for murder.

CHAPTER 2

HOW DO I HATE THEE? LET ME COUNT THE WAYS

All husbands think they're gods. If only their wives weren't atheists . . .

During my twenties I thought I'd developed tinnitus, but it was just the endless ringing of wedding bells as all my friends got hitched. I married Rory, a vet, which is ironic as I've never been much of an animal person – possibly because I teach them all day. (Little bit of pathetic staff room humour there.) To me, animals are at their best on a barbecue. I especially hate dogs. Dogs have far too many teeth for a supposedly friendly nature. If I *had* to have a pet it would be a crocodile – so it could eat all the others.

And it's not just our four-legged friends I loathe. I'm paranoid about all creatures, two-legged, one-legged, eight-legged. Each night before getting into bed, I check my sheets for scorpions – *in England.*

You may think you like animals, but believe me, if you were married to a vet you'd soon be cured. At any one time we have seven or eight dogs in the house, the same number of cats and a lot of mice which *aren't* pets. When I was pregnant, Rory told people that I was 'whelping'. Quite often he absentmindedly scratches me behind the ear and says, 'Good girl.' Pretty soon he'll start throwing me a tennis ball to chew on.

If I had to imagine Rory as an animal, he'd be a Labrador – faithful and fun. I met him when he was dangling from the minute hand of the clock tower at college, which he'd climbed whilst inebriated, just so he could use the pick-up line, 'Do you have the time?' Rory is an outdoorsman. He has thighs the width of two seven-year-old kids put together and biceps the size of a guest bathroom. He's built for outward-bound survival quests. A born frontiersman, he could ford a mighty river, scale a snow-capped mountain, fell a redwood forest, build a ranch house and have 'vittels' simmering in a pot – and all before I could say, 'Who wants to eat at McDonald's?'

For me, the Great Outdoors is the bit between Bond Street tube station and the front door of Selfridges. I grew up in Sydney (my parents moved here when I was sixteen). The only geography I have of London is how to get to Harrods then home again. When friends ask me to their country retreats in say, Scotland, their directions consist of, 'Go to Harvey Nichols and turn right.'

I married Rory because he made me laugh.

The first time he took me to meet his mum in Cricklewood, he referred to the phenomenon of a son having lunch with his mother as the 'edible complex'. The aquamarine eyes and the tawny curls springing out of his cranium in all directions kinda helped too. As did the way his face is lit up by that ready smile, which renders him instantly likeable. I also adore the way he cocks his elbow onto the window ledge of his car whilst whistling a tune. Oh, and his compassion. Even back then he was devoting half his time to voluntary work in homeless animal shelters. And nothing much has changed. He now has his own veterinary clinic adjoining our house in Kilburn, but does a lot of work for free.

Still, we are – or we were then – allies, spun together like silkworms. My love has always covered him, like treacle. And when he looks at me, a fondness spills and ripples over his face in a way that has always set my nipples on fire. After fifteen years of marriage, I'm far from oblivious to his downsides. He wears a battered leather jacket in all weathers, and owns the largest collection of T-shirts in the Western world. Formal wear for Rory consists of an *ironed* T-shirt. Even worse, he doesn't like my friends. He says that London dinner parties account for three-quarters of the world supply of Condescension. He attends Jazz and Hannah's social gatherings under duress, slumps in a corner and says nothing. 'Oh, that's your husband? I thought he was a bookend.' Which is why he didn't want us to go to Jazz and Studz's twentieth wedding anniversary party last January. If only I'd listened to him . . .

★　　★　　★

17

It was meant to be a quiet celebratory dinner, with their oldest friends from university. But thanks to Studz's inability to separate work from pleasure, the whole thing had become bigger than Dolly Parton's hair.

Jazz married David Studlands while he was a young houseman on a surgical team at a big teaching hospital in Cambridge. She fell for him the first day they met. 'He's gorgeous,' Jazz told me. 'I just want to pop him on a canapé and eat him whole.' Jazz, who graduated as a Home Economics teacher, supported him while he climbed the hospital ladder, by cooking in restaurants. Studz is now so wealthy he has a walk-in wallet and drives a rhymes-with-banker Jaguar, which he parks outside his private clinic in Harley Street. The man is not only handsome but so tall he has to radio down to us mere mortals below to see what the weather is like at street-level.

Even nearing fifty, Studz's body has remained slimmed and gymmed. He has a profile so sharp you could shave your legs with it and an equally cutting tongue. His style is mocking, although he mainly mocks himself – but in a way which only amplifies his charms. As a top surgeon in re-construction and burns repairs, Studz gets his academic kudos by working in an NHS teaching hospital as a consultant. The family's luxurious lifestyle is financed by his private practice in cosmetic surgery. ('You're a neurotic time-wasting

18

narcissist. However, if you want to consult me privately, just lie back and open your chequebook wide.')

To absolve his conscience for operating on people who don't need it, Studz regularly takes unpaid leave to work on medical ships which sail around Africa, providing free surgical treatment to war victims. He talent-scouts doctors for aid organizations and is famous for advising his junior registrars to do six months' volunteer work with Médecins Sans Frontières for the sake of their souls. He also donates his time to the Medical Foundation for the Care of Victims of War and is an expert adviser to the World Health Organisation. Yep, the man has already been summoned to Buckingham Palace for a halo fitting. And it was in honour of this altruistic part of his nature that Jasmine Jardine, our very own scintillating and saucy It Girl on campus, carved his name into her headboard.

Jazz had actually wanted to cancel the wedding anniversary party, as her mother had died, after a protracted battle with breast cancer, just before Christmas. However, Studz had insisted the celebration go ahead. Hannah and I hoped that this bash would be our friend's passport out of her state of grief. To achieve this, it was our job to make sure there was no mention of the dreaded 'C' word.

It was 8 p.m. and I was running late. Hannah had ordered me to look chic – which for me means employing a special effects movie stunt team, since the dress code for female teachers, in case you hadn't noticed, is flat shoes and 'interesting' earrings. My shambolic clothes are usually missing buttons, always trailing hems, and are often Rory's. I base my daily fashion sense on what doesn't need ironing. Jasmine has looks which turn heads. Mine turns stomachs. You think I'm exaggerating? Lately I've taken to wearing shell suits – and not because I like to put them to my ear to listen for the Atlantic, either.

When we met, Jazz used to say that I was the classic 'girl next door' – attractive enough to be special, but not pretty enough to be hated by other women. However, I didn't care if I was pretty or not because, meeting Rory, I was beautiful at last. Nearly two decades later, I would have to say that I still look good from a distance . . . a distance of, say, 200 miles. So what happened?

Motherhood, that's what. As a girl, I hated exposing my scrawny limbs. The day I got married I weighed seven and a half stone. A few years later I was in Top Shop, hyperventilating as I tried to pull a pair of size 10 jeans up over my hips. I looked in the mirror and there was my mother – all small boobs and big bum.

When did I pass nine stone? I'd meant to go to the gym after the baby was born, but who would look after him? Being at home so much in my pyjamas meant that pretty soon I was pregnant again. Now that my kids Jenny, eleven and Jamie, thirteen, are older I *could* go to the gym but, as a working mum, it's amazing that I have the energy to turn on the microwave to defrost the store-bought dinner. And kids are so calorific. As you cook their tea, leftovers just get hoovered up into your mouth – sausages drenched in ketchup, buttery mashed potatoes, ice cream left melting in bowls, all so sensationally slimming. Well, you can't waste it, can you? So you store it on your waist. Luckily I adore my mother, which is fortunate, seeing as I've become her!

When I was finally ready to go to the party, dressed in an M&S pre-baby trouser suit, with the trousers pinned together beneath the long-ish jacket, I noticed that my hair was moving. It seemed to be waving at me from the mirror. Oh God. Nits. An occupational hazard of teaching in a primary school. My choices were to run through the streets ringing a bell, shouting, 'Unclean! Unclean!' and perhaps painting a big X on the door, or, a less Dickensian option, to Chernobyl my scalp with chemicals. Which I did. The only way a nit could survive in there now was in a flame-retardant wetsuit and an aqualung. I was no longer contagious, but I don't think 'chic' quite covered it.

As Rory angled his beaten-up Jeep, reeking of dog piss and guinea pig poo, into an illegal parking spot half on the pavement outside Jazz and David's Georgian Hampstead home, I looked through the bay windows and could see all sorts of chic people who didn't have nits, boiling around the drawing room. We could hear the jumbled roar of their exclusive badinage, punctuated by men laughing smuttily. My husband did his Lamb-to-the-Slaughter look.

'Shit. Jazz and Studz have become the Edmund Hillarys of social climbing. You know I have no head for heights, Cassie. We'd better rope ourselves together in case one of us falls.'

Jazz and Studz were what the papers called a 'power couple'. They were plugged into the right social socket. Although it was mid-January, the Prime Minister's personal Christmas card would still be up on the mantelpiece, next to one from Kofi Annan and, no doubt, Nelson Mandela. The most chichi card on *my* mantelpiece, came from the local dry cleaners to thank me for my custom.

Champagne flûte in hand, Hannah Wolfe answered the door. A quicksilver woman with dark, glassy eyes like those of a doll, she has a soft knob of a nose, a red helmet of hair, eyebrows plucked into two sceptical arches, a granulated voice and opinions as strong as her trademark espressos. She speaks three languages in the same rapid-fire South African Jewish accent and has an endearing bark of a laugh. Hannah is approaching forty, but from the wrong direction. The woman isn't getting older . . . What she's getting is injected twice a week with collagen and smeared in foetal lamb membranes.

With her duck-like deportment, hyper-arched back and flattened chest, it's obvious that Hannah had been tortured in tutus by her mother from a very young age.

Having given up teaching art in a comprehensive and moved into interior design before it was fashionable, Hannah is credited with bringing feng shui (like chop suey, only not as tasty) to the West. In the early days she was compared to Martha Stewart, but insists that she was a rotten, two-faced bitch YEARS before Martha came on the scene. I adore Hannah, despite her grating, 'Let's get on with it, already!' approach. Ms Wolfe always knows exactly which beaded pashmina or faux-chinchilla throw will be this year's 'must have' accessory. This Design Diva could wear a tarpaulin cleverly draped so as to look like a ballgown and get away with it. Every time Hannah sees me in saggy leggings or ink-stained jeans, she adopts the sort of pained expression which makes me think she's trying to suck her face out through the back of her skull.

After making her first fortune advising heiresses on whether to paint their houses peach or pistachio, Hannah decided she no longer wanted to 'accept any employment which might interfere with my nails, dah-ling'. Shortly afterwards, she opened her own art gallery in Old Bond Street, and made her second fortune.

This world of spin and spittle provided her with a house in Regents Park so big there's a toilet for every occasion, and a marriage proposal from Pascal.

When I first met Hannah at teacher training

college, she prided herself on only ever dating men whose professions began with P. There was a Polar explorer, a poet, a pornographer, a pianist, a philanthropist, a political dissident and then finally a painter. Well, Pascal *called* himself a painter. Jazz and I saw him more as a lapsed Satanist.

With his dark good looks, insolent pout, lazily half-closed lids and Medusa dreadlocks aureoling his head, Pascal was the hot-to-trot Love God of Art School. Let's face it, 'My name is Pascal Swan. And yes, I mate for life,' is a pretty persuasive pick-up line. And it seemed to be true. Even if his hair hadn't lasted, their marriage had.

While Hannah is ever-optimistic, Pascal sees the bad side of everything. If he had his way he'd be skywriting *There is no such thing as Santa!* over EuroDisney.

Although we hated the way he sponged off Hannah (when Pascal put his arm around his bride at the wedding, Jasmine whispered, 'Wouldn't it look more natural with his hand in her purse?') and even though we got Rory and David to tell him on his stag night that the marriage was not going to work unless *he* did, what we really resented was the deal he'd struck. He would only marry Hannah if they never had kids, or 'ruggis ratti' as he called them.

Whenever Jazz and I complained about our children, Hannah would do a little jig. 'I'm celebrating National Childless Day, dah-lings. I'm dancing and leaping to celebrate my infertility!'

24

In short, she brought home the bacon – but not to go with eggs.

Standing now on Jasmine's threshold, Hannah shook her head in disbelief at the sight of me, silver earrings jangling jauntily from the four holes in her chic little earlobes.

'What? You're trying to sell me a used car?' She pointed at my slicked-back hair. Hannah is the most disloyal person I've ever met. That's what makes her such fun.

'It's nit napalm. I have to leave it in for twelve to sixteen hours. Who's here?' Shedding my coat, I watched Rory retreat at speed to the kitchen, mumbling about checking on the family's animals – even though I knew that the only animal Jazz had allowed her son Josh was a pet *rock*.

'Oh, the Good and the Great. A few Prime Ministers from Third World fledgling democracies,' Hannah sighed, 'a couple of Nobel Prize winners, the World's Greatest Living Playwright . . .'

'Oh fab. The Cultural Commissars. Is Jazz at least enjoying herself?'

'Well, nobody's mentioned the C word. They're all besotted with that pop star the United Nations has just appointed as a Good Will Ambassador – at least, I think she's a pop star. With a name like Kinkee she could also be a hooker. She's American, blonde, and you can still see the price tag on her store-bought boobs. Says she's moving into acting, dah-ling. No doubt as Paris Hilton's pussy double.'

25

I laughed. 'Oh, the Parma Syndrome, huh? Thin and hammy. Christ!' I caught sight of my Al Capone hairstyle in the hallway mirror. I looked underdressed without a sub-machine gun. 'I can't go in looking like *this*.'

But like a sky-diving instructor with a reluctant recruit, Hannah had already shoved me through the drawing-room door. And there was Jazz, all laughing eyes, luscious breasts, honeyed hair and velvet glances, coiffured and sublime in a colourful silk cocktail frock, smiling at me quizzically as I parachuted in.

I kissed her hello. 'You look like a holiday. I want to go on you.'

She held me at arm's length whilst scrutinizing my nit napalm. 'Nits? Just pretend you're into tits and clits,' she suggested. 'Then everyone will just presume that you've slicked it back because of the lesbian chic look.'

But there was no need to turn the other chic because all eyes were on the Pop Princess. In her mid-twenties, with lacquered lips, conical breasts and the obligatory flawless dentition, she was cadaverously pale and, like a jockey, way under her normal weight. All the better for riding, I supposed. What can I tell you? The girl was born to limo. This gym junkie was so determined to show off her time in the ab lab, she was only wearing a boob tube and matching hot pants made from mesh. The woman was so vain she'd no doubt installed a follow spotlight in her bedroom.

Despite the hours we girls had dedicated to looking good, the men were not even aware there were other women within a ten-mile radius. With a Pop Princess present, we were ranked somewhere below lesser invertebrates. As Kinkee jabbered on inanely about Kabbalah and hot-cupping, London's male so-called intelligentsia hee-hawed appreciatively.

To my alarm, the Pop Princess suddenly broke off and shimmied towards me. A feather boa coiled and writhed like an exotic snake around her snowy neck. 'Wow! Lesbian chic. I like it.' The boa jerked as though really alive. 'Bi-polar, bi-coastal, bi-sexual. Everything is bi, bi, bi right now. I've been thinking a little lesbo action could broaden my career options, ja know?'

The geriatric males, who all had high hopes of turning up sometime in the future on a postage stamp, turned their droopy eyes in my direction. As the centre of their fleeting attention, I tried a simulation of coquetry by giggling and hair-flicking. Only trouble was, I'd forgotten that I was infested so accidentally sent a plague of dead and dying lice into the atmosphere. Perhaps she'd like to come up and see my itchings? It was a bad pun I'd save for Jazz, who'd love it. 'Well, actually it's nit lotion,' I confessed.

This spokeswoman for vermin-afflicted children in the Third World gagged, shrieked and then ricocheted across the room at the speed of light. The United Nations had obviously selected her for her survival skills. Couldn't wait to see how she was going to endure those field trips to the Congo.

Jazz rode to my social rescue with a call to dinner, and even though Studz had not yet arrived, we filed into the ornate dining room where the elite male intellectuals jockeyed for position next to the Pop Princess. As we devoured the eggplant soup and pimento coulis, the human rights lawyer once imprisoned in Burma, the journalist from Chile who'd written about his torture, and the poet still living under a Fatwa all began to compete to see who had been the most heroic and self-sacrificing, who had received the most death threats. 'The reward for sticking one's head above the political parapet,' sighed the Pulitzer-winning journalist. It was the intellectual version of comparing penis sizes. Basically these pacifists would have *killed* for a Nobel Peace Prize.

I myself had never got close to active combat, unless you counted the supermarket check-out queue. How inadequate not to be on a hit list, or to have my phone tapped. Mind you, if I want terror I just attend my son's parent-teacher night.

Oblivious to the men's posturing, the Pop Princess jabbered on about tofu face creams, while we wives rolled our eyes, sharing a silent laugh at the girl's inanity and the men's vanity.

Jazz, the hands-on-hostess, was carting platters of vegetables to the table. She paused by my chair as a mildewed political activist talked of his brutal imprisonment in South Africa. 'Truth be known,' she murmured in my ear, 'his only experience of real pain was when a BBC interviewer asked him if he was tortured by the guilt of inherited wealth.'

I glanced in his direction. Not only was this Oxford Mandarin an antediluvian, but he had the kind of face which would frighten a gargoyle. 'Don't mock. Some day his looks will go,' I whispered back to Jazz.

Giggles were rising up in us like champagne bubbles. Men are so egotistical they never think they're too old for a girl – not even when they lose their dentures during oral sex.

The lawyers, heads down, chins tucked into their other chins, were now competing to see who did the most *pro bono* work. Jazz confided to me that she was only pro Bono if he was headlining a concert. It was like watching a room of flat-chested women fighting over a 36C cup bra.

Hannah, Jazz and I were crossing our legs and biting our lips to contain our glee. Good girl-friends have an emotional patois only they can understand. We can speak fluently to each other without using words. I was just pondering how much easier it would be if men had antlers (perhaps then they would at least stop driving those stupid cars), when David Studlands swept into the room and eclipsed every one of them.

The all-over tan, the tailored teeth, the coronet of luxuriant greying hair, his bouffant was so distinguished there was talk of giving it its own knighthood, the freshly laundered silk shirts and racy Paul Smith cufflinks – he commanded respect. When Jazz rose to greet her husband, the air around her lit up with love.

'Sorry I'm late,' he said briskly. 'Urgent meeting with the PM on our AIDS funding in Uganda.' Studz was so in demand, so over-scheduled, so heroic – always coming straight from scaling the cliff-face of fundraising for torture victims or something equally important – that he was also invariably forgiven, fussed over, indulged.

Studz flashed his dashing smile – the smile of a gambler who only plays for dangerously high stakes. When he spoke, the room became illuminated by his eloquence. As he expounded on his latest project in the Sudan, praising the Pop Princess for her contribution to the health of underprivileged children, with amusing little asides and witty, self-deprecating remarks, managing to flatter every single person present by referring fleetingly to their own unique and selfless qualities, Jazz just smiled fondly and went to the kitchen to fetch the main course.

A steaming vat of her famous osso bucco appeared, complemented by leeks and red beet essence. As the guests marvelled greedily, Jazz started to relax. It was the first time I'd seen her laughing and joking since her mother died. And there was still no mention of the dreaded C word. I was just breathing a sigh of relief when the Pop Princess bayoneted a piece of veal on her fork and held it aloft as though it were a medical experiment gone wrong.

'I doan eat meat. It gives ya colon cancer, yer know,' she drawled.

Jazz jumped as if something had bitten her. Hannah and I locked eyes in dismay. I thought now would be a good time for Rory to hold forth on the mating habits of the Giant Squid, but it was a difficult concept to communicate to him using only sign language.

'Have some wine,' Hannah offered in an effort to derail the Pop Princess. The smiles of the other guests, aware that Jazz had just lost her mother to cancer, seemed spackled on as we all telepathically begged her to shut the hell up.

'Them preservatives they use in wine are carcinogenic too,' Kinkee lectured. Perhaps it was an opportune moment to tell her that she'd left the price tag on her tits.

The skin on Jasmine's smooth cheek tic-ed. All night there'd been an ocean of chatter, eddying around the table, but we were now conversationally becalmed. The dinner party suddenly seemed to have been going on longer than the war in Iraq – and we were only on the main course.

'Worrying will give you wrinkles,' I cajoled, but the Pop Princess shot me a censorious look.

'You should be like really, really, really like worried. I mean, what's that shit in your hair? Chemicals?'

'Sure is. You could nuke al Qaeda terrorist cells with this stuff.'

'Ohmygod. That will *definitely* give you cancer.'

Jasmine's eyebrows quirked as though she were about to cry.

The screech of Rory's mobile relieved the suffocating silence. No doubt some hamster-related emergency.

'Oh, you use a cellphone? *I* don't,' said the actress self-righteously as my husband rushed off to assist some lemming to suicide or something equally 'urgent'. 'Not any more, anyways. Because—'

'Yes, yes, it's carcinogenic,' snapped Hannah.

'I think too much, doan I? That's my trouble,' the Pop Princess giggled.

The men nodded in eager agreement. Could have fooled me. I would have guessed that her ambition was to be a contestant on *Big Brother* – only she didn't have the IQ.

As the Pop Princess rabbited on about the cancerous tumours caused by mobile-phone masts, Jazz kept looking at her lap. And Hannah kept gesturing helplessly at me, to which I responded with my own social SOS hand signals. There was so much semaphore going on around that table we could have landed an aeroplane.

What topic could I raise that would divert her? I racked my brain. A barbed comment utilizing the F word would cover things nicely. What did people normally talk about at London dinner parties? School league tables, foreign policy, remortgaging. The one time I actually wanted them to discuss how much they'd paid for their houses and how much more they're worth today, what did I get? Nothing. What suitable subject-matter would interest a Californian pop star? Then I hit upon the foolproof small-talk safety net. 'I know – what's your star sign?' I asked enthusiastically.

The entire table of guests looked at the Pop Princess in eager anticipation.

'Cancer,' she replied.

With that, Hannah, Jasmine and I were up out of our seats, dashing to the kitchen on the pretext of culinary duties. Once there, we exploded into helpless laughter. We fuelled our hysteria with comments about ending world hunger by eating more pop princesses and references to genetically modified vegetables i.e. aged male intellectuals. By now we were rolling around on the floor as only old friends can. I laughed so hard I had to take off my jacket, exposing the big silver safety pin securing my trousers, which only made us howl more.

The hilarity subsided slightly when Hannah announced that she'd laughed so hard she now had a headache. Jazz tripped upstairs for Panadol. 'I'm sure David's got some in his bathroom,' she said, still chuckling. 'He is a doctor, after all.'

While Jazz was rummaging in her husband's bathroom cabinet, I examined her kitchen. The Le Creuset, the whole range, matched the aubergine-tiled splashback. On the walls, around the Bang & Olufsen plasma television screen, were tasteful black and white photos of their working holidays in Namibia and Sri Lanka. With her Neff stainless steel double oven, Miele fridge, cappuccino machine and breadmaker, everything was *Vogue Perfect Living*. Flowers in coronets of tissue paper lay on the counter waiting for vases. I thought of my own kitchen – the bowls of leftovers growing fur, the Himalayan piles of plates in the sink, the forgotten hot dogs in the microwave which savaged me when I discovered them three weeks later – and felt a pang of envy for my friend's perfect husband, perfect son, perfect life. I would have gargled Satan's sperm to have a life like hers.

'Right, I've got Panadol, Aspirin . . .' As Jazz handed each packet to Hannah, she read aloud the names of the pills. 'Nurofen, Ibuprofin, Viagra . . .'

The word was out of her mouth before she could catch it.

'Viagra?' Hannah asked as we formed a clot around the offending packet. 'How long has Studz been using Viagra?'

Jazz's face took on a cloudy cast. 'I didn't know he was.'

'Oy veh!' Hannah exclaimed, wide-eyed, before recovering her composure. 'Not that it matters that you didn't know. It's rather nice that he wanted to keep it from you. We'll stay shutum, won't we, Cassie? Cone of silence.'

'Of course. Cone of silence,' I added. 'I'm sure

34

Pascal takes Viagra as well and Hannah doesn't know. He'd only have to take quarter-strength Viagra, though, 'cause he's such a wanker,' I teased.

Normally, Jazz delighted in any remark which belittled the pseudo-artist, but now her face remained frozen.

'And Rory is *def*initely taking Viagra, on account of the fact that he's got so much taller,' Hannah rejoindered, but Jazz was still doing her Easter Island statuette impression. 'Oh, come *on*, Jazz,' she soothed. 'It's no big deal, dah-ling. All men of David's age pop the odd pleasure pill to help them shtup.'

'Well, I wouldn't know,' Jazz replied stonily, 'as we don't have sex. Haven't had any sex at all for one year, one month, two weeks, five days and um . . .' she checked her watch '. . . seven hours.'

The air around us suddenly thickened. 'Oh,' was pretty much all Hannah or I could say as the penny dropped.

'My husband gives very good headache,' she went on dully. 'I just thought it was something to do with our stage in life. Well, *his* stage. *I'm* so desperate for sex that I had a cervical smear test from a male doctor last week and actually enjoyed it.'

If Jazz had meant it to be funny – well, it wasn't. Hannah and I tried to mumble something conciliatory, but Jazz oscillated her hands through the air as though shooing away an invisible wasp.

35

We watched as she started manically rushing around the kitchen organizing desserts.

'Even my fantasy life is boring. When I order a pizza, the pizza boy is not cute. He's acned and fat and anyway, after I pay him, he leaves.' Her valiant attempts to take this lightly were falling flat. She had now laid out twenty plates and was frisbeeing mango slices onto each one like Fanny Craddock on amphetamines. 'But I didn't know he was seeking satisfaction elsewhere. I'm obviously too dumb to notice.' She lifted up a chunk of her blonde hair by way of explanation. 'If I were a brunette, I'd have been on to him straight away. I suppose he's only stayed with me for my cooking. An oral orgasm to Doctor Studlands means a fine gourmet meal. Honestly, if I were to serve myself up naked for dinner with a bit of watercress up my bum, David would just ask what's for dessert. And tonight it's papaya, mango and kiwi compote with lime mint salsa and coconut chocolate cake, as it happens,' she said, squirting curlicues of cream onto the ziggurat of puddings she'd assembled frenziedly on consecutive plates.

'Jazz, dah-ling.' Hannah steadied our friend's arm. 'David's obviously had an erectile problem, but he's clearly trying to fix that now. This Viagra is obviously for you.'

'Jazz's face flickered and tensed. She shoved the Viagra packet into our hands. It was half-empty. And it was a repeat prescription. Sadness seemed to devour her. Then she threw the bowl of whipped cream at the wall where it detonated. Looking back, it was this moment which pinpointed her change from frustration to something much more ferocious. She turned on us, blonde hair flying. 'Mind you, the world's best-kept secret is how bad married sex actually is.'

'Speak for yourself, dah-ling,' said Hannah huffily.

'Don't tell me your sex-life is good, Hannah. Any wife who starts decorating the house as compulsively as you do is NOT having good sex. Basically, if the floor's getting laid, then you are not.'

Hannah flared her eyebrows. 'There is time for both, Jasmine. In marriage, couples develop a sort of sexual shorthand. Short and sweet. A sensual haiku.'

'Ha! Sounds like that joke: Why don't married women blink during foreplay? Because they don't have time.' Jazz spat out the punchline.

'Well, I'm sorry for you, Jazz, but Pascal makes me very happy in bed.'

'Yeah, right. And Doctor Shipman was a mercy killer.'

'Well, Pascal *should* make you happy in bed, Hannah,' I said, in an effort to dissipate the growing tension. 'He spends enough time in it! That man has only got up before midday once in his life – and that was at Uni when his mattress caught fire, do you remember?'

Hannah cut me a slit-eyed glance. 'Just because

Cassie and you have awful sex-lives, don't presume that—'

'Hey! I didn't say that Rory and I have—' But before I could counter Hannah's claim, Jazz reared her head defensively.

'You're just of the Hear No Evil, See No Evil, and Marry No Evil school, Hannah. At least Cassie is honest about how lousy things are in bed.'

'My sex-life is not lousy!' I reiterated. I thought of the joy of feeling my body all relinquished and pleasured and hot beside Rory's, my nightie squelched up around my waist and the pleasant ache in my groin the next day as I minced, bow-legged up the tube escalator to work . . . Hang on – when exactly *was* the last time my walk was all John Wayned like that?

'I don't want to discuss this now. I have a headache,' Hannah said irritably.

'And I'm about to get one,' I sulked.

'Oh, then it must be bedtime,' Jazz concluded bitterly.

A crespuscularity of mood crept over us. It was only shattered when Jazz's seventeen-year-old son, Josh, ambled downstairs for food supplies. There was a Penguin Classic in one jean pocket, a half-written poem in the other. Jazz waved her hand like a windscreen wiper in front of her face to sweep away her emotions. She ruffled her son's sandy-coloured hair as he raided the fridge. 'Try and leave me the odd crumb this time,' she said affectionately. 'So much for your father's medical prowess. He hasn't found a cure for adolescence yet, has he?'

Jazz maintains that she spoils and pampers her son because one day he'll be picking out her nursing home. But in actual fact she has to make up for David's lack of paternal interest. Ever since Josh was born, she's carried her own body weight in castor oils and Calpol, baby walkers, Play-Doh and unsweetened kumquat and guava juice – enough baby stuff, in fact, to establish a comfortable wilderness homestead.

David, on the other hand, did not take to parenthood. He took to travelling to war-torn environs instead. 'That's the trouble with marrying an activist – they're so damn active!' Jazz told people breezily. But as far as she was concerned, her son was the cleverest person on earth – now that Einstein has kicked the bucket. And Josh *was* clever. I wouldn't have been surprised if he'd changed his own nappy as a baby. But David seemed oblivious. Josh is an only child, but he still isn't his father's favourite.

So it was for the sake of her son that Jazz reapplied her lipstick, put on her bright hostess look and returned to enjoy her wedding anniversary party. Only Hannah and I noted the tiny, uncharacteristic dab of lipstick on Jazz's eyetooth, and that one of her shoes, a little too big, was sighing as she walked, as if in sympathy with her true feelings. Bearing trays of dessert, Jazz swept back into the dining room to find the Pop Princess sitting on her husband's lap. She noted David's concupiscent glance down the Pop Princess's cleavage and smiled until her face cramped and her teeth looked ready to fall out.

'You doan mind, do ya?' Kinkee purred in explanation, clutching Dr Studlands's hand as she heaved her ample bosom. 'I just wanted to shake the hand that has saved so many lives in Africa.'

'Oh, I'm sure it's shaken a few other things as well,' Jazz retorted with contrived friendliness, handing out her confectionary delights. 'Although, darling, don't you think she's a little young for you?' she said to her husband. 'Of course, it's the height of bad taste to point out the onset of your baldness, so I suppose that's why I do it.'

I held my breath as my eyes jumped in Studz's direction. But his face just creased with amusement.

'My lovely and long-suffering wife is cross about my midlifecrisis motorbike. Pathetically clichéd, I know.'

'Oh no, I don't mind the bike, darling. I'm sure it must be reassuring to finally have something hard between your legs.'

My head spun to scrutinize my friend. Jazz's mouth rose at the corners, smile held stiffly in place as if for an invisible photographer.

A murmur ran around the table, but Studz simply chuckled and raised a glass to his wife. 'In celebration of twenty wonderful years with the only woman in the world who can keep me grounded.'

Jazz, now back at the opposite head of the table, raised her glass in reciprocation. 'Darling,' she enthused, and even I couldn't tell if her buoyancy was counterfeit. She smiled luminously at her husband and we guests all exhaled for the first time in five minutes.

'Yes, my love?' Studz gave a languorous smile of anticipation.

'Do you realize,' she said sweetly, and we prepared for a loving statement of mutual warmth and respect on their twentieth wedding anniversary, '. . . that if I'd shot you the first time I seriously contemplated it, I'd be out on parole by now? Now, who's up for a little partner swapping? Car keys in the centre of the table, please!'

As a way of bringing a dinner party to an abrupt end, it was fantastically successful. Under the circumstances, I could only refer to it as premature social ejaculation.

At the door, while I waited for Rory to collect me after his veterinary call-out, Jazz took my arm.

'If you do have sex tonight I bet you it's from behind so you don't have to worry about not kissing . . . Or face the truth – which is that you don't want to.'

'Our sex-life is fine,' I told her emphatically, flinching from the cold January draught. 'In fact, it's fabulous.' I felt sorry for her. Her disappointment and humiliation were understandable, but I wouldn't be contaminated by her rage. Rory was a kind, genial man with a big heart.

'Sexual freedom?' Jazz scoffed drunkenly as I fled down the steps and into Rory's warm car. 'Ha! Well, for married women do you know what that means? THE FREEDOM NOT TO FUCK THE BASTARD!'

Her voice echoed around the Georgian square. 'Bastard . . .! Bastard . . .! Bastard . . .!'

'I told you we should have roped ourselves together for safety,' Rory grinned as I buckled up.

I squeezed his hand as we sped home. Jazz was wrong. Our sex-life was intimate and loving and tender and orgasmic. It truly was – wasn't it?

CHAPTER 3

THE HAND – A MODERN GOTHIC HORROR STORY

It was a dark and eerie night. With rain thrumming on the windowpane and the wind nagging in the treetops, our heroine was just curling up against the shadows into a cocoon of sleepy contentment when her skin pinpricked in dread as she felt *The Hand*. Her heart thudded against her ribcage and she stifled a scream in her dry throat. She flinched. She winced. She wound herself up tighter than the white lace nightie twisted around her quivering frame . . .

It is the stuff of horror movies. Every woman's worst nightmare.

Men make horror movies about The Blob or The Alien or The Thing. What terrorises men is Wolfman, the Zombie, Dracula, Frankenstein. What terrorises women – well, weary mothers, that is – is *The Hand*. The Hand groping over the sheets for you when you're on the cusp of sleep.

You shrink from it. 'No! No! Not *The Hand*, I'm a sleep-deprived mother!' You feign catatonia, pneumonia, death. Anything to get away from those wandering digits.

The Hand creeps stealthily over from its side of the marital bed and clamps demonically onto your tit, tweak, tweak, tweaking. *The Hand*, that most predictable of matrimonial gestures that signals conjugal rights are being requested despite your bone-achingly deep state of exhaustion. Forget *The Silence of the Lamb's* cannibal Hannibal. *The Hand* would be the scary movie which *I* would make. Cue creepy music, the goggle eyes of the terrified heroine. 'Tie me to the railway tracks! Lock me in a tower! Anything but leave me to the mercy of *The Hand*.'

It was my own fault. When we got home from Jazz's dinner party I'd kissed Rory goodnight on the ear. How could I have forgotten that husbands invariably interpret the smallest act of affection as foreplay?

As Rory ran his tongue around my upper molars, once, twice, around and around and around until the titillation became so intense that I was tempted to flick on the telly to watch the Darts final, I realized with dismay that Jazz was bloody well right. A wife will do everything to discourage her husband, bar stretching razor wire around her bed and setting bait traps. While men want the tumbling in the hay to recommence six weeks after childbirth, mothers want to tie up the sheaves and

44

put them in the barn. Sure, I'd joked with my girl-friends about how my favourite position in bed was the doggy position – 'where he begs, and I just roll over and play dead', but I hadn't admitted to myself that it was actually true. As Rory climbed aboard and pounded away at me as if I was his latest bit of DIY, I made a mental list of all the excuses I'd concocted to get out of sex in the last year.

WAYS TO GET OUT OF SEX WITH HUSBAND:
1. Contagious flu. Nobody could have as many cases of influenza as me in the last year and not be in an iron lung.
2. Thrush, from the taking of imaginary penicillin capsules to cure the fabricated flu.
3. The yoghurt up the fanny to cure the imaginary thrush.
4. Addressing him in baby talk. 'Who is Mama's iddy, biddy baby boy then?' whilst trying to put your nipple in his mouth.
5. Taking a child into the marital bed because of a nightmare. The playing of scary videos before bed greatly helps in this department.
6. Setting off the smoke alarm. Talk about dampening his spirits.
7. Asking him what position he'd like to do it in, then laughing hysterically when he answers.

8. Being too demanding. 'Hey, I feel like stripping each other naked with our teeth, wrestling in Jello, hiding strawberries up my twat which you have to retrieve with your tongue, slathering ourselves in chocolate, and then executing the *Kama Sutra* for seven hours before climaxing outside on the pavement for an added erotic frisson. Then we can recover for ten minutes and do it all over again! Are you up for it?' For added effect you then squeeze his balls as though testing the air in a tyre.

If these usual contraceptive ruses don't work, there are the regulation insults to the penis. A wife can always take to saying loudly, 'Is it *in* yet?' Followed by 'They always say that men with tiny equipment have great personalities. And you do, darling! You really, really DO.'

Or you could try a variation on this theme: 'It's not the size of a man's penis, it's the . . . no, it's the size.'

Of course, there are more tried and tested detumescents like –

1) 'What am I supposed to do with it . . . *floss*?'

2) 'So, which dwarf are you exactly?'

3) 'A toothpick! Why? Do I have food in my teeth?'

4) 'You know, love, I saw an episode of *Nip/Tuck* where they performed surgery to fix that.'

If more imagination is required, one day simply explain to your husband that you can only really enjoy sex if you bring along your best friend and just when he's getting excited, wondering which of your girlfriends is up for a threesome, drop in the fact that your best friend these days is a gay manicurist called Merlyn.

If you're really desperate for a good night's sleep, you can employ my tiptop favourite sex-stalling technique. Warning: this must be used sparingly so as not to induce heart failure. Just when hubby's snuggling up and you feel the prod of his penis in your back, mention casually that the Inland Revenue telephoned and want to audit his accounts. Not only will he lose the inclination for sex, he'll also lose the desire for sleep, which means you won't have to put up with his snoring either.

More drastically, you could just finish all your sentences with 'in accordance with the prophecy'. Although that could also lead to divorce. Or the sudden appearance of a few more wives.

As I ruminated on the above, I noted how the bedsprings were mourning beneath us as if mocking my misery. Having stopped contemplating new colours for the ceiling, I took to wondering exactly how many shoes I owned? Twenty-eight pairs, I deduced. Oh, the things you can fathom when time is on your side!

I sucked in air in alarm. What had happened to me? I wasn't even faking orgasms, I was *flunking* them. On those official Name/Address/Age forms, after it says Sex – I would have to write 'NOT IF I CAN POSSIBLY HELP IT'.

Predictably, Rory then rolled me over on my side without a nuzzle or a kiss. Jesus. Come to think of it, there never was any kissing any more. *Just as Jazz had predicted.* When had we stopped kissing during sex, I wondered. Rory thrust away once, twice. As usual, each move was so mechanical, I could draw a diagram of it. He'd never asked me my favourite position – which is, by the way, Deputy Head Teacher. A promotion I'd never achieve if I didn't get some bloody shut-eye. I was just about to point this out to my husband when he began groping round for my clitoris. And groping and groping and . . .

Why is it that men can assemble a hand-held rocket grenade launcher off the Internet, and yet they can't find . . . Oh wait. Yes. Houston, we have lift-off! But as a feeling of pleasure began to spread through me, I stayed quiet. God knows I didn't want to *encourage* the man! That would delay sleep even further. Then he might want to keep going. It used to be that women faked orgasms. Now we faked NOT having them! But I didn't need to pretend that I wasn't being pleasured for long because Rory then began prodding at me as though he was running late for a meeting and my clitoris was the elevator button. Prod. Prod. Prod. Oh, just take the stairs! This lift only stops at one floor, anyway. The pelvic floor and, God knows, that needs some work. But hell, so did the rest of me. My hair, full of nit napalm, was encased in a plastic shower cap. As if that weren't unattractive enough, I was also wearing saggy, baggy flannelette pyjamas and airline bedsocks. Flannelette pyjamas are the sexual equivalent of soldiers laying minefields across the entrance to their tunnels.

When, I speculated, did this slow-drip sexual ennui set in? Exactly when did sex become more dutiful than enthusiastic? We used to do something that involved a fair bit of nestling and stroking – I couldn't remember what exactly, but I do remember that I liked it. What happened to those sex-surfeited days we once had where we dinged furniture, took headboard divots out of the wall, broke beds, destroyed mattresses and ran up chiropractic bills? Nooky nostalgia, that's all I had now.

Rory had settled into his usual metronomic rhythm with habitual grunting. Did all married couples practise this kind of sexual samba, with its well-worn steps? When had things deteriorated? With the onset of motherhood, perhaps. There was no denying that childbirth had wreaked havoc with my sex-life. A little something to do with stretching your vagina the customary five kilometres. Despite the bean bags and the water births and the plinky plonky harp music, giving birth still boils down to a doctor putting a knee on your chest, spreading your legs and diving in with a pair of barbecue tongs. As if that's not traumatic enough, no sooner

49

have the lactation leakage circles dried on your shirtfront than your husband wants hanky-panky. Needless to say, the woman with the recently stitched perineum does not.

Rory wanted to discuss my waning desire, I remember that. But all I wanted to discuss were my post-partum haemorrhoids. Besides which, by that time my husband's needs were no longer on my radar. I was in that mind-numbing, mother-baby netherworld. A baby is the greatest love affair of a woman's life. If you *do* notice your partner at all, it's to think, Who is that tall, hairy person hanging around ME AND MY BABY? But once the kids started sleeping through the night, we'd still enjoyed the odd bonk-a-thon, hadn't we?

Rory was still pounding away. If he *were* working on a DIY creation, I'd have been a bookcase with built-in music cabinet and television swivel panel by now. I wondered if he'd get the hint that I wasn't exactly enjoying myself if I took out the nail file Hannah had given me and started pushing back my cuticles?

I realized with relief that his momentum was building up.

Rory always came precisely the same way. A series of identical moans, crescendoing into a sequence of mini-moans which rose towards one giant inflection, concluding in a loss of amplitude on the final surge, followed, a few minutes later, by thunderous snoring.

I lay on my side, looking at the landing light

sliding in under the bedroom door. Perhaps I should try harder. Don a filmy gown, get a prescription for She-agra – even make the first move? After all, one good turn – gets most of the blankets, I thought, as Rory lurched and the arctic air groped my body.

With a sickening heart, I admitted to myself that Jazz was spot on. The thought of her gloating was unbearable. Drifting off to sleep, I determined not to tell her that 'sexual freedom' was, indeed, the freedom not to have sex with your husband.

CHAPTER 4

IS THERE LIFE AFTER INFIDELITY?

'You're right. Our sex-life sucks,' I couldn't help confessing to Jazz the moment I heard her voice. I was on the phone to my best friend first thing next morning.

'The only thing in the married boudoir which does, sweetie,' Jazz replied, her voice thick with hangover.

'I've just been in denial, I suppose,' I went on. 'What about you, though? What happened after the dinner party? Did you confront Studz about his little honeymoon at Viagra Falls?'

'I went to bed in a huff. He followed and tried to have sex. Can you believe that? He said that ever since I'd taunted him at dinner, he'd wanted to make love to me so badly.'

'And what did you say?'

'I told him he'd succeeded.'

I snorted with laughter down the phone. 'But did you ask him about the Viagra?'

'He said it was for me. That he'd been experimenting privately, on his own, and it hadn't worked. But that he'd now perfected the dosage.'

'Do you believe him?'

There was a pause. 'Does Elton John have his own hair?'

'So what's the plan?'

'It's time to spy.'

'And exactly how are you proposing to become Commander Jane Bond?'

'You know that little holiday to Sri Lanka we were supposed to be going on, to celebrate our wedding anniversary?'

David Studlands, humanitarian doctor, only ever took holidays, where there were torture reports to be made. The Congo, Algeria, Sudan, Burma, Aceh – these were the poor woman's holiday highlights. David wasn't happy unless in some fungal jungle teeming with malaria-riddled mosquitoes or terrorists. Finally Jazz stopped travelling with him. 'I don't like to go on holiday anywhere that's been too recently traumatized,' she explained. One year, when Studz announced a trip to Disney World, Jazz was baffled. 'Disney World? Really? Wow.' What she hadn't realized is that Florida has the death penalty, and that Disney World is in close proximity to the maximum-security prison at Gainsville. So, once again, she was on her own, traipsing with a small child around the gigantic funfair – a death sentence of its own for any mother. *Call Amnesty*, she'd texted me. *Help urgently needed. Dead Mother Walking.*

'Sri Lanka?'

'Yes. David chose it so that he could treat tsunami survivors between pina coladas. Well, he's cancelled, because of work in London allegedly, but he's insisting that I still go.'

'And are you?'

'I shall tell him I'm going, but . . . Cassie, are you busy for the next few nights?'

'I'll probably just be sitting around tweezing my stray facial hairs. Why?'

'I'm going to pretend to leave for the airport then hide at your place and see what kind of house calls the good doctor makes while I'm supposedly away. Will you help me?'

My heart sank to *Titanic* depths. 'Stalking? But isn't that illegal?' A day-glo orange jumpsuit beckoned. Yet I couldn't say no. Jazz always backed me up in any emergency. Hannah was the opposite. '*Oh dah-ling, I'd like to help but I'm allergic to children.*' But, as I explained to Rory later, I did try to put her off.

'Of course you're always welcome, Jazz,' I said now. 'But you do realize that I'm married to a vet. A vet whose office is next door to our house. A vet who brings his work home. At night, well, I can never sleep in case something has *escaped* . . . Something with envenomed fangs which it fully intends sinking into your flesh.'

I warned her that my husband Rory thinks a thwack with a tea towel is the best defence. While I, on the other hand, would prefer a SWAT response team.

But nothing would put her off. She was in Miss Marple mode.

54

The upside was that for an entire week I got what I'd always wanted. A wife. While I was at school teaching, Jazz cleaned my ramshackle little Kilburn terraced house. She corralled various escaped canines, shopped for food, did the laundry and cooked the most spectacular dinners. Whereas Jazz serves vintage champagne in crystal glasses, at my place you'll be lucky to get some leftover cooking wine in a recycled jam jar with dinosaurs running around it and the label half-peeled off. The kids call my evening meals YMCA dinners – Yesterday's Muck Cooked Again.

She also helped Jamie and Jenny with their homework – a task which sends me into a coma. While I adore my kids with a primal passion, I actually got morning sickness *after* they were born.

Kids are like desktop computers. You have no idea how much assembling is required until it's at home in pieces on the study floor and you and your husband are screaming at each other about whose idea it was to get one in the first place. Parents, on the other hand, are so simple that even a kid can operate them. My kids have been running rings around me since they were born.

Anyway, the calm Jazz brought to my chaotic home was a small price to pay for a little light stalking. Or so I thought at the time . . .

At first it seemed almost a lark. As I slid into Jazz's Hertz rental car outside my school gate after a late staff meeting, I noticed she'd dressed for the

55

occasion in all black with a Beanie hat, and had swapped her regulation high-rise heels for some sturdy trainers. She held up her foot. 'Lesbian shoes, sweetie. Very comfy, actually. No wonder dykes look so happy.'

'Do you really think this is worth it, Jazz? I do have thirty English compositions to mark.' I like teaching. Yes, I know, I've obviously been working with glue for *way* too long. And with a promotion on the cards, I really needed to put in the extra effort.

'Do you know what they call a woman who knows where her husband is every night? A widow,' Jazz retorted and floored the accelerator.

Winter had come violently. For the whole of January there'd been nothing but this thick, low, leaden sky. London was as cold as a giant meat locker. It had been so bleak that the entire population of Britain was online, chasing availability of last-minute flights to the Canary Islands.

We trailed Studz from his gym in Marylebone to a cabinet minister's cocktail party, then on to a fundraising banquet for the starving of the Sudan at the Victoria & Albert Museum.

The museum mausoleums on Cromwell Road looked even grimmer beneath the clotted night sky. Jazz and I sat shivering, our faces mashed up against the side windows of the car, me correcting English homework by the glow from the cigarette lighter ('A conjunction is the place where two railway lines

56

meet') and blowing smoke rings of our breath in the icy air as we ate something from a fast-food vendor; it couldn't technically be classified as food, but at least it was hot. Just when I had become so cold I thought it was time to amputate my extremities, Studz sprang agilely down the museum's marble steps and Jazz fired the engine.

'Maybe he is telling the truth,' I ventured to my friend as we tailed him towards Hampstead. 'He's nearly home.' I yawned. 'Can we call it quits now?' I still had an hour's marking to do. (*Q*: What is grammar? *A*: Grammar is how to talk good and stuff.) And I was desperate for a pee.

Finally even Jazz was ready to admit defeat. 'Okay, Cass. Maybe I *was* over-reacting.'

We were just about to abandon the chase, when Studz hung a suicide right off Haverstock Hill and headed back down towards Camden. Our hire car juddered around the corner after him on two wheels. The upside of being female undercover agents is that you can hang onto a car seat using labia suction. After I'd recovered from this heart-stopping manoeuvre, we stooged around looking for his car, before finally spotting it idling, kerbside, outside a row of snaggle-toothed tenements decayed with age and leaning erratically.

Studz was on his mobile phone, engine still running, when a young woman in a brightly-coloured poncho strode from the fluorescent foyer of a block of council flats, phone to ear, and vaulted energetically into his passenger seat.

Jazz lurched forward, fingers gripping the dashboard as though on a white-knuckle ride at a funfair. 'It's Phillippa. She researches for him.'

'Maybe he's just got something for her to research,' I hazarded, but anxiety was skittering through my belly. 'If it makes you feel any better, only about seven females in the world look good in a poncho. And they're all under nine years old – or Nomads tending their yaks.'

But Jazz was in no mood to banter. We followed unobtrusively, and in silence, as he drove Phillippa to the marital home. We watched, from two houses back, as he led the young woman inside.

It was midnight. London lay grey as a grave-yard. Dark clouds sloshed across the bruised sky. The smoke of our breath steamed. A single light appeared in the master bedroom.

And, soon afterwards, it went out.

Despite the fact that we were on a covert operation, Jazz emitted a howl loud enough to be heard in one of those base camps in Antarctica. Something seemed to crack open inside her. This was open-heart surgery. There she sat sobbing, with this gaping wound. Is there a doctor in the house? Ah yes, but he was showing off his bedside manner to another woman at the precise moment that his wife lay bleeding to death outside his house in a hire car. I moved Jazz over into the passenger seat, took the wheel and swerved toward home, too upset to drive straight.

Jazz cried for an hour before I could coax her

inside. 'He took her home to our bed! Actually it's not my home any more. It's Fuckingham Palace.'

She was in agony. Childbirth with no epidural would hurt less than this. 'Come on, darl,' I said gently. 'You need a drink.'

'What I need is to climb into the bath with an electrical appliance,' she replied between wracking sobs.

Once inside, I made inadequate comments along the lines of how most men are like worms, only taller, but Jazz just took to the spare bed in the flat behind Rory's surgery, curling herself foetally around a whisky bottle. The sight of her burned itself indelibly into my retinas. Rubbing the small of her back, I reflected that husbands should come with a warning. *This person could be dangerous to your mental health.* I also got a feeling that Jazz had never read the small print on her marriage licence.

On Tuesday night the mood in our hire car was sombre as we followed Jazz's husband to a fundraiser for AIDS in Africa organized by the Prime Minister's wife in a marquee at Kensington Palace. High-pitched quartet music twanged in the background. Two freezing hours later, Studz and others adjourned to Chinawhite for a nightcap.

'How long do you think they'll be?' I asked. Clouds were scudding low across the night sky as though it was cloud rush-hour and they were in a desperate hurry to get home. Everyone was in a rush, except for us, apparently. 'I've got loads of maths homework to mark. "A circle is a straight line except that it goes around and has a hole in the middle of it",' I quoted from one kid's paper. 'These children need help!'

Jazz shrugged dismally, too miserable to speak.

'Oh, okay,' I conceded. 'But let's not stay for too long. Should I go for food supplies?'

She shrugged again, then said weakly, 'Get something vaguely healthy.'

I returned with two low-fat muffins. 'Would madam like the banana Styrofoam or the blueberry Styrofoam?'

But Jazz left her banana cake after one bite because her husband had just emerged, along with the Pop Princess recently appointed a Good Will Ambassador by the UN. We trailed them back to the Savoy Hotel – the more discreet River Entrance. Studz parked the car on a double yellow line and tossed the keys to the doorman as though this were routine.

'Maybe they're just going to the American Bar, for a cocktail of puréed unhusked wheat kernels or whatever the hell is her preferred non-carcinogenic tipple,' I suggested feebly.

Jazz just stared grimly ahead. Here, by the river, the streets were creamy with fog. Having parked, we just sat watching the leering grille of Studz's Jaguar. After one hour, I reminded Jazz that a celebrity is nothing but a nonentity who got lucky. The Thames twitched beside us, pale as milk in the misty moonlight. After two hours, I pointed out how one day Kinkee's youth would fade and she'd end up going 'Whoo, Whoo' behind a J-Lo female impersonator tribute band. My only answer was the seagulls squawking like teething babies. I tried to mark geometry sheets by the streetlamp glow, 'An angle has wings and comes from God', but quickly lost the will to live. After three hours, my best friend started crying without any noise at all; she just hunched there, shuddering.

'What do you want to do?' I asked dispiritedly. 'Perhaps a call to one of the tabloids would be appropriate? You know, the *News of the Fatuous Gossips*? or *Louth mouthed, Inane, Ill-informed Perspectives OF THE WEEK*.' I was trying to cheer her, but Jazz curled up into a ball.

'I couldn't do it to Joshua,' she said in a whisper, before the smell of banana vomit invaded the car.

On day three of Jasmine's Indian Ocean holiday, we took yet another trip down Infidelity Lane. From the anonymous safety of our hire car parked opposite, we saw Jazz's husband waiting at the stage door of a West End theatre where they were performing a revival of *Cats*. The side alley where he had parked was urinous, villainous and dark as a ditch. But with the nocturnal accuracy of a bat, David Studlands could home in on any pretty woman. He was waiting for a kitten who appeared wearing spray-on snakeskin trousers, killer heels and a fedora hat. He took her arm and steered her into his Jag.

In silhouette, we saw them kiss. We then watched open-mouthed as they clambered over into the back seat and the car started shaking and quaking. The Jag was rocking so hard on its springs that I thought it might be in labour. I kept checking the exhaust pipe to see if two or three miniature versions of Studz's Jaguar had popped out.

'Really she's in the wrong musical. It should be "Guys *In* Dolls",' I said. It was a little laboured but I was desperate to kick-start some of Jazz's trademark caustic humour.

Jazz blew her nose cacophonously. 'I think it's time Andrew Lloyd-Webber sold those cats to some lab for cosmetic testing, don't you?' she said with melancholic acerbity.

One thing was for sure. Three women in three nights? It was no wonder he was mainlining Viagra. Jazz's surgeon husband obviously thought he was in a *Carry On, Doctor* movie.

Day four and Studz was appearing in a live debate on the use of torture to combat terrorism. We knew because the programme had been flagged on the BBC all day. I tried to talk Jazz out of stalking and into having an early night. Three nights of no sleep and my face had gone a fetching shade of green. The livid semi-circles beneath my eyes gave me the look of a suicidal racoon. It was my turn to drive, but I was so tired I was manoeuvring the hire car to Shepherd's Bush like a pill-crazed, long-haul truck driver. 'There are only two jobs where eye bags don't count against you. President of the United States and a Vulcan crewmember on the *Starship Enterprise*,' I whined, parking by the security gate.

But Jazz maintained that her husband was a snake. And that snakes always hunt at night – their sensors striking in the dark at anything warm . . . even a famous BBC interviewer, I realized, as Studz flashed past us in her chauffeured car. Jazz had an eerie calm about her which I didn't like. 'You're thinking about how to kill him, aren't you?'

'Let's just put it this way. I wouldn't advise him to start watching any long-running soaps on TV,' she said grimly.

When Jazz's husband disappeared into the presenter's house in Notting Hill Gate, my best friend suggested I get a mop and bucket because we would need it when she removed her husband's kidneys with her nail scissors to sell on the black market. 'Well, why not? He's got two of them . . . just like he's got two faces.'

Scrutinizing Jazz in the wan light, I realized that she wasn't joking. If I were David Studlands, I'd be thinking long and hard about what happened to John Bobbitt.

I touched her arm tenderly. 'Is there anything I can do to cheer you up?'

'Yes, I must cheer up. After all, I read somewhere

that it takes forty-two muscles to frown but only four to pull back my trigger finger on my father's hunting gun,' she replied menacingly.

'The only shooting you're supposed to do are the rolls of film from your tropical holiday,' I reminded her. 'Speaking of which – you must get to a tanning salon before Sunday.'

But Jazz wasn't listening. She put her hands in the prayer position. 'God grant me the patience to tolerate the things I cannot change, change the things I cannot tolerate, and to find a really good hiding-place for the body of my philandering arsehole of a husband.'

Day five found Studz in the company of a glamorous Mayfair feline. She was a mink-lined-hatbox, white-poodle-on-a-diamond-lead, invitation-to-spend-summer-on-Valentino's-yacht kind of woman.

'Ohmygod. I sat next to her at the quiz night to aid the campaign for the abolition of the death penalty in the Caribbean,' Jazz reported amazedly.

Actually, at that moment I would have liked nothing more than to bring back the death penalty, in *England*. Not for every crime. Just for, say, breaking your wife's heart.

'Oh, I know the breed. One of those glamour-puss models who married for money and is now busily developing a social conscience to compensate for her fading career,' I guessed.

'But David hated her! God! I'm overheating.'

Red-faced, Jazz opened the window to guzzle down the chilly air. 'He said she had the IQ of a school of plankton.'

We trailed them to an exclusive restaurant in Piccadilly. 'You wouldn't believe how mean Studz is with me. He makes me reuse my dental floss! He cleans it with alcohol and then hangs it out to dry. "I do so hate to discard a length of essentially unworn floss, Jasmine" and then he takes *her* to the *Caprice???*' she said tragically. 'Is there air conditioning in this car? I'm burning up here,' she gasped, fanning her flushed face, as I sat shivering.

By the time we shadowed them to the woman's Mayfair mansion, Jazz was gesticulating like the heroine of some Jacobean tragedy.

'*You're* upset because you're faking the odd orgasm with Rory? But men! Men can fake a whole fucking marriage.'

On day six, Studz ventured into the wilds of Hackney. I couldn't believe that he could possibly seduce another female. I mean, if so, David Studland's appendage would be a celebrity in its own right. It would need its own agent. 'Your hubby is a spermicidal maniac,' I observed dubiously as Studz got out of his car.

For this excursion Jasmine's husband had dressed down in jeans and leather jacket. Having beeped his Jag locked, he ventured into a grimy-looking Irish pub which boasted live music by bands called, invitingly, 'The Red Hot Sticky Helmets' and 'Right To Devour'.

As we loitered outside in our hire car, a group of yobs swaggered by, kicking vehicles. We'd discussed the danger of muggers here and had decided that telling them, 'Jesus says I am the Chosen One' would act as a suitable repellent. In the end, we settled on a demand from me in my best head-mistressy voice as to whether or not they'd done their homework? And did they know that a hooligan was just a polygon with seven sides?

At this, the yobs dispersed in double-quick time, so we alighted and pressed our noses up against the pub windows. Studz was sharing pints with a twenty-something girl with caramel freckles and thick honey-blonde hair which she'd torniqueted into a ponytail.

'Good God! It's our masseuse, Carmel,' Jazz said damply, as damply as the low sky which bulged with rain.

'Et tu, cutie,' I surmized as the wind slapped our faces.

We watched agog as Studz loosened the girl's ponytail so that her fair hair fell wantonly over her shapely shoulders.

'She's been our masseuse for three years. I mean, how long do you think he's been seeing *her*?'

The man really was a dastardly moustache twirler. All that was missing was the railway track. It shocked me how we all thought of Studz as being so brave, bringing medical help to war-torn,

66

disease-riddled countries, when it was clear that Jazz didn't even have to leave her home to find a hostile environment.

'You should have frisked the bastard for cruel intentions when you first met at Cambridge.'

We'd parked outside a seedy Japanese restaurant, beneath the neon gaze of its electronic sign – *Nippon Tuck*. By its harsh strobing light, I saw my friend's face creased with pain. 'Trouble is, like most intellectuals, he's just a clutch of paradoxes,' Jazz adjudicated sourly. 'Like the dedicated spanker of teenage prostitutes who publically campaigns against smacking children. Or the sixteen-year-old anti-materialistic vegan daughter who drinks all your Krug and steals your fur coat. And the Human Rights doctor who hates humans. Not in general,' she amended, 'but in particular. He can save the lives of people he doesn't know while decimating the lives of the people he does. I just don't know him any more,' she said desolately. 'Who is this man I married? He's alien to me.'

An alien from Planet Shag, I thought to myself, turning the hire car for home.

'The stupid thing is, I still love him, Cass,' she said with melting vulnerability. Love was a feeble word for what Jasmine felt. David Studlands was her whole life.

It was starting to seem that love prepares you for marriage the way needlepoint prepares you for round-the-world solo yachting.

★　　★　　★

67

Day seven was the Sabbath. Surely this had to be Studz's day of rest? What was the jerk doing – auditioning mistresses? He'd had sex with so many women this last week his penis must have developed scar tissue.

Not only was I haemorrhaging money on babysitters as Rory was away at a conference, but I was so tired from a week of late nights that I was throwing clothes into the washing machine with the kids still in them. When I was making my daughter's breakfast, I buttered my hand and placed it on Jenny's plate.

But no. The very day Jazz was due back from her allegedly tranquil seaside sojourn, Studz was in their marital bed with a lithe, blonde-highlighted, forty-year-old university lecturer Jazz recognized as one of his private patients.

Sitting in the rental car opposite Jazz's house watching them draw the blinds in the master bedroom, I made a stab at jocularity because, really, we were both beyond shock now. 'My husband's a vet. Let's just hope Rory doesn't sleep with *his* patients.'

'Maryanne, that's her name,' said Jazz. 'I saw her at our house once. After her face lift, she started suffering from fainting fits, as I recall. Obviously I had no idea that the cure was to take deep breaths, lean forward . . . and put her head between the legs of her doctor.'

I laughed tartly. 'What does she lecture on, this Maryanne? Husband rustling?'

'Sylvia Plath.'

'So she's Plathological,' I punned.

We roared at that. Great belly-wrenching guffaws. Exhaustion and emotional overload had kicked us up into a state of near-hysteria.

'I think it's time I left David a note. *Hello, darling. Dinner is on the table and . . . your wife's head is in the gas-oven.*'

We laughed until we cried . . . Only when Jazz stopped laughing, she just kept right on crying.

CHAPTER 5

IF HE WANTS BREAKFAST IN BED, TELL HIM TO SLEEP IN THE KITCHEN

Marriage, I'd now realized, is for Extreme Sports enthusiasts. It's a highwire act with no safety net. *The Amazing, Dare-Devil, Flying Married Couple! Trapeze Artists Extraordinaire!* And Jazz had fallen. Splat. Leaving Hannah and me to try to pick up the pieces. It was Sunday afternoon and we were sitting around my crowded kitchen drinking neat Scotch and painting Jazz's naked body with fake tan before a fan heater. She was due back at Heathrow from her Sri Lankan holiday in an hour. Hence this crisis meeting.

I was slightly nervous as I don't often entertain visitors. This is mainly to do with the abundance of methane-gas-producing canines. Guests were constantly reeling back, eyes smarting, lungs scrambling for oxygen, great-grandfathers reliving the mustard gas attacks they endured in the trenches . . . or worse. The one and only time I'd attempted sweet-talking my Headmaster, Mr Scroope, over dinner about the up-and-coming Deputy Head vacancy, he'd fled in humiliation after one of Rory's

70

pet rats tried to mate with his hairpiece. But this was an emergency. My kids had been banished to their rooms and some dental-drill rap was now vibrating down through the ceiling.

Predictably, the conversation kicked off with Jazz blaming herself. As I sloshed whisky into chipped glasses, she began to make a squeaking noise like a stuck drawer.

'It must be my fault.' She peered through her wispy fringe like a startled woodland creature. 'David just doesn't find me sexy any more.'

Hannah and I immediately went into our roles as human Wonderbras, uplifting, supportive and making our girlfriend look bigger and better. But with Jazz's melted-lemon-drop hair and skin as pale and smooth as vanilla ice cream, we didn't need to exaggerate.

'Jazz, darl, you are so beautiful. I mean, look at your hair. It never has a bad day. And you're *soooo* slim. Unlike me. Which is bloody unfair when I'm the one always dieting,' I complained, goodnaturedly. 'In my life I've lost 147 stone, do you know that?'

Grief was devouring our friend and I ached for her. Banging your head against a wall also uses up 150 calories an hour and that seemed to be Jasmine's current form of exercise.

'Yes. And I'*m* the one who's bought every cream. Creams for toes, tummies, eyelids, inner goddamn insteps even. And all for nothing,' Hannah added lightheartedly. 'I have more lines than British Telecom.'

But Jazz couldn't be cheered. She just stared mournfully at her whisky glass, as if it were a crystal ball.

'Turn,' I ordered. As though basting a chicken, I began slathering fake tan onto my girlfriend's haunches. She looked pensive and delicate in the wintry light. Naked, her thinness shook me. She seemed to have dropped seven pounds in the last week.

'Maybe I breastfed too long? My tits have gone all tribeswoman. All I need are the bongos. Then there's my stretchmarks, crepe-paper bum, pelvic-floor muscles shot to pieces. That's the one thing about childbirth which nobody tells you. That you will never be able to laugh again without peeing yourself,' Jazz whimpered.

'It's true,' I confirmed. 'At your dinner party the other night I laughed so hard, tears were running down my legs.'

Childfree Hannah squawked a laugh, but at the mention of pelvic floors Jazz and I suddenly got that expression you see on the faces of people whose dogs are crapping on the street: that vacant, preoccupied, this-isn't-my-dog look, as we secretly contracted our vaginal muscles.

'Listen, dah-ling, it's surprising how many women your age are a lot younger than you are. Time is a great healer, Jazz, but it sure ain't no beauty therapist,' commiserated Hannah, handing Jazz her cosmetic surgeon's card.

'You're right, Hannah. These are not laughter

lines around my mouth, they're fucking fjords.'
Jazz swigged at her whisky. 'I think I'll just have
my whole head cosmetically removed.'

With forty-five minutes till touchdown, I
ordered Jazz to turn again and began massaging
the brown globules into her belly over the
small corduroy ridges of her baby marks. We'd
often shared our post-natal woes; confessional
stretchmark-comparing conversations were a
regular. But we hadn't taken it seriously, until now.

'If we want to keep our husbands, we need to do
the maintenance,' Hannah prompted, crunching
noisily on a dry cracker – no doubt her main meal
of the day. 'I think you should catch whatever's
falling – including your face, dah-ling. You too,
Cassie. Don't you ever want to be desired for your
body instead of your cryptic crossword abilities?'

'My answer is two down, five letters, past
participle abbreviated,' I replied.

'Ugh.' Jazz caught sight of herself in the bank
of mirrors above my kitchen table. 'My skin just
doesn't fit me any more,' she sighed, a funereal
droop to her shoulders.

'Chin up, Jazz,' I said gently. 'Despite what
Hannah says, you do only have *one* of them.'
Oh, the hours of my life I had wasted having
conversations like this one. If only time would
stop flying. If only it would sit it out at the
airport duty-free store. If only it would walk,
stroll, take a slow bus and stop tormenting
women.

'Everyone knows David has an impending saint-hood, so how can it not be my fault?'

'Saint? More like the Prince of Darkness.' I moved on to painting Jasmine's biceps. 'Tell me, when you first met Studz, couldn't you *see* those clouds of sulphur he was trailing?'

Hannah turned on me, while irritatedly attacking another cracker. 'Cassandra! You are talking about the woman's husband, you realize. The putz, despite it all, whom Jasmine loves.'

I rolled my eyes so far into the top of my head, I could see my brain cells renewing. Hannah reprovingly confiscated the faketan bottle and swept Jazz's fair hair on top of her head in order to paint her shoulders.

'Okay,' I amended. 'Studz is not quite the devil incarnate, but you could easily confuse them in an identity parade. He's behaved like an evil pig.'

'He's behaved like a man, dah-ling. Men rotate car tyres, they put three-in-one oil on their hedge trimmers and they fuck around to prove their sex-ismo. Now eat. You need to regain your strength.' Hannah lifted the cheese plate towards Jazz, who just crouched over it, eating nothing.

In the silence I thought about what Hannah had said. As a wife and mother of a son, I could definitely testify that the male brain is made up of an Internet obsession lobe, a gi-normous football gland, a minuscule personal hygiene particle and a teeny-weeny, incy-wincy relation-ship molecule. But surely sexual incontinence

74

was an optional extra? Rory was faithful to me . . . wasn't he?

'Boys will be boys, dah-ling, and so will a lot of middle-aged men who should know better,' Hannah stated.

Jazz put down her whisky glass so decisively that it nearly shattered. 'If David's having a midlife crisis, couldn't he just, I dunno, buy an impractical car? Or cross the Channel on a homemade raft? I mean, wasn't that ridiculous motorbike enough?'

Hannah was daubing on the fake tan as though she were Michelangelo. With twenty minutes till landing, a Fast Pass through Customs and an estimated hour ride home from the airport, I became so frustrated I snatched back the bottle and began frantically slathering tan around Jazz's imaginary bikini line and under both rounded boobs.

Hannah munched disgruntledly on another cracker. 'Look, nobody ever said marriage was going to be easy. In sickness and in health and all that . . . and believe me, dah-ling, if you marry into allergies like *I* did, there's always going to be a little *some*thing wrong. He'll always have a niggling ache *some*where.' She topped up Jasmine's glass. 'All husbands have their bad points. It could be worse. He could be a gambler or a child molester. Or,' she shuddered, 'play golf.'

But Jazz remained inconsolable. Despite being only half-painted, she began pacing now, naked, back and forth across my chaotic kitchen, with me and the tan bottle in pursuit.

'In my twenties I took up two new hobbies, marriage and insanity. I mean, Cassie is right. Good God! Why couldn't I see what Studz was really bloody like?' The husband Jazz had worshipped for twenty years was wavering in the heat of her scrutiny. What she'd thought was real had become nothing more than a marital mirage. 'I . . . I thought we were h . . . h . . . happy.' She gave another desolate howl.

Hannah sloshed more whisky into Jasmine's glass. 'Come on, dah-ling. Let's not get all Sylvia Plath about it.'

Jazz's cry was like a rusty hinge. She pressed her hand against her forehead. It was a silent-movie gesture of a helpless damsel in great danger.

I kicked Hannah under the table. 'What?' she mouthed at me. 'What did I say?'

'I put that wanker through his hospital training!' Giving vent to feelings long hidden, Jazz yowled even louder. 'I devoted myself to Studz, body and soul.' Her voice seesawed with emotion. 'I loved my job but I stupidly gave that up too! All for *him*.'

'Well, dah-ling, I for one have never understood why you gave up chefing,' Hannah the career woman tut-tutted as she smugly crossed her lithe, lasered legs.

Jazz levelled Hannah with a steely glare. 'I decided to stay home and mother my own child so that Josh would inherit *my* personality flaws, and not those of the Czechoslovakian au pair with the eating disorder. Okay?'

As I manoeuvred my half-basted friend in front of the fan heater (we had about five minutes till touchdown), I thought how Jazz really did have a point. I'd never met any female executive, no matter how senior, who didn't jettison the financial pages to turn to the scare story about how the children of mothers who work fulltime have less chance of progressing to A level and are more prone to collect Nazi memorabilia in later life.

Jazz had her arms outstretched as though on the cross so I could paint her sides. 'Haven't I been a good wife?' She stuck her chin out nobly. 'Good God! The things I've put up with. The medical emergencies. The Human Rights campaigns . . . My house is always full of one-legged landmine victims. Or literacy-challenged homeless lower Voltans with no refugee status and haemorrhoids. Black trade unionists who talk about "equality" then snap their fingers at me for coffee because I'm a mere female. Oh yes, I've graciously entertained them all.'

When Jazz blew her nose, it sounded like the HMS *Britannia* foghorn. 'Funny, isn't it, the delusion among the Bridget Jones set vomiting drunkenly in gutters at three a.m. that marriage will be a step up!'

Hannah corrected her. 'Not all men are shmucks.'

'True. Some of them are dead. Men – can't live with them, can't slip them a cyanide tablet without being jailed for murder. Oh, I feel sick.' Clutching her abdomen, hair limp with sweat, Jazz looked like an overripe mango. She mopped at her brow.

'Your heating's too high, Cassie. I feel so queasy. And I have a headache. Do you have any peanut butter? I've had such a craving for it lately.'

'Christ, you're not up the duff, are you?'

Hannah's eyes rolled like a pantomime dame's. 'Yes, that must be it, Cassie. It's an immaculate conception.'

'The reason I'm feeling so rotten,' Jazz went on, 'is because I've only just realized how women are still putting themselves last. Look at you, Hannah. You didn't have children because Pascal didn't want them. And . . .'

This was dangerous territory. I glanced at the kitchen clock. Jazz could easily be through Customs now and at the baggage carousel. I made a pathetic attempt to steer us towards safer conversational ground. 'I can't understand why you didn't have kids, Hannah. If only as an excuse to leave parties early.'

But Hannah was already bristling. 'My first commitment is to Pascal. We have the life we want.'

Jazz, fuelled by whisky, guffawed. 'You have the life that *he* wants. Pascal just wanted to be your only child. The centre of your universe.'

'Well, at least *we're* happy,' Hannah retorted, a little cruelly.

'Come on, Jazz. Hannah's soft furnishings are actually far too nice to have sprog pee all over them.' I was doing so much defusing I could get work with the Bomb Disposal Squad.

'Eeeew! I detest children. I detest animals too,

78

but I thought admitting to the former would bring me fewer death threats,' Hannah crabbed.

Whenever Hannah and Jazz found themselves at each other's throats, they would reunite by redirecting their dissatisfaction towards me. And we had definitely entered a Hard Hat area.

'Come on, Jazz, get dressed,' I insisted. 'You'd be driving home from the airport by now.'

'My life is fine,' Hannah reiterated, flicking dog drool off her fingers in disgust. 'It's *Cassandra* we should be worried about. Cassie should be appearing on a Jewish *This is Your Life* called *THIS is Your LIFE*?!' She gestured around her, repulsed, before cringing away from a Doberman which was licking her hand under the table. 'What the hell *is* that dog? It looks like the kind of creature which would drag you into the Underworld.'

'Hannah has a point, Cassie. I mean, why is it that you have a full time job and yet Rory does fuck all to help you?'

As usual, I was exceeding the Daily Recommended Allowance of Cowardice. I bleated for a bit about what a good partner Rory was and how he did half of everything.

'Half! Women are so crap at maths,' Jazz exploded. 'This is why men are able to trick us into believing that they're doing fifty per cent of the housework, childcare and cooking. It's like that joke: the reason the bride wears white is because it's good for the dishwasher to match the stove and the fridge.' She paused to blow her nose once more. 'Which is why your sex-life sucks, because underneath you resent him.'

I glared at Jasmine in horror. How could she blurt out my secret like that? Hannah gave me a gluttonous look and for a minute I thought she was finally going to spread something on her cheese cracker – *moi*.

'Your sex life sucks?' she repeated, voraciously.

'Well, I wasn't actually planning on broadcasting my sexual secrets i.e. *that I don't have any*, but . . .' I glowered at Jazz once more. Stalling for time, I busied myself wetting Jasmine's bikini and scrunching it up in a plastic bag, then sprinkling sand from the cat litter into her suitcase. 'Cone of silence?' I requested and Hannah nodded. 'I've . . . I've . . . Oh God. My pussy has lost its purr,' I confessed reluctantly.

'Like most married women, her sex-life is terminally blah,' Jazz elaborated resentfully.

'Really? I thought Rory was an animal in bed.'

'Oh, he is an animal – a hamster.' I winced. Once, having loads of sex made a woman feel guilty and cheap. After marriage, not having loads of sex made a woman feel guilty and cheap.

'You two should really hit the road. I mean,' I tapped my watch, 'what if there's traffic?'

'Rory has the patience to spend hours and hours trying to hit a teeny weenie golf ball into a teeny weenie hole, but hasn't got the time to find her G-spot. Isn't that right, Cass?' Jazz said, testing the dryness of her tan with a fingertip.

Hannah looked at me with horror. The news had obviously scandalized her. 'Rory *golfs?*'

I shrugged non-committally. Rory may golf but I was the one with the handicap – my pathetic personality. Why could I never stand up to anyone? In my book, caution was always a good risk to take.

'We were told that our generation could Have It All,' Jazz continued, 'but what they really meant was that we can *Do* It All. Which is why I gave up work.'

'I don't Do It All,' I protested feebly. 'Rory helps me – he does. Get dressed, Jazz. It's time to go. Come *on!*'

'He helps you, eh?' Jazz echoed sarcastically as she pulled on trousers, boots, jumper and gloves to face the winter weather. 'Because the average working mother gets the kids up and off to school, does the housework, finally racing to her job, exhausted, panting, unbreakfasted, with kids' egg-dribble on her blouse – totally unaware that there was an earthquake in Pakistan. While her husband has read the papers, showered, shaved, listened to the BBC news and arrived at his office, refreshed, relaxed and warmed up for his day – and *that's* why you've lost your orgasm. Because you're angry. You're trapped in a hamster wheel of resentment and recrimination, and subconsciously you begrudge the prick, which is why you've stopped enjoying fucking him. It's just one more bloody demand.'

Jazz straightened up, fully dressed, with nothing

left to do but go and confront her awful wedded spouse. 'Marriage,' she declared, 'is the only war in which you have to sleep with the enemy.' She picked up her orange scarf and lassooed her neck in a noose. The symbolism wasn't lost on me.

'Rory is not the enemy!' I carped. 'He's a very hands-on dad, I'll have you know. He helps me a lot. With the kids, with the cleaning, with the—'

'And with your career? Aren't you up for a promotion? Mazel tov!' Hannah threaded her arms into the satin lining of her coat.

'Yep. I've got a meeting with the Head tomorrow morning.'

'Well, let's just see how much the shlemiel helps you get that job.'

I wanted to retaliate, but had no wish to fight with my friends. Would I never be cured of my lack of sass? It was a wonder David Attenborough hadn't made a documentary on me – half-woman, half-mouse, with the backbone of a jellyfish.

'Just remember that no wife has ever shot a husband while he was vacuuming,' were Jazz's parting words as Hannah left to drive her home from the airport, supposedly all tanned, rested and relaxed.

After they'd finally left, I slumped back against the hall door, exhausted.

Jazz was wrong. My Have It All dream had not turned into a Do It All nightmare. Rory and I were true partners. He did half of everything. He really did . . . Didn't he?

CHAPTER 6

THE WORKING MOTHER'S WEEK OR *'WHERE THE HELL'S YOUR FATHER?'*

Monday morning

The Dunkirk evacuation must have been easier to organize than a working mum getting her kids up and out of the house in the mornings.

7.00 a.m. Start breakfast. Sound alarm call. My kids always know it's time to get up when they hear me sharpening the toast.

7.10: When they're still not up, make their beds with them still in it.

7.20: Start sobbing that they can either get up now, or after their mother is institutionalized. Whichever comes first.

Ten minutes later it looks as though my friends will be getting a *lot* of woven baskets for Christmas.

'Come *on*, we'll be late,' I beg, running my daughter's morning bath to ease her eczema.

'Fish are in schools. And they're not learning anything,' my teenage son smart-arses from beneath his duvet.

It crosses my mind that it was so much easier to love your children unconditionally before they learned to speak.

7.23: In desperation, go into Attila the Mum Mode. 'Get up immediately or I'll fetch your father! Where the hell *is* your father?'

'On the loo,' they chorus.

After I slip a disc tipping them both out of their respective beds, I find Jenny's favourite cucumber and grapefruit shampoo with 83 added vitamins, ginger-nut bodywash and super-absorbent towels (two), then track down the cream for Jamie's wart, plus his fish-oil supplements.

7.30: Stand by sobbing as daughter plays Musical Clothes for the regulation ten minutes before choosing *the very outfit I had laid out for her the night before.* Informed by son that his uniform is caught between the wooden slats under the mattress of his top bunk.

'Where the hell's your father?' I plead, plaintively.

'Eating breakfast.'

There's nothing else for it. Manoeuvre top bunk-bed mattress onto own back so Jamie can retrieve snagged shirt. Catch sight of myself in mirror. Bent double from the weight of the mattress, look like two-legged turtle. Make mental note to go to chiropractor and to remind husband to put together Jamie's new Ikea single bed bought bloody *weeks ago.*

7.38: Hurtle into kitchen. Kids enter after me like a rush of wind. A squall of limbs and cacophony of complaints about what they will and won't eat. An Impi of Zulus doing close order drill would be less noisy than . . . Oh God! No!

7.39: Cereal fight. Bowl hurled at the fan heater. Cereal and milk globules splatter Jackson-Pollock-like, everywhere. Where is a Turner Prize judge when I need one?

'Where the hell's your father?'

'Shower.'

7.42: Trundle out vacuum cleaner. Start to hoover up rice bubbles. Just in time, see escaped guinea-pig. Bend down to coax it to safety. Hair sucked up in hoover nozzle. Now have impromptu perm on one side of head. Will have to teach in profile.

7.46: Dehair shower plug. Will let the water beat down on me for five minutes and tattoo out a soothing rhythm to stave off nervous breakdown. Turn on taps. Shriek. Water arctic. Thank *you*, Rory. Fucking hell! Bloody bugger it! Shit! Shit! Shit! Slip on puddle because husband has showered with plastic curtain outside bathtub.

7.50: Taking cold sponge bath with a flannel when daughter barges in. Needs cake for school fête. Oh fab. All the other mothers will have been up all night baking and all *I* have in the cupboard is a novelty, anatomically correct Gingerbread Man left over from the school librarian's hen night. Oh, and could I rustle up a few wood-nymph costumes for today's school play while I'm at it?

7.57: Finally have one leg threaded into tights

when son pokes head around bedroom door. He's just remembered he has rugby today. 'Rugby! You tell me that *now*?!!' I scream, rummaging through drawers, cupboards, laundry baskets, washing machines in frantic search for sports kit.

'Where the hell's your father?'

'Shaving.'

In a moment of blinding insight, I peek into Jamie's gym bag. There's something down there, something reeking and harbouring wildlife. Prod. It's brittle with mud but at least it isn't moving. What *is* it? A science experiment? When it doesn't bite me, realize that it is indeed Jamie's sports kit. No time to wash it. Spray it with perfume and stuff it back in again.

8.05: Fifteen minutes left for me to manoeuvre my way though peak hour traffic, drop off two kids at two different schools, find a spot in the school car park and get to my meeting with the head-master about the promotion. Nearly out the door, bags and books in hand, teeth brushed, lunches packed, when there's a last-minute request for excursion money. Then I'm rummaging again, in bags, drawers, coat pockets. End up stealing neighbour's milk money.

'Where the hell's your father?' comes my maternal mantra as I grope for keys to lock the front door.

'I'm right here, kitten.'

'Rory! Where the hell have you been all bloody morning?'

'I knew I'd just get under your feet. You're so brilliant at multi-tasking!'

Monday evening

'Well?' Jazz demands. She's on the phone the nanosecond I get home from school. 'Did Rory help you get to your meeting on time?'

'Maybe women are just better at multi-tasking?' I venture as I dust skirting boards. Dust? Who am I kidding? My skirting boards have *topsoil*. 'I know from teaching that boys definitely don't have the same finely tuned motor skills . . .'

'Let me get this straight, Cassie. Even though your husband can unhook a lace bustier with one hand in the dark, you think he's too clumsy to screw on a milk bottle top? Don't tell me you were late for your meeting?'

''Fraid so. And believe me, my hideous Headmaster accepts no excuse. He won't even take a doctor's sick-note because he says that if you're well enough to go to the doctor, then you're well enough to go to school,' I say, phone cradled to my ear as I hunt through the fridge for food that hasn't turned to penicillin. 'Anyway, talking about the Husband Hall of Shame, did you confront that low-life hubby of yours about his sexual multi-tasking?'

'Not yet. I'm still in shock. I don't know whether to vent my spleen or rupture his. I did get a call from the UN though, asking me to measure him for his bulletproof vest. They wanted me to measure him standing and then "sitting when erect".'

'Gosh! Have you got a tape measure big enough?' I ask facetiously as I attack the downstairs bathroom basin.

'And when I was measuring him . . . well, I didn't measure quite correctly.'

'Revenge of the Human Rights surgeon's wife. You're evil, Mrs Studlands,' I cackle, chipping away at Rory's beard stubble which enamels the porcelain.

'I'm making light of it, Cass, but I have been feeling so awful. I can't sleep. I have headaches, depression . . . and I'm so hot I'm creating my own micro-climate here!'

'Really? Should weather girls start including you in their reports? East Anglia, cold and windy. Jasmine Jardine, humid and sticky with warm front approaching.'

'Don't joke. I've made an appointment with the doctor even though I'm sure it's just stress. I wish I were more like you, Cass. You have the patience of a saint.'

'No. Two kids, a husband, a job and seven hundred animals to feed. That's what I've got.'

'Well, just remind that hulking great hubby of yours to help you more, okay?'

Tuesday morning

Rory's helping method is to set the clock an hour earlier.

'The early worm gets eaten by the bird,' my hubby mutters groggily, resetting the snooze alarm and rolling over.

Still, by 7.55 I am out of the door. Breathe a sigh of deep relief. Will make it to the meeting!

'Bye, tiger,' Rory waves as he slides into his Jeep.

'Rory! I thought you were doing the school run today? I have that interview with Scroope.'

'But I have a seminar. It's recently been discovered that research causes cancer in rats. Anyway the kids' schools are on your route, Cass. Oh, and could you drop off Mrs Pinkerton's Doberman in St John's Wood? I mean, it's right on your way.'

Oh no. Not the Hound of the Baskervilles. 'But—'

'That's what I love about you modern women. You really can Do It All,' he beams, blowing a kiss.

At eight o'clock, Rory roars off, 'Stairway To Heaven' blasting from both speakers.

Rory always seems to get a parking spot right outside our house whereas *I* can only ever find a space so far away I actually contemplate catching a taxi to my car each morning. Set off on a cross-country trek to find my Honda, me, the kids and the Doberman – with a compass and a list of edible berries.

★　★　★

Whoever wrote that bull about it being better to travel hopefully than to arrive has never done a school run.

The children start to fight about who gets to sit in the front. Solve battle by ordering them both into the back and strapping the Doberman into the passenger seat. It's a mystery of parenthood that your son can give mouth-to-mouth resuscitation to stray, worm-riddled dogs, share a piece of rechewed gum from a kid with bronchitis and pick his nose and eat it on a regular basis, yet won't sit next to his sister because of 'Girl Germs'.

The kids are at each other's throats by the end of the street. This chiefly entails trying to push each other, or sometimes *me*, out of the car windows. I don't think the Highway Code has a clause about not pushing the driver out of a moving vehicle because no one with a rational mind would ever imagine this as a possibility. Traffic lights were invented, not as you might imagine to ease the flow of cars in each direction, but to enable the distraught mother on the school run to flail around insanely at anything within striking distance – which in this case ends up being the Hound of the Baskervilles. Scream in pain as arm gnawed off by offended Doberman.

Miss one green light because busy stemming flow of blood. Miss second green light because picking chewing gum out of Jenny's hair and making Leaning Tower of Pisa from toothpicks for Jamie's art assignment. Miss third green light writing late notes on yesterday's parking ticket with eye-liner. Now so late I don't even stop outside my kids' schools. I just slow down long enough to hurl my eleven and thirteen year olds out onto the pavement like mailbags. Same with Cujo the killer dog.

Turn car for Primrose Hill. Put foot flat to the floor on the accelerator and land smack bang in a gridlock of 4 X 4s. Why do London mothers on the school run opt for four-wheel-drives which would only come into their own in, say, the Kalahari or Kathmandu?

Their only motto seems to be *Death Before Giving Way*. Sandwiched between the high bumpers of motorized monsters, my little Honda only comes up to the hubcaps of what Hannah self-deprecatingly calls 'Jews in Jeeps' and what Jazz refers to as 'derangerovers'. Panic rises in chest. I've five minutes to get to school and present myself, all calm and capable, before my headmaster. Reverse up one-way street – and become the first person in motoring history to be given a ticket for speeding backwards.

Might have got away with this radical manoeuvre if I hadn't drawn attention to myself by crashing into a miniature Smart car. But the policeman reckons he's been following me ever since I veered into the bus lane whilst talking on my mobile.

'Sorry, Officer,' I gabble. 'I think I'm high on library paste from making a Leaning Tower of Pisa in rush hour. And anyway, I'm a mother – a working mother – and we really should have our own lane. A pink lane. Right next to the bus lane. I mean, we need *help*, goddamn it! Anyway smart cars are not all that smart if they can be crushed like a cigarette packet from one incy wincey little bump. They're just a good way of keeping the population down, don't you think? So actually I've done society a service by demonstrating this design fault – which should cancel out all the road rules I broke during this slavering-animal-instigated whining off-spring inspired, deranged Working Mother (now *there's* a tautology) incident,' I plead, showing him my bleeding dog bite. 'Don't you think?'

The cop cocks an amused eyebrow, says he feels sure the insurers are bound to frame my statement of claim, then books me, before escorting me and my mangled arm to the Royal Free Hospital.

As the nurse stitches my wound, I ring Rory. Tell him what happened. Suggest in a thin-lipped way that he do the school run from now on, concluding with the fact that children in the back seat cause accidents.

'Accidents in the back seat cause children. That was how Jamie was conceived, remember?' he hints lasciviously.

'Rory! I'm in a hospital! I need looking after. And all you want to do is take my temperature WITH YOUR PENIS?' I notice that Casualty has gone terribly quiet all of a sudden and lower my voice.

'You have to look after the kids tonight, okay? I rang the Head from the car to say I'd be late . . .'

'Of course you were late, Cassie! How can any teacher be on time when there's that sign outside which says *School Ahead. Go slow?*'

'Rory, this is no laughing matter. Scroope informed me over the phone that he's devised something called a Threshold Assessment Form for job applicants. I have to fill it in before my meeting with him, rescheduled for tomorrow morning. It's fifty-seven pages long.'

'Hey, have I ever let you down foxy?'

'You're right. I couldn't ask for a better husband,' then, under my breath, 'as much as I'd bloody well like to.'

'Well?' Jazz asks when we bump into each other in the chemist in Camden during my lunch hour. She's at the counter. 'I'll have some soluble vitamin C tablets, a jar of Echinacea tablets and,' she raises her voice by ten decibels, '*tampons.*' She clocks my arm wound. 'Let me guess. You missed your meeting?'

'Not a bit,' I reply sarcastically. 'It's rescheduled for the morning. Rory's going to mind the kids so that I can swot. Scroope is making the contenders fill in some ridiculous questionnaire.'

'Don't forget the TAMPONS. The biggest box you've got!' Jazz calls out to the assistant. 'But you're the best qualified, Cass. You've been in charge of Year Six for five years. You get the best

93

SATS results. The Head's always receiving letters from happy parents saying you're fab for getting their kids into their first choice of schools. Ofsted Inspectors give you top marks all the time for innovation and creative flair. The staff love you, as do the rug-rats. So what's he waiting for?'

'He prefers the Chalk and Talk method of teaching, where the teacher stands at the board writing stuff and the kids learn by rote. He's devised this questionnaire as a way of catching me out. Then he'll have an excuse not to promote me.'

'Really? You think you'll have trouble with the questions?'

'No,' I said patiently. 'It's the *answers* I'll have trouble with.'

'My TAMPONS? . . .' Jazz nags the attendant. 'Thanks. Actually I need SUPER TAMPONS, if you don't mind.'

'What did the doctor say?' I ask.

Jazz's face takes on a stricken expression. She lowers her voice to a scandalized whisper. 'Apart from discovering that what you thought might be the menopause is really a three-month pregnancy, what is the worst thing that can happen to a woman our age?'

'I dunno. What?'

'Discovering that you're having an early menopause, of course! I'm peri-menopausal, apparently. Can you believe it? *Moi*?'

'Lucky you. My periods are so bad I have to

wear pads down to my knees. I'm positively *uphol-stered*. So . . . what's with all the tampons?'

'Good God, Cass! I don't want anyone to *know*. Cone of silence, promise? No wonder Studz has gone off me.' Tears rim her green eyes. 'What man in the world would want a woman who has,' she can barely utter the words 'passed her use-by date?'

'Um, Prince Charles? He gave up a supermodel for an older woman.'

'That's true.' Jazz rallies a little, blowing her nose. 'Actually, I've really liked Prince Charles ever since he wanted to be a Tampon. Although it is a metaphor for his whole life, don't you think? Always in the right place at the wrong time.'

We laugh and hug before parting, with promises to speak the next day. 'Where is Studz?' I ask.

'I don't know. No doubt off fornicating with a couple of crack-whores somewhere.'

'Are you going to confront him?'

'Not yet. He's off to Haiti. Here, look.' She fossicks through her Kim Novak bag and extracts a handwritten note. The letterhead declares it to be from a prison in Port-au-Prince. She reads it aloud. '*My grateful thanks for coming to meet my Prime Boss on Death Row. I need not tell you that you and your family will always be welcome to my perfumed land fondled by the sun and the Creole beauties whose charms are unknown to the world . . .* Which, I presume, is why Studz hasn't asked his family to go with him,' she post-scripts bitterly.

'Maybe he thought it was too dangerous – that you'd be kidnapped before you could say "I wonder who that man is, with the handcuffs and the tranquillizer daaaaa . . .""

'No. That cheat of a husband of mine is just too busy saving the world to save his marriage.'

My Rory may not be famous for healing the world's wounds, but he suddenly looked so good by contrast. You may be only one person in the world, but you can also be the world to one person. 'I do love Rory, you know, Jazz,' I say on an impulse. 'Tonight he'll redeem himself. I know he will.'

'Yeah, sure . . . And Melanie Griffith is aging naturally.'

Days in the houses of working parents pretty much conclude as they began – in a state of chaos and confusion.

4.30: Somehow manage to shoe-horn car between two massive Range Rovers only one hour's walk from my house and trudge home without getting mugged. Oh happy day!

5.30: Rory still not home. No Jeep outside but lots of rubbish. Rory hasn't tied the drawstring on the garbage bag tightly enough, much to the joy of the urban foxes which have recently invaded London. Littering the garden are all my guilty working-mother secrets – the frozen food packets and fast-food containers which I don't particularly want my stay-at-home organic mum neighbours to see.

5.40: Inside, find kids gazing mystified into fridge waiting for something edible to materialize. If ever I get time I'm going to hunt down Martha Stewart and ram that bread maker right up her jacksey! Domestic Goddesses from Mrs Beeton onwards have made the lives of ordinary women a misery. My favourite recipe would be to roast one slowly on a spit. Domestic Goddess *en croute*. Settle on chicken nuggets in the shape of comical cartoon characters which will no doubt introduce an array of inoperable tumours into my offspring's delicate systems.

6.00: Whilst cooking dinner, yell at kids to do homework. Express regret when can't answer their questions. From Jamie, 'I took the Religious Studies exam at school, Mum, but shouldn't my grade be determined by God?'

6.30: Pick up phone sticky with Nutella. Ring Rory's mobile. 'Rory? I've got to start filling in my Threshold Assessment form.'

'Just write "etc" a lot. That's what you write when you want bosses to think you know more than you do,' he says, promising to be home soon. A Golden Retriever has died in surgery during foreign object removal, and he's apparently on his way to break the news to the owners.

Try to revise my notes during dinner but kids keep up a stream of ridiculous questions.

'Mum, wasn't Hitler's first name Heil? Tell Jenny, she won't believe me.'

'Mum, when that ad on TV says that dog food

is new and improved tasting, well, who tests it? How do they *know*?'

Look at my offspring in bewilderment. Hadn't I ingested gallons of fish oils during pregnancy to optimise brain development? Hell, I'd eaten so much fish oil I'd probably soon grow gills and start spawning. And for *what*?

8.00: Ring Rory. 'The kids are driving me insane.'

'Hmm. Obviously you're still carrying a little residual anger over the whole breech-birth thing, pet,' is his reply.

'Come. Home. Right. Now,' I beseech, burping the lids on the Tupperware.

'But I'm just taking the dead dog owner for a beer to cheer him up. Turns out I forgot to get him to sign a consent form for surgery. I'm going to slip it under his nose when he's had a few. You don't want him to sue, do you?'

'Oh great. Which pub?'

'The Hobgoblin.'

'Isn't that the pub with the super wide-screen TV? God, there's not a match on, is there?'

'Won't be long. Love you.'

I groan. A pub with a wide-screen TV is the earthly equivalent of the black hole in space. Once a man goes in, he won't be coming out for an eternity. 'Rory! Rory! No, don't hang up on—'

9.00: Try to get Jenny to pack her school bag. Can't get her off the phone. Actually, can't remember what she looks like without half a phone growing out of her ear.

9.15: Give daughter phone-ectomy. March her into the bathroom to clean teeth.

9.30: Ring Rory again. Finally he answers, sounding inebriated. 'I know kids are hard work but they really are so rewarding, kitten. Just get them to bed earlier and you'll have loads of time. Even better, I won't be there to annoy you. Lovely peace and quiet, eh?'

'But Rory, I—'

9.45: Through bribery (what Jazz calls 'rewards'), I manage to get the kids into bed. Ironic how you can't get kids *out* of their beds in the morning, but can't get them *into* their beds at night. Pour glass of wine. Finally settle down to write Self-Assessment form.

9.50: Piercing scream from Jen's room. Steeplechase furniture and gallop upstairs in athletic spasm. Having run out of clean linen, I'd made her bed up with her brother's old Batman sheets. The fluorescent illustrations of the Joker and the Riddler, all grinning maniacally, has induced the world's first linen-related nightmare. Try to replace the single Batman duvet cover with one of my king-sized ones, but get lost inside it. Feel like an Arctic explorer, having a white-out. Give up. Put her in our bed.

10.00: Settle down to decode Scroope's obfuscatory educational jargon when suddenly remember I must record *The Six Wives of Henry VIII* for Jamie's school assignment.

Japan's revenge for losing the war is to manufacture

goods with indecipherable booklets; a psychological torture more painful than bamboo shoots under the nails. While lying on stomach on floor prodding various VCR buttons, I notice tumbleweeds of dust. If only houses could be like ovens and self-clean – but with the weekly cleaner not due till Friday it's down to me again. I spend the next hour scrubbing and scouring. Remember how diligent I was as a new bride. When Jamie was born everything had to be sterilized. By the time Jenny arrived, I sterilized the dummy by sucking on it – the old saliva disinfectant process. A decade later, my domesticity has dwindled to using a grey flannel to wipe down anything that doesn't talk back.

At 11 p.m. I make school lunches to save time in the morning. Take meat out of the freezer for next day's dinner. Put on a load of washing. Iron clothes for meeting with Head. Talk to pot-plants, which are wilting. Feed menagerie of animals. Make shopping lists. Put away *Monopoly*. Load dishwasher. Finish fairy costume for *A Midsummer Night's Dream* onto which tinsel refuses to bloody well stick bloody bloody bugger it! Just knuckling down to work – when Rory swaggers in.

'You see? How peaceful. Aren't you glad I stayed out of your hair all night? Don't worry about getting me any dinner either. I ate out. Got the surgery consent form signed too. Let's go to bed and celebrate, shall we?' He winks.

Oh great. The perfect way to top off my horror movie of a day – *The Hand*.

Then I remember that Jenny's in our bed. Phew. Safe. It's the first time Rory had been right in ages: *Children really can be so rewarding at times.*

Wednesday

'So?' Jazz asks me over lunchtime coffee at the deli near school. It's Wednesday, halfway through my week, thank God. 'How did it go with the Head?'

'Slept in.'

'What?! I thought Rory was going to take over last night?'

I shrug. 'Some surgery emergency.'

'Stop concocting excuses for that lazy pig. It's hard to make a comeback, Cass, if you haven't been anywhere.'

I watch in alarm as Jazz extracts a packet of fags from her bag. 'Since when did you take up smoking?'

'I haven't.' She lights up. 'I'm just faking it, so that when I wear my HRT patch, you still get periods you know. I can tell everyone it's an anti-smoking device.'

'If only they made Husband Patches, so that we can slowly withdraw from *them*,' I say, blowing on my toupee of cappuccino froth.

'How true, sweetie. Husbands are becoming less and less relevant. They're probably going to devolve – like tonsils and appendixes.'

The Incredible Shrinking Spouse. As there's no way I can be late again for my Deputy Head interview, and Rory's busy with his seminar, I decide to take matters into my own hands. I'm deluding myself of course. But still, a girl never knows what's she's incapable of, until she tries . . .

Thursday morning

Having made the kids sleep in their uniforms, I pack them off in a minicab to breakfast at the McDonald's near their schools, meaning I'm out of the door by 7.45 a.m.

8.00: Finally find car. Somewhere near *Wales*.

8.03: Start engine. Dashboard making funny, blinking signs. Unfortunately my car only speaks to me in Japanese. Using all my powers of mechanical genius, deduce that flashing light signals empty petrol tank. Bloody Rory. He'd promised to fill it up for me last weekend.

8.08: Fill up at garage. Go to pay. Computers down.

8.15: Sprint to cash machine opposite. Five people in front of me. We're all waiting behind a man of the heavily bearded persuasion who is probably a shoe bomber. He is shoving his card upside down into the slot. He looks at the card. He looks at the slot. He looks up to God. Ignores offers of help. Shoves card back into slot and pushes in the wrong number – three times. And the machine gobbles up his card, prompting him to scream and curse and no doubt shortly reach for his backpack detonator. Proof of my deranged state is that all I can think is that at least if he *is* a suicide bomber it will mean I won't have to make up another lame excuse for being late.

In desperation, I leave my car in the garage forecourt and run the rest of the way to work. My Headmaster is cut from the same tweedy mixture of snobbery and violence that supplied the warp and weft of the colonial empire. When I barrel into the admin block, eight minutes late, sweaty chest heaving asthmatically, he breaks off his chatty little conversation with my rival, Perdita Pendal, raises a thick pelt of eyebrow and says thinly, 'This lateness of yours is getting to be a habit, *Ms* O'Carroll.'

'Well, I've tried being early, but the trouble with being punctual, of course, is that there is usually nobody there to appreciate it,' I wheeze.

He gives one of his meagre little smiles. What will follow will be a softening of his voice which all his staff, me included, find very menacing as it usually precedes one of his furious tirades.

'Do you think these issues with time management make you Deputy Head material?' he says quietly. 'Mrs Pendal is always perfectly on time.'

Perdita Pendal is not only punctual but also well connected. Seems to me that the only way to survive in England is to pick an ancestor, whack on some fertilizer i.e. bullshit, and simply grow an extra branch of your family tree. Perdita doesn't just have a family tree, she has a forest, including a father who has been Chief Inspector of Schools. I, on the other hand, come from a long line of felons. My ancestors were transported to Tasmania for stealing a lace hanky and a stale loaf of bread . . . oh, and for dealing in A-grade narcotics. Perdita is the sort of woman who has coasters, matching hand towels, padded hangers, fish knives and a special little dish for the butter. She also has a well-off husband. In the staffroom one day she was actually heard to say, 'Oh, I'm completely exhausted! I've spent the *entire* week agonizing over which au pair to take skiing.' The female staff members could have killed her then and there. And do you know what? A jury of working mothers would have acquitted us.

'And your excuse *this time*?' The Head seems to be taking grim enjoyment from my discomfiture.

'Um . . .' During my time at North Primrose Primary School I've run through the pantheon of excuses. Unbeknownst to my relatives, most of them have met a premature demise. My children's illnesses have ranged from diarrhoea and diphtheria to whooping cough and weasel bites (married to a vet means I can occasionally resort to the zoological). I glance up at my boss. His eyebrows are raised in anticipation of my answer. When he waggles them, they look like copulating caterpillars. I rack my brain for a fresh excuse. I think about telling him that my cult leader kept me back for throat-slitting practice . . . Well, it

104

may not get me the promotion but it will *definitely* get me early retirement on full pay. Then, genius strikes!

'Actually, I was up so late relishing your Threshold Assessment form which, by the way, is scintillatingly insightful, that I slept in a little this morning,' I lie. 'It was just so penetrating, so, well, stimulating that I just couldn't sleep.' I really should stockpile Chapsticks so I can kiss yet more ass, I think to myself, but it does take the wind out of his vitriolic sails.

'Oh. Yes. Well. Right. Do you have it on you?'

'*I* have mine. Brilliant title, by the way. *To Teach Is To Learn*!' Perdita chirrups unctuously, handing in her form.

I think about explaining to Scroope that a job application is just a piece of paper with lies written on it. But settle instead for, 'Oh! Gosh. In all the rush of being late, I must have left my form behind,' I ad-lib. 'First thing tomorrow morning I could—'

'You *could* give Mr Scroope a verbal assessment,' Perdita suggests sweetly.

Shit. Out-foxed by a Chalk and Talker.

'Excellent idea,' Scroope says heartily. 'Normally I would see you separately, but as you've missed so many appointments, *Ms* O'Carroll, I've had to squeeze you into Mrs Pendal's preliminary session. Would you say that you . . .' the Head reads from Perdita's sheet, 'consistently and effectively use information about prior attainment to set well-grounded expectations for pupils, and monitor progress to give clear and constructive feedback relating to the curriculum?'

'Curriculum?' I cling to the only word that computes in his entire sentence. 'The inner-city London school curriculum? Oh, you mean how to read, write and do a drug deal?' I bluff. 'Oh well, at least it teaches the kids how to do metric.'

My smile is not reciprocated. In fact, my Headmaster's response would make a piece of granite look animated.

Perdita then volunteers to give her self-assessment verbally, enabling her to sing her own praises for approximately eternity, before running through the history of her illustrious family since, oh, the Crusades.

'Excellent. Well, *Ms* O'Carroll, Mrs Pendal and I have had a meaningful dialogue about what I'm looking for in a Deputy Head during this probation period . . .'

I'd like to have a meaningful dialogue with Perdita too – armed with a cricket bat.

'But as I now have school assembly, perhaps you could take the time during your lunch-hour to write me out your Teacher Appraisal, listing your strengths . . .'

'Not punctuality, obviously,' Perdita slips in so she can share a little conspiratorial chuckle with the Headmaster.

Trying to explain what makes you a good teacher is like nailing jelly to a wall. 'My best qualification, Mr Scroope, is that I adore my pupils and love my job.'

Strangely, the Head seems unconvinced of my genius. He pushes to his feet. 'Thank you, Mrs Pendal,' he dismisses Perdita with a smile. 'But *Ms* O'Carroll, if I could just have a quick word . . . You may have been at this school for longer than Mrs Pendal,' he tells me when we're alone, 'but you know she did get a first-class Honours degree. *And* she's written a thesis – "Control and Structure in the Classroom",' he parrots approvingly.

My most accomplished skill as a teacher is knowing who is pulling faces behind my back and which kid's dog really did eat the homework. Not things they can really teach you at college.

'Tell me, why did you choose primary-school education?' he says finally.

'Well, I suspect that educating high-school kids is probably more rewarding than primary-school teaching because the kids are tall enough to head-butt,' I joke, 'but kidding aside, I actually like teaching younger children because of their sense of humour. Just last week little Rosie Myttas-Perris wrote in her geography lesson that what joins the Red Sea to the Med is the Sewage Canal! And when I asked Adi Greenberg to count from one to ten backwards, she turned her back to me and started counting.' I laugh, cutting it short when I realize I'm the only one who is amused.

Mr Scroope draws in a fractious breath. In the staffroom we often joke that our Head would have been discharged from Saddam Hussein's hit squad for being too brutal. When he loses his temper, which he does daily, one suspects he's missed his vocation. The man should definitely have followed the career path marked *US Postal Worker*.

'ARE YOU SERIOUS ABOUT THIS PROMOTION, MS O'CARROLL? MR DUNDEE IS LEAVING AT THE END OF THE SUMMER TERM AND I WILL NEED TO REPLACE HIM WITH A CAPABLE AND CONSCIENTIOUS TEACHER. YOU ARE THE MOST SENIOR APPLICANT, AND THE INSPECTORS AND THE CHILDREN LIKE YOU, TRUE, BUT I AM *NOT* SEEING LEADERSHIP QUALITIES IN YOU.'

As he rants on about 're-engineering priorities' and 'downsizing' and 'rightsizing', I study his comb-over. It looks like limp spaghetti draped over a hardboiled egg. Examining the coffee-cup rings on his desk as he interrogates me about what I've allegedly written on my forms, I contemplate asking him what he writes on his passport under *Hair colour*, seeing as he is, you know, borderline BALD.

Behind him I see Perdita sashaying across the playground in her twinset and pearls, rested, relaxed, poised and, well, perfect. Ah, I think, there but for the grace of a househusband, go I.

Friday

What teachers drink in the staffroom tells you a lot about them. Most stagger into school clutching Starbucks hard-core espresso. Mr Scroope is a milky tea, two sugars type. Perdita – a rosemary-infused herbal. The rest of the day we boil the old kettle full of limescale and drink randomly from ironically sloganed mugs – *Teachers Do It With Class, Teachers Make You Do It Till You Get It Right.* Perdita's tea mug, on the other hand, was sacrosanct. It was also emblazoned, ominously, with *Best Teacher.*

I slump onto a threadbare sofa which resembles a yak that has been dead for some time and sip a cup of staffroom coffee. It tastes as lukewarm as I feel. I dwell dispiritedly on my past week. Like tidemarks left around the bath, like toenail clippings abandoned on bedside tables, the evidence has begun to mount up that Rory has truanted from the How To Be A Good Husband School.

Whoever said, 'Life is just one thing after another'? For working mothers it's just the same thing, again and again and over and over. But at a very fast pace. Like jogging in quicksand. For working mums, every day is a lot like holding a live hand-grenade with the pin pulled half-out.

No matter how much I wanted to be one of those women who can change a nappy with one hand whilst whipping up a soufflé with the other at the same time as I'm taking a conference call, what I had become, instead, was a cliché. When I heard those homilies coming out of my mouth like, 'Where were you born? In a *tent*?' it's as though I've been secretly brain-washed during my sleep by suggestive tapes entitled *Wifely Clichés, Vol. 2*.

Was it any wonder that by Friday night I'd developed the demeanour, aching legs and mood swings of a long-haul flight attendant? Maybe Jazz was right after all. Maybe I *was* angry with Rory, which was why I didn't feel affectionate towards him in bed. Oh great. Now I had to add sulking to an already over-booked schedule.

I also had the feeling that it was time for a coup in the Holy State of Matrimony.

CHAPTER 7

LADIES WHO LYNCH

In my opinion, advice is like syphilis. It's better to give than to receive.

Should I leave my husband? That was the typed question blinking out at me from my computer screen in the staffroom as Jazz and I emailed each other a week later.

I quailed. It was one of life's unanswerable questions, equivalent to why 'monosyllabism' is such a long word.

But I was not going to contaminate her with my influence. I looked around the shabby staffroom at the rest of the female staff. Two divorcees. Three separated. Four unhappily married. The trouble is, women marry without a Matrimonial Safety Drill. No one ever said to us, 'Your exits are here, here and here.' But I was *not* going to be the one to ever tell a girlfriend to parachute into the unknown.

Another message zapped up on the screen.

Jazz: *When Studz got home last night from Haiti I told him how and why he'd broken my heart. The Great Healer's advice? To take two aspirin and lie down. With him. He put my constant crying down to 'excessive lachrymonal activity'.*

Cassie: *Sensitive bastard.*

Jazz: *He said that the awful reality of trying to stitch together landmine victims has made him numb. He said that war has chloroformed his compassion, and that the grim sights on his operating table have left him etherized . . . And that he only has affairs to feel alive again.*

Cassie: *Ironic, as you're about to **kill** him! What a conman! As he's taking Viagra, that makes him a hardened criminal. (Pathetic, I know, but the best I can do, having taught science all morning.) What else did he say?*

Jazz: *He asked if I wanted him to sleep in another bed. I said yes, preferably in another hemisphere.*

Cassie: *Is he going to stop seeing those other women?*

Jazz: *He said that obviously affairs fulfill some need that isn't being met within the marriage and, as long as that need continues to be unmet, so the dissatisfied partner will continue to be unfaithful. Rather than destroy the marriage, he said it was kinder to look elsewhere for things that are missing. According to him infidelity is a strategy for **maintaining** our marriage. It is an act of **preservation**, rather than **destruction**. That's how he justifies being a repeat cheat.*

Cassie: *Justifies being a duplicitous, lying maggot, you mean. What are you going to do?*

Jazz: *Kick him out, I suppose. Well, I don't want to spend the rest of my life counting his condoms, do I?*

Cassie: *You could always attach a tracking device*

to his undies – a Shag Tag. Shit! Gotta go. Scroope in playground sniffing the air like a bloodhound. It's parent-teacher evening.

Jazz: *C U 2night at Hannah's opening do at the gallery. Plse don't be late. There's something else I need to discuss with you.*

Cassie: *How to find a proctologist with really cold hands to do your husband's next rectal examination?*

Jazz: *I've found a lump. In my tit.*

A lump? I looked at the little green cursor on the computer screen as it blinked neurotically. Jazz's mother had just died of breast cancer. And wasn't it hereditary.

I taught my afternoon class and sat through my parent-teacher meetings in a state of bowel-knotted angst. The ten-year-old girls in my care had just endured their 11-plus exams to see which high school they would get into. The competitiveness between the parents was sickening. London parents are so desperate to get their kids into the right school they sprint to the doors of top nurseries, clutching their pregnancy kits, pink sticks still dripping with urine.

'My daughter got straight As, so we're confident she'll get her music scholarship. She's only grade Five, but she got top distinctions. She wants to be a soloist and a brain surgeon. You have a daughter, don't you? What did *she* tell prospective school principals she wanted to be?'

'A trampolinist and a spy, I believe is what Jenny said.'

113

'Oh.' Brief silence, followed by pitying smile. 'How, um . . . original.'

The overly ambitious parent wears the dazzling but terrified smile of a highwire acrobat. One of the beaming mothers was concerned that her son was reading cowboy comics instead of the classics. What was my advice?

'Um . . . not to squat down with his spurs on?'

My *own* son had just joined a band called 'Jerk to Inflate' and penned a song titled 'My Dog Ate Hitler's Brain', so really I was in no position to give advice to anyone.

It was 8.35 p.m. before I staggered out of the classroom. Usually I'd meet the other female teachers for a drink to finalize 'The Most Fanciable Father Competition', but tonight I had to get to Jasmine. I was stampeding for the door when the Head slid out of his office like an eel from under a rock.

'During assembly, when the children were told to stand for the National Anthem, apparently several of your class stood on their heads. When sent to my office, they maintained that you told them that that nobody had actually specified which part they had to stand *on*.'

'Well, actually nobody did. And blood to the brain does revitalize the—'

'I would appreciate it, *Ms* O'Carroll, if you would keep your anti-Royalist sentiments to yourself – if you want to pursue a career in education, that is. And do you really think trousers are acceptable for a woman to wear to work?'

What *I* wanted to know was how acceptable it was to have a Head Teacher who was so fat and wore a suit so small he looked like a condom full of porridge. And how unacceptable it was to be told off in front of my rival Perdita, who was lurking behind him with a cat-that-licked-the-cream countenance.

'Yes, sir. No, sir,' was my gutless reply. I was too submissive, I knew that. I possessed the kind of compliance that foretold a long career in check-out-chicking. It also meant that from now on I'd have to sport the Modified Nun Look. Lovely.

'Cassandra,' said Perdita, after the Head had steamed off down the hall, a sixty-year-old battleship with moral guns blazing, 'I know we're both up for the same job and may the best girl win! But that doesn't mean we can't still be chums. Why don't we go for a drink one evening?'

I'd rather be staked out by my labia over an ants' nest. How about never? Does never work for you? is what I thought. But, 'I'll have to check my diary,' is what I said. I really did need a course in Cattle-Prodding for Beginners because Perdita didn't want to be friends. She wanted to pick over my brain as though it were a chicken carcass. School Inspectors were now looking for creativity. Perdita was thorough but unimaginative. When she saw my kids' whacky art on the wall, she expressed a condescending curiosity, but was well aware that it got me *Excellence in teaching* on my reports from Inspectors.

When I finally made it to Hannah's gallery later that night, for the Private View of her latest show, I was not only shattered from thirty parent-teacher interviews, a bollocking from the Headmaster, and anxiety about my exile in Orgasm Siberia, but I was also gibbering about the state of my best friend's breasts.

Outside the gallery I shucked off my trainers and tortured my toes into the high heels I was carrying in a plastic bag. As I balanced precariously on one leg, steadying myself by holding onto the arm of the steroid-addled doorman, I could hear the murmur of voices; of laughter, smug and luxurious. I peeked through the window and groaned inwardly.

I am not good with posh people. Hannah took me fox-hunting once with one of her clients and I got my jodhpur caught in my stirrup, lurched into a bramble bush and was bitten by a hound. The fox died, yes, but only because he was killing himself laughing.

I milled around pretending to look at the paintings, but really ogling Liz Hurley, Mick Jagger, Elton John and an overweight movie mogul whom Jazz always described as 'the man who ate showbiz'. Their noses were so high in the air, I kept expecting trolley dollies with trays to appear by each nostril.

Also attending were the usual aristocratic cliques – the lusty patriarchs and their long-suffering, alienated wives, the Number 1 mistresses, the slightly eccentric cocaine-sniffing outsider elder sons back from rehab – all being buttered up by Hannah to buy paintings from her latest discovery. It seems to me that good art is in the wallet of the beholder. No doubt this was why Hannah had the fat taken from her buttocks and injected into her lips because 'kissing ass' was part of her job.

I wished Rory was with me for support, but he hated modern art. He refused to come and look at dead sharks in formaldehyde. He felt that a dead shark was not an *objet d'art*, but a mouldy fish finger.

Unaccustomed to wearing pointy high heels, I minced painfully around the party, looking for Jazz. 'The work speaks to the inner beast, yes?' a man in a dress asked me. Help! I had to find Jazz and fast, if only because I was the only guest not fluent in designese.

Jazz was sitting on the stairs in a funereal cock-tail dress, her long hair loose, nursing a glass of chardonnay and pretending to smoke a cigarette for HRT patch camouflage.

'Sorry I'm late, darl. What happened? Did you have a mammogram? How was it?' I perched on the stair below her.

'Well, they squash your tits into a blender until your brain erupts through your ears, but it's no worse, painwise, than your average divorce.'

A comment like that should be stepped around as carefully as a dozing anaconda. 'But what did the doctor find? What did she say?'

'She found a lump, which looked malignant. I had the biopsy straight away, because of my history,' she said flatly. 'Results in a week.'

'Oh God. It's bound to be nothing, Jazz. It's probably just a cyst.' I sounded calm but my heart was thudding against my Wonderbra. 'Did Studz go with you?'

'No. He had another lump in mind. That lump of land in the bloated midriff of Europe solely interested in the pursuit of Michelin starred extramarital affairs, otherwise known as France.'

She'd obviously had plenty of time to work on that line in the hospital. I squeezed her leg sympathetically. 'I would have gone with you for the mammogram, love.'

She shrugged. 'Silly me. I thought he'd realize at the last minute that his wife is more important than a meeting at UNESCO. It's no wonder I've contracted cancer really. Except for playing with asbestos, there's no greater health hazard than an unhappy marriage.'

I was groping for a reply when Hannah swanned past. She was blending into the background, as usual, in an orange velvet dress and a turquoise turban. 'Oh, there you are, you two!' She rested one Jimmy Choo on the bottom stair and looked us up and down. 'Cassandra, how little you must think of yourself to buy shmatte like that when I keep offering you my cast-offs,' she said. Hannah's motto is *If the dress fits, buy it in at least four colours.* 'Where's Studz?'

'Addressing UNESCO. Allegedly. He's coming straight here from Waterloo Station.'

'That man will work himself to death.'

Jazz shrugged one delicate, bare shoulder. 'Oh well. We've all got to die sometime.'

I gave Hannah a 'shut up' look.

'What?' she mouthed at me. 'What did I say?' But she was looking up at us with such rumpled perplexity that Jazz just burst out laughing.

'I've had a lumpectomy,' she announced. 'And I'm divorcing my husband.'

If Hannah could have raised a brow, I'm sure she would have, but being Botoxed, all we got was a tiny flutter of lashes to show her distress.

'A lump? Fuck. Well, do you really think you should be smoking?' Hannah snatched the cigarette Jazz was pretending to puff and put it in an ashtray. 'And Divorce? You can't possibly divorce. What about Josh? What kind of role model will that make you?'

Jazz defiantly lit up another fag. 'Being a role model for your teenagers takes all the fun out of middle age, don't you think?'

Hannah placed her perfectly painted hands on her Atkins-dieted hips. 'My parents divorced when I was in Kindergarten, but anyway, enough about why I bit my nails till they bled until I was, oh, twenty-fucking-seven.'

'Look, sweetie,' Jazz amended, 'I didn't believe in divorce either – until I got married.'

'Anyone can divorce. Lasting is the hard thing,' Hannah lectured. 'I'm sure Studz is just having a little midlife crisis, dahling. Can't you keep an open mind until he gets over it?'

'My mind hasn't been open, it's been vacant. I've had enough of the small humiliations, Hannah,' Jazz explained, her voice a miserable whisper. 'I think, therefore I'm divorced.'

'Speaking of which . . .' I nodded in the direction of the door. Jazz's dashingly handsome husband had just swept into the gallery, briefcase and black leather coat in hand. He glittered. He shone. He outblazed the chandeliers. The room was full of models thin as skittles. And it was Dr Studlands who bowled them over. Women were leaping onto him as though he were the last helicopter out of Saigon.

For a moment Jazz put on her Madame Defarge face, as she watched, gimlet-eyed, from the side-lines. Then her expression cracked and she abruptly turned her back. 'I'm so sick of watching my husband parade around like some Medieval King taking his pick of fertile maidens.'

Hannah's ring-encrusted hand was on her arm, reassuringly. 'When do you get the biopsy results?'

'End of the week.'

'Let's deal with that before you undergo any marital chemo,' I suggested kindly. 'Okay?'

'Yes. Don't do anything till then, dah-ling. We need to talk it through,' Hannah advised.

So talk we did. We talked so much our lips lost weight. It was like facial aerobics. The Talkins Diet.

We talked in the loo queue at a West End theatre with its usual combination of 250 desperate women and two backed-up toilets.

'But why divorce?' Hannah was putting on red lipstick expertly without the aid of a mirror.

'Because, sadly, the use of the hemlock-poisoned chalice seems to have died out in modern marriage,' Jazz said facetiously.

'Does his infidelity really matter when you have so much else?' Hannah wanted to know.

It struck me as extraordinary that wives consider a husband staying faithful a far greater achievement than, say, a cure for whooping cough.

'Pascal predicts a return to nineteenth-century values. *Fidelité et séduction,* he calls it,' she continued. 'Pleasing and charming and caressing the tender feelings.'

'That just means he doesn't fancy you any more,' Jazz pronounced.

'How dare you!' Hannah said with rigid grace.

'If all you're doing is a lot of connubial cuddling, well, it's over, sweetie. Truth is, sex is like air,' Jazz pronounced. 'No big deal unless you're not getting any. Especially when *he* obviously is,' she concluded poignantly.

The interval bells were sounding the five-minute

warning, but the loo queue seemed to be enjoying our private mini-drama much more than the critically acclaimed Ibsen.

'You could agree to an arrangement. You know, the way the French do,' Hannah suggested. 'Couldn't she, Cassie?'

One of life's great truisms, like the fact that nudists are always the very people you don't ever want to see naked, is that you should never interfere in a girlfriend's marriage. 'Um . . .'

'An arrangement? Yes, that's a splendid idea,' Jazz jumped in. 'David can arrange to fuck around and I can arrange to kill him.'

The loo queue cheered their support. It seems that wives are recycling husbands so fast there should be a recycling bin at the bottle bank just for them. Green glass, brown glass, clear glass, and then the *Boring Cheating Husband* bin.

Back in the foyer, we were swept up in the exultant crowd exploding from the bar like champagne, yet I took my seat feeling flat. Even the play, *Hedda Gabler*, was really just a kind of Norwegian *Desperate Housewives*. Our angst was nothing new. I definitely had the feeling Hedda had lost her orgasm too – and look where *that* had got her! Judging by the mounting evidence, marriage was turning out to be as exciting as thrush, only much harder to be rid of. Like a drummer with an IQ a quiet American or a fat model, it seemed that a happy marriage was an oddity of nature. But Rory and I were still happy, despite a few disagreements and a little dis-enchantment of late . . . weren't we?

We talked when shopping.

'The good thing about being a woman is, no matter how bad things get, we can always go shopping,' Jazz declared as we rode the Selfridges escalator.

'Armani who art in heaven, Hallowed be Thy name,' Hannah genuflected.

'I read this article that said the typical symptoms of stress are eating too much, impulse buying and driving too fast. Are they kidding? That's my idea of a divine day,' I added excitedly. I had one whole hour of indulgence before the kids were due to be collected from tennis.

While we lost ourselves in rack-pawing, sales delirium and guiltless gimme, Hannah tried to convince Jazz that she needed to dress more seduc-tively to win back her husband's devotions. I was also in the stylistic firing line.

'You'll never get a promotion in shoes like that. Where did you *get* those anyway?' Hannah said, pointing at my suede loafers.

'Somewhere at the back of my closet.'

'Dah-ling, your shoes are so far back in the closet they're *gay*. Now . . .' She checked to see if Jazz was out of earshot. 'We need to talk. Jazz can't divorce. There's so little difference between husbands, she might as well keep the shmuck whose disgusting eating and farting habits she's got used to.'

In truth I would rather listen to a Yoko Ono CD than hear Hannah lecturing me on reasons Jazz should stay in her marriage. But as I tried to move away, she seized my arm.

'You really want to condemn your friend to a life on her own, nibbling microwaved Lean Cuisine meals and watching repeats of *Sex and the City*?'

'I don't think Jazz is interested in finding another husband, Hannah, although an aged billionaire with a great art collection who is quite ill could hold some appeal, I guess.'

But Hannah refused to be amused. 'Divorce is a bad, bad idea, Cassie. And you'll back me up, yes?'

Besides manually masturbating caged animals for artificial insemination, I couldn't think of a worse request. I was going to procrastinate but, as usual, I didn't quite get round to it.

'Um, yeah, sure.'

We talked, naked, in the changing room of the gym after water aerobics.

'If swimming's so good for losing weight, how do you explain walruses?' I panted, balancing on one leg like an asthmatic flamingo as I threaded a damp foot into a knicker leg hole. Jazz remained stony-faced. 'Cheer up, love. George Clooney's still single. Now *that's* something to smile about.'

'No. The reason to smile is that every seven minutes of every day, a husband, somewhere in the world, dies.' Jazz glanced around to make sure Hannah was not eavesdropping, but our suave friend was still in the showers rubbing on her latest anti-aging cream – some mix of minced Transylvanian fluke fish and puréed sloth.

'We need to talk. You've got to back me up against Hannah,' she said urgently. 'Without the lubrication of love, the cogs of a marriage grind away into dust. Don't you think?'

What I thought was that she'd been listening to too much Leonard Cohen. 'Um . . .'

Her fingers dug into my shoulder. 'There's nothing lonelier than an unhappy marriage,' Jazz went on. 'Gloria Steinem once said that the surest way to be alone was to get married. I'm like a married single mother, and so are you, Cass. But Hannah's so judgemental. You will back me up, right?'

Gnawing an Albanian weight-lifter's jockstrap would be a preferable option. 'Yeah, sure.'

My best friend jumped for joy.

So did I – right off the nearest bridge.

The day Jazz's results were due the hospital called to say they needed to do more tests. This did not bode well. Hannah and I immediately dropped everything. After a frantic ring around to arrange play dates and vowing yet again to get an au pair (most middle-class English kids have no idea that their au pair is not their mother until they're about ten, which can be quite a trauma as they can only speak Croatian), I went straight to Jazz's house after school.

I was not prepared for Studz to open the door.

It was one of those rare winter days where the sun, low in the cloudless blue sky, slices into your eyes. David Studlands was lit as if in a stage spotlight. And as usual, he dazzled.

'Come in,' he said in his mellifluous voice, a warm hand on the small of my back. 'Can I get you a drink? Jasmine's doing the school run.'

He steered me into the sitting room. 'No thanks. I'll—'

But Studz was already pouring me a glass of Merlot. In the sunlight he looked suddenly younger. I had a flashback to his student days – all tousled hair, faded jeans, a half-smile playing on his lips. When had he undergone his Bastard Transplant, I wondered. When had he transmogrified into Snidely Whiplash? A surge of fury went through me, overcoming my lack of confidence.

'I'm not going to make small talk with you, Studz – even though I know how much you like talking about your dick . . . not to mention, thinking with it. Why? Why the hell have you hurt Jazz like this?' I flopped down angrily into the sofa.

'Oh I see. The coven have been consulted around the cauldron.' Jazz's husband threw his hands up in the air. 'Stress. Exhaustion. I'm practically running the Medical Foundation for the Care of Victims of War single-handedly.'

'Really?' I looked at him, as unblinking as a lizard. 'What are you doing with your other hand?'

But instead of taking umbrage, Studz just laughed. He was Teflon Man. Insults slid right off him.

'You know that Jazz is about to ask you to go down on bended knee and say, "Will you be my ex-wife?"' I paused and Studz looked down at me with his hooded, slightly bloodshot eyes. 'How could you do it to her?' I asked again. 'You've broken her heart.'

He shrugged. 'Men go with younger women for a little something extra,' he said matter-of-factly, 'fearing humiliation and gruesome handbag injuries if we asked for those "extras" at home.'

Studlands centred me in his gaze once more. His eyes, a tart mix of orange and green, were made even more marmaladey in the afternoon sunlight. As he moved towards the couch I shifted to make room for him, but he sat too close to me. I could feel the warm length of his thigh against mine.

'On the other hand, unlike most wives, I always thought *you'd* be very creative in bed, Cassandra.'

'Oh yes, I am,' I replied coldly. 'I do origami, macramé and needlework.'

'Is there life after infidelity? Of course there is,' he continued, smoothly. 'Monogamy as a workable concept is dead.'

'For you blokes maybe. Men being good at

fidelity is like saying that . . . I dunno – that Gandhi was good at catering.'

'Come on, Cassandra. How long have you and Rory been married? Wouldn't you like to feel the thrill of a strange hand on your skin? The heat of another man's mouth?'

He was staring at me – no, *into* me – a certain savagery in his look and then his hand was on my thigh. 'Aren't you a little old to be playing doctor?' I slapped his hand angrily. I would have said more except my best friend had just arrived at the front door.

Josh strolled in behind her. 'Mum,' he waved at me, dumping his bag and heading for the fridge, 'will you help me with my art assignment?'

'Of course, darling.'

Studz gave a snort of laughter as merciless as a nose blowing. 'Your mother? Using her brain? She's been a lady of leisure so long I think it's rusted, kiddo!' he condescended, sauntering back towards his study.

'You're right, I *must* be stupid,' she riposted. 'I mean, *look who I married.*'

Once we were alone, Jazz gnawed fretfully on the inside of her left cheek. She poured herself a drink. She was so upset she forgot to light up one of the cigarettes she didn't really smoke.

'I've been thinking, Jazz' I said. 'You know how you keep asking me what you should do. And you know how, next to shoving a fork into an electrical socket, my least favourite thing to do is give advice to a girlfriend about her marriage? Well, I've decided that yes. Yes! You should divorce the scumbag. The man is evil. It's a wonder he's not off somewhere tossing virgins into volcanoes.'

'Thanks, Cass.' She visibly relaxed. 'The way Rory treats you, you should think about divorcing too. Just remember that, statistically, one hundred per cent of divorces begin with marriage.'

I looked at her agog. Was she serious? Did she really think I could just put Rory in the cupboard under the stairs with all the other broken domestic appliances?

'I'm going to talk to him. Once Rory realizes how selfish he's been . . .'

'Talk to him? Ha!' Jazz hooted. 'He won't remember what you say. Men have a carp-like attention span. It's a kind of empathy amnesia. The only good thing is that you can make cracks in front of them about how inadequate they are, 'cause they're not listening anyway.'

'Once I explain my feelings, he'll—'

'*Feelings!*' In purple Prada, Hannah was arriving. Josh had let her into the hallway where she was subduing a quarrelsome umbrella. 'Of course men have feelings! My Pascal is very emotionally inarticulate, dah-ling.' She expropriated the red wine bottle and air-kissed Jazz with an 'Are you okay?' look.

'That's utter tosh, Hannah. Women spend more time thinking about what men are thinking about, than men spend thinking.'

'Well, I'm going to give Rory a chance to change,' I decided.

'Change? Ha!' Jazz scoffed. 'It won't ever happen. It's as likely as the washing-machine repair man turning up at the appointed time on the appointed day.'

'Love can exist in marriage. I mean, you love Pascal – right, Hannah?' I pleaded.

'Dah-ling. We're so far above Cloud Nine we have to look down to see it. He's searing salmon for my dinner as we speak. Proof of how much he loves me!'

'Pascal *has* to love you,' Jazz said. 'You support him. The mixed-income couple is the new inter-racial couple. I now pronounce you Man and Mansion.'

'I know you're anxious about your results, Jasmine, and I should be nice to you, but you can be such a bitch,' Hannah scorched back.

'No, I can't.' Jazz lit up a fag and smoked fakely. 'If I were a real bitch, I would tell Cassie that her husband is a lazy, misogynistic bastard, and I haven't, have I?'

'Just because *you're* unhappy in your marriage, Jazz, don't undermine Cassie's or mine.' Hannah stubbed out Jazz's cigarette with vehemence and primly steepled her hands.

'I do still adore Rory, Jazz,' I added. 'We aren't exactly on Cloud Nine. But Cloud Seven and a Half, for sure.'

'Maybe so. But women need emotional intimacy

to stay attracted to a bloke. And how can you feel emotionally intimate with a man you resent for not helping around the house?'

She had a point. Yes, I adored Rory but, of late, my biggest sex fantasy in the bedroom involved me discovering that he'd picked his underpants up off the floor. But divorce? It sounded so scandalous. So satiny underwear and sloe gins. If hostages in Iraq could survive being shackled together to a radiator, surely I could stand a little ball and chain? My parents had been married for nearly forty years. How had they done it?

Spending time with most family members is like eating brussel sprouts, a dreary duty we endure at Christmas. But I was close to my mum and dad, who divided their time between Sydney and Surrey. So, the next Sunday, as we endured a traditional English barbecue, eating half-raw, carcinogenic sausages made from pigs' lips and cows' nipples, while being wind-whipped in the back garden, I cornered my mother.

'Mum, I need advice. Lately with Rory, I dunno, I just feel that I do everything and that I'm totally taken advantage of. He's so emotionally withdrawn.'

My mother laughed caustically. 'Wait until you both retire and he discovers the Internet, dear. Whenever your father gets back from a trip he rushes into the study, embracing his PC crying, "Hi, honey, I'm home." I mean, he completely ignores me all day, even eats his meals at the computer, then comes to me for a bit of slap and tickle at night! When we've hardly even spoken! It's bloody infuriating.'

My heart sank. Is this what I had to look forward to? 'But haven't you talked to Dad about it? Haven't you complained?'

'Talk? Oh no, dear. There's no point. Wives must just drink gin and bear it,' she quipped, topping up my glass.

I may have started to resemble her physically, but did I really want to turn into my mother emotionally? To become acquiescent and compromising? To wander around, endlessly sighing, with my freeze-dried feelings and vaccuum-packed dreams?

My mother may have pressed *Ctrl Alt Delete* on her self-esteem, and Jazz's marriage may have been *Brigadoon*-ing before her eyes, but mine was not melting into the mist. It was just that Jazz was so unhappy I'd begun to get maritally psychosomatic. Yes, that was it! I'd started to develop divorce symptoms. But Rory was not lazy or misogynistic or emotionally inarticulate. Okay, recently the air had been seeping out of my marriage like a tyre with a slow puncture. But it was time to patch things up.

My girlfriends warned me I was gullible . . . I only wish I'd believed them.

CHAPTER 8

TO LOVE, HOOVER AND OBEY

In a marriage, no news is bad news. I therefore determined to talk to my husband on Saturday morning, over breakfast.

'Rory, I don't seem to remember that my wedding vows were "To Love, Hoover and Obey".'

'What exactly are those Japanese researching on whales?' was his answer. He was scrutinizing an Animal Welfare report.

'Rory, are you listening to me?'

He munched on some cereal, sending milk splattering. 'I mean, they've killed so many and yet made no announcements. Are they suddenly going to reveal that whales can tap dance? Yodel? Do calculus?'

'Great! You can't even *hear* me asking if you're *listening*!' (Note to self. Never attempt conversation with man if newspaper, sports programme or work folder is within one-mile radius.)

'Huh?' Rory was so unused to me shouting at him that he looked up in wounded bewilderment. But for once I was *not* going to do the traditional Anglo-Saxon thing of bottling it all inside and

133

then finally psychologically imploding one afternoon by the cheese counter of Sainsbury's.

'YOU NEVER HELP ME AROUND THE HOUSE ANY MORE.'

'Huh?' A schoolboy head of floppy hair fell into his eyes. 'That's not true, puss.'

'Rory, your only contribution to anything domestic of late was when your brother and his new bride were coming to stay and I asked you to get the bedroom in the surgery flat ready and you put the baby monitor under the bed so you could hear them having sex. I mean, how old are you exactly?'

Grinning cheekily, he answered my query with a melodious belch.

'I had hoped one day that you might grow up and perhaps discover that a burp is not an after-dinner speech,' I sighed, stacking newspapers into the recycling bin. 'All I ask of life is a hygienic toilet environment. Peeing on the loo seat, leaving your underwear all over the floor . . . you're like an animal marking its territory.'

'But we have a cleaner.'

'So? You still have to clean for the cleaner. Besides, she only comes once a week which is not enough to clean up all the mess you make.'

'Where?' Rory smiled lazily. 'I can't see all this mess I've allegedly made.'

'My point exactly. Why is it that you can see a naked boob a hundred miles away, but you can't see a dirty sock in the middle of the floor?' I snapped, clearing away his breakfast plates. 'And then there's the childcare . . .'

'Hey, that's not fair. I help with the kids. What about Jenny's last birthday? I brought that retired sheep dog in from the surgery and it had all the kids rounded up into a holding position in the garden for the entire party.'

'Exactly. You do all the fun stuff, making me the ogre who has to bully them into eating vegetables and brushing teeth and—'

'I make them balanced meals!'

'Yeah, you give them dark *and* white chocolate! Not to mention the nagging over homework.'

'That Lego I bought them was very educational.'

'Yes. You spent six hours building a space craft with rotors and working moon modules while I took the kids to the park. And that was five years ago.'

'But you're such a great mum, Cass. Of course a dad should have a say in his children's upbringing and welfare, but what he should say is "Your mother is right".'

My anxieties had grown too big for me to laugh. They were *sumo* anxieties by now. 'I'm also always the one who has to take a day off when the kids are sick.' I hated the shrewish tone to my voice, but I couldn't stop my complaints from piling up on top of each other, like a Chinese acrobatic group. 'Why am *I* the only one who can find a lost library book or football boot?' It was as if someone else had written the words and I was merely miming – a marital karaoke with the banality of a pop song.

'I do things . . .'

'Rore, I've been waiting two months for you to put together that new Ikea bed we bought for Jamie.'

'I'll do it, okay? I'm a man – I love rising to vacuous challenges.'

I looked at my husband. This was as meaningless as Republicans saying that they were going to do something about global warming.

'But *when*? Why don't you do it today? And you could wash up while you're at it. Plates don't levitate, clean, into cupboards of their own accord, you know.'

'Boy, it's so nice to see you so positive this morning.'

'Hey, I like to start out right.' Once, Rory's flaws had made me feel more tender towards him, a little ache of attraction and affection. Now these same endearing foibles had my skin crawling with irritation.

My husband got up from the table and wrapped his muscular arms around me. 'Of course I'll help, chicken. You go off and have a nice time.'

I had been about to forgive him, but these words froze me in my tracks. '*Nice time?* I won't be having a "nice time". I'll be doing the food shopping.' This was my 'day off' so of course I was taking the kids for hair cuts, dropping one off at dance class and the other at tennis, stopping by the dry cleaners, renting videos, buying garden fertilizer, filling up the car with petrol, selecting Rory's brother's birthday present, renewing my pill prescription and then depositing the kids at various parties, Ten Pin Bowling and Rock Climbing, and at absolute opposite ends of the city. The thing that drives a mother mad, is driving her offspring everywhere. 'And I expect you to clean up while I'm away too, okay? I was going to say this house is a pigsty, but no self-respecting pig would set a trotter in here!'

Judging by the peculiar odour emanating from under the couch, herds of wildebeest had obviously gone there to die. Or maybe it was just the smell of our relationship rotting. But then my husband said a surprising thing. 'Of course, angel.' And blew me a kiss goodbye.

The cockles of my heart, not to mention other parts of my anatomy, warmed. I couldn't wait to tell Jasmine how wrong she was. Rory wasn't autistic or emotionally inarticulate. I had complained, he had listened, compromised and changed. He was sensitive and caring and my darling and there was absolutely no need to put this marriage to the sword.

Three and a half hours later I was back, laden down with bags of groceries. I could hear the music blaring from two blocks away. As I struggled into the house, the throb of the amplifier rattled my bone marrow. I'd dropped the bags in the hall and burst into the sitting room to see Rory gyrating manically. My husband is the Jimi Hendrix of air-guitardom. He knows all the various stances. He can play on his back, behind his head. The man can play with his teeth. He once sold an air guitar on ebay for £50.

Using my pot-plants as the other band members, a lampstand for a mike, and the mirror as an adoring audience, he was belting out the lyrics to 'Smoke on the Water' whilst giving himself a bad case of thrash.

Needless to say, the house did *not* look like the model home I'd envisaged. It looked more like an SAS training ground. The dirty plates were still underneath the couch and the Ikea bed remained in its flat-pack at his feet. Rory wasn't even embarrassed when he saw me standing in the door, but just strummed his invisible guitar even more enthusiastically, dropping to his knees at one point for a particularly harrowing solo.

I felt it might be time to share with him a wife's most handy household hint: that a husband's bloodstains can be effectively removed from carpet using a mixture of starch and water.

Surprise, surprise, a fight ensued. There was quite a lot of incredulity on my part i.e.

'What have you been *doing* all this time?'

'Well, I have cleaned up a bit.'

'Cleaned . . . ? Why is it that there can be rutting rats romping across a coffee table, creating a bacteria colony capable of devouring a small child . . . and a man thinks that's clean? Hmmm?'

There was also quite a bit of sarcasm i.e.

'What about a Power-Point presentation on whether empty orange-juice cartons belong in the fridge or the bin? Would that help you?'

Quite a lot of open hostility i.e.

'Any husband's ass left here on the couch watching sport on the telly for over four hours will be towed away and impounded at the owner's expense. Am I making myself clear?'

And quite a lot of martyrdom i.e.

'I suppose *I'll* have to do it, just like I do Everything Else.'

Graduating to full martyr mode, I then ripped the plastic off the wooden slats of Jamie's Ikea bed and scrutinized the instruction pamphlet. *Take a Phillips-head screwdriver.* I slammed open the toolbox and surveyed the bewildering contents. Who the hell was *Phillip*? And why was he such a sadist?

'Oh, all right then.' Rory begrudgingly turned the music off and cancelled the rest of his imaginary rock concert. 'If you help me, it shouldn't take too long.'

Three hours later it began to dawn on me that Mr Ikea and his Allen key are responsible for more marriage break-ups than infidelity. They should be renamed 'The Divorce Bookshelves' – only they weren't supposed to be bookshelves, they were supposed to be Jamie's new bed, but that's not how they turned out. Six tantrums later I finally found a good use for the Phillips-head screw-driver. It's a very handy implement for spouses to use when stabbing each other to death.

Rory hit the whisky bottle. I was so depressed I thought I might need something stronger – a swig of paint-stripper, perhaps.

'Look,' I relented, 'why don't we book a babysitter tonight and just go out and talk.'

'Out? Where? Going out pisses me off. Restaurants always have those menus where it takes sixty words to describe something which then arrives at your table on a lettuce leaf, looking like a diseased frog with a sprig of basil sticking out of its backside. No, thanks, Cassie. Besides, what is there to talk about?'

'Gee, I dunno. Our impending divorce?!'

The next day, 2 March, was my birthday. A mother's birthday takes second place to the guinea pig's, of course – we women know that. But I would have thought a cup of tea and a bit of burned toast in bed might have been in the offing. Even from the kids.

When it's *Rory's* birthday, I buy and wrap presents from the children, plan a birthday dinner, complete with heart-shaped cake and generally make him feel like a Sultan. By Sunday lunchtime when there had still been no mention of What Special Day It Was, I spoke up.

'Look, I wasn't expecting a light aircraft sky-writing *I Love You, Cassie* in the clouds. Or a neon sign lit up with a love message at Piccadilly Circus, but, you know, a flower or two for my birthday might have been nice. Did you at least remind the kids?'

When Rory told me that he'd forgotten and hadn't bought me any presents, I knew he was just trying to put me off the scent. Obviously he had a surprise party planned! By 9 p.m., I felt a twinge of doubt. An even bigger twinge at 10. A panic at 11. Followed by a manic declaration of 'now or never' at 11.45.

'But I *told* you I hadn't bought you anything,' he replied, perplexed.

'But I thought you were joking! How can you spend twelve months researching five hundred Internet sites and remembering every comparative price before buying an electrical appliance, but you can't remember your own wife's birthday?'

'It's not my fault I forgot. I mean, it's not like you dropped any hints. Did you stay in bed all morning shouting, "Where's my birthday break-fast?" at intervals? No. Did you send yourself flowers from a mystery admirer? No. Did you circle the date on the kids' kitchen calendar? No. Besides, how could I remember it's your birthday when you never look a day older?' he concluded sycophantically.

Good try. But I was beginning to think that Rory and I just didn't match any more. If life were linen, suddenly he was a king-size top sheet and I was a single fitted bottom. God! Even my analogies had deteriorated into the domestic. What the hell had happened to me?

There was only one course of action left. Sulking. I decided not to talk to him. For the next five days I served his meals in silence. I turned my back on him in bed. By the end of the week, I was a nervous wreck, as were both children. We'd been walking around on eggshells. The strain and tension in the air was palpable. The cat had taken to looking at me in a superior way as if to say, 'You're new at this, aren't you?'

By Friday night I could take it no more. 'Oh Rory. Rory darling,' I sobbed with relief.

'Huh?' he replied, giving me his full peripheral attention.

'Let's make up, Rore. I just can't stand it any more. I've been crying myself to sleep at night. I mean, the tension, the angst, the atmosphere!'

He just looked at me and said, 'What?'

HE HADN'T NOTICED.

PART II

CHAPTER 9

DON'T GET MAD, GET BAD

As I rang the bell at Jazz and Studz's Hampstead mansion a couple of evenings later, I was still brooding about Rory's shortcomings. Why is it that a man would rather watch a rerun of some badminton championship between two Croatians he's never heard of than communicate with his wife? Although I wondered if Rory actually fitted the category of 'man' any more. He was more of a warm-blooded pot-plant – he just sat there, waiting to be fed and watered.

I stopped brooding then because as we moved into the lighted hallway, I realised that Jazz had greeted me at the door topless. That is to say, she was wearing lipstick and glitter on one pink nipple and a sequinned tassel on the other. I scanned her face. This could mean good or bad news, I wasn't sure. Was it a celebration? Or did she want to take her little darlings out and give them one last great time before the removal of a ravaging tumour – which, by the way, we'd already nick-named 'Studz'. Jazz had warned us that over the coming months she might be ringing to make unreasonable requests. I now steeled myself for a night of male dancers in latex Lederhosen at short notice.

'It's only a cyst,' she laughed and did a little tapdance, sparkly nipples jiggling. She seemed anointed with joy.

I hugged her hard enough to get sequins all over my chin and a nipple tassel between my teeth. 'Where's the International Man of Mystery? Why isn't he here to celebrate?'

'Amnesty mission to Darfur. Part of his ongoing Wife Avoidance Programme,' she told me. 'I may not have cancer, Cassie, but I'm still in the terminal stages of a lengthy disease called wedlock.' She paused to pour me a glass of Krug Rosé, pilfered from her husband's cellar. 'Side-effects? Self-loathing and excessive alcohol intake.'

'Well, it must be contagious because I seem to have the same symptoms.' I glugged down the exquisite vintage vino. 'Yep. We're both so happily married, except for one thing – our husbands.'

When Jazz suggested all wives put crushed glass in their hubby's coffee, I dazzled my sozzled self by replying how that really would be grounds for divorce.

Jazz raised a shapely brow. 'Divorce? Oh no. I'm not divorcing.'

'But . . . but I thought . . .'

'It takes a superhuman effort to demolish a marriage, sweetie. And the time is never right. Studz's mother is sick, Josh's A level exams are coming up. Divorce would be so damaging to

Joshie. Why should a child born in love be condemned to . . .' she lit up a cigarette and launched a halo of smoke ceiling-ward, '. . . .seeing his mother pouring concrete down the loo and stealing the light bulbs.' Recoiling from the image, Jazz tucked her long legs, which were slinkily clad in black leather trousers, under her on the sofa. 'Eeeeew. No way.'

'But I've just come round to the idea of divorce,' I said. 'I mean, we've both stayed put in the one position for so long, that marital deep vein thrombosis has set in. We need the psychological version of support stockings.'

'No. What we *need* are frequent-flier miles for surviving the journey – frequent-flier points in the form of a lover. Studz said that the grim reality of his operating table had left him etherized. Well, I've been left etherized too – *on my marital bed.* I'm going to take his advice and just go and have affairs to feel alive again.'

'Revenge fucking?'

'That's the one.'

'Crikey. Won't you feel guilty? *I* feel guilty about everything. I just know one day they'll find out it was me who stole the teacher's peanut butter sandwich in Year Two and my life on the run will finally be at an end.' I extracted the cigarette from between my friend's painted talons and extinguished it with a hiss in her half-empty champagne glass. 'I'm pretty sure that guilt is to adulteresses what lung cancer is to smokers.'

Jazz's mouth, lipsticked bright orange with bravado, broke into a bitter smile. 'My husband cheats on me with everything that walks and now I'm going to have my revenge by fucking the pool boy. Gosh. Perhaps one day I'll be *flooded* with remorse,' she concluded sarcastically, shrugging a black cashmere cardigan over her naked shoulders.

I looked at my friend in amazement. After her brush with mortality, there was a new flinty exterior to her. Curled on the couch in her black clothes, she looked like a comma. And passers-by would pause when they saw her and catch their breath.

'The best thing about being a woman . . .' she hesitated while her lips took a brief hiatus to light up another fag.

'Is never having to make a best man speech?' I guessed.

'. . . is that we live longer than our partners and can spend all their money. Which is why I'm staying married, but cooking all Studz's food in double cream and not draining the fat off his bacon. I'm feeding him up like a Strasbourg goose. After his coronary, I'll buy a Home Autopsy Kit so I can check for myself if the creep actually *has* a heart. However, until he's dead and buried, you're going to have to cover me for any clandestine carnal activities.'

'Oh, a dream come true. What I've always wanted to be – an under-the-covers agent.' I squirmed. 'Do you honestly think an affair is the answer?'

'Affairs may not be the answer, sweetie, but it sure as hell will help you forget the question.'

'Which is?'

'Why the fuck did I ever marry that pig?'

To illustrate her point, the phone rang. 'No, he's not home. But do give him a disease for me, will you?' Jazz suggested in a vinegary voice before ringing off. 'It's that patient of his – the expert on Sylvia Plath. You see? They even ring him at home now.' Her green-gold eyes glinted with tears. 'It's so hard not being loved, Cassie. I just don't want to feel dead any more. Yes!' she rallied. 'Just look on me as a mortician, sweetie. I can't bring my marriage back to life, but at least I can make it *look* better.'

'So don't get mad, get bad. Is that your new motto? But where exactly are you going to find this hot – to-trot lover of yours?'

Jazz poured herself some more Krug in a clean glass. 'I dunno. Internet chat rooms, dating agencies, ads . . .'

'Relying on the kindness of passing serial killers?'

'You're right,' she said with a taut laugh. 'Much better to stay unhappily married with no sex-life and contract cancer from being so bloody miserable.'

She pointedly twirled a nipple tassel. It seemed that her mammogram had in fact been a telegram from Mother Nature – a wake-up call to live.

'The hardest thing about middle age, sweetie, is

149

that we grow out of it,' she said wistfully. 'Tonight, I'm going on line to see what I can bait.'

A few days later, when I told Hannah that Jazz had found a potential lover, she nearly drowned. We were in our weekly aquarobics class, splashing around energetically to a wavery tape of 'Let's Get Physical'. Once Hannah had been given mouth-to-mouth resuscitation from a lifeguard and the jets of water had ceased erupting from her nose, my well-groomed friend defied her Botox and raised her eyebrows higher than her hairline.

'The clitoris is clearly the least intelligent part of the female body. So why is Jasmine thinking with it?'

'Jazz says that all women secretly want an affair.'

'Hmm. On balance I think I'd rather take up heroin. Less dangerous. What you both should do is rekindle your passion. I saw some sex guru on the telly saying that married couples should liaise in the bedroom mid-afternoon.'

'Mid-afternoon? Are you mad? Where am I supposed to put the children? Under the sink with the lethal household substances?' 'Liaise' sounded so full of Gaullist suavity. But the only vaguely French thing about *me* were the tufts of armpit hair I'd sprouted during the winter.

From her supine position in a poolside lounge chair, Hannah's eyes interrogated me. 'And where exactly has she met this lover of hers?'

'An Internet chat room,' I verbally fumbled.

'Oh, how romantic. What's it gonna be, *your* homepage or mine? So we're talking about a perfect stranger?'

'Yes – except I doubt he's perfect. He listed his hobby as "aura grooming". Oh, and there was a star sign mentioned too, I think.'

Hannah grimaced, her small face a knot of opinion. 'Some women like to just pack a pair of spare panties, paint on their lipstick, go to a bar, see what gorgeous Love God fate throws into their laps, then go home with him for a night of wild, rampant sex . . . Most of these women are never seen again.'

'Jazz says his emails are really sweet and polite.'

'Oh, *that's* reassuring. She's found the most polite sexual psychopath in London. Great.'

'That's why she wants me to drive her there. To the rendezvous. Just to be careful.'

The pool area was flooding with mums and toddlers for junior swim class so Hannah didn't speak again until we were in adjoining shower cubicles, dodging Band Aids and verruca viruses. Her shampoo-foamed head giraffed over the partition.

'It's such meshuggeneh talk. Completely crazy. And we have got to stop her, Cassie.'

We? We was rapidly becoming my least favourite word in the English language. No way, I thought. 'Of course,' I said, even though I'd rather lick the sneeze hood over a salad bar.

* * *

151

'So what are you saying? That I should just give up on sex?' Hannah timed her confrontation with Jazz until we were midway through our Sunday-morning power walk on Hampstead Heath. We were standing atop Parliament Hill, panting. Beyond the inky calligraphy of trees, the city lay scribbled below. The smoggy air in the basin of London was thick as broth. You could almost spoon it.

'Having sex three times a week burns about seventy-five hundred calories a year and is the equivalent of jogging seventy-five miles,' Jazz enthused.

'Shtuping a man you meet on the Internet will be about as much fun as jogging seventy-five miles,' countered Hannah. She was on all fours, executing her push-ups rhythmically, mindlessly.

'Man? Did I say *man?*' Jazz smiled in an almost regal way. 'He's twenty-two.'

'*Mind the gap,*' I said, in the scratchy voice of a tube announcer.

Hannah sprang to her feet. 'Ohmygod. What if he rapes you? Or beats you? Or kills you!'

'There are far more effective ways to destroy a woman, you know. You can just marry her,' Jazz said in an aggrieved tone. 'Anyway, statistically most women get murdered by their husbands, not some stranger. He sent his photo. His upper arms look like two footballs caught in a stocking.'

'Oh, for fuck's sake, Mrs Robinson.' Hannah glanced at Jasmine sharply. 'Cassie, did you know Jazz had taken up residence on Sunset Boulevard?'

I paused in my bench presses and flumped onto my back on grass thickly buttered with daffodils. 'Um, well, I dunno. I do think Missy Eliott CDs are slightly unseemly at our age, Jazz.'

Jazz gave us both a sidelong, withering look. 'Another nice thing about being a woman, even a woman of "our age",' she said thinly, 'is that, unlike men "of our age", we don't have to pay for sex.' She lifted a leg onto the bench and bent into a stretch. 'We can just take a toy boy.'

'Having a toy boy, you have to pay for everything anyway; dinner, theatre, holidays,' I said light-heartedly, gazing up at the interlaced limbs of the trees. '*Paying* for sex actually would cost you less!'

But despite our attempts to saw raggedly through Jasmine's fantasies like a bread-knife through a frozen loaf of wholemeal, she remained determined. Hannah urged me on with her eyes.

'Besides, do you really want to start going to comedy clubs again?' I added. 'And putting up with his nagging about recycling? And endless talk about the fate of the ozone layer whenever you use your hairspray??'

'Oh sweetie, I don't intend to be *talking*!'

And with that, Jasmine pranced off down the hill, dismissing us with a perky, four-fingered wave.

'You are *not* to help her. Is that clear?' Hannah ordered me, before moving off after Jazz in a miffed manner.

Oh yes, as clear as the view from Parliament Hill.

⋆　⋆　⋆

And so it was that on a day in late March, Jasmine Jardine, a forty-three-year-old housewife and mother of one, left her home in the leafy environs of Hampstead, climbed into the family Volvo estate and drove down to the grimier environs of Southwark. Her husband was under the impression that she was going to the cinema. But she drove straight past the Swiss Cottage Cineplex and on and on over the river until she reached a dilapidated terrace, where she parked, adjusted her hair, straightened the seam in her stay-up stockings and sashayed to the paint-peeled door. It was the first time she had been on a date for more than twenty years. And the first time she had ever been with a man who could lick his own eyebrows (the toyboy's latest Internet revelation).

I know all this because I was with her in the car, armed with a can of mace and the local police number. It was bad enough we'd had to go south of the river, which North Londoners see as apache territory. Southwark's local industries are kneecapping and drug dealing. The area has cockroaches so big you can hear the pitter patter pat of their huge hairy feet. As I waited in the car and time crawled by, one hour . . . two . . . it crossed my mind that I'd been looking out for Jazz's welfare for so long I really required a clipboard and a white coat. Four crossword puzzles, three Mozart CDs and two packets of chocolate biscuits later, Jazz staggered onto the street, her clothes dishevelled, all wide-eyed and wild-haired. She looked like a haircare magazine reject.

'Are you okay?' I jumped out of the car, ready to pick up the pieces. 'Shall I call the police?'

'Only to tell them I've invented a new game: "Pin the Tongue on the Clit".' She suddenly leaped about as though auditioning for *Riverdance*. 'Wow! OhmyGod. Wow! Wow! WOW!!'

'Really? How were his teeth? Did he have a nice bum?' Words tumbled out of me. 'Do you feel guilty? Is the guilt eating you alive?'

'*Guilty*? I feel euphoric!' she said jauntily. What I'd taken for dismay was in actual fact a state of pure elation. The woman had the thrilled sense of achievement of a bungee jumper.

'Christ. All those years at Catholic school taught me fuck all. The sin of omission is passing up sin! Do you know that I once sat next to George Clooney at a fundraiser? And he asked for my number?'

'Yeah, well. It's obviously why he's never got married,' I put in sarcastically.

'Men are like books. So many out there, so little time!' Jazz grinned coyly. 'Look, if the Good Lord hadn't meant us to have affairs, She wouldn't have given us lingerie.' She twanged her stocking top as she got into the car. 'Women are the new men! Oestrogen is the new testosterone!' She punched the air.

'Yeah. And bullshit is just the same old bullshit.'

'Look,' she justified, 'it's not a perfect set-up, but life isn't perfect, is it? Will you cover for me tonight, if Studz asks . . .'

'I dunno, Jazz. I hate lying. I—'

'Otherwise,' she grabbed my arm in a ferocious vice, 'I'm going to turn into the kind of deranged woman who hatches abandoned bird eggs in her bra.'

'Well, when you put it like that . . .' Starting the engine, I kicked off my shoes and drove in my stockinged feet.

'You know he shares the flat with a mate. Music student. Sooo cute. We could double date!' she enthused as we crossed the inky Thames.

'A student? I'm forty-bloody-four! I'm so old I've put Doctor Kevorkian's number on my speed dial. Besides which, I'm married.'

'You know, you really can't blame Madame Bovary or Anna Karenina for wearying of their wearisome husbands. The only reason to get married is so that you can have furtive affairs . . . otherwise life would be so boring you'd have to get married!' Jazz laughed mirthlessly.

For a moment I was partially persuaded by her nimble rationalizations. All those unhappy wives, rows and rows of battery hens, cooped up, hatching eggs in our terraced hutches, our bad-tempered, arrogant roosters strutting around on their matching, identically mown lawns. The predictability of it was so claustrophobic. I wanted to be free-range! To roam from home! To be taken in the wild . . . or perhaps backwards over the dustbins by Russell Crowe.

'Hannah says that I should try to rekindle my

passion with Rory. You know – afternoon liaisons . . .'

'Ha! You can't rekindle passion. I'm a chef and believe me, soufflés don't rise twice. Besides, life, like cooking, is much more palatable when you deviate from the recipe. Come on a double date with me instead. Get in touch with your Inner Vixen!'

'You're really going to see him again?'

'Good God, yes.' Jazz beamed, humming gaily to herself. 'Some mistakes are just too much fun to only make once. So forget rekindling passions, okay?'

'Okay?'

'Just remember, All Men Are Bastards And Evermore Shall Be So Unless They Are Johnny Depp Who Is Crumpet. Got that?'

'Got that.'

I thought of the way Rory had looked at me when we'd first got married. Of course, now he only looked at his pets like that. Maybe if I got fleas or foot rot he'd be more attentive. For the first six years, oh, how happy we'd been. But then, after the babies were born, he'd compartmentalized me. That was the trouble. Women love all day, all night; it garnishes the whole pizza of life. For men, it's just one slice. Work, friends and sport comprise the other slices. But Jazz was right. Rekindling passion was a ridiculous idea. It was pointless trying to get back on my husband's menu . . . Wasn't it?

CHAPTER 10

THE REASON I DON'T TELL YOU WHEN I'M HAVING AN ORGASM IS BECAUSE YOU'RE NEVER THERE

I was sitting astride my husband, pitching precariously like a retired rodeo rider. It was Saturday afternoon, the kids were at the cinema, the surgery had closed at one and we were 'liaising' to 'rekindle our passion'.

I attempted another halfhearted kiss, avoiding Rory's beery breath and quite possibly the food he had stuck between his teeth. I remembered fondly when we were drunk on nothing but excitement. The Annie Oakley routine was chafing so I dismounted, positioning myself robotically first this way, then that. It was not fore but boreplay; a total waste of leg waxing. I snorted with tedium – a noise Rory evidently mistook for a groan of passion as he then began tweaking this and twanging that. His touch felt as erotic as a wet shower curtain sticking to my body. My responses were automatic, like the reflexes of a knee when hit by a hammer. God. What had I become? A *clam?* Did all married couples go through this routine of pawing each other uselessly until one or other passed out? He persevered for another, oh, two seconds tops, then licked his finger to manufacture some moistness. It was then it struck me that I was truly miserable.

To bring about a rapid conclusion, I wet my own finger and tickled his prostate – a sexual short-hand learned by most bored and busy wives. Rory ejaculated with all the exhilaration of a burp.

As he showered, I lay in a bed which smelled of nothing but the meaninglessness of our encounter.

Rory splashed back into the room, more or less wearing a towel. He opened the door leading onto the hall and a German Shepherd with stitches bounded onto the bed, my brand new and now half-gnawed leopardskin slipper between his foaming incisors.

'That's *it*!' I heard a voice raised in anger and real-ized that it was mine. My emotions were spinning round like a jam-jar lid dropped on a hard slate floor. 'You may not have noticed in all the years we've been married, Rory, that I actually hate animals.'

'Oh come on, Cass', Rory, loin-clothed in terry towelling, struck his Johnny Weissmuller pose, hands on hips, chest puffed out, lats splayed. 'He's just playing. Satan – down, boy.'

'*Satan*?! The fact that all German Shepherds are invariably called Hitler, Adolf, Eva or Satan slightly belies the notion that they're "fun loving", don't you think? This is the sort of dog which rips the face off a baby for its teething toy.'

'Actually, he's a very upmarket dog. He was paper-trained on the *New York Review of Books*.

This dog won't even mount a leg unless it's clad in Armani,' he replied jovially, as he dressed.

'Even if your patients aren't having sex with my leg, they're doing hideous things behind my Conran couch, which wouldn't happen if only you were a *real* doctor instead of a vet.'

I couldn't see his face beneath his floppy fringe, but I felt I'd scored a direct hit. 'There's nothing second-rate about veterinary science,' he replied tensely. 'My patients have certainly had to learn to be quick on their paws around *you*, Cassie. Come on,' he tickled the big dog under his slathering jaw. 'How could you not love animals?' he asked, regaining his cavalier composure.

'Oh, I do. They're so good with gravy.'

'What is wrong with you lately?'

'Nowhere did it state in my marriage vows that I would have to cough up fur balls.' I was up now, tugging on jeans. 'I mean, this house is filthy enough, thanks to your domestic blindness.'

'Oh, Cassie,' he sighed. 'Why must you always sweat the small stuff?'

'Because it is all about the small stuff, Rory. Reality is about mundanity.'

'But you're clinically obsessed. It's been years since I've seen you without a toilet brush in your hand.'

'Oh, and you think I'm doing that for pleasure? No, I'm doing it because you claim psychological brutality if I ask you to put your dirty underwear in the laundry basket.' Giving a melodramatic sigh, I set about tidying up the bedroom.

Rory waylaid me, turned me to him, took my face between the palms of his large hands and gave a cheeky smile. 'But, Cass, that's why I love you. Because you cope so well.'

Anger bulged up in me – big as a submarine surfacing, the wake rippling out. 'They're just words, Rory – those things that actions speak louder than. Just think about it.' I broke free and recommenced tidying up with ferocity. 'How many acres of toast do you think I've buttered for you? How many flocks of lamb do you think I've baked for your Sunday dinners? How many schools of fish have I fried? Pascal does all the cooking for Hannah, you know. The man sears salmon! Well, I want a salmon searer, goddamn it!'

Rory steadied my hand. 'Would you please stop fluffing pillows for a second?'

'Oh God, I hate that,' I scowled. 'I hate the way I can be lecturing you about how you should help me clean up the house while you just stand there watching me clean up the house. I work fulltime too, in case you hadn't noticed!'

'But you girls can juggle. A woman's brain has a ten per cent thicker connecting cord between the left and right lobes. Men's brains can only concentrate on one thing at a time. If I'm hammering and the doorbell rings, I'll hit my thumb. I just can't help it, you see.' He beamed cockily, thinking himself off the biological hook. 'It's genetic.'

'Oh really? I bet you wouldn't have trouble multi-tasking at, say, *an orgy.*'

Rory was trailing after me now as I slammed drawers, shoved clothes in cupboards and kicked dogs.

'If you didn't have so many people over all the time, you wouldn't have to *do* so much housework,' Rory said with a studied air of truculence. 'If it's not your Witches Coven brewing husband-poisoning potions, it's the Motley Whatsits for fondue.'

'You are *so* anti-social, do you know that? "Oh no, we can't go out tonight because we went out in October . . . "Well it's now March – and what exactly are we staying in *for*? It's not the sex, that's for sure.'

'What's that supposed to mean?' Dark crescents had begun to bloom in the armpits of his shirt. 'Here's a novel idea, Cassie. *You* could initiate sex now and again – and try different things. Couples do swap positions occasionally, you know.'

'Yes. Let's swap positions. *You* stand by the sink washing-up and *I'll* lie on the couch farting and watching the footie. Believe me, a husband sprawled drunkenly before a blazing television is not exactly foreplay for a girl – not that you'd care. You don't seem to have even noticed that I haven't had an orgasm for over a year.'

He looked stunned. '*What?*'

'You're a surgeon. You're good with your hands. You can fashion a temporary cistern ball float with a squeezy bottle and a coat hanger in five minutes flat, and yet you can't find my G spot? Location! Location! Location! That's all there is to say about the G spot, really.'

'And you're just telling me this now?' Rory gave me the sidelong glance of a maltreated pet. 'After how many years of marriage?'

'A sensitive man would have noticed – he wouldn't have to be told. But shucks, as long as *you've* had *your* pleasure . . . Then you just roll over and snore, like some caveman.'

'Look, I told you if I'm snoring I'll sleep in the surgery bedroom.' He flopped back onto my dressing table chair, flummoxed.

'Rory, your snoring is at a decibel level which would only be tolerable if the spare bedroom was in, say. Nova Scotia.' I attacked the bed now, wrestling the duvet into submission. 'But of course you don't want to talk about it. The only thing we do talk about of late is how little we have to talk about!'

'Actually, you know, I *can* talk about feelings – like how bored shitless I feel having conversations about feelings all the fucking time!' Glaring hotly, he knifed to his feet. 'I mean, what are you trying to turn me into? A female impersonator?'

'No. I'm just *sooo* sick of living with a Neanderthal. Why don't you just go kill a bison with your bare hands and get this macho shit out of your system?'

'Hey, if it weren't for us macho blokes, human beings would still be passing through the digestive systems of bears and tigers and lions. I mean, what are you suggesting I do?' I could see Rory digging his fingernails into the pads of his palms in an effort to control his temper. 'Go and find a cave somewhere and hibernate until you feel like starting an argument again?'

'*I* don't start them. *You* do.'

'Look at us, Cass! We argue and then we argue about why we're arguing. What is happening to us?'

'We need help, Rore. That's what I've been trying to tell you.'

We looked at each other for a silent eternity; though the clock recorded it as twenty-seven seconds. Then my husband's eyes narrowed knowingly.

'You know who you sound just like? Jasmine.' He shook me by my shoulders. 'Who are you? What have you done with my wife!'

'I know you hate Jazz. You always have. But tell me, do you hate her more or less than you hate all my other girlfriends?'

'I don't hate her. It's just that she's encamped in the gender jungle, conscientiously patrolling her little patch of territory, just like those Japanese soldiers of the Second World War who occasionally emerge from obscure bits of Borneo to discover that the war is over and nobody bothered to tell them.'

'The sex war's *not* over. This is just a new front in the existing skirmish. I have tested this theory under scientific conditions and—'

'Meaning, you've asked your girlfriends over cappuccinos.'

'Well, um, yes. But the point is, Rory, if we were

in a plane right now we'd be assuming the crash position.'

'It's not all my fault, you know. All I get from you is the cold shoulder and the hot tongue.'

'Lucky you. 'Cause the only tongue I've felt for years is one in my shoe.'

'Well maybe if you stopped emasculating me, I'd be more confident between the sheets. I mean, how can you knock my profession like that? You know I was the youngest in my year to graduate. I got there faster than anyone else!'

'Oh, that is true of so many things you do, Rory.'

My husband looked at me like a kicked dog. 'I would say sorry,' he said sarcastically, 'only the Testosterone Treaty obviously prohibits me from conceding defeat.'

'Obviously. Does it allow some kind of Husband Relocation Programme?'

'So what are you saying?' he went on. 'That the warranty on our marriage has expired?'

'If our marriage were one of your pets you'd have it put down. Seems to me we're at that stage where we either divorce or seek an "interesting couple for hours of uninhibited fun!"'

Reflexively he took a step backward. Judging by Rory's expression, I might as well have pulled a pin on a live grenade. The clock's luminous hands creaked into the suffocating silence.

'So you really have lost your orgasm? Christ. What happened to us, Cass? We used to fuck like rabbits.'

I shrugged. 'We got marital myxomatosis.'

CHAPTER 11

THE THREE MUFFKATEERS

arriage is definitely Nature's way of promoting masturbation. *Only to me, wanking is like dancing without music*, I confided to Jazz over the email.

You're too young for the Pope to be ringing you for tips on celibacy, Cass, she replied. *You need a toy boy. Think about it.*

And I did think about it. A lot. I thought about it when I cricked my neck and found myself lying on my belly getting a massage from a bulky, bulky gym masseur, and I had to fight the urge to roll over like some beer-bellied businessman and ask for 'extras'.

I thought about it when the sports mistress told us a joke in the staffroom. 'Why are married women fatter than single women? Because when single women get home they look in the fridge – and go to bed. When married women look in the bed – they go to the fridge.'

I thought about it while reading the *Guardian*'s report on marriage, which stated that forty-two per cent of women surveyed said they often thought about running away with someone else.

Half wished they'd never married. And a third found sex boring. I thought about it when I woke up crying, then realized I hadn't been asleep yet. I ground my teeth during nightmares, only to discover I was wide awake.

I thought about it while visiting my parents. In England, fathers are often found at the bottom of their gardens, like fairies. My mum called my father's shed his 'anteroom to death'. He disappeared there for hours at a time. 'I just pop down occasionally to check he's still breathing.'

I was huddled with my half-pickled rellos by his shed one Sunday, freezing around a damp barbecue fire – when my father announced it was my wedding anniversary. 'Go on, Rory. Kiss your lovely bride.'

I'd been studiously avoiding the subject. The biggest surprise Rory could give me on our wedding anniversary would be to remember it. And if he was reminded, I'd only have to endure some kind of dismal, pseudo-celebratory anniversary sex later. Cue *The Hand*. (Parents, can't live with them – can't be born without them.)

My mother was the only one who noticed that I'd become small, lumpen and anchored by anxieties. 'I need a change,' I told her. 'A thrill . . . And I don't mean a pilgrimage to Santiago de Compostela or white-water rafting.'

Her advice was to just throw myself into my work.

And so I did. For the next week I threw myself

into writing term reports. I was so distraught that on two occasions I nearly wrote the truth to the parents. *Do not allow this child to breed under any circumstances.* And, to the father of the school's most disruptive pupil, *Get a vasectomy. This must not happen again.*

But at the end of the week, with the kids cascading down the corridor after lunch and the air electric with the buzz of their banter, I felt successfully diverted from my marital angst. If only I could have been similarly distracted from my Headmaster. But there he was, striding towards me, his trousers up around his chest, the turn-ups not quite reaching his ankles. 'My office,' he said ominously. If Scroope had a chin he would have jutted it out.

Once I'd sat down opposite his desk, he asked me if I thought he was the type to 'fall prey to the enervating parasitism of staffroom gossip?'

I told him that once I'd worked out what that sentence meant, I'd let him know.

'Did you really say to Mr Ratzinger that his child was born intelligent but that education had ruined him?' If a power company could harness the steam coming out of his ears, London's energy problems would be over.

'Well, yes, I do think Jasper would benefit from some home schooling . . .'

'Do you have any idea what an image of failure that creates for our school? Do you think that's a confidence-building initiative?'

Mr Scroope always spoke in these terms. The

man would call making love an 'on-site merger'. He would call an orgy an 'off-site team-building event'. He would call his wedding anniversary a 'performance review of core competencies'. His children 'pilot projects'. A divorce – 'emotional downsizing'.

'Um . . .'

'I think it's time you reassessed your critical success measures.'

And I think it's time you did something about your chronic halitosis, I wanted to say in reply, but instead smiled meekly. If being pathetic were an Olympic category, I'd be a Triple Gold Medallist, I really would.

'Your classroom skills are creative, as the Inspectors keep pointing out, but we must also stick to the curriculum. I've had a round-table discussion with the Governors and I think, to be on the safe side, it's time you took some advice from a more . . . disciplined colleague.'

And I thought it was time he took a direct hit from an asteroid, followed by a round-table discussion about whether or not he's the world's greatest asshole. (Including open forum and role-play.) I bristled. Could people smell submission on me? Eau de Useless. 'What sort of advice?'

'Mrs Pendal has generously offered to go through your coursework and make sure that it's in keeping with school policy. Despite being a rival, she's kindly allowing you to drink at the fountain of her knowledge.'

Actually, I needed a stiff drink and I needed it now. I'll have knowledge *on the rocks*, please.

And so, for the next week, I had to face the ignominy of Little Miss Priggy poring over my lesson plans. 'Never forget, you're unique, Cassandra. Just like everyone else!' Perdita oxymoroned. Worse, she had also been put in charge of inset day. This was, usually, a relaxed, kid-free day where the teachers got to drink more tea than usual and indulge in some badly needed preparation time. But Perdita had the brainwave of the staff 'bonding' by playing games.

'What shall we play first?' she chirruped to a sullen crew, come Monday morning.

I looked at our Headmaster with loathing and thought, Pin the Toupee on the Bald Bastard'?

Gee, this throwing myself into my work thing was proving so rewarding, I might just as well go back to agonizing about my private life. Work, as we all know, is a pain in the ass. Funny isn't it then, how people are always putting the word 'work' next to the word 'marriage'.

'It's all organized. A double date.' Jazz tossed her car keys in the air and kicked up her leather-mini-skirted legs, her eyes sparkling with mischief. I felt in awe of her brilliant, shifting surface. I so wanted to be Jazz, to enjoy her ease in the world, her way of knowing just how much to tip, just what to quip . . . and how to cross her legs to make every man she met want to part them immediately.

'You should come as well, Hannah, for a little extra-curricular carnal activity.' Bending into Hannah's fridge, Jazz swung her tush pendulum-like, back and forth, as she helped herself. 'While we're still young enough. The Three Muffkateers.'

Hannah's shoulders twitched towards her earlobes and she replied loftily, 'You may only be young once but obviously you can be immature for ever.'

'Hannah's just been advising me to go to marriage therapy,' I volunteered, then tried to make light of it. 'You know, to stay Jung at heart in my own little Nietzsche.'

'Therapy?' Jazz cringed. 'Are you insane?'

'That's the reason people normally have therapy,' I replied, crestfallen.

'Having counselling for a failing marriage is like, I dunno . . . the coyote in the Bugs Bunny cartoons, trying to stop a freight train with a twig.'

'Not thinking you need counselling means that you obviously do.' A by-now familiar frostiness had crept into Hannah's voice.

Listening to their gaggle of contradictory opinions about my life made my brain flip flop like a dying fish. I looked from one to the other of my best friends. Here I was once again – the ham in the friendship sandwich. 'Well?' they demanded in unison.

I didn't want to join Sad, Middle-aged Adulteresses Anonymous. Nor did I want therapy – the only profession in the world where the client is always wrong. 'Um . . .'

171

One thing was for sure. I'd definitely skipped over the 'for better' bit of my wedding vows and was very firmly in the 'for worse' section now. I had to do something. And soon.

But how to choose between my friends? As usual, my indecision was final.

PART III

CHAPTER 12

GENITALIA FAILURE

The volume of her orgasm made the *objets d'art* – lean mahogany phallic things collected by the therapist on her travels to New Guinea – rock precariously on their bookshelf perches.

'A few months of my classes and you too will be able to orgasm at will!' the couples counsellor promised in a velvety voice. This didn't seem to reassure the pear-shaped woman with dry flaky skin, lank hair and defeated, astonished eyes sitting next to me, who was surveying the sex therapist with horror.

The spontaneous orgasm had emanated from a curvaceous thirty-year-old redhead who was wearing emphatic lip-liner, a push-up bra and a nametag which read *Bianca*. This Life Coach, Clinical Hypnotherapist and Marital Healer had the endless vitality usually associated with cruise-ship directors. Bianca stood up from her chair behind her desk . . . and then she kept on standing up for what seemed like hours. Her long legs were finely shaped and fishnet clad.

'So, how many months have you and your wife

been sexually dysfunctional?' She sashayed towards Rory, who was smouldering in a beanbag the shade of dog poo. She flicked her tangerine-coloured tresses over her shoulder, took my husband's hand in hers and smiled. This woman smiled as the sun shines over the Aussie outback of my childhood – relentlessly.

Rory glared savagely in my direction. When I'd suggested therapy, he'd told me he'd rather have steel spikes jack-hammered up each nostril. But after I threatened to deny him sex for the rest of his natural life, he'd sullenly relented – although driving to Muswell Hill in rush hour with an angry husband on the wrong side of the road was probably *not* the kind of marital therapy we needed, actually.

My beanbag, which was attempting to eat me alive, was so tatty and cheap it could only be made of *imitation* vinyl. My thighs stuck to it in pools of nervous sweat.

'Dysfunctional, yes . . .' Bianca checked her clipboard. 'Your Significant Other feels you haven't noticed that she takes longer to reach arousal. What's your reaction to that . . .' Bianca peered at the crayoned nametag I'd stuck to my husband's chest, 'Rory?'

Rory turned his prisoner-of-conscience countenance in my direction and glowered even more angrily.

'Well?' Bianca insisted, squeezing his meaty palm.

'Well, ugh . . . um. According to my wife, our marriage has . . .' Rory sank further into his sludge-coloured beanbag as he groped for the right words '. . . blown a gasket. Got a flat. Needs a tune up.'

The therapist's mint-green eyes, hard as peppermint candies, glittered. A husband who talked of emotions by using car terminology? She was mentally reaching for the speed dial number of her accountant to inform him that she *would* be able to afford that gazebo, after all, as this was obviously going to take *years*!

Bianca sidled around the rest of the group introducing herself. There was a pallid pair of newlyweds. A bloke whose John Lennon specs were overwhelmed by his jowly face and lugubrious expression, and by his large librarian wife, who announced that he could only get an erection when wearing her underwear. In the beanbag beside them was a client who was in the middle of a third hysterical pregnancy . . . and he was *male*. The man whose toupee resembled a dead animal which had just happened to pass away on his head, had brought an imaginary friend.

In other words, just the sort of people with whom you'd like to share your most intimate sex secrets.

As Bianca put on her Enya CD, lit her essential oils in the infuser and made her little introductory jokes (i.e. 'How many therapists does it take to change a light bulb? One – but the light bulb has to really *want* to change!') I took the opportunity to examine my surroundings.

The Therapy Centre, a utilitarian, two-storey brick building in North London, had the décor of a shabby motel lobby on a motorway. It was all exhausted pot-plants, worn, grey carpet, cheap beige desks, fluorescent lighting and unwashed windows. The room had the friendly ambience of a concentration camp.

I could see it was also the kind of place where you needed to look at your shoes a lot, because when I tuned back into the conversation, my husband was telling Bianca that, yes, his wife took a little longer to reach arousal, 'Say a day and a half!'

'Um, you can shut up any time now,' I interrupted, embarrassed.

But no matter how squeamish it made me and how much Jazz would disapprove, to agree to pay £35 an hour to have my sexual shortcomings paraded in public proved beyond a doubt that I really did need therapy.

'And then . . .' said Jazz, kittenishly brushing her hair from her eyes, 'he ate strawberries out of my fanny. They were halfcooked and well marinated by the time he devoured them!'

'I'm so pleased to see you're both looking after your nutrition,' I replied, trying not to sound flummoxed.

It was later the same night and we were sitting around my kitchen table, listening in awe to details of Jazz's erotic adventures with her Internet toy boy. It was like a sexual tutorial.

'And then, after we'd drunk champagne in the bath, I let him fuck me gently with the neck of the bottle. The bathwater was so hot and the bottle neck was so cold . . .'

'Oy veh! Obviously dignity is the only thing alcohol doesn't preserve,' Hannah put in primly, but nothing was going to interrupt Jasmine's epiphany.

'And then, he took some of the ice cubes from the champagne bucket and slipped them inside me, while he licked me. Oh, the sensation of my hot juice and his hot tongue and the melting ice trickling down my thighs,' she reminisced in a sighing staccato, before concluding with breezy impudence, 'So, how was *your* day, Cassie?'

'Oh great,' I replied dispiritedly. 'I learned to put a condom on a cucumber.'

The second worst thing about therapy is the communal waiting room. The compulsive gamblers invariably make the sex addicts wager bets with the passive aggressives about who can make the bulimics throw up first.

The worst thing about therapy is the therapists. Early on in our treatment, about late April, Bianca decided I had a 'hostile vagina'.

'Excuse me?' Surely something was being lost in translation?

'From everything Rory has told me in our one-to-one, I think you have an arousal disorder, Cassandra.'

'No,' I countered, 'what I *have* is a job, kids, an angry spouse, high blood pressure, an overdraft and a promotion in the offing.'

'Hostile vagina, eh?' Rory rocked back in his beanbag and cocked one leg over the opposite knee. His face broke into a smug smile. It was the first time I'd seen him cheery for weeks. 'You know what, Cass? I'm beginning to think maybe there really is something to this therapy malarkey after all,' he gloated. 'It does seem to explain your lack of horniness.'

'Hey, how horny would *you* feel, having worked all day then coming home to spend your time cooking, cleaning . . . and teaching small people to construct oil derricks out of coat hangers? And what about *your* hostile penis, hmmm?'

Bianca, who obviously didn't like to be interrupted, clapped her hands to regain the attention of the class. 'Right. Who knows the basic ways to please a woman?'

I put my hand up. 'Stacking the dishwasher. Not snoring. And telling a woman she doesn't look fat in stretch Lycra.'

It was Rory's turn to speak. 'To become more cliterate, right?'

Cliterate? God, I thought. Where had he got *that* one?

180

Bianca bestowed a 'go to the top of the class' beam at my cunning hubby.

'I'd just like to say that ninety-nine per cent of men give the rest of us a bad name,' Rory chirped shrewdly, flashing our therapist his most endearing grin.

Bianca's reciprocating smile was so intense I felt sure it could irradiate soft fruit. 'Well, *I'd* just like to say that I'm sure we can help your wife overcome her inhibitions,' she assured him in her honey-buttered accent.

'My inhibitions!' I scorned. 'Huh! We're talking about a man who can calculate the total surface area of every room in our house, determine the exact mile-to-the-gallon ratio of a trip from Calais to the South of France – where he effortlessly locates the remote fishing village that's not even on a map – yet he can't find my clit? No, the truth is he just can't be bothered to find it!'

The women in the room barked laughs of recognition. The men grumbled about women demanding too much. Bianca's embarrassing solution was to make us sit through a sex video, depicting 'willing' couples in acts of intercourse which were so graphic and badly lit, that it made my legs go to jelly. Classmates whose legs still functioned properly rose shakily to their feet and fled, leaving human-shaped holes in the walls. One thing was for sure. I would soon be over my sexual inhibitions. Mainly because I would now be *celibate* for the rest of my life.

★   ★   ★

By mid-May, the only thing on my mind was whether or not I was going out of it. Why else would I ever have insisted on dragging Rory to therapy? Hannah was adamant that I must persevere. All therapy was confrontational and difficult, she assured me as we had our heels pumiced at the local Chinese nail bar. Things would turn a corner if I just stuck with it. 'And whatever you do, don't mention your misgivings to Jasmine, dah-ling. She hates you seeing a shrink.'

'Oh sweetie, I don't hate you seeing a marriage therapist,' Jazz said, wafting late as usual into the nail bar. 'I'm seeing one too.'

'What?' I nearly fell off my stool into a bucket of pedicure shavings.

'. . . and a Pilates instructor and a dentist, and a yoga teacher and a dog walker.'

Hannah jerked so violently she accidentally kicked over her foot-soaking bucket. 'What happened to your Internet toy boy? Don't tell me you've contracted some kind of CTD – Computer-Transmitted Disease.'

But Jazz remained immune to goading. 'Well, my main squeeze is still my divine little toy boy. But I do have this small, emergency back-up Love God called Zen who trims my trees. We had sex for the first time yesterday morning, then the second, third, fourth and fifth time during the afternoon.'

'Um, Jazz, I think you'll find that running two or three simultaneous relationships for more than a month and you stop being an adulterer and officially qualify as a Mormon,' I told her. 'And what about Studz? Is he still cheating on you?'

'Well, I'm not stalking him any more, sweetie. But last night he told me he was out with our neighbour, the dentist. And well, that was impossible. Because *I* was – but obviously I can't say anything, can I? A rather modern situation, no? Love thy neighbour, but don't get caught. That's my motto.'

'Jasmine,' Hannah said seriously, 'all these one-night stands, no matter how much you deny it, are just a shelter, however fragile, against the terror and despair of a broken heart. You do realize that?'

Jazz's face crumpled for a second, before she steadied herself. 'I've never had a one-night stand, Hannah,' she corrected airily. 'Just a few one-night relationships.'

My relationship, meanwhile, had no idea what side its bed was buttered on. It seems to me that there are very few aphrodisiacal bonuses to being able to visualize the 8,000 nerve endings in one's cervix contracting during orgasm. This is what I thought as I stood before eight strangers holding my crutch and moaning in an effort to liberate my sexual chi. Blushing and sweating, I was suffering from a performance anxiety I hadn't felt since those hedonistic hours of enforced folk dancing in Kogarah Bay Primary School.

'Are the nerves in your vulva sensorium quivering?' Bianca demanded of me.

'Um . . .'

'Fewer than fifty per cent of women actually achieve orgasm during intercourse.' Bianca's voice was syrupy with sincerity. 'And I am going to show you how to fix that. Class, open your eyes.'

We were greeted by the sight of an anatomically correct inflatable woman lying, legs akimbo, on the floor before us. 'Now, I'd like a volunteer.'

I stifled a laugh. Finally we had a partner for the toupeed man's imaginary friend. Our 'therapist' had at last pushed the boundaries of reality too far. But to my amazement, all the men put their hands up to volunteer. A minute later I watched in a state of dazed disbelief as my husband was instructed on how to stroke his inflatable date to orgasm. He was advised on what pressure and rhythm and digit to use. Having mastered the finger, thumb and palm techniques, Bianca then instructed him on when to apply pressure to the pubic bone, when to pull on the plastic clitoris and when and how to rub her rubber labia. 'Manual over other forms of stimulation are preferred,' Bianca advised. 'You don't drive a car with your tongue, now do you? Once we've mastered manual stimulation, we can move onto cunnilingus. Now, if this doll were me, my genitals would be swelling with blood, my pulse would be racing, my muscles contracting involuntarily. My feet would be arching and shaking. My breasts would heave . . .' As her voice crescendoed, Bianca's cleavage, which was levered up near her chin by her lace underwear, jumped up and down. 'Sweat would be surfacing on my breasts. My heart would pump frantically as my breathing becomes fast and shallow. Oh yes. Faster, harder, faster. Harder!!'

As the doll neared its imaginary orgasm, Bianca helpfully provided the soundtrack and running commentary. 'Oh yes . . . Yes . . . YES!! Excellent, Rory! Don't stop! Don't stop!'

I noted my husband's flushed cheeks and panting breath. For someone who hated therapy, he sure could put on a brave face.

'My nostrils flare and now my climax, with contractions at consistent 0.8-second intervals, will put me into an orgasmic spasm. Faster! Faster!! Harder!! HARDER!! FASTERRRR . . .'

Rory's fingers were flying in and out and up and down the plastic pudenda. And then Bianca moaned so loudly it shook the cheap walnut panelling.

'Ahhhhhhhhhhhhhhhhhooooohhhhohohohohoh . . .'

As Bianca's purrs subsided into silence, the only sound was the pinging of men's fly buttons popping across the room.

'Very good. Note how a warm glow envelops my waist and chest. Even my toes relax. At my sexual summit, a total paroxysm of pleasure was reached. Well done, Rory.' Then she pulled the plug on her inflatable woman. 'This week's revision is for you all to try these techniques at home.'

I looked at the plastic woman who was crumpling

in on herself with a sad sigh. But we were amateurs! Wasn't it dangerous? We didn't have a licence to operate such heavy machinery.

But at Bianca's insistence, that was how Rory and I spent the next week, just the two of us, cosied up on the bed – a searchlight trained up my fanny, *Karma Sutra* open on page 362, studying diagrams and consulting the text. What, you ask, could be better? Well, from my point of view, just about bloody anything.

'Just about anything' was also starting to sum up Jazz's recreational sexual activities. She had dyed her hair blonder, no doubt so that men could find her more easily in the dark. First came her plumber. 'He really has sorted out my pipes,' she chirruped gleefully.

'I need a man who is good at DIY too – so he can fix my pelvic floor.' I crossed my legs, needing the loo, and glanced around Sotheby's auction room. Sotheby's is like an orphanage for heirlooms. Hannah was bidding on a bulging commode, which looked like a chest of drawers that had over-eaten.

'And he's such a man. A real man, you know?' Jazz added dreamily.

'Man? He's not a *man*,' Hannah scoffed. 'He's a marital aid. Getting yourself secretly serviced by a bit of rough is not a fulfilling alternative to a more intellectual relationship.'

'Maybe not. But by God it's fun! Look, you can

smell him in my hair.' Jazz leaned towards us. 'Here, take a whiff.'

'Ugh! Get away! Can't you just use hairspray, like any *normal* woman?' I asked her, appalled. But had to admit to a twinge of jealousy. Fun? What a long-forgotten F word that was.

Her next conquest was an alternative comic.

'Alternative to what? Being funny?' I asked, peering at the 'windswept and interesting' photo on his flyer. We were making our monthly sortie up the motorway to Costco, the wholesale warehouse on the North Circular, in Jazz's Volvo estate.

'Let me guess. He performs a one-man show . . . and there are more people on the stage than in the audience?' Hannah chortled, crumpling the pamphlet. 'What on earth attracted you to a putz like that?'

'Because his opening line was to ask me did I know which two fingers are the most effective for women to use during masturbation. Then held up his own hand and said, "*Mine.*"'

Hannah barked out another derisive laugh. 'I cannot believe you fell for that.'

'Yes, Jazz. If only laughter really were the best medicine, we'd be *so* healthy now!' I added. But why did I feel sick with envy?

The next man on her menu was her car mechanic, a biker named Jism. 'Apparently he changed his name to get back into the pubs which have banned him.'

187

'Really?' I asked, intrigued. 'Now *that's* what I call Alcoholics Anonymous.'

It was a Saturday afternoon and I'd brought my kids around for a swim in Jazz's basement pool while she waited for a man Studz had organised to evaluate the property for insurance purposes.

'He's mad about me,' Jazz giggled. 'My bikie.'

'Must be a condition of his probation,' Hannah retorted.

'When he wants sex he says that it's time to "unleash the meat sabre". Isn't that ad*o*rable? And he's not kidding. One night he wore a fluorescent-coloured condom. When I turned off the light, I thought I was going to bed with Darth Vader!'

'Okay, okay, enough already,' Hannah huffed, thin-lipped. 'The baroque ecstasy, the grotesque compulsion of your conquests is, frankly, disgusting.'

'Oh well,' I rationalized to Hannah. 'At least with a man with tattoos, if the sex gets dull there is always something to read.'

Next in Jazz's game of relationship roulette was the lead singer of the 'Suicide Bombers'.

'A rock star? Ugh,' I cringed. 'How can you put him in your mouth? I mean, you never know where he's been!'

'Hey, don't knock unhygienic until you've tried it. He won't let me shower before he goes down on me,' Jazz divulged, with sassy insouciance. 'Actually he prefers me not to shower for a few days!'

'Bravo,' Hannah countered, with equal cool. 'You must send away for the Germaine Greer Feminist gift pack.'

We were lurking up the back of our Pilates class.

'Don't pretend you aren't jealous. That man has made masturbation pleasurable for millions of women. He says he loves my ass.'

To be honest, I could understand her excitement. To have your bottom admired by a famous rock star, who not only counts them to get to sleep at night, but has also had more bottoms than hot dinners, often simultaneously, is a compliment indeed. I felt an unsettling twinge of chagrin.

'It's sooo exciting, sweetie, don't you think?'

'What I *think* is that you should be put on some register and shunned by polite society,' Hannah decried.

'You're so bland, Hannah, you could dilute water, do you know that?' Jazz told our mutual friend affectionately. 'Have you any idea how lovely it is to feel desired again?' There was a trace of grief in her voice, which she quickly extinguished. Jazz was like one of those 3-D cards you buy in a gift shop which change depending on how you tilt them. Sometimes she was a femme fatale, other times I could see the wounded wife in her. 'Feeling desired is my new hobby,' she said, leaving for the changing room. 'And so much more fun than Pilates.'

And a lot more fun than couples' counselling, I mused. Jazz may have a rock star, but I was beginning to think that I had rocks too . . . *in my head*.

Last and most definitely least, was a performance poet she picked up at Tate Modern. The reason he didn't last was that he lost her keys. When I received Jazz's SOS phone call to come and pick her up from the Marriott Hotel, I thought she meant he had lost the keys to her car.

'No. To the handcuffs.'

'Jazz, handcuffs are only acceptable if you're an undercover cop with Scotland Yard,' I chided.

When Hannah and I collected her from the side entrance of the hotel in Swiss Cottage to drive her to the locksmiths, a coat flung around her negligéed shoulders, her hands shackled before her, Hannah shook her head disapprovingly.

'Dah-ling, aren't you afraid you're going to lose your amateur status?'

'Amateur' just about summed up my feelings about my counsellor too. By the end of June I had enough advice to see me through several husbands. I also had a hunch that if I told my therapist I had suicidal feelings, she would have asked me to pay in advance. So far, she had talked me into buying a state-of-the-art vibrator which was 'totally realistic'. 'Oh, so it cums, coughs, farts, goes limp then switches off?' I asked bleakly. When I saw the size of the cheque Rory wrote her, I was tempted to insert her slide projector, pointer and maybe even a beanbag into an intensely private part of her own anatomy.

Next, she pressured me into buying testosterone patches to cure my 'Desire Disorder.'

'Testosterone?' I looked at her in disbelief. 'Oh yes. That's bound to make me more attractive. To *gay* men!'

She also tried to book me in for Laser Vaginal Rejuvenation, a mere snip, literally, at £3,000. 'A little labial trimming would give you a designer vagina. An Armani Punani would solve all of your sexual inhibitions,' she purred.

The only inhibition I had now was Baggy Fanny Phobia. I could never again have sex with my husband for fear of losing him in that aircraft hangar between my legs.

Just when I felt that it was pretty well impossible for my counsellor to be able to counsel me into feeling any worse about myself, she decided that what I lacked was experimentation. I tried to develop kinks, I really did. I wore Rory's underwear. I even went commando. But, believe me, as a mother of two with no pelvic floor, one must be cautious about not wearing any knickers. On one occasion, one of the Benwah balls Bianca had made me buy, fell out in a staff meeting. I had to pretend to be a player of miniature bowling.

When I complained, Bianca insisted on a one-on-one session during which she pursed her lips before crisply placing crosses in boxes on her questionnaire. 'Do you like the lights on or the lights off?' she grilled me.

191

'I like to have the lights on,' Bianca's eyes lit up for a moment, until I added, 'so I can read.'

'Do you like S and M?' she persevered, pen-wielding.

'Certainly not! I don't like to be beaten. Not even at Monopoly.'

'Well, what about talking dirty?' Bianca asked exasperatedly.

'Talking dirty for me is "James, wash your face. Jenny, your room is a pigsty!"'

'Do you talk in bed at all?' she asked, in despair.

'Oh yes – usually about whose turn it is to do the school run and when the plumber's coming to repair the leaky loo.'

'Well, do you have any questions for *me*?' the therapist asked tetchily, smacking her clipboard down onto the table.

'Well, yes, my most burning question is . . .'

'Yes?' Bianca leaned forward expectantly.

'Can you use flavoured yoghurt for thrush or not? It's all I've got in the fridge.'

Bianca was not amused. 'You need to develop an erotic portfolio,' she announced curtly. 'I understand that you are not that comfortable with or good at oral sex. You should start by practising fellatio on a phallically shaped organic vegetable.'

I reeled back. 'My husband told you that?'

'Well, that's what he implied.'

'Did he now? Well, I'd just like to imply that I'm not that comfortable with premature ejaculation either.'

'Really?' Bianca, eyes glinting, made a note. 'I'll be back in a mo.' She swept out to the waiting room.

'It is *not* premature ejaculation! It's what's termed in the popular vernacular as a "quickie",' Rory said defensively, surfing into Bianca's office on a wave of self-justification.

'Ha! You're so premature, Rory, that last night I wasn't even in the room! Who were you fantasizing about, by the way, when I walked in?' I demanded.

'Perdita Pendal, if you must know.'

'*Perdita?*' It was his turn to score a direct hit.

'Yes. In her prissy little pinstriped suit.'

'Ugh!' I recoiled. 'I can't believe you'd let that woman have sex in my bedroom!'

'There's only one way to deal with a premature ejaculator,' began Bianca, trying to regain control.

'Have your orgasm first?' I suggested crossly. 'And anyway, isn't it too early in the therapy course to be having this conversation?' I said to really annoy her.

Bianca shook her head at her wayward pupil, before insisting that I help Rory master the art of the slow build. What this meant, apparently, was logging on to the London School of Striptease Website of Empowerment. My heart sank. Funny, isn't it? How one woman's empowerment is another woman's sleazy degradation.

Trying new things sexually is *not* my favourite pastime. For one thing, it creates terrible eye wrinkles caused by puckering up into a squint and shouting, 'You want me to do *WHAT*?'

This feeling was reinforced when Bianca demonstrated the Peek-a-boo home pole-dancing kit which she suggested we purchase from her, complete with choreography manual, fake dance money and a garter to tuck it into. 'The Peek-a-boo dance pole goes up or down in sixty seconds,' Bianca assured us.

Story of my life, I sighed dismally.

I'd pushed so hard for Rory to come to marriage therapy and now, as I watched women gyrating on Bianca's computer screen, all I felt was a profound sense of desolation. Bianca was adamant that she could lay us down beside the still waters – all we had to do was be more patient with each other's desires. And she was right. Any slight irritation I had from then on was soothed by simply burying my face in the pillow for a few hours and screaming and screaming and screaming.

I was beginning to think that the only tip a marriage counsellor should give is: NOT TO HAVE ANY MARRIAGE COUNSELLING UNDER ANY BLOODY CIRCUMSTANCES WHAT-SO-BLOODY-EVER.

CHAPTER 13

UNHAPPILY EVER AFTER

Part of my job as Head of Year Six was to create a 'happy work climate'. Unfortunately, in most staffrooms the work climate is damp with high wind approaching. Having to check the teacher roster first thing didn't do much to brighten the day. If there were any absences I had to assign the duties to other disgruntled staff members. Teachers break into two groups – the Sneerers and the Okayers. The Chalk and Talk teachers nearly always fall into the sighing and sneering 'I sup*pose* so' category.

But Perdita, her smile cement-rendered onto her face, now had a permanent excuse. 'I *would*, but I'm just soooo busy going over your work,' she said today, in answer to my request to cover playground duty at break. 'I know it's a little embarrassing to have your classwork checked by a fellow member of staff, but Claude – Mr Scroope – did insist we make it inspection-proof. And it's best to keep the old boy happy. As I'm a people person, I'm willing to help you out.' She gave a long-suffering sigh.

The minging staffroom, with its rusting chrome

sink and threadbare armchairs, is situated directly behind the children's dining hall. Positioned as it is at the back of the cafeteria, it's nicknamed 'the Bacteria'. Well, the Bacteria was now buzzing with activity as teachers milled about making last-minute cups of tea and coffee before the bell rang. Perdita's reply had been loud enough to ensure maximum overhearing. The graveyard of apple cores in the cluttered ashtrays, the grape-cluster skeletons, the glove of banana peel on the floor and being belittled in front of my colleagues – this must be why I became a teacher. I just couldn't resist the glamour of it all.

I drank in air languid with kids' wet shoes and marmite sandwiches, feigned a shrug, then diverted the curiosity of the other teachers by sharing my latest batch of biology homework. '*Benign is what you can't wait to be when you're eight,*' I read aloud, to mild tittering.

But inside I was seething. I had begged Mr Scroope to reconsider, but obsessed with the impending inspection, he just kept repeating his order, like a Dalek. 'The Inspectors are coming. Perdita must supervise your lessons. The Inspectors are coming.'

And so my free time after school was spent in my rival's classroom which she had cluttered with cuddly toys, gonks, ornamental flowers and 'amusing' signs of the type sold in shops called *Bitz* or *Nick nacks*. Red pen in hand and dotting all her I's with smiley faces, she excised all the

196

frivolity from my class notes, replacing fun phrases with obfuscatory jargon about 'building team commitment to action' and 'clarifying individual roles and responsibilities'. How deftly this Hackademic turned my simply worded educational aims 'meeting yesterday's challenges tomorrow' into meaningless drivel about aiming to 'grow skills in speedy problem-solving ideas' and 'barrier breakdowns'. Whatever the hell that meant. The woman's course notes were so convoluted that I would just grasp the end of one sentence, when the other end would wriggle away like a slippery leg of an octopus. It was like being trapped in an elevator with a Seventh Day Adventist recruitment officer.

Fed up, I tried to get out of going over my science notes. 'Don't worry,' I told Perdita gaily. 'I'm planning a more practical than theoretical approach. I'm taking my class on an excursion to the Science Museum.'

Perdita's professional manner cooled a few degrees. 'But the Science Museum told me all their school slots are taken. I rang last week.'

'Oh, well, I booked up a year ago.' And with a perky flutter of my fingers, I was gone. As to the work climate? Let's just say I felt a distinct frost in the air.

But half an hour later, things got very hot indeed. Mainly under my collar.

'I'm afraid I'm declining your request for the Science Museum excursion,' the Headmaster told me, his large lips slapping together in a wet percussion of rebukes. I'd been summoned yet again to his office.

'It's been brought to my attention that during the last school trip you organized to London Zoo, as the children were leaving for the bus, you suggested they sprint towards the parking lot yelling, "Run for your lives! They're loose!" It has been reported to me that this so startled the tourists that it started a small stampede. Is this an accurate description of said incident, Ms O'Carroll?'

My Headmaster's manner is so severe that he causes the people around him to squirm and blurt things nervously.

'Um, well, um . . .' Come on, I told myself. Even a turtle has to stick its neck out to get anywhere. 'The kids were really tired and I was just trying to wake them up.' I tried to keep calm by listing all the jobs that would be worse. A judge in Baghdad, say. An official car-starter for a Mafia boss. Animal faecal identification expert. Defroster of Walt Disney's head. Food taster for Kim Il-sung. 'It was funny at the time,' I concluded, timidly.

'And do you find it funny, how badly this reflects on my school?'

All it reflected on was the sneaky nature of my fellow teacher. Perdita had been the only other staff member on the zoo excursion that day.

'Oh, hello. I'm not interrupting anything, am I?' came her lilting voice from the doorway.

198

She placed a cup of strong tea on the boss's desk. 'Thought you might need a little pick-me-up.' Honestly, this woman could network at a funeral. 'Can I get you anything, Cassie?' All this was said through the most courteous of smiles.

Yeah, you could take this knife out of my back. 'No, thanks.'

I was beginning to think that if Perdita were a dog, *I* was her tree. I told myself not to sink to her level, as it was, after all, such a *long bloody way down*. Little did I know that I was about to fall flat on my face anyway . . .

'Well, it gives new meaning to "personal training",' was my only comment when Jazz, our resident sausage jockey, pointed out her newest ride after school later that day. Hannah, Jazz and I were at the Regents Park Tennis School, taking turns to half-heartedly knock a few balls at each other, while Jamie and Jenny had their lessons on nearby courts.

'Oy veh, Jasmine,' snapped Hannah, having examined the coach in question through her opera glasses. 'In general I think it's best not to shag someone you could have given *birth* to.'

'As I see it, any male of legal age on the planet the same time as me, is up for grabs, girls.'

Hannah fiddled with the lenses then fixed the opera glass to my eye. A muscled Adonis jumped into the frame. 'Yowzah! He's gorgeous, Jazz. I think I'll shop you to Social Services so that *I* can have him! So, where do you do it?' I probed, looking around voyeuristically. 'In the club-house?'

'Of course not. We do it at his house.' Jazz dropped onto the lawn to re-lace her tennis shoes. 'He's um . . . sharing a place with some old friends of his.'

'You mean his *parents?* You shtup him at his *parents'* house?' Hannah remonstrated. 'That's pathetic, dah-ling. And does the tennis coach know about all your other men?'

'No. And don't tell him! He's a little naïve. He only slept with me because I told him it was my first time, you know, with someone else besides my husband. Well, it was my first time *that day*!'

My laugh died in my throat as I glanced across the courts.

'Fuck a duck.'

'It's about the only thing she hasn't.' Hannah's sarcasm was cut short by my frantic finger-pointing and arm-waving, because there, crossing the courts, was Bianca, in an immaculate white tennis skirt, her hair swept up into a coronet of slightly burned profiteroles.

'Who is it?' Jazz asked languidly, looking up from her shoes.

'Bianca – our Couples' Counsellor. I've missed her class for weeks. Said I had terminal flu. Left another message today saying I was at death's door.'

Jazz followed my gaze. 'Oh my God! I know her.'

'Really? You and Studz had therapy?' I marvelled.

'No. Her daughter does swimming training – you know, squads, at the Y, where Josh trains. Serendipity's her name, can you believe it – she goes to your daughter's school. Didn't you know that, sweetie?'

'No. I didn't even know she *had* a daughter. Poor kid.'

'You better believe it. Bianca only dresses her in unbleached cotton from Fair Trade. Sends her to swimming practice with lentil sandwiches on home-made rye. The woman has been irrigated in every orifice. She once told me she knew the other mums must always say about her "How does she do it! What an inspiration!" Well, let me tell you, what the other mums *really* say is "Quick! Hide! Here she comes!"'

'Quick! Hide!' I found myself saying. 'Here she comes.' I ducked down behind an ornamental shrub.

'How can you take advice from *her*?' Jazz scoffed. 'The woman's insane! Has she sat on your husband yet? She's a real husband-sitter from way back. The female version of a marauding Viking. She's had affairs with the swimming coach and two of the fathers. Yep. A total truffler of other women's hubbies.'

'Really?' I experienced a colonic flutter as my sphincter battened down its hatches.

'She's also a marital bulimic,' Jazz insisted.

'Marry, divorce, marry, divorce . . . You've got to be suspicious of the "till death us do part" bit when the bride makes a habit of catching her own bouquet . . . I can't believe she's teaching couples how to stay together! That's hysterical,' Jazz shrieked.

A cold shadow loomed over me and I squinted upwards. If only I weren't so wimpy. I needed a wimpectomy, urgently.

'My, my. What a speedy recovery you've made, Cassandra. I am glad. Although I'm sad you've missed my class.'

To my amazement, I gave her a tart, withering look.

'I think I'll be missing it a whole lot more from now on, actually.' It was as though I'd undergone a bravado-transplant and chutzpah transfusion.

'Oh really? I think Rory is getting quite a lot from my self-help group.'

'A self-help group is a contradiction in terms, you know,' I pointed out, pedantically. Jazz and Hannah, astounded at my uncharacteristic outburst, applauded my sassiness.

'I'm sorry you're not as committed to your marriage as your husband is,' Bianca seethed.

'If I listen to you any longer, I'll be committed alright. To an asylum.'

Which is exactly what I told Rory later that night. I was weary of being pushed around. It was as though my self-esteem were solar-powered, and it had done nothing but rain for day after day. But no more. I was no longer going to Cringe for Britain. The next morning, instead of cancelling the Science Museum excursion as instructed, I urged my pupils to get their parents to write to the Head expressing their disappointment. I also emailed Bianca to cancel the rest of our therapy sessions. But unfortunately, if I wouldn't go to the sermon on mounting, the sermon on mounting started coming to me. Bianca was just suddenly always around. Inexplicably. Like carrot in vomit. You know how you can never remember eating any carrot, but there it is? Well, neither Rory nor I could ever remember inviting Bianca, but *there* she bloody well was. All the bloody time.

At first she popped over for advice on pets, which, as far as I could see, she didn't own. Another June day, she zoomed over from Camden because her washing machine was on the blink. She then proceeded to confound and delight a neighbourhood full of horny husbands by prancing to the clothesline and pegging up a line of erotic lingerie; making my devotion to the Cottontail God pale a little in Rory's eyes by comparison.

One day in early July, she arrived wearing a bikini top and minuscule shorts. 'It's just *way* too hot to wear clothes today,' she sighed.

'Yes, clothes are just so last season,' I said ironically.

'Yeah. I'm with you, Bianca,' I heard my husband say, boggle-eyed at her curvaceous body. 'Cass, what do you think the neighbours would say if I took the rubbish out naked?' he said, palming the beard he'd started growing against my wishes.

'Why bother? The neighbours already think that you're a total Sex God. I mean, look around you. They obviously *know* I didn't marry you for your money,' I tried to joke, but was feeling nauseous with distrust.

'My, my, my, Cassandra.' Bianca seized on my comment with raptor-speed. 'Do I sense a hint of animosity? Let's examine your motives. Could it be because you're a passive-aggressive co-culprit?'

'No, it's because I think you're a charlatan. I mean, you therapists are the ones who need therapists. The care of the id by the odd. Which is why we don't want you coming around here any more.' I moved to stand next to my husband. 'Do we, Rory?'

Bianca wore the calculating expression of a praying mantis. Before my husband could answer, she said in her sumptuous, satiny voice, 'Rory's tragedy is that he has a huge capacity for loving, but the one person who should respond has rejected him. No wonder he retreats to the clinic.'

'Ladies, ladies,' Rory said, 'I think Bianca's clinic *is* making me a more evolved person. I relate to her energy.'

Relate to her energy? Evolved? Was this my husband speaking? The beard, the dire chill-out CDs, the incense, the candles . . . Mr I'd-Rather-Die-Than-Have-Therapy had become a poster boy for karmic laundering.

'I mean, this was *your* idea, Cassie,' he went on. 'It was you who wanted me to get in touch with my emotions.'

'I'd say you're in touch with your emotions, Rore. Your selfish, arrogant, mean emotions.'

'Well, he'll be in touch with a whole lot more next week,' Bianca boasted.

'What's that supposed to mean?'

'I was going to tell you,' Rory said sheepishly. 'Bianca's holding a little graduation class.'

'What's that?'

'Well, I prefer to call it a sensual, interactive surprise,' Bianca preened. 'At my home.'

I felt my chest tighten. I had a feeling that any party at Bianca's would only require one etiquette tip. 'Take off underwear – mingle.' The woman's front door no doubt had a sign: *Come In! We Are Never Clothed!*

'Shall I take it you'll be coming?' she asked archly, before laughing fakely. 'I suppose that's pretty much the point of an orgy!'

I wondered how many times she'd made that little joke. Still, Rory laughed uproariously.

Perhaps now would be the right moment to pretend to her that my husband was just recovering from the surgical part of his sex-change operation. One thing was sure. It was time to page Doctor Freud to reception . . .

CHAPTER 14

THE SENSUAL INTERACTIVE SURPRISE

I don't like surprises. Most surprises are so surprising that you could die of a heart attack. And this was to be a week of surprises.

The first surprise was actually pleasant. I was in the staffroom when Scroope strode in to announce that he'd had a change of heart about my Science Museum excursion. This was due to the number of disappointed letters he'd received from parents. He grudgingly congratulated me on having the foresight to book the museum trip a year in advance, reiterating for the benefit of the 'chalk and talkers', how much the Inspectors approved of field trips. 'Therefore, I'm allowing you to take your class. As planned,' he pronounced crisply.

As he then lectured me on Health and Safety and the endless Risk Assessment forms I would need to fill in i.e. risk of choking to death on a grape in the museum cafeteria, risk of falling into a canal, risk of a terrorist attack; and whether or not the perceived risks were high, medium or low, I sneaked a glance at Perdita, hunched over her herbal tea. She was giving me a splenetic stare.

Saying that Perdita was competitive and jealous is like saying that Al Qaeda are only a little fanatical. Risk assessment for Perdita back-stabbing me was very, very high. I feared for my promotion more than ever.

I was ambushed by my next surprise whilst ambling down Marylebone High Street the following Saturday morning on my way to collect Jenny from her drama class. A sleek black Merc purred past me before coming to a tyre screeching halt halfway over the zebra crossing. As pedestrians scattered, the driver's window whooshed down and Jasmine's highlighted head popped out.

'I'm fucking a murderer!' she called gleefully at me across the road from her new car (the Volvo estate didn't suit her new, vampish image), much to the bewilderment of passers-by. 'I'll pop by later.'

The 'murderer' turned out to be prison playwright Billy Boston, newly celebrated for his début drama, written whilst incarcerated, which was being staged at the avant-garde Tricycle Theatre. 'Not only is he BIB, sweetie,' (her shorthand for Brilliant in Bed) 'but I'll also finally be able to get rid of my husband! Do you have any idea how hard it is to find a lover with advanced weapons' training?' she'd laughed.

Billy Boston had tattoos, a pierced penis, nipple rings, a youth spent in boys' homes and orphanages, two convictions for GBH and theft, one for manslaughter, a court case pending and a drug habit. In other words, a difficult man to seat at a dinner party.

'Oh, I see,' I said at my place later that day. 'So, he used to be a drug-taking, violent thug – but then it all went wrong?'

I was halfway through a basket of ironing when Jazz had arrived, high on her own scandal.

'The manslaughter conviction was really self-defence against a drug dealer. But he doesn't do drugs now. He just does me!'

'Come off it, Jazz. A man like that could find a heroin needle in a haystack,' I retorted, pressing the iron over one of Rory's recalcitrant cuffs.

'Do you know the average number of times a person has sex in their lifetime? Two thousand, five hundred and eighty. Well, we've had more sex than that in a week! I've given up all other men.'

'What?!' This was so surprising that I burned my finger. 'Christ!' I licked the sizzled flesh. 'Bit prim for you, isn't it, Jazz – only having one lover and one husband at a time?'

I immediately phoned Hannah. It was time for reinforcements. She was briefed and at my house in all of ten minutes. 'You're just spunk-drunk, that's all,' she said to Jasmine.

'No, it's more than that. I'm so in love with Billy it renders me incapable even of shopping.'

'Christ,' I conceded. 'That *is* serious.'

'You're just having some D.H. Lawrence fantasy,

already. You're slumming it, Jasmine Jardine. To cure your broken heart,' Hannah commiserated.

'Well, it's better than broken legs – which is what Studz is going to have by the time my murderer boyfriend has finished with him. The man has stolen my heart,' Jazz sighed.

'Well, of course. He is a thief after all,' Hannah warned.

The doorbell rang and I looked at my watch. My husband's heart, not to mention other parts of his anatomy, were being unlawfully acquired at the home of Bianca in exactly half an hour. 'It's my babysitter.'

'Perfect timing. Come out with me tonight, Cass. I'm meeting Billy in the Boom Boom bar, in Shoreditch. Full of low-lifes and Ladies of the Night. Very rough trade,' Jazz thrilled. 'Billy's got a very sexy friend. Prison poet. Ex-cons are so intense. He'll worship you. The prison vernacular, I believe is "cunt-struct". It's just what you need, sweetie.'

'Let me get this straight,' Hannah interrupted. 'You're double-dating *criminals*?' She looked up to heaven. 'Heal them, Oh God, for they are injured in their taste buds.'

'I can't. I've got an orgy to get to.' I feigned joviality, but was wretched with dread. 'Oh well, at least I don't have to worry about what to wear.'

'Well, if you change your mind and feel like a Slow Comfortable Screw in the Boom Boom bar . . .' Jazz interrupted.

'I'm sure it's not a group-grope, Cass,' Hannah comforted. 'It's probably just a sales spiel for a more Advanced Counselling Course.'

'A slow, comfortable screw?'

'It's the name of a cocktail, silly.'

I was surprised to find I was disappointed. But in actual fact, it was so long since I'd had sex, I'd probably get motion sickness. I'd have to tell the guy to pull the bed over to the kerb.

The one accurate bit of information I did learn from therapy is that if you arrive late at a whipped-cream orgy, chances are it will have curdled.

Having vacillated for so long about venturing to Bianca's basement flat in Camden, by the time I got there things were pretty much in full swing. Literally. As my eyes grew accustomed to the dark, I could see that couples were locked together, legs around each other's waists, like sexual Siamese twins. The rather large librarian was flailing around like a sperm whale in flummery while the accountant nibbled at her nipples. The toupeed man with the hairy ankles and the grey socks was making out with the inflatable date. An orgy, one you're not taking part in, looks about as much fun as an anal probe by aliens. And then my heart stopped with a jerk. I peered into the candle-lit gloom. Was that Rory? Was that Bianca? And were they kissing? My stomach roiled. My toes curled up as though I was wearing a pair of Turkish slippers. The image bored like titanium augers into

210

my brain. It must have been a good kiss because Bianca was thrashing around so much, I presumed she was giving birth – and to a woman pretty much her own size. The range of reactions available to me as a Homo sapien seemed completely inadequate to the situation. I needed to spontaneously combust. Or go to another galaxy, warp factor 5.

When Bianca saw me, she broke off from kissing my husband and encouraged me to join in, with the line, 'It's just experimentation. A new technique of mine – tongue-reiki.'

'Rory,' I said, 'if you could manage to extricate your tongue from our therapist's navel, I think it's time to go now.'

'Where's your sense of adventure?' Rory asked. 'Bianca says you have no feel for the erotic.'

'Actually, it's not erotic, or exotic. It's *psy*chotic. There are not enough circuses for all the freaks in this room. You don't need a therapist – you need an exorcist. You're possessed. I don't exactly know how Bianca got the job of marriage counsellor, but I'd be very surprised if it didn't involve a satanic ritual at some point.'

'You are so straight, Cass,' my husband sighed. Unlike the sexy and sophisticated Bianca, whose limits were obviously limitless.

'If she bores any more, she'll strike oil,' Bianca giggled.

Rory laughed with her and I felt my face burn.

'Listen, Rore. You can stay here watching

strangers licking each other's genitals or wait until your wife is sectioned under the Mental Health Act. It's your choice.'

He answered me by dropping a kiss, or rather 'tongue-reiki', on the nape of Bianca's bare neck.

I lunged then, trying to wrench Rory from the Husband Truffler's embrace, but slipped in my leather shoes on a melted patch of cream. I skidded and in the fall, must have hit my head because when I came to, my forehead was being bathed by a self-confessed coprophiliac. Does it get any better than this? I asked myself.

Yes, it does. I had a sensual interactive surprise for Rory too. I was off to meet Jazz and her prison pals in the Boom Boom bar for a slow, comfortable screw.

CHAPTER 15

HIGH INFIDELITY

Billy Boston was not that hard to spot. A Pointillist portrait of a naked Pamela Anderson lay supine on his left bicep; Marilyn Monroe on the other. He had small, close set eyes, which made me wonder if the guy's frontal lobe had been hammered. They were eyes that screamed 'maximum security prison'. He looked so much like a hardened criminal, I couldn't believe that the bar manager wasn't already sending off the CCTV footage to the police.

If Jazz, who was wearing what can only be described as Slapper Chic, had been a dog, she'd have been sniffing at his crotch.

I made my way towards them through the Boom Boom bar, which was full of sherbet-eye-shadowed teenage girls and their scrofulous, shaggy-haired male companions, dancing like things in pain, curling and coiling and jumping from foot to foot. There wasn't a defined side-parting in sight. But past the dance floor, there was another breed prominent. The forty-year-old hottie. From their hipster jeans to the Justin

Timberlake tracks on their iPods, these women were the opposite of the alcoholic Mrs Robinson. And Jazz was the most glamorous of them all.

My best friend patted the bar stool next to her and introduced Billy, whose opening remark was, 'More posh totty, eh? I like youse birds from the big end of town.' He crushed my fingers in a chiropractic handshake. 'Youse talks so good, ja know? Youse have got articulate-ness.'

Then Billy moved off towards the end of the bar to buy me something called a 'Slippery Nipple'. He walked as if on a trampoline, bouncing along, buoyant on his own hot air.

'Isn't he sex on legs?' Jazz thrilled, readjusting her micro-mini for maximum stocking-top glimpses. 'When I look at him, all I can think is "take me".'

'Really? When I look at him all I can think is "pubic lice".'

It was clear to me that Billy was in his late twenties – and possibly always would be. But the prison poet friend Jazz introduced moments later was another case altogether. The Trinidadian who sidled onto the stool next to me, cocked an elbow on the bar and said hello in such a silky voice with lips curved into the most dreamy smile, that the overall effect, the voice and smile, so at odds with his stealthy eyes, was completely unnerving. I wasn't sure whether his splayed nose was the original edition or had been broken, but it gave Trueheart Jones a certain devilish, dangerous charm. This was only accentuated by his opening remark.

'I didn't know angels could fly so low. But hey.' He placed his large warm hand on my shoulder-blades. 'Here are your wings.'

To a sane woman, a woman who only used the word wings when it was attached to the other word 'pantyliner', this might have sounded trite. But to a deranged female whose husband was at a whipped-cream orgy, it was music to her neglected ears.

For the past fifteen years, a 'stud' had meant little more than a drawing pin on the school noticeboard. But here was one flirting with me. Things like this didn't happen to married mothers of two. Let me just check my self-esteem-ometer. Yep – empty. Who was this delicious stranger? Jazz had been wolfing down men as though they were hors d'oeuvres and I was beginning to see why. I wanted some magical, mysterious hours, learning other men's stories and inventing my own. That wild recklessness I could hear in the music, where was that in my own little life? My timid existence had all the excitement of a tin of tuna.

'Are you flirting with me? I am way too old for you,' I flirted. I hadn't felt this excited since I went up to a 34B when breastfeeding.

'I like to feel time passed in the skin. No less than I like to see it in the face. Where there's no record of event, I can have no curiosity. And where there's no curiosity, there can be no desire.'

215

Okay, so it was poetry on L-plates, but I found it oddly enchanting. I couldn't even use alcohol as an excuse. I was just disarmed and charmed. He was all mouth . . . *and* all trousers.

'So you're a poet?'

He shrugged. 'Won a prize. While I was in Pentonville. But in the tradition of all great Oscar acceptance speeches, I couldn't be there to make it,' he grinned.

I laughed. It felt like an age since a handsome young man had talked to me like this. 'Poetry is a great literary gift, mainly because you can't sell it. Am I right?'

He chuckled and I experienced an unexpected pang of pleasure as I realized with a jolt that it had been too long since I had felt amusing.

And then he placed a companionable arm around my shoulders. Goose pimples as big as acne erupted on my skin. I suddenly felt so hot I was worried the sprinklers might start gushing and the smoke alarm would wail. This was the sort of guy who knew how to wake a girl up smiling. Walking might be difficult, but smiling would be a cinch. And he was schmoozing *me*. I would have to keep my legs crossed for the entire duration of the evening. Actually, they were so tightly crossed, I doubted I'd get any feeling back for – oh say, the next two years.

But what was I thinking? I was at the age where, if a man asked me to 'slip into something more comfortable', I'd put on Ugg boots and trackie bottoms. 'You know, I have to go. I have a husband and kids and homework to mark and . . .' I blustered, flustered. 'I just came down here in a moment of irrational madness. I—'

But the poet saw straight through me. 'So tell me, baby. Were these feelings of irrational madness prompted by anythin' unusual? Or did they develop naturally in the course of a normal marriage?'

Here I was, a *Guardian* Woman's-Page-reading, Simone de Beauvoir worshipper, yet I loved it when he called me 'baby'.

I hurried home to Kilburn, to a house dull with despair. The children, sensing something was up between their parents, had become so clingy and whiney of late, and unruly when I was out. They'd put Jamie's Red Ant Farm under the babysitter's chair with the trap door left open and she was threatening not to come again. I was so guilt-riddled about having abandoned them for the Boom Boom bar I felt sure they'd grow up to write the sequel to *Mommy Dearest*. Rory's dogs, also deprived of attention, whimpered to be taken for walks. There were piles of unpaid bills, unopened mail and urgent requests from irate pet owners. I tried to wait up for Rory, jealousy thumping in my head like a migraine, but fell, eventually, into a deep sleep. When I awoke at dawn to see his crumpled, rumpled head on our pillows, a wave of relief washed over me.

I stretched a tentative hand across the sheets. Men suffer not from ADD but *E*DD – Erection Deficit Disorder. Rory might forget birthdays and favourite foods, but he always paid attention when sex was on offer. However, he pulled away from my touch.

It was as though I'd been thrown headfirst into the cold embrace of the sea. Water filled my ears. The silence was unnatural.

'Rory,' I finally whispered. 'I'm just so sorry I ever made you go to therapy. All therapists should be put on a spaceship and launched into a black hole with no booster rockets for earth reentry. Let's forget her.' I touched his arm, aching for the smallest gesture, the faintest softness in his voice to reassure me. 'Let's just go back to how we were. You can play air guitar and I'll chase the hamster around and we can be happy again.'

I gently laid my cheek against my husband's mouth, but his lips stayed stony. And cold.

'I think you're right, Cassie. Our marriage *is* lacking something. I think I should move into the surgery flat for a while.'

Every word burned me. 'The flat?' I repeated blankly. 'Why?'

'Because . . .'

I resolutely steadied my lips to stop from crying. I just didn't think there could be a good end to that sentence.

'Because I need some space.'

'Space?' Who was he, Buzz Aldrich? 'What do you mean, space? Are you . . . leaving me?'

'No.'

'Has someone put you up to this?' I steeled myself to absorb the blow. 'What exactly went on last night? Did you have sex with some other woman? Was it B . . . B . . .' I couldn't stand the taste of her name in my mouth. 'That woman?'

'Who are you – the Crown Prosecutor? It was just tongue-reiki, that's all.'

I buried my face in the pillow for a moment so that he couldn't see what I was feeling for him. 'I think you just officially forfeited your chances of winning Husband of the Year,' I said, yearning for the miraculous comfort of his smile.

But no smile lit up his face. 'I'll be back for some clothes and stuff.' His chilly monotone signalled that the conversation was over. Then he left.

It was that simple. It was that easy. To assassinate a woman.

CHAPTER 16

WET ADULTERESSES OF NW1

'**E**eteezotorault,' Jazz mumbled, pouring me a glass of whisky and cracking open an emergency packet of Green & Black chocolate.

'What?' In a state of numb despair I'd dropped the kids with their friends at the Sunday cinema club, giving me exactly ninety minutes to sort my life out. Like a creature in a nature documentary with homing instincts, I'd then driven on remote control to Jasmine's place.

Jazz removed her tooth bleaching trays and tried again. 'It is not your fault.'

'Do you think he's left me? God! What am I going to tell the children? I mean, how can they not notice their father is sleeping in the surgery flat? Maybe I could say he has to give pills to post-operative cats in the night or something? I'm so worried, Jazz.'

Even though it was a Sunday, Jazz was waiting in once more for another valuation expert for a second quote on their property for insurance purposes. When I enquired why Studz couldn't wait in, she replied, 'Oh, he's off at Number Ten. Winning some award for his humanitarian work.

No doubt they'll reward him with an even bigger stethoscope.' But there was a bitter edge beneath her jokey bonhomie. She poured herself a whisky now and downed it in one wincing gulp. 'Billy's been invited to a writers' festival in Australia and he's asked me to go with him.'

'If you really are in love, why don't you just run away with the guy?'

Just then Josh strolled through the kitchen. He was so manly in his build, yet grinned impishly as he handed his mother his washing. There's a peculiar indeterminacy to teenage boys; Josh was simultaneously childish, yet prematurely adult.

'He still needs me,' she shrugged, after he'd sauntered off.

'And is Studz still cheating on you left right and centre?'

She sighed. 'Well, he does get a lot of odd calls. You remember that Sylvia Plath expert? She's just getting bolder and bolder. It's mind-boggling. She texts him all the time. It's textual harassment. Stuff like: *Was your father an alien? 'Cause there's nothing like you on earth.* She also sends postcards. I know her writing now. 'What's your favourite position on extramarital sex?' She slugged down another hit of Chivas Regal. 'Which is why I go revenge-fucking. As should you. Billy's poet mate, Trueheart Jones – isn't that the best name ever? He's sooo cute and he really, really fancies you. If anyone could cure you of bore-gasms, it'd be a Trinidadian poet named Trueheart.'

I looked at my best friend in alarm. Dating at forty is like being a teenager again. Then you avoided bright light because it showed up spots. Now because it shows up wrinkles. I was just way, way too old for this. 'I am not at the age where I grope at parties then rush home and write about it in my diary, Jazz. I couldn't cheat on Rory. It's just all so . . . slutty.'

'Oh really? Well, next time you go to a dinner party, take a close look at the sluts – sorry, married women – sitting around the table. Latest research? Half of them are having affairs. They're easy enough to spot once you know the telltale signs. She's given up her trouser suit for a Moschino mini. She's not eating any carbs. Her arse is two sizes smaller, her tits two sizes bigger. She's suddenly an expert on things she knew nothing about before – hang-gliding, ghetto rap, Mahler, mountaineering, Tibetan nose flutes – whatever her new lover's into. Her teeth are as bleached as her hair. Her Manolo-Blahniked legs are now as long as the tales she spins about working late at the office. Having been chronically under-valued, she's suddenly full of self esteem.'

'Really?' Oh God, how I craved letting off some esteem. 'But I'd be betraying the person with whom I've shared my life, my children, my greatest confidences . . .'

'Yeah, the husband you're now sharing with your marriage therapist.'

'Rory is not cheating on me, okay? So he kissed

Bianca. Big deal. Maybe it really was just tongue-reiki. Maybe he just does need some time alone. He would never be unfaithful to me.'

'Get real. Men will shag anything. Including body-temperature pies or tethered, reasonably domesticated livestock. You just have to make him jealous. You're so pretty, Cass. Our dreams may have collapsed but not our faces. Why don't you just work out a little more?'

'Hey, at my age, I just try to be neat and punctual.' It was my turn to slug down a gulp of acidic Chivas Regal. 'What I hate about gym classes,' I gasped, my throat searing, 'is the instruction to wear loose-fitting clothing. If I had any loose-fitting clothing, I wouldn't have to come to the gym now would I? But that's also the reason I can't have an affair. I mean, say we go to bed at eight? If I stay the night that makes it twelve hours. I just can't hold my stomach in that long. Besides, what would I say to him?'

'"My, what an enormous cock you have" seems to work wonders.'

'I just couldn't do all the lying and cheating, Jazz, I'd feel like, I dunno, Iago! Anyway, there's nothing serious going on between them, I know it.'

'Anything unserious is serious enough. And you *can* lie. Good God, it's not like you're testifying under oath. Look, you weren't searching for an affair. It's just that you're sexually frustrated and emotionally famished.'

Well, that was true. The encounter in the bar lingered in my memory with a crystalline clarity, as though I'd taken a drug which intensifies the senses. The feeling of Trueheart Jones's hand on my back burned on warmly in my mind. Despite my denials, oh how desperately I wanted to explore the sweet empire of sexual satisfaction.

'At our age it's probably wise to stock up. I mean, we never know where the next penis is coming from, right?'

'Gosh, Jazz, if I'd known I was going to have an affair, I wouldn't have let my legs grow together,' I replied facetiously. 'Besides which, I just don't have the underwear. Victoria's Secret is that nobody over size eight can bloody well wear them.'

'We'll go to Agent Provocateur. They have lingerie for all sizes.'

'Actually, I was thinking of something more substantial. Say, a ski suit. Or the Turin Shroud.'

How could I get naked in front of a twenty-nine year old? How could I get naked in front of a strange man for the first time in twenty years? Because that's the trouble with cheating – sooner or later you have to take off your clothes. Jazz advised me to leave the heating off and the windows open, and then suggest we both undress in bed, because it was soooo cold . . . But what if the cheap motel we'd no doubt end up in had no opening windows? No, no, I would just have to engineer situations where I only met him whilst lying on my side – the only foolproof position guaranteed to make a woman's post-breastfeeding boobs look bigger . . . Unfortunately, in this position men tend to regard you as either a drunken retard or a tragic paraplegic. I could just walk with my arms crossed to push my cleavage out . . . But the only look *this* achieves is of an insane asylum escapee contorted into a permanent straight jacket position. And I suspected that neither option was particularly conducive to seduction.

'By the time you've got him into bed, none of that will matter. The trick is getting him in there. And for that you can just cheat,' Jazz suggested. 'Men lie about their sporting feats and childhood heroics all the time. So, why can't we lie a little? Silicone-gel bras, padding . . .'

'Okay! Bring me my breasts!' I demanded.

'Oh goodee!' she thrilled. 'You soooo need a stint in image rehab.'

Her first attempt involved insertible bra pads, only they kept working their way out of my bra, so that I left a trail of white miniature petal-shaped cushions wherever I went. Mind you, this was very handy when people were looking for me. Especially my husband. I would just lead him, Hansel and Gretel like, to my wanton whereabouts.

Gel inserts were her next technique for making mountains out of my molehills. These are silicone pouches you wear in your bra, only I'd no doubt forget they were there – until, that is, Trueheart found one during foreplay.

'Shit, what are these?' he would ask, holding the illicit quivering jellyfish between forefinger and thumb.

'Um . . . would you believe, an innovative way of defrosting poultry?' No, this was ridiculous. I was not going to sleep with him.

'I know you're not going to sleep with him, sweetie, but you might as well pop on a party thong to be prepared. Just in case you're in an accident or something,' Jazz replied, steering me into the lingerie department of Selfridges.

Now personally, I favour 100 per cent cotton knickers the size of a small emerging nation. You know, pants you could also use as a spinnaker on a yacht. But Jazz soon had me in teddies you need an engineering degree to operate. After ten minutes of wrestling with a frilly teddy, my head was sticking out of the crotch slit, one breast was in the neck hole and my pudenda tufts were fetchingly framed in lace portholes.

'What are you up to in there?' Jazz knocked on the changing room door.

'Oh just busily flunking femininity.'

'You certainly are not!' The next thing I knew, I was in the beauty salon being waxed. Believe me, the pain of waxing will kill you – and there's not much point in being smooth and hairless, if you're *dead*. Then I was coiffured, after which my bouffant was so heavy I could hardly move my head, such was its cargo of hairspray. Bouffy the Vampire Slayer looked back at me from the mirror.

Finally, I was plucked. 'They're not chin hairs. They're just eyelashes which fell down.' Men are so lucky. Not only do they need only one pair of shoes, and in one colour, for their entire adult lives, but they also have an option about growing a moustache.

Determined to spin gold from straw. Jazz's sartorial Rumplestiltskinning began with her trying to squeeze me into the latest designer skin-tight trousers, but found the space already occupied with *legs*.

'I like that dress,' I said to the sales assistant in Joseph, 'but have you got it in a heavier bone size?' The only dress I found which was vaguely flattering, sported the price label *Guess*.

'Gee, I dunno. More than a week's salary?'

In the end, I settled on a new wardrobe from Top Shop and just sat up all night writing *Pucci* and *Prada* onto all my cheap bags, shirts and shoes.

Jazz also believed in the King Canute property of face creams and made me buy every lotion and potion which promised to hold back the sea of time. Needless to say, she did not seem very impressed by my make-up drawer which contained one minimascara I'd had for four years that dried up after the third eyelash, plus a freebee lipstick the colour of which was so vile that a mortician wouldn't use it on a cadaver. But Jazz's beauticians did finally manage to transform me . . . Only trouble was, I could never go anywhere spontaneously ever again, because I needed to start getting ready at least forty-eight hours before.

Then there were the control-top tights, as easy to get in and out of as, say, a wetsuit. It was hardly striptease material. I wore them to school for practice and they were fine, but struggling out of my Extra-Hold Thigh Shapers that night proved so strenuous that I pulled a muscle and had to be taken to hospital.

I sat in the Accident and Emergency room rapidly going off the infidelity idea. Affairs sounded easy, but they were actually so bloody dangerous. And not just physically. I mean, what if Trueheart got serious? What if he got cloying and annoying? I could always call out my husband's name in bed. *That* would probably be enough to put him off . . . Or perhaps I could become more sexually demanding – in a weird way. Or I could tell him I had a stalker and police protection. That would make an ex-con run for his life.

But what if Trueheart *became* the stalker? Then I could just tell him that I had a restraining order out on my husband because he'd threatened to kill any man who slept with me.

Christ. But what if I got serious about *him*? There never really is a good time to tell your husband that you're divorcing him for a twenty-nine-year-old poet with serious pecs appeal – oh, and a criminal conviction for cannabis dealing. No, no, I couldn't go through with it.

To cement my view, I was at Jasmine's when the blonde-haired Sylvia Plath academic telephonically doorstepped her. 'Look,' Jazz barked down the phone, 'I know you're having an affair with my husband. Just as long as *you* know you are one of many, sweetie.'

No, no. I wouldn't put myself in such a vulnerable position. But then again, the thought of Trueheart Jones kept triggering that heat between my thighs. Something had to give and it could be my knicker elastic. Maybe he was the one to shift my sex-drive out of neutral?

I booked and cancelled a double date with Jazz. And booked and cancelled. But in the end, my vacillation was pointless. I came out of the school gate one Wednesday evening after choir practice, glum at the prospect of the long night ahead of me – Jamie was away at school summer camp, Jen was on a sleepover and Rory was still living in the flat – when he was just there beside me, dexterous as a cat burglar.

Against my better judgement, I felt a delightful throb of expectation. I floated towards him. Cosy in the shelter of his huge arm, I was led by Trueheart Jones on a walk towards Regents Park. I could feel the warmth rising up off his skin as we strolled over the lawns and down amongst the roses. Behind the Open Air Theatre he brushed a fingertip along the nape of my neck. A hunger spasm shot through me, and not for food either. I had a craving for the meat and bones of a man.

He traced the neckline of my T-shirt, where it ran along the collarbone, and electricity rushed through me from neck to knee, and quite a few places in between. I was so turned on I forgot to feel guilty. I was so turned on, I forgot to cry 'bring me my breasts.' There was no fumbling as he expertly got beneath my old grey bra, found my nipple and squeezed it. Not softly, the way Rory did. But hard.

'I have breastfed two children . . .' I spluttered apologetically.

I'd hardly finished the sentence before his lips were on my breast, warm, wet, startling. He didn't suckle as Rory did, but bit me, lightly. Sensation juddered along my spine and down my legs. He crushed me to his body. I was under a libido attack. And oh, how happily I surrendered as his hand crept beneath my skirt and up my thigh, slow as Tai Chi. He was under the knicker elastic of my big white cottontails and inside me, two fingers, circling. 'I want you so bad.' And suddenly I knew why half of all married women are apparently having affairs. Not because they want mind-blowing orgasms. Although, yes, yes, yes!!! They do want those. But because a woman needs a man to desire her. At least half as much as he desires victory for his country in the cricket.

As sensation built, I found myself writhing up against Trueheart Jones. I was about to be in my prime! Just like Miss Jean Brodie! My muff would no longer be in a huff! Any minute now I would cry out in an urgent, animal way before I collapsed wrecked, in a sweaty, panting heap . . . But no sooner had I imagined it, than I found myself pulling back from the brink, like some sappy romantic heroine in an eighteenth-century novel. The sensual mist, the cocoon of breath and skin he'd spun around me, tore.

'I need to go.'

'Yeah well, I need to lie ya down so I can lick ya.' His hot voice was thick with lust.

I swallowed hard. My body gave in straight away, yes, yes . . . but a warm storm of feelings took me over. I loved my husband. I belonged to Rory. He had soaked into me, body and soul. He was my man.

'Hey, I thought you wanted to go all the way?'

'Oh, I do – But it's got to be in opposite directions. I'm so sorry, Trueheart. So, so sorry.'

Racing round the Inner Circle to Baker Street tube, I realized I'd recycled Rory too easily. He was like the stuff you keep for years and years, only to throw out two days before you need it. There's a fine line between lust and insanity. And I had just stopped myself from erasing that line.

CHAPTER 17

TILL HOMICIDE DO US PART

The night was warmly scented with honey-suckle, which buoyed my spirits as I let myself into the surgery and went straight to the little flat behind. All I could think about was the dreamy, creamy warmth of my husband's embrace. I was burning up with need – the need to feel Rory close to me. That was my matrimonial mantra. Rory wasn't back yet from his home visits so I crashed into the spare bedroom, determined to wait for him, but after a couple of hours, I passed out, fully clothed, face down on the bed. In my light-headed relief at having escaped from folly, the last frivolous thought on my mind was that it had been so long since I'd seen my husband I was frightened I'd shoot him as a burglar. But *I* was the one hell-bent on theft. Emotional break and enter. I would steal my way back into my husband's heart.

I woke in a mist of adrenalin and angst. The dawn gave the surgery bedroom a melancholy, vanquished look. Much like me. The pillow beside me was empty. *Where was Rory?* I felt the zig zag of doubt go through me as the pendulum of suspicion swung back and forth. Clambering off the bed, I searched the room for clues. I prodded at the message button on the decrepit answerphone. The tape was so old that the message which had been left was scratchy and warped, but the voice was definitely female. And it was arranging a time to meet. I frantically tried to come up with other excuses for why my husband would be meeting a female. Perhaps his mother had come back from the dead? Perhaps he'd developed Dr Doolittle traits and could talk to the animals – and they could talk to him? Perhaps Rory was a cross dresser making an appointment with his seamstress? All these excuses were more palatable than the fact that he might be having an affair. Especially when logic dictated that there was only one possible candidate.

I wanted to call the police and get them to throw fingerprint dust all across her naked body, because I was now imagining my husband's hands all over her. Bands of anxiety circled my ribcage, tighter and tighter. Nervousness beaded my lip with perspiration as I fell into psychological quicksand. Men are creatures of habit. They don't leave the comfort of their homes unless it's for another woman. Terror slammed through me. Of course he was falling in love with her. One encouraging word from the Husband Rustler and he'd fled from our marriage so fast he'd left nothing but the outline of his body in the wood of the front door as he went through. Why had it taken me so long to admit it? I was a Mensa candidate, obviously.

As I blundered my way out of the veterinary practice, I felt sure the animals were mocking me from their cages. Can rabbits smirk? Because I was convinced I saw one chuckling snidely.

The Dickensian houses of Camden cast tombstone shadows across my car as I sat outside Bianca's flat. I felt oppressed by fear and wound down the window for a blast of oxygen. It was 8 a.m. Rory opened the surgery at 8.30, so if he was here, he'd have to appear soon. Sure enough, a heart-stopping moment later, Bianca's yellow front door squeezed open and they were there, together, on the doorstep. Peering between the suctioned feet of Jenny's Garfield doll, I saw him kiss her. I strained my eyes until they stung, watching them. Oh. I clutched the steering wheel and despaired. My skin prickled as though *I* was being secretly watched, instead of the other way round. Rory looked so muscular and handsome. Yes, the entire world loves a lover – unless he's your bloody husband.

'I thought it was experimentation?' I was out of the car and screeching across the street before I knew what I was doing. I gulped in air as tart as she was. 'I thought it didn't mean anything?' I felt as though I'd been hollowed out by the wind. 'Rory, I want you to get in the car and come home with me right now.'

Rory stood stock-still. Bianca, however, nuzzled his ear, no doubt whispering her spells. She was wearing a pink silk camisole with lace scanties.

Her hair was fetchingly tousled and she was sporting false eyelashes which would have been more at home on a giraffe. Just the way all working mums look in the mornings. Not.

'Rore?' But Rory just stood there, staring. 'When I say I'd like your answer soon, what I mean is, *within my lifetime*.' It sounded bold, but I could feel a great floodtide of grief behind my tonsils.

'Actually,' answered Bianca, 'we're moving in together.'

Pain came, rapid and intolerable, like opening the blinds on a summer's day when you have a hangover. A malicious smile shrieked across her face.

'Where to? Your eco-sensitive igloo? Rory, she's a fake. Can't you see through her?' The street, the world, seemed to tilt and start sliding slowly toward some dreadful abyss. Fear began to ooze from me. I looked at my nemesis. Bianca had obviously been to the Eva Braun School of Mistressing. 'Don't you care about the family you're destroying?'

'I care about Rory, in all his complexities,' Bianca cooed in her creamy tones. 'I can fulfil his needs in a way you never can.'

'Gee, how many years of yoga did you have to do, to be able to kiss your own ass like that? It's quite an achievement.' I could feel my blood coagulating with rage.

'*I* can nurture his creativity and tap into his untouched potential. *You* have done nothing but smother him.'

I wanted to make a Wildean quip, a Shakespearean

reference, a caustic aside. But instead, I just smithereeened into tears. 'Rory!' If he didn't hold me, I was going to fly apart, like an exploding land-mine. 'Can't you talk to me alone?' As addled as I was, I knew that it was a sure sign that your marriage is not going well when your husband has a loaded woman pointed at your chest. 'Stop pointing that thing at me.' I gestured towards Bianca. 'It's making me nervous.'

'I'm sorry. But where Rory goes, I go. That's the kind of devotion he's been missing from his marriage,' Bianca said with practised aplomb.

I had been hit by a psychological truck. And my husband was driving. 'Listen to me,' I told him. 'You're having a midlife crisis, obviously. But couldn't you just worry over male pattern bald-ness, like other men your age?'

Rory palmed his new beard. He'd been sprouting the look of a revolutionary leader for a few weeks now. But it was me he was revolting against. Or maybe, just me he found revolting?

'I know it was my fault, dragging you to therapy,' I went on, 'but when I told you to show more affection, I didn't mean you to take a lover!'

Bianca shook her head. 'Truth is, you just don't satisfy him sexually.'

'Well, you know I have a sex tip for you, Rory. The way to ensure that a wife stays moist during inter-course is to keep your bloody mistress out of sight!'

'Mistress? For your information, Cassandra, Rory and I are soulmates. We are emotionally and psychologically simpatico. But of course, we also have so much to discover sensually about each other.' She squeezed his hand and gave him one of her velvet glances. 'In fact, he's going to star in a video I'm making called *The Body*.'

'Oh really? How big is his part? Must be quite small.' Which wasn't a bad reply, considering I was in the midst of an anxiety attack. I felt an ache of disgust grip my intestines. How could she do this to me? To us? A murderous fury took hold of me. Die! Die! But all I had in the car was Jamie's giant water-pistol. I had a sudden vision of all the brunch-crumb-coated Camden arty types, sipping their champagne and shaking their heads condescendingly as they caught sight of me chasing my husband and his mistress down the street pumping watery rounds into them from an aqua-gun.

'Rory, what about the kids?' I implored. 'If you can't think about me, at least think about them.'

'Oh, but we are. I've already had a text from Jamie saying he can't wait to meet me. Look.' Bianca displayed Rory's phone with a message illuminated. *She sounds cool, Dad* it read. 'Aw,' Bianca gushed, 'thassadorable.'

I had to wait for the crashing in my ears to fade away before I could talk again.

'Rory, don't be fooled,' I said desperately. 'Bianca hates children. She makes her own kid play with gender-non-specific toys from economically disadvantaged Third World craft fairs. I mean, it's child abuse. And before you move into Tofu

237

Towers,' I gestured to her flat, 'just think about this. Bianca may pretend to be all organic, hell she's no doubt given you your first organic orgasm, but the woman's full of Botox. Don't you find that a little hypocritical?'

'And he's taking me to meet Jenny today,' Bianca miaowed.

I tried to answer, but what erupted instead was a cry of anguish. 'Where?' My life was suddenly a cracked mirror.

'Sports Day. Our daughters are at the same school.' Rory spoke at last. I reached for him, but he brushed me away as if I were a gnat. A gnat he wanted to swat. 'Serendipity is a year younger, but I'm sure the girls will get on.'

'But, Rory you never go to Sports Day! *I've* always gone. This is the first year I've not run in the Mothers' Race, but the dates conflicted with my school excursion to the Science Museum.'

'It's okay. Bianca's going to run.'

'Yes,' she gloated. '*Some* of us like to keep in shape.'

Warning! Warning! Danger! Klaxons of terror trumpeted in my head. My face was pinchy with indignation. How could he do this to me? Rory might be the vet, but I seemed to be the one with a degree in Animal Husbandry. 'So, you really do want my husband, do you? Well, just let me go and get his water bowl and chew toys. And hey, that might be a good way to get rid of you too, Bianca. If I throw a stick, no doubt you'll run after it.'

Bianca abruptly pulled Rory back into her

garden flat and slammed the door. I felt desolate at the loss of him. What really upset me was that *I* was the one who'd battled with and then retrained him; who'd finally got through to him the importance of birthdays and anniversaries and that there is only one answer to the question, 'Does this make me look fat?' Only for another woman to waltz off with the New and Improved Version. It was like renovating a house, making it perfect – only to be evicted. That was it. I'd been sexually gazumped by a new owner. A younger, thinner, firmer new owner, with better underwear.

And it was all my own wretched fault. Jesus Christ. By dragging him to couples counselling, I might as well have lit up a cigarette next to a petrol tanker. And soon Bianca would be meeting my daughter, and running with all the other Yummy Mummies in the Mothers' Race.

Driving to school, I fantasized about killing her off and making it look like a lawnmower-related accident. I could see myself now on a maximum-security prison wing crocheting doilies and pleading that I suffered from Multiple Personality Disorder. Multiple? Who was I kidding? Hell, I didn't even have *one*! Well, all that was about to change.

I steeled myself. The chequered flag had been dropped. The race was on. And I would win back my hubby fair and square. Even if I had to cheat to do so.

CHAPTER 18

SURVIVAL OF THE PRETTIEST

When a woman finds out that her husband is having an affair, most of the immediate options seem puerile.

1. Writing on his driver's licence under *any distinguishing features* – NO PENIS.
2. Dating the bloke he hero-worships on their Saturday footie team who never passes him the ball.
3. Spreading a rumour that you ended it because he's incontinent.
4. Signing him up to some embarrassing websites; websites under surveillance by Scotland Yard.
5. Giving up chocolate. You'll miss it so much, you won't have time to miss your husband.
6. Getting hold of his chequebook and on all the cheque stubs writing *for sexual favours*.
7. Beating the bitch in the Mothers' Race.

Sports Day is an exercise in ritual humiliation. Most mums like to spend the Mothers' Race hiding in the toilets. Needless to say, I was looking forward to it only slightly more than I would have my own execution by lethal injection, but my hatred of Bianca overrode all other feelings. The only problem was how to get out of my school excursion to the Science Museum?

There was no point calling in sick. Mr Scroope doesn't even accept a certificate of death as an excuse. But it would be my own funeral if I didn't beat Bianca in the Mothers' Race.

As a teacher you become au fait with every excuse imaginable. The absentee notes from parents provide much mirth in the staffroom.

Please excuse Kylie for being absent on the 29th, 30th, 31st and 32nd of February.

Please excuse Jackson for being. It was his dad's fault.

Please excuse Chardonnay for being absent yesterday. Me and her Dad had her shot coz she was real sick.

Even adulterers like Rory had excuses. *Please excuse me from my marriage but I have fidelity fatigue.* He was the one having the affair, yet I was the one made to feel at fault. But what excuse could I give for abandoning twenty children at the Science Museum?

Planning is a vital part of any trip. Just ask Scott of the Antarctic. I planned to take my class to the museum, then leave them there with Lucy, the other teacher from my form who is a good mate, and the six parental helpers drafted in for the day. I would then dash to my daughter's Sports Day in Hampstead Heath, compete in the Mothers' Race, and catch the Northern Line back in time for the return coach journey to school.

I knew the dangers of bunking off from a school excursion. It was no doubt a sacking offence. However, the school policy cited that a teacher had to be given three written warnings, before he or she could be sacked. Which was at least fairer than marriage. Three written warnings then divorce would be preferable to the sudden rejection Rory had sprung on me.

Oh yes. Preparation can make all the difference between not getting a promotion and not even getting close.

On the way to Jenny's Sports Day, I was so nervous, I devoured two Mars bars, swigged down a cappuccino and crunched my way through a packet of crisps. Not the ideal way to train for a race. I had to sprint from the tube to the sports ground, a matter of some 300 yards, but that left me bent double at the waist, wheezing and praying for death. I was so bloody unhealthy I could hardly stand upright. I traversed the last stretch with the speed of a tree sloth through treacle. Hampstead Heath had been chock-a-block for weeks with deranged mothers panting along with their personal trainers, trying to achieve Olympian stamina for their mothers' races. And here was me, shuffling along, as though trekking across snow.

There was also the drawback of what I was wearing. Having crashed out in the surgery flat, I'd slept in the clothes I'd worn teaching yesterday – a skirt and a short-sleeved top. Luckily, I'd put on my trainers before leaving the flat for Bianca's. But I'd hoiked off my old grey bra during the night and, in my haste that morning, hadn't put it back on. Never mind, I told myself. My bras weren't that supportive anyway. A truly supportive bra would tell me that I'm not half a stone overweight and have no stretchmarks.

Once I got to the sports ground, the children's races were coming to an end. I was just in time to cheer Jenny on. I sat with the other parents, writhing in our seats, as though being tickled by gigantic invisible fingers, as we craned for the best view of the finishing line. Heads bobbed like popcorn exploding in a pan, amid the flash of digital cameras and the whir of camcorders.

'*Mu-um!*' Jenny cringed when I hugged her at the finishing line, ecstatic that she'd come third, 'You're not wearing a bra. *Eeeww.* You're just sooo embarrassing.' In a spirit of reconciliation, she offered to run away if I embarrassed her again. All I could think was that she'd better start packing, because pretty soon her mother would be sprinting, skirt tucked into knickers, tits to the wind.

'Have you seen your dad?' I asked, trying to keep the hysteria and pain out of my voice.

She hooked a thumb towards the amenities block. I meandered as casually as possible in that direction. The wind whipped through the long grass, this way and that, making it seethe and twitch like a sea of green snakes. It was quiet behind the toilet shed and quite secluded. Trying to quell my emotions, I peeked around the corner of the building. And there they were, stealing a kiss. I couldn't breathe. I was gasping. It was an emergency situation. If I'd been on a plane, an oxygen mask would have been dropping from the overhead lockers.

After they'd sauntered back to join the other parents, I walked to the place where they'd been standing. They'd left two perfect casts of their shoes pressed into the soil. Like the scene of a crime. But at least Bianca was wearing kitten heels and a summer frock, which meant I might not have to run after all.

Then the mothers' race was cracklingly announced over the Tannoy. Devoted mums suddenly flung their children out of their arms as though flamenco dancing and hurtled towards the starting line.

Once upon a time, there would have been a few fun, gentle heats, mums running in their stockinged feet, perhaps balancing an egg on a spoon; the biggest danger being if your wrap-around skirt came undone and fell down. But not now. Not since the advent of the alpha mums, those women with their polished granite kitchen worktops, down lights and number plates which read *A1 Mum*. They'd had their meteoric careers, then bred late; giving up their high-powered jobs to be high-powered mummies. But the killer competitive instinct still oozes out of them. The traditional big-thighed mothers, women testing the limits of Lycra, were so cowed by the ferocity of the supermums, each muscle and sinew flexing intimidatingly, that they'd given up competing and now just sat glumly on the sidelines.

Bianca suddenly peeled off her frock to reveal a state-of-the-art, high-tech Lycra running ensemble, which wouldn't be out of place in the Olympic village. She kicked off her kitten heels and bent to lace herself into trainers, too white to be anything but brand new and purpose bought, I reflected wrathfully. She then rose like an Amazonian warrior. The flowers seemed to curtsey in the wind before her. Christ. Even Mother Nature adored the man-eating bitch.

Strolling to the lane next to mine, Bianca, in full make-up – including fake eyelashes, looked me up and down. 'It doesn't matter if you win or lose because . . . you're gonna lose.' She stretched, as languorously at ease in her skin as a cat.

'Well, I just hope you've got a spare medical team on hand, because you are going to need it,' I bluffed, tucking my skirt into my knicker-leg elastic, a look I felt was probably *not* going to catch on at the next Olympics. 'With any luck your eyelashes will break your fall.'

I was tortured by thoughts of what the other mothers knew. Was I imagining the furtive glances behind my back? These perfect, cake-baking domestic goddesses, the type who make you want to stick your head in your food processor, aren't competing for the attention of men, but to out-perform each other. 'Did you see she's getting cellulite?' 'Her children are feral. Why doesn't she discipline them?' 'I'm sure she got a boob job for Christmas.' They were more judgemental than the High Court.

'On your marks . . .' We all leaned forward into our starting positions. The white finishing-line tape looked nauseatingly far away. I glanced down the row of runners. Normally mild-mannered mothers had acquired a look reminiscent of hunters about to bludgeon baby seals at the North Pole. Nails outstretched, elbows jutting, they pawed at the starting line like bulls who've seen their matador.

'Get set . . .'

'Jenny and I got on wonderfully, by the way,' Bianca imparted. 'She has such . . . potential. It's a shame you haven't maximized it. But there's still time and a girl her age is so malleable.'

'Go!'

If Bianca's comment had intended to unsettle me, it actually had the opposite effect. Fuelled by hatred, I ran as though I were on crystal meths. I ran as though there were free Jimmy Choo shoes at the finishing line, being given out by Brad Pitt, naked.

The woman on my left moved forward like an ostrich, head and neck outstretched, her upper body apparently having nothing to do with her legs. Others ran with bent, averted heads, like small harvest animals. But I felt myself passing them all. Waves of wind spanked my face as I ploughed ahead, pinballing off other runners. As the crowd thinned, I glanced over my shoulder. And there was Bianca. She was flinging other women out of her way, hurling them into bushes. That glance cost me a few seconds and I turned to focus on the white tape, held by the school secretary and the music teacher. I could feel Bianca running up behind me, close as a whisper. The finish line came closer, closer. I was panting, panting, legs like pistons, when I felt the push. I executed a dervish thrashing of arms, but could feel myself falling. I caromed sideways, missing giving the Headmistress a full frontal lobotomy by half a millimetre. Other runners tripped over my falling body, until we lay on the lawn, our tangle of black leggings and brightly coloured tops giving us the look of a large liquorice allsort having an epileptic fit.

'You fucking idiot,' spat one earth mother. 'What the fuck did you do that for!'

'I . . . I . . . was p . . . pushed.' My lungs scrambled for fresh air.

'You should be banned, you stupid bitch!'

'But . . . but . . .' My justifications were lost in a general hubbub of disgruntled fury. Talk about

a fall from grace. The light under the trees thickened, turning malevolent. Ill-will surrounded me.
I was finding it hard to breathe.

'Mum, are you all right?'

'Sure. I always bleed from the ears like this,' I
wheezed. 'And my ankle often flaps off the end
of my leg in this rather curious manner.'

I found Jenny's calf and groped for purchase,
pulling myself up. 'She pushed me, did you see
that?' I gasped. 'I was winning and Bianca pushed
me.'

'Oh Mum, don't be a bad loser.'

Rory was moving reluctantly in my direction,
with Bianca not far behind, clutching her winning
bottle of champagne.

'You should be awarded something for
competing without a bra. A bravery medal
perhaps. Are you okay?' he asked begrudgingly.

'She pushed me! That cow pushed me. Doesn't
anyone believe me?' I inwardly cursed my name,
Cassandra – one whose warnings go unheeded. No
one had believed *her* about the Trojan Horse either.

'Bubbles!' Bianca's eyes were aglow with a
chilling triumphalism. 'I just love bubbles.'

'Yeah? Well, why don't you just go fart in the
bath.'

'Mum,' Jenny shushed me. 'Stop it. Haven't you
been embarrassing enough for one day?'

'Do you want to, um, you know, join us?
Bianca brought a picnic lunch,' Rory asked,
half-heartedly.

Of course she had. 'No. I've, I've got to get back to work.'

In the midday sun, the wedge of shade from the amenities block had retreated to a thin line. I limped there to lick my wounds before making the crazed dash back to my science excursion. Desolate and ruined, I thought I might start crying, but then rallied. I hadn't wet my pants, so all in all, it was a success of a kind.

As I said, planning is a vital part of any trip. I had timed things so that I had an hour to get back to my class. But what I hadn't planned on was firstly, a sprained ankle and secondly, a 'person on the line', which is a London Transport euphemism for suicide on the track. And finally, an uncharged mobile.

After hobbling to the tube, there was a delay which meant when the train finally came, I had to work my elbows like oars to fight my way into a carriage, where we sat motionless for the next ten minutes. There is no air conditioning on London's underground. My T-shirt, already wet with sweat from the run, stuck to me like a cotton skin. When the announcement of the line closure came, I staggered above ground to find a taxi. When no taxi appeared, I lurched onto a bus.

The roads were blocked with North London standard parental-issue behemoths. The bus trundled along at a geriatric pace. I reached for my mobile to call my fellow teacher, Lucy, but the phone was as flat as I felt. I had slept in the surgery the night before so hadn't had the chance to charge it. I tried telling myself it was all part of the great adventure of living in London, but was quietly having a panic attack. I began making inventive promises to God about all the charitable acts I would perform if only I was able to make it back to the Science Museum in time.

When the bus lumbered into Baker Street, I hopped off, literally, and doddered into the underground once more. Two changes and I'd be there. As I waited and waited for a tube, with more and more delays announced, I began to think of career alternatives; jobs as a chicken de-sexer or armpit sniffer for deodorant testing clearly beckoned.

At South Kensington station, I kangarooed all the way to the museum. By the time I lumbered into the foyer, there was no sign of my class. I shuffled about a bit, pain oozing from me in rancid sweat, frantically crying out the name of my fellow teacher, 'Lucy? Lucy!!' My T-shirt had been torn in the race, I was covered in grass stains from the fall, my hair was knotty and dishevelled, I was jigging around on one foot, bra-less boobs bouncing, and the security guards seemed to be looking at me in an over-attentive manner. When I pushed ahead of the line to ask whether North Primrose Primary School had left the premises, I was told to wait my turn or go to hell.

Since I was limping from a very painful and swollen ankle, mid-heart attack and three-quarters of an hour late for the coach back to school, at this juncture hell actually seemed like the better destination.

One £40 cab fare later, I was back at Primrose Hill. While stuck in traffic, I'd prepared my defence. I would plead mental unfitness and retire early on a pension. To back up my claim, I'd put mosquito netting around my staffroom chair and only play bongo music.

As it happened, I was getting plenty of practice at jungle warfare. The only way to sneak into the school was to sidle, back to the wall, underneath the security camera and then crawl on my belly commando-style past Scroope's office window.

It was three o'clock when my covert operations concluded with a successful infiltration of the first floor and a Geronimo-type entrance through the side window into Lucy's classroom, where she was entertaining my pupils as well as her own. Not being a 'chalk and talker', Lucy whispered that as she'd covered my rear so well I owed her a beer. Exhausted with relief, I slunk into my classroom to retrieve the register – and stopped dead with shock, gorgonised to the spot by her steely stare.

'And where, may one ask, have you been?' Perdita Pendal moved into my path faster than the Pentagon Rapid Response Force, and with just as much dedication to passive diplomacy. 'Do you know the penalty for leaving your class on an excursion?' When Perdita talked, her thin, lacquered lips looked to me like two pink worms wrestling. 'I believe it is a sackable offence.'

Thousands of illegal immigrants, possibly packing Anthrax, are setting up terror cells around England, and can the security forces find them? No. One and a half hours late back from a school excursion and Perdita was on to me. Why she isn't on Scotland Yard's anti-terror pay-roll remains a mystery. I closed the door behind me and prepared to grovel.

'Look, it was an emergency. The kids were fine. On excursions you're supposed to have a one to ten parent-child ratio, right? Well, I made sure there was a one to six ratio, by drafting in extra parents. And Lucy was there. It was a family crisis. Nobody needs to know. I mean, everything's worked out fine.'

'Hasn't it just,' she said, with the demeanour of a Victorian governess.

'Perdita, I'm begging you. Please don't tell Scroope. I'll do all your playground duty for the rest of the year, if you just don't say anything.' I had gravel rash on my knees from grovelling, but persevered. 'Have some compassion. Some teacherly loyalty. Some sisterly solidarity?' I begged. But Perdita had the compassion of a Medellin drug cartel.

'Duty before friendship,' she replied ominously. Her crisp tone told me that it was pointless pleading.

At four o'clock when the kids exploded out of the

252

door for home, I saw Scroope in the quadrangle. His face was rigid, his mouth pinched up like a rectum straining for a bowel movement. 'My office,' he ordered.

Dragging my hurt foot towards my doom, I wondered if it might help to tell him about much worse things that had happened on school excursions. A friend of mine from college had taken her Year Six girls camping in the New Forest, where they went mushrooming . . . only they turned out to be magic mushrooms. Her entire class were in Intensive Care for a day, hallucinating. It gave a very literal meaning to 'school trip' . . . But I changed my mind when I saw his eyes at close range. I looked around for a weapon to protect myself, wondering desperately if perhaps I could set his laser printer to 'Stun'? My Headmaster's moods ranged from obnoxious to Satanic. And that was on a good day. His rage, when it came, was tornadic.

'YOU LEFT YOUR CLASS?!!!'

For the next half an hour, he just went off, like Hurricane Katrina, words pouring out of him instead of rain. He was apoplectic with rage about breaches of Health and Safety. The cords of his neck stood out like cables as he screamed about the risks, the dangers and hazards, the possible outcomes of such a reckless act. I was irresponsible, immoral, immature . . . If it were up to him, he said, he would sack me on the spot. Yes, teachers had to receive three written warnings before they could be fired. But this was so serious that he was going to take it before the Board of Governors and ask them to consider dismissing me immediately.

I should have stood up for myself, but now I simply wondered how I could ever have thought I would get away with it. If I wrote an auto-biography it'd be called *It's Time To Take a Good Hard Look at Your Pathetic Excuse of a Life, You Bloody Idiot*.

I kept my eyes on the wall behind him which was painted institutional beige and, as he ranted, found myself pondering what subjects he'd been good at teaching before his inexplicable rise to Headmaster? Cringing and Quaking perhaps? Torture Techniques? My parting gift would be a sign for his office which would read *You don't have to be a misogynistic, misanthropic bastard to work here, but it helps*.

After Scroope had ushered me from his sight, no doubt so that he could play some more with his gun collection, I thunked my head against the wall. But the school and all its tribulations might as well have been on Pluto. They seemed so paltry by comparison to the rest of my woes. I had lost my husband's heart. And embarrassed my daughter, which meant I'd practically thrown her into Bianca's sinister embrace. I had a feeling that the light at the end of the tunnel was from a train. And I was tied to the tracks.

CHAPTER 19

I'M HAVING MY PERIOD SO CAN THEREFORE LEGALLY KILL YOU

'He's bonking his therapist? You're kidding. Where do they make love? On her couch? After fifty-five minutes does she say, "Your time is up"?'

'It's not funny, Jazz. I tell you though, if things get any w . . . w . . . worse, I'll have to ask you to stop h . . . h . . . helping me,' I sobbed.

After school, I'd shoved some money at Jamie and Jenny and dropped them at McDonald's, cursing myself for being such a bad mother. Guilt gland throbbing, I recalled how I'd asked the doctor the day Jamie was born to wake me after the Caesarean – when he was oh, say *seven*. But the guilt wasn't enough to stop me from abandoning them to a McShit meal while I careered to Jasmine's.

She was showing another property valuer around. Apparently, Studz wanted yet one more house evaluation for insurance purposes. Lately, estate agents were constantly coming and going in their black, shark-like cars.

'Here,' Jazz said to me. 'Drink this while I get

rid of this guy.' She plonked a stiff gin and tonic on the kitchen table, rescued her freshly baked bread out of the oven, then turned her attentions to the sharp-suited salesman.

'So, before you *go*,' she said pointedly to him, 'just out of interest, how much do you think I'd get for the place?'

'Oh, the house is worf free mill, easy. No doubt 'bout that. It's a fine property. Georgian master-piece. State-of-the-art kitchen, magnificent spiral staircase, underground swimming pool, unique double height wood-panelled library, bewdifully presented.' He spoke like a brochure as he gazed admiringly at the crystal decanters, the neat piles of Christies' catalogues, the gleaming grand piano. This house had been Jazz's labour of love.

'Gosh! You'd certainly get a juicy commission, wouldn't you? If I wanted to sell, that is,' Jazz small-talked, opening the hall door in way of a hint. 'What would you earn on that?'

The ginger-haired man snapped his briefcase shut. 'Peanuts on this joint, Mrs. It's owned by the bank.'

Jazz stood as straight as an exclamation mark. 'What?'

'Mortgaged up to the hilt, love.'

'That's a mistake. We paid it off a decade ago.'

'Yeah, but then youse remortgaged a few years back and then again recently.'

Jazz barked out a nervous laugh. 'No, we didn't.'

'Well, whoja fink keeps employin' me to come

round 'ere and do the evaluations? I'll let meself out, shall I?'

'It must be a mistake.' She moved after him down the hall.

I hurried to her side. Jazz held onto my arm as though she were drowning. Before she could find her feet, Studz padded into the kitchen from the basement swimming pool. He was as taut and trim as a tennis pro.

'Oh, look who's here. That heroic champion of the underdog.' Jazz's voice dripped with sarcasm as she marched back down the hall. I instinctively ducked out of sight into the living room. 'I've just had a very interesting chat with that valuation chap who tells me that you've remortgaged our home. Is this true?'

'Yes. Actually it is,' he replied calmly. 'I needed more money to fund my new invention . . . I've got a team working on an anti-ageing serum. Far more effective than collagen. That's what's taking all my money. It's also taking longer than I thought to perfect. We've been conducting trials in Africa. But there have been a lot of setbacks and side effects . . .'

'You're using your poorest patients as guinea pigs?'

'Why not? I've done enough for them. Now they can do something for me.'

'I thought you preferred the prestige of helping the underprivileged?'

'Yes, yes, I have cachet. Now I want cash. But

I need to spend it to make it. Hence the re-mortgaging.'

I saw Jazz reel as though he'd hit her. 'And you did this without consulting me? What am I? A child? But wait. The house is in both our names! I paid the bloody down payment, when you were still a junior doctor.'

'Remember those papers I asked you to sign once, when I was rushing to the airport? They weren't insurance papers. They were papers granting me emergency signature rights.'

Jazz bent double as though winded from the punch. 'This is my home! Don't you care about your family? Your son?'

'It will be good for him to grow up the hard way, like I did. I didn't have anyone holding my hand . . .'

'Yes, you did! You had *me*! Me, for all those fucking years. How can you do down your own son? It's sick. It's insane.'

Studz still didn't know I was in the house. I tried to think of a good excuse to leave, like, 'Oh dear, I think I've gone into labour!' But then the phone shrilled. Jazz snatched it up from its cradle. 'Look,' she barked into the receiver, 'he's got no money. You might as well find some other fool to fuck.'

'Give me the phone,' Studz ordered. He wrenched it from her and spoke monosyllabically. Gone was his famous flippancy. There was no warmth in his tone. Only anxiety and anger.

Jazz scrutinized him shrewdly. I found David

Studlands as indecipherable as his doctor-like handwriting. But Jazz knew him inside out.

'What's going on? It's your Plath-alogical ex-patient, isn't it? Don't tell me she's stalking you!' Jazz let out a harsh burst of nervous laughter. 'That would serve you right.'

Studz looked momentarily unsettled. 'How did you know about Maryanne?'

'Oh, I don't know. The imprint of her vulva on your face kind of gave it away. That's where the money's going, isn't it? On diamond pendants and Mayfair penthouses. It's not all going to your anti-ageing research. Is it?'

It was awful to witness the throes of a dying marriage. They were like two gasping fish out of water. I was sitting out of sight on one of Jazz's antique chairs. Its slender, shapely little legs gave the impression that it could canter away. And I was willing it to do so now.

'She's threatening to report me to the General Medical Council,' Studz sighed. 'I could escape with a two-year supervision order, but . . .'

'What? Are you serious? This woman is black-mailing you?'

'Thanks to you, yes. Because you blabbed to her about me seeing other women. Then she got nasty. She's threatening to sue my arse off.'

'You're a surgeon. Can't you just sew it back on?' Jazz replied frostily.

'Not if I'm struck off. And what would my life be without my work?'

Jazz clenched her fists. 'What will my life be without my house?! You bastard! The first duty of a doctor is to do no harm. That's what Hippocrates said. You *should* be struck off the Medical Register. Having sex with a patient is completely off-limits. Every doctor knows it's a career-ending offence.'

'Christ! It's not my fault. Female patients often fall in love with their doctors. Freud calls it transference. It was nothing more than a faux pas . . .'

A faux pas? I thought to myself. Yeah, a faux pas right up there with 'never get involved in a land war in the Middle East'.

'At first it was stimulating. Maryanne's an intellectual. Conversations with her were so invigorating,' Studz said, unaware of how he was crushing his wife. 'Then she became besotted. Leaving poems in my briefcase. Sticking love notes on my car. Turning up at places she knew I would be. I mean, I should be able to sue *her* for harassment. Anyway, when she found out about the other women, she became psychotic. Unhinged. She followed me everywhere. The woman needs help. What did she expect? It's the biological destiny of men to pursue new sexual attachments. We are programmed to—'

'Programmed? What are you, A VCR?' Jazz scoffed.

'It's the natural cycle of—'

'Only washing machines have cycles, David.'

'Of course, I broke off with her. But that's when things got ugly.' His shifty eyes jumped around the room. 'She went to a lawyer and made an affadavit claiming that she came to me looking for help for depression and I took advantage of her insecurity. And that the affair only exacerbated her illness. She will testify that I exploited her physical and emotional vulnerability.'

'What proof does she have?' Jazz demanded, ashen-faced.

'Well, there are my text messages – which she kept, I'm afraid. You might as well know the worst of it. She's threatening to sell her story to the *News of the World* with details about how I took her to sex clubs in New York and Paris, where I asked her to have sex with strangers so that I could watch.'

Jazz slumped down into a chair. Through all this I had been doing my very best impersonation of a pot-plant. In fact, I kept trying to tiptoe to the door, but every time I made a move, lost my nerve. 'If only you practised safe sex, David, and would just go fuck yourself,' she said quietly.

'You have no idea what a poor opinion I have of myself – and how little I deserve it,' Studz sulked egotistically. 'Haven't I spent my life trying to help people?'

'Yes, the world so needs more men like you, Studz, willing to tackle its problems and challenge injustice . . . That's a quote for the notes I've written for your eulogy because I am going to kill you. Why didn't you tell me about the blackmail earlier, before you re-mortgaged our home for the second bloody time?'

'It would have been a breach of patient/doctor confidentiality,' he joked darkly, carving himself a warm slab of the bread Jasmine had baked.

'*Now* you have morals! That's fucking helpful. I took you for better or for worse. You just took me for everything . . . I'm about to do what I should have done a long time ago, David. I'm divorcing you.'

'I can't afford a divorce. Or the scandal. If you divorce me I'll get custody.' From my hiding place I watched as he casually slathered homemade marmalade onto his bread. 'And then you'll get no maintenance. That "sleeping rough on the streets of London" look. Do you think that will work for you?'

Jazz guffawed. 'You'll never get custody. Who would ever believe *you* are a good dad? You don't even know you have a son. You're just vaguely aware of someone a bit shorter living in the house.'

'Still, a father like me is better than a whoring mother.' He re-knotted his swimming towel, offering me a choice view of his infamous manhood.

'*You're* the whore, David. The girl from *Cats*, the Hollywood bimbo for UNICEF, the *Newsnight* reporter, our masseuse, your researcher, the . . .'

'Ah, but can you prove it? Whereas I have a whole dossier on your Bedroom Olympics. Including your current ex-con. What was he in for? Murder, wasn't it? Oh, the judge is going to love that.' He took a hearty bite of his bread and munched appreciatively. 'When you stopped pestering me for sex, I guessed you were getting serviced somewhere else and had you followed.' He mopped crumbs from his cruel lips. 'Some rather good snaps too. Especially the ones on that student's mobile phone, which he "lost" didn't he – of you being penetrated with a champagne bottle. *Very* embarrassing when *that* comes out. I mean, it wasn't even vintage. Good God, I don't even think it was *French*!' he concluded viperishly, licking the marmalade from his fingers, one at a time.

Jazz looked at her husband in staggered disbelief. If my eyes could shoot out lethal rays like Disney superheroes, I would have vaporized him on the spot.

'Remember on our wedding day when you said you would die for me, David? Well, I think it's time you kept your promise!' Jazz then launched herself with a bestial cry at her husband's throat. She had raked two deep scratchmarks down his chest before he could push her off him.

'There is no way you will ever get custody,' Jazz panted. 'I clean for you both. Cook every meal for you both. I doubt you even know Josh's birthday! What makes you think I won't go to the *News of the World* myself?'

Studz smiled maliciously, mopping at the faint trickle of blood on his cheek. 'The blaze of publicity, the door-stopping, the lurid accounts in the papers . . . You just wouldn't do it to Josh.'

Studz casually cracked open a beer and looked down on his wife with smug impertinence. So much for his image of humane champion of the underdog. Dr Studlands seemed to have the caring compassion of, say, Don Corleone.

'Josh is seventeen. He gets a say in who he lives with, you know,' Jazz said. 'And he'll want to live with me.'

'Not when I tell him he has a slut for a mother. And that if he doesn't choose to live with me, I might just have to prove it in court. Photos and all,' he stated with bloodless indifference.

The man seemed to have had his remorse nerve extracted.

Jazz fell back against the kitchen counter. I watched in horror as she picked up the six-inch breadknife lying there and lunged. But her husband seized her wrist, squeezed hard, and the knife clattered onto the kitchen tiles, having only grazed his arm.

'Do you have any idea how easily I could dispose of you? I'm a doctor. I know how to eradicate people so that nobody ever finds out . . . Not a bad idea, actually. I must up your life insurance.'

Studz laughed as he sauntered down the hall. I emerged from hiding in time to see Jazz snatch up the knife and flash after him. Dread sliced into my stomach as I too lurched into the hall. The front door was banging against the wall. I was down the stone steps two at a time, despite the agony in my foot. And there she was, slashing again and again, plunging the knife in up to the hilt.

David's Jaguar car tyres hissed plaintively, then wheezed a dying breath. And then she sat in the driveway, devastated, wailing with anger at what her husband had done and sobbing with self-loathing for the way she had lost control.

'Who ever would have thought that I could behave in such a way? A mild-mannered, middle-class mum like me?' she whimpered into my shoulder.

It was then I found myself agreeing with Jazz. It was time Studz died a slow, wretched death, involving multiple orifices.

CHAPTER 20

WHEN HUMILIATING THINGS HAPPEN TO DESPERATE WOMEN

There are two inevitable things in life. People die and husbands leave you for younger women. That's all I could think about as I nuked something vaguely edible in the microwave for the kids, garnished it with the guilt I felt for leaving them yet again, found a babysitter I could bribe at short notice (if only supermarkets stocked a babysitter in a can; simply open and heat up), hunted down Hannah at a Charity Ball for the Serpentine Gallery and persuaded her the situation was urgent enough to abandon the event. In the car to Jazz's place, I filled her in on the fact that Studz had not been playing with a full deck of credit cards. We finally arrived, with heavy hearts, at Hampstead Heights.

When our two-woman cavalry pounded on her door, Jazz greeted us in an apron, her hair bundled onto her head, flour on her hands, beaming broadly despite the fact that her eyes were puckered into squints from crying – and clutching a syringe.

'Jazz, what have you got in the needle?' Hannah

coaxed, taking in her wild-eyed demeanour with unease.

'Oh, something life-threatening.' Jazz waved the needle around cavalierly. 'My husband threatened to kill me. Cassie was my witness. Survival of the fastest. That's my new motto. I'm going to kill the Good Doctor before he kills me. By inducing a heart attack. Easy-peasy really.'

'Jazz, love, give me the syringe, there's a good girl,' I sweet-talked, as though cajoling a child. 'You know Studz didn't mean it?'

In the grapple, the needle was discharged. An oozing globule of yellow slime hit the stone step between our feet.

'Lard! Lard! Lard! From now on, I'm going to inject all my husband's food with heart-attack-inducing amounts of lard. David has always loved my cooking – I think that's why he stayed with me, in fact. So, I'm making him dinner.'

I trailed her to the kitchen, where she proceeded to reload then plunge the fat-laden syringe into a pale plump chicken in a roasting pan. 'But you're cooking a half-thawed chicken,' I noted, scraping icicles from the puckered flesh.

'Oh yes, I know. In fact, I've already half cooked it, then frozen it again. Now I'm cooking it again. It's a new recipe, called Salmonella Chicken.'

'But Salmonella poisoning can kill.'

'That's right. And where there's a will . . . I want to be in it.' She was like Blanche Dubois in an amateur production of *A Streetcar Named Desire*.

'Jazz, you're a convent girl! What would the nuns say?' Hannah remonstrated, appalled.

'Funny you should say that. I gave up on religion at the age of fifteen. But this afternoon, after you left, Cassie, I realized that there is an afterlife, you know. It's after your husband dies.' Jazz twirled, her dress fanning out around her, like a demented Doris Day. 'We must devise an advertisement for our next boyfriends. Only happy, supportive, non-alpha males may apply. Men who will cook and clean for us while *we* work.'

Hannah's countenance took on a sucked-on-a-lemon look. 'There is more to life than work,' said the woman who had been known to call out in her sleep, 'Take the highest bidder! But get him up by ten per cent!' 'Why don't you sit down and I'll pour you a nice stiff drink?' Hannah suggested, sympathy spilling across her face.

'Doctor David Studlands has taken a Hypocritical Oath. The reason he's in Africa so much is because he's guinea-pigging those poor people to perfect some anti-ageing invention. And he's remortgaged our house to do so. Apparently he's taken leave without pay so much these last five years and has so many debts that the bank's foreclosing. And he's being blackmailed. Did Cassie tell you?' Jasmine pushed the hair from her face with pink-varnished talons, leaving flourmarks. 'I understand Sylvia Plath now, I really do. Marriage truly *is* a fun-packed, frivolous activity – occasionally resulting in death. Lard! Lard! Lard!' She reloaded the syringe and injected the half-thawed carcass once more. 'How else can I get rid of him? I mean, men often punch themselves in the stomach to show how tough they are, but rarely when they're holding a ten-inch carving knife. However, if I kill him and make it look like an accident, which is what he's no doubt planning for me then I'll get his life insurance money. Like most wives, I can always use an extra one or two million. Especially now that I'm h . . .' She paused, not quite able to bring herself to say the word 'homeless'. 'Now that I'm domiciliary-deficient.'

I looked at Hannah in alarm. Jazz wasn't the most subtle or cautious person. Whatever she did to Studz might be originally reported as an accident, but not after those highly advanced forensic tests proved that his heart had been gouged out of his body by his wife's nail file.

'You know what he wants now, Hannah? Did Cassie tell you? He wants custody of Joshie.'

'What? I would have thought that putz would sue for *less* custody.' Hannah positioned herself on the kitchen banquette, orchestrating her taffeta evening gown around her.

'It is ridiculous,' I commiserated. 'I mean, they may sit on the same twig on one branch of the family tree, but that's about all they share.'

'If he gets custody, you see, he won't have to pay me any maintenance.'

'But Josh is an adult, nearly.'

'Not till he finishes school. And then he's got Uni so he'll still be living with me in the family home. And that maniac of a hubby of mine doesn't want to have to pay for it.'

'Apart from that it'll be an amicable split,' I elaborated to Hannah sarcastically. 'They'll both get fifty per cent of the acrimony.'

'Look what I found today.' Jazz thrust a torn-out bit of newspaper at me. 'A phone number for a Forensic Cleaning Service for Victims of Violent Crime. It deals with Decomposition, Blood and Related Stain Removal. Rather handy if I chop him up and put him through my food processor. Now *that's* the kind of tip a wife needs. How to Kill Your Husband – (and other handy household hints).'

'Stop this crazy talk right now!' Hannah demanded. 'Let's all sit down and get practical.' She patted the banquette beside her. 'Who's your accountant? Do you have his or her home number?'

'It's not crazy talk. The reality is, there are only two days when a husband is great fun to be around. The day you marry him – and the day you bury him.' Jazz cackled like one of the witches in *Macbeth*.

'Studz will never get custody of Josh.' I put my arm around Jazz reassuringly. 'It's the mother's job to be the eye of the storm.'

'Boys need their mothers.' Hannah slid her arm around Jazz's other shoulder. 'You must be strong for the sake of your son. Mother Courage, that's where the expression comes from, dah-ling.'

Pained at the memory of how the predatory Bianca had ingratiated herself into my children's lives, my skin, which already felt as though it were made of paper, was scorched by her words. I could feel my face burning.

'I know Josh's friends, his dreams, fears, hopes. What he's thinking, how he's feeling, what mischief he's plotting. What do I live for? My son's jeans still warm after he takes them off for the wash. The smell of his hair when he hugs me goodbye in the morning. Is that too much to ask out of life?'

'No, darling,' I soothed, kissing her forehead. 'It's not.'

'Jazz. Think straight. Accountant's number. Bank account details. Do you have a lawyer?' Hannah insisted, sitting back down and marshalling pen and paper. 'If only he didn't have that private eye's evidence. Gevalt! And that photo! I *told* you cheating on Studz wouldn't fix anything. But did you listen to me? No.'

Jazz leaned back against the sink, cocked her head to one side and looked down at Hannah through screwed-up eyes. 'Are you suggesting that David and I should have gone to couples counselling? Oh, that soooo worked out for Cassie, didn't it? Her husband is now living with his therapist – thanks to you.'

It was true. All therapy had done was to encourage Rory to leave our marriage. One word from Bianca and he'd left so damn fast he had G-force cheeks. I bit back a tear.

Hannah bristled. 'I'm sorry, but you're the one who ruined Cassie's life. She was fine, she was happily married, until *you* interfered, Jasmine.'

271

That was true too. At Jazz's insistence, I'd been hurling myself against the bars of my relationship to test its endurance levels, as though I'd been a special effects stuntwoman. And guess what? It hadn't endured. My lower lip trembled.

'I didn't interfere.' Jazz prodded Hannah in the chest with a stiletto nail, not hard, but enough to make Hannah stand up, her evening dress creaking floorward. 'I just pointed out how she was being exploited. Cassie worked the rest out for herself. Self-enlightenment is just one of the services I offer,' Jazz then gave another deranged twirl.

Hannah, who'd been dragged away from her charity dinner for this, tossed some nuts into her mouth with startling violence. 'Your trouble, Jazz, is that you openly despise every man on the planet and secretly despise the few exceptions.'

'And I'm bloody well right too. Look at what Rory has done to Cassie. It's male nature to be lying, two-faced and rodent-like.'

'Do you agree with this puerile analysis, Cassandra?' Hannah asked imperiously.

I took a breath while trying to devise a way to earth the electrically charged atmosphere. 'Look, all I know is that Jenny had this mouse she named after her dad, who was extremely messy and slob-like. He lived up in the mice tower in their cage and only came down for a feed or sex. Well, one day, a mate of my husband's, who's a mobile vet, popped in for a cuppa and I asked him to de-sex Rory. Once he'd worked out that I wasn't referring to my spouse, I got him to neuter the male mouse. The next thing, Rory is cleaning the nest, nurturing the babies. Crikey, he was practically reading *The Female Eunuch*.'

'You see! That's what all husbands need. Castration! Or maybe we should replace their Viagra with Oestrogen? Sprinkle some on their cornflakes? Or . . . I know!' Jazz's apron strings were unravelling as she danced around the kitchen. 'I could get Billy to take him out! Why didn't I think of it before? My boyfriend is a *murderer*, after all. He could kill your husbands too – the cheating, duplicitous scum. He could award them a Prison OBE – One Behind The Ear. Three for the price of one.'

Hannah drummed her nails on the tabletop. 'Not all husbands are dishonest. Pascal is faithful to me. He supports my career. We are very, very happy.'

Jazz stopped flitting about abruptly. '*Is* he now?' There was something menacing in her voice. It was as though a switch had been thrown. 'I am so sick and tired of your Holier Than Thou attitude, Hannah. All husbands have things to hide. Including yours.'

A spasm of irritation darted across Hannah's forehead and she thumped the table again. 'This is your modern take on the sewing bee, isn't it? We bitch and stitch. Bitching about, then stitching up every man we know. I'm sorry you're so unhappy, Jazz. I really am. But why are you hellbent on destroying your girlfriends' happiness too? So that we'll be as miserable as you are?'

Jazz raised a combative eyebrow. 'I am *not* the kind of friend who goes round ruining girlfriends' lives – otherwise I would have told you about your husband's secret life and I haven't, have I?'

'What secret life?' Hannah stared at Jazz, nonplussed.

'Well, let's put it this way. I suggest you call the mobile vet because you have a very large rat on your hands.'

I nervously ripped off a hangnail with my teeth. I don't like to be scared – it scares me. After all, getting scared half to death, twice, could be fatal. And this conversation was definitely headed into unchartered waters.

'Why would you say Pascal is attracted to you?' Jazz went on sweetly. 'What's your best feature, do you think? Your marble Jacuzzi or your Mercedes convertible?'

Hannah waved a dismissive hand. 'Bitch and stitch. I should worry.'

'Well, you know what they say. A fool and her money are soon married. And in you, Pascal found a wife he can really bank on.'

'If they made a movie of your life, Jasmine, do you know who'd play you? Bette Davis,' Hannah announced off-handedly, but her face flickered and tensed.

'The man you love and worship and sing the praises of constantly has a whole other life. I'm sorry to have to tell you, but . . .'

Hannah gave off an air of aloofness, but her

voice had become high and girlish. 'You've gone quite mad, do you know that?'

'David has been Pascal's doctor since they were students, writing out prescriptions for this and that. He always treats old mates and family, here at home. And the needy, of course – asylum seekers claiming torture et cetera. Well, as you know, I've been snooping on Studz for months. So, I was riffling through his filing cabinet last week, the one he keeps locked, and, well, I read your husband's entire confidential file. Pascal's been seeing David privately because of a very private matter. The thing is, Hannah, he's – well, he's shacked up with an art student. She . . .' Jazz hesitated before delivering the final blow. 'She . . . I mean *they* have a son.'

Hannah relaxed then, snorting with laughter. 'I thought you were going to tell me he had a gambling addiction or something. Pascal hates children! He's always laughed at those fathers, padding around Sainsbury's on invisible dog leads called "commitment". You know that.'

'It's not that he didn't want children. He just didn't want children with *you*. I'm sorry, Hannah, but the man's just been using you as a cash cow all these years.'

I looked at Jazz aghast. The woman was obviously self-medicating from David's doctor bag.

'Where is your proof?' Hannah stropped, but her pursed mouth was as taut as an archer's bow.

Jazz clicked down the hall in her satin mules and clattered up the stairs, with Hannah and me in

275

tow. We were like a human fuse burning towards a bomb. On the mezzanine was an office which doubled as a small surgery. There was an examination table in the far corner and sherbet-toned walls the colour of a nurse's uniform. With its medications and bandages, the room exhaled an antiseptic breath. Jazz took a key from its hiding place inside the hollow leg of a bronze statuette, unlocked a filing cabinet, then threw open the drawer with a flourish. She flung a manila folder onto the desk as though it were contagious.

Hannah moved towards the desk so slowly it was as if she were underwater. She put one foot in front of the other as gingerly as a novice ice-skater. Quailing inwardly, I came to a ragged stop beside her and also began to pore over the contents. The file contained the medical records of Pascal Swan, a twenty-six-year-old woman named Shona Sarpong, and a five-year-old boy – Dylan Swan.

My blood was throbbing like a diesel engine. This could not be happening. Since Rory's betrayal I hadn't been able to regain my equilibrium. The floor in front of me seemed to be constantly undulating. Hannah leaned on to the desk for support, equally unbalanced. At first she said nothing. There was just an aching, tourniqueted quiet. Then, when she finished reading, a single tear crawled down one cheek. She closed the file on Shona last. 'She only has three per cent body fat,' she said, her voice suddenly thick-throated with sobs.

I didn't want to believe it, but pieces were suddenly

falling into place – Pascal's holidays with male friends abroad, like the truffle hunting in Italy when he failed to bring back any truffles. The heli-skiing in Russia – when he couldn't ski. The weekends he went painting in the Cotswolds, returning with a curious lack of canvases. His studio in Shoreditch, the one Hannah was never allowed to visit, even though she'd bought it for him. This, no doubt, was where Dylan and Shona resided.

'Why would he stay married to *me* if he has a child with *her*? Why would he stay if he didn't love me best?'

'Um . . . what's the phrase I'm looking for? *Joint bank account*? Holiday house in France? First-class air travel?' Jazz replied bluntly.

'Jazz, that's enough,' I begged.

'Oh, but does infidelity really matter, when you have so much else?' Jazz parroted what Hannah had said months before when Studz's sexual incontinence had been discovered. '"It's only sex" – isn't that what you said to me? And "Can't you move on?"'

'Jazz. Stop it!' Jazz may be stunningly attractive but if her inner beauty were on the outside right now, she'd be Boris Karloff.

'Why? Why did you have to tell me?' asked Hannah numbly.

'Come on.' Jazz softened her tone. 'You must have known something was wrong when you saw stiletto marks on the leather roof lining of that new jeep you bought him.'

'I didn't know anything.' Hannah's voice sounded creaky and old.

'I see. So you kept your eyes wide open at work and half-closed at home – is that it? Would you really rather live in ignorance?'

'Yes,' Hannah said sadly.

'If ignorance is bliss, then why aren't more people happy, huh? Besides, if I *hadn't* told you and you'd found out, you'd be screaming "Why the hell didn't you tell me?" I've agonized over this for a week. But how could I know something about your life which is this monumental and not tell you? I wish someone had told *me* about Studz. Then I wouldn't have wasted my whole fucking life. Maybe you did know and didn't tell me, is that it?' Jazz turned the tables with the expertise of a furniture removalist.

'You want me to feel sorry for you!' Hannah exclaimed. 'But you're the kind of female creature my husband is with now. You sleep with other women's men.' Her lips were drawn tight, as thin as a paper cut. And her words scissored out sharply. 'You've become the female version of Studz. You've become the very man you hate.'

Jazz recoiled at the idea. 'You're just taking your anger out on me because you can't believe how stupid you've been. Pascal's wedding vows should have read "Do you take this woman to the cleaners, for fifty per cent of her income, from this day forth, for richer and richer?" You bloody well bet I do!'

'You've ruined my life,' Hannah moaned. 'You've ruined Cassie's life too, making her find fault with Rory. You practically pushed her to the abyss she's in now. You're evil. You're Machiavelli in Miu Miu!'

I, too, looked at Jazz astonished. 'Chaos, heartbreak, despair. I'd say your work here is done, Jasmine.'

Jazz made a placating gesture and began to speak but Hannah silenced her with a traffic cop hand.

'You're like some psychological butterfly collector. An emotional lepidopterist. You just pinned us both onto a board, to watch our painful flutterings, for your own sadistic enjoyment. But do you know what I've just realized? *You're* the poor, pathetic moth, flitting from flame to flame.'

At Hannah's harsh rebuke, Jazz's bravado evaporated and sadness flowed down her face.

'Constantly telling us we'll be cured by taking toy boys.' Hannah snorted. 'It might be okay behaviour for Joan Collins and Cher, but for we mere mortal women, it's pathetic. Look at you. You're walking around in orthopaedic nightmares to make your legs look longer. You're losing circulation because your clothes are so tight. You spend the whole time reversing out of bedrooms so that younger men can't see the backs of your thighs.'

Jazz looked suddenly pitiable and faintly ridiculous in her ankle chains, henna tattoos and rubber message bracelets.

'But what you didn't realize, you silly cow, is

that all those toy boys only have sex with you because they're too lazy to masturbate.'

Jazz rose to criticism like a cobra, striking Hannah's face. With slapstick timing, Hannah hit Jazz right back. Mimicking premenstrual school-girls they started tearing at each other's hair. Their argument was silenced by the crash of Jazz's crystal vase. I gasped. It was her most treasured possession, given to her by her mother before she died. Watching the pink flower petals fall to the carpet with gentle implacability, Jazz dissolved into silent tears. Hannah, however, began howling like a wounded creature, falling to her knees, beating her breasts, tearing her hair and ripping at her taffeta frock. Her day had started as calmly as any other and then she'd just drifted into disaster, like a boat without a rudder, ending up shipwrecked.

What a trio we were. Women fantasize about being 'taken'. Well, we'd been taken, all right, but not quite in the muscley-thighed, half-naked Adonis way we'd wet-dreamed of.

Jazz was being taken to the cleaners by her husband.

Hannah had been taken for a ride by her husband.

And I'd been taken for granted.

Wedding vows really need updating. They should read: *Have faith in your husband. Respect your husband. Idealize your husband . . . but get as much as you possibly can in your own name.*

PART IV

CHAPTER 21

UNDERACHIEVERS ANONYMOUS

Now is the summer of my discontent. Well, our discontent really. Hannah, Jazz and I needed a Low Self-Esteem Support Group, but the class would be cancelled as no teacher would want to hang out with such losers. Besides which, it would be a very small class because Jazz and Hannah were not on speaking terms. I was so low, I changed the joint 'We're out' message Rory and I had left on our answer-machine to say instead, 'I'm out of my mind – but leave a message.' When feeling blue, it helps to start breathing again, but just in case, I took to reading impressive Booker Prize-winning tomes, so that at least I'd look intelligent if I died in the middle of one.

Early in August the bank foreclosed on Jazz's house. Too frightened to divorce, she had to move with Studz into a minuscule, rented two-bedroom flat on Finchley Road. Her beloved Josh, traumatized by all the change and tension, turned remote and withdrawn. He was suddenly quoting Goethe and becoming intellectually precocious. Jazz thought he might be seeing someone, but he wouldn't tell her anything. 'I've done everything except a polygraph test,' she confided in me anxiously.

She couldn't even cook for him as the poky kitchen was so decrepit. I suggested that we shop for some new fittings. 'There must be something cheap and cheerful we can stump up for?'

'Oh, good idea!' Jazz replied sarcastically. 'Just what I need when I'm this depressed and my husband's being blackmailed by a Sylvia Plath expert – *an extra oven lying around.*'

For Hannah, it was all over bar the shouting and the exchange of real estate. Her twenty-year marriage was now confined to a file in a divorce lawyer's office. A marriage is about as manoeuvrable as a supertanker, but at least she had started the process of changing course. Her husband, who had promised that no sperm of his would ever get near an ovary without written permission, had moved in with the mother of his child.

Hannah was so humiliated by the realization that her life had been nothing more than a mirage of convenience, that she was threatening to change her name and move to another member state of the European union. And I had a strong desire to join her.

My marriage to Rory had dwindled to one affair, a mortgage and two children between us. As news seeped out, women friends clucked sympathetic-ally, but were secretly relieved that it was me and not them. I felt like a rubber glove which had been turned inside out.

Rory, meanwhile, had gone on holiday to Greece with Bianca. As she always seemed to be drawing on our savings, I now referred to her as Biancaccount, and our dwindling finances as Rory's Bonk Statement.

Otherwise things were great. Fab. Hunky-fucking-dory.

Like a war-weary soldier, I crawled back to my parent's house to seek refuge over the holiday month. It's the only time in my adult life that I've cried in my mother's arms. I was always teasing my parents with complaints that they should have screwed me up more when I was a kid as 'I've got nobody to blame now.' Well, *my* kids would have nothing to worry about in that department because I was about to screw them up big time. When I told them that Rory and I had separated, they looked at me with huge, dismayed eyes, no longer tough and cool, but frightened little babies. Jenny, who'd now turned twelve, shattered into tears. I set her down on my lap gingerly, as if she were a Ming vase. How could I have coquetted with divorce? I was like a woman who flirts with a sex offender and is then surprised to be indecently assaulted.

I tried to distract them with endless excursions to funfairs for rides on the 'Twist and Vomit' or the 'Plunge and Chunder', but nothing could lift their gloomy spirits. My marital chaos must have been contagious because by the end of the summer, my parents were also fighting. My mother maintained that she was a computer widow, a shed widow and a golf widow. She told my dad that the reason he loves his computer is because he *is* a computer – hard to figure out and never enough memory.

'You're lucky to have got rid of your husband,' Mum told me, loudly over dinner one night, within Dad's earshot. 'You must be so relieved you no longer have to make a pretence of finding him attractive in the bedroom.'

But I did still find Rory attractive. Rory was my rock, my lighthouse. I missed the blinking, inter-mittent warmth of him. Every time the phone rang I lunged for the receiver – but it was never my man.

I heard from regular clients and neighbours that the surgery was no longer taking mottled strays or giving freebie consultations to the poor and the elderly, but only administering to pedigree pooches. When neighbours did glimpse Rory, he usually had a pair of poodle clippers in his hand. Not a good look on a red-blooded man. Now that Rory had two households to help finance, Bianca had initiated a more lucrative line of work which she called 'feline feng shui'.

All Rory's years of rigorous medical training were now being utilized to run pet masturbation workshops for overly sexed cats. (It gave a whole new meaning to 'Heavy Petting'.) The rest of the time he spent on 'pet bereavement counselling'. *Losing a beloved pet can be as devastating as losing a spouse*, Bianca's brochure blurbed.

No, it couldn't, I thought acrimoniously.

By the time the kids and I got back to London at the beginning of September, our Kilburn house had a meek, defeated look. Much like me, I thought. I tried to make myself feel at home – until I remembered that's where I was, goddamn it.

When my husband, as I still thought of him, in the odd proprietorial spasm, came to collect the children for a meal at the local Chinese or a movie, it was like a hospital visit, formal and tense. This is how it went on all through September, borrowing and returning the kids as though they were library books.

Once I was back at North Primrose Primary, supposedly refreshed for a new school year, the octopus tentacles of misery really took their stranglehold. Six months ago, I'd been so blasé about our marriage, but now the wild panic of no longer having Rory made me lose my moorings. Without him, I just failed to add up to a person. A whole person. For a while I thought his attraction to Bianca would pass, but by October I had to face the vertiginous terror of being alone. It was worse late at night, when the silence of my world would roar steadily in my ears. Then I would sit in Rory's favourite chair, so I could feel his contours in the way the seat moulded under me – and ache for him. I missed the hot rush of his laugh, and his rather gruff adoration. I would sleep in his shirt and cry all night. I even missed the animals. Oh for a pet piranha in the bath; an incubator full of snakes in the airing cupboard; a sabre-toothed llama in the living room.

Stupid little things would ambush me, leaving me tsunamied in tears – the sight of the knee-guard he wore for squash, or stepping on his spearmint dental floss. The worst night was when I went to the flat, at the back of the surgery, to retrieve some books, and there on the floor were a pair of his jeans, the legs pointing out at an angle of half past seven, as if he'd just stepped out of them. Jagged black edges sliced and tore me up. Time fractured, and it was two hours before I could climb the steps back into my house, arms clutched around myself, attempting to contain the dreadful hurt inside.

I tried to sleep but was savaged by nightmares. I shrank from my thoughts as if they were blows. Was it all my fault? I went over and over it in my mind; fingering the rosary of guilt, each bead well worn by my mental touch. Bitter regrets, like ghosts, skulked out of my shadowy subconscious to claim retribution.

I began listening to country and western songs with cheery, up-beat titles like 'What Can You Expect From A Day That Begins With Waking Up'. I took to tearfully singing 'Wichita Linesman' and Tina Arena's 'Chains', in between sloping to the shops wearing slippers, a duffel coat and pyjama bottoms to buy more booze.

I took to cooking with wine – and forgetting to add any food. The warmth of the alcohol sinking into my body was all that would calm the chaos of my heart. Some mornings I was still drunk from the night before. Then I'd have to rummage around my brain for a few remaining cells and attempt to strap them on to a bit of caffeine so I could get to school on time. What a way to start the day, trying to saddle up a coffee bean then ride it round the kitchen. But I couldn't risk being late.

With the Deputy Head announcement due in November, Perdita had become terminally syco- phantic. I was one strike down already. And a second was looming. Raw with lack of sleep and excess emotion, I was not at my best to handle a confrontation with a pushy father.

'My daughter is in the choir. When I come to the choir performance, will I be able to hear her individually?'

'Um . . . it's a choir. They all sing together.'

'That's not good enough.'

'Actually, do you know what's not good enough? The way you push Lilly. Your daughter is already top of the class, yet you're always insisting she has more holiday homework; more tutoring; that she's failing. *You're* the one who is failing, Mr Farber. An infant prodigy is nothing more than a rug-rat with an overly ambitious parent.'

If that didn't get me the sack, nothing would. I had the distinct feeling I'd soon be making both weekends meet.

Sure enough, the next day I received my second written warning. When Scroope called me to his office, he was using his deceptive voice, as mild as a kindergarten teacher. Once the door was closed, he just laughed flatulently. 'You might have been the Board of Governors' favourite choice and pet of the Inspectors, but this is just one more reason for me not to promote you. Thank you, *Ms* O'Carroll.'

I tried to tell myself that it could be worse. I could be a teacher at the Robert Mugabe Charm School. Or the Gary Glitter Dating Academy. But I just sank lower into despair.

I would have booked in for some really serious drinking time, if it hadn't been for Jazz and Hannah. The best thing about having girlfriends is that when you don't know what you're doing, someone else always does. When I stopped answering her calls, Jazz came around and banged on the front door until I opened it, to see two of her standing there. I blinked frantically and reduced the two Jasmines to one.

'You should answer my calls now and then, sweetie. Look on it as a useful distraction from daytime television,' Jazz lectured me. 'You look awful,' she added tactfully. 'Where the hell have you been?'

'Oh, obviously at my Joy and Euphoria Seminar,' I replied sourly.

'Oh, haven't we all.' Jazz gave a dispirited sigh. 'That flat. Ugh. Thank God Studz is rarely there. I can hear entire neighbourhoods through my walls. Someone flushes the toilet two houses down and I reach for the loo roll. I'm finishing my neighbour's sentences, crossword queries, arguments. Yesterday I said yes to someone else's marriage proposal.'

'Lucky girl,' I moped, snivelling.

'You are joking?'

I shrugged dismally. 'I was born married, Jazz. I don't know how to act any different. I like obsessing about single fitted bunk-bed sheets, I do. I'm so heartsick and petulant and furious at myself for driving Rory away. I should never have dragged him to therapy.'

'Ain't that the truth. Bloody Hannah! She's the one who sabotaged your marriage. *You* only acted out of love,' Jazz said. And then she consoled the way she knows best. She cooked. Lasagnes, curries, beef bourguignon, all individually frozen in Tupperware containers for the kids' dinners. She also spoon-fed me chicken soup made to Hannah's recipe until I thought I'd grow feathers.

When Jazz wasn't cooking, Hannah was cleaning.

Hannah, usually so well-groomed, was now sporting hair which stood in a frizzy corona around her head and there were food stains on her Juicy Couture.

'Pascal says that living with a woman who is

291

more successful drains you,' she reported, working her way through the Mount Everest of ironing in my laundry basket. 'He says it made him clinically depressed. Having a baby with Shona cured his depression immediately. Which, he says, proves beyond a doubt that I was the cause of it.' The iron hissed angrily. 'Here.' She handed me a load of washing to sort into piles of whites and colours.

I had intended staying welded to the sofa for the rest of my natural life, but Hannah had threatened to use an oxyacetylene torch to prise my body from its permanently prone position.

'He says that being a kept man is hard work. It saps a chap's confidence and destroys his self-respect. In short, it turns him into a woman. He says that he had to schtup Shona, to make himself feel like a man again.'

'Pascal has enough chips on his shoulder to open a casino,' I said moodily. Then: 'But what about the baby?' I demanded, fossicking for tissues in Jamie's jeans pockets before they went into the wash. 'I thought he said that his sperms were blunt-nosed couch potatoes which couldn't travel?'

'There's worse.' Hannah now began ironing manically, the iron spitting. 'They're having another baby.'

It took a moment for the enormity of this to sink in. *What?*

'And I'm forty-four. My eggs are fried. Stale. Scrambled.'

'But . . . but I thought you didn't want babies?'

'Only because *he* didn't. I child-proofed my life, but somehow they'd still get in. I feel judged every day, Cassie.' Hannah was ironing even more furiously, her anger-gorged face sweating. 'I don't know what's worse. To be judged heartless and unfeeling for not wanting children, or the unbearable waves of pity when people hear how I pretended I didn't want babies to keep my husband happy, only for him to then run off and have babies with a younger woman. Pascal is also citing "fiscal neutering", which means he plans on inflicting terminal palimony.'

'So, he wants custody of the cash? Oh, it makes my blood boil. When wives divorce, they've raised the children and run the home. They deserve recognition,' I said defensively. 'But Pascal has done fuck all! Forget the thirty-five-hour week. He's been on a thirty-five hour *year*!'

'He maintains that he helped support me emotionally, which enabled me to have such a successful career. And that it's only fair that I make up for ruining his life by giving him half of everything. He's insisting I sell my favourite paintings.'

'He's worse than a cockroach, Hannah. I mean, Pascal doesn't scuttle under the fridge. He picks the fridge up and carts it out of the kitchen on his back.'

'And you'll soon be in the same financial boat, otherwise known as the Titanic. Your ship will come in all right – your hardship. Thanks to Jasmine Jardine.'

Hannah was adamant that it was Jazz who had whisked up my emotions, like some deranged chef stirring up chaos to make everybody as wretched as herself. 'She put this big hole in your life, Cassie. That gash is not self-inflicted. No, there was someone holding the knife: Jasmine Jardine, marital assassin.'

All I knew was that I'd lost my husband, my orgasm, my mind and quite soon perhaps, my job. I wanted to make my mark in the world, but all I seemed to have was an eraser.

All through October and November, it was as though a time bomb was ticking on beneath our lives. What happened next, the whole drama of it, was an accident that wasn't so much waiting as *begging* to happen.

Jazz and Hannah, with their duelling broken hearts, had been avoiding each other since the showdown. We were all entwined in a slow motion game of Emotional Twister.

It was a sunny, crisp-as-a-Granny-Smith autumn morning when we three women met accidentally. The kids had gone gokarting with Rory and I was panting my way through a morning walk on Hampstead Heath before starting my Sunday ritual of housework and homework marking. The earth steamed and sunlight glinted on the rust-coloured leaves. As they fell around me in the dappled woods, I felt my spirits lift a little. It was such a glorious day, I was not the only one who'd been lured out of her pyjamas. In our favourite coffee shop on Hampstead High Street, I bumped into Hannah. The next voice I heard belonged to Jazz.

'Look at us!' Jazz exclaimed, peeling off her gloves and hat. 'All on the dating-market again. Just like when we met at college. Love is the dirtiest four-letter word. Marriage is to love, what thermal underwear is to sex. We are soooo much better off without it.'

Hannah merely grunted. My two best friends were conversationally circling each other like wrestlers.

'When a woman runs off with your husband, there is no better revenge than to let her keep him! Just remember Lot's wife and don't look back,' Jazz breezed, strolling to the counter to order a semi-skimmed latté. When she returned to our table, she seized my mobile phone from the tabletop and scrolled through my call register.

'*Why* does your phone register ten calls an hour to Rory's mobile?'

'Must be the kids,' I lied, even though I had worn my fingerprint off pressing 'redial'. Rory's mobile phone beeped entreatingly, but he never picked up. Like the rare Spotted Finch, there had been some sightings of him though, trailing after Bianca with ice-skates or roller-blades over his shoulder, looking exhausted, limp no doubt with fatigue from mapping Bianca's most elusive erogenous zones.

Like the pet poodles he now pampered for a living, Bianca kept him on a very short leash.

'I see,' said Jazz, handing back my phone in a peeved manner and peering over Hannah's shoulder at something she'd ringed in the paper, 'Taurus? That's Pascal's sign. Even though he's told you he's marrying Shona as soon as possible, you're still reading the bastard's horoscope?'

When Hannah had heard the news of Pascal's impending nuptials, all she'd done was weep copiously. If it were *me*, I'd have turned up at the wedding in a hearse, wearing a black veil with the stake I was going to plunge into the bride's heart.

Jazz then launched into yet another diatribe on the usual theme, that a husband is something you make do with once you're too old for a toy boy, when Hannah stopped her mid-sentence with a momentous announcement.

'Stop lecturing me already. I have actually heeded your advice and taken a lover,' she blinked neutrally, 'for your information.'

Jasmine sloshed coffee accidentally down her front. 'Really? Since when?' she probed.

Hannah's expression remained unfathomable. 'Oh, a little while now.'

'That's just what you need, sweetie!' Jazz was more excited than by a 'free gift with purchase'. 'Well, who is it?'

'I'd rather not say,' Hannah replied coolly. She finished her coffee, stood up and moved outside. We followed suit.

'How old is he then?' Jazz interrogated, buttoning up her coat.

Hannah's face flushed elusive expressions. 'Young enough.'

'Oh, tell us! Younger men are so much fun. You can educate them, *Pygmalion*-style,' Jazz enthused, pulling on her gloves. 'How old is he? Come on – make us jealous.'

'He's an art student, actually.'

Jazz made a fist and jerked her elbow back hard. '*Yes!* A student? When I said take a younger man, Hannah, I didn't mean adopt!' She laughed. 'So, what did you say to him? "You have been a very naughty boy, now go to my room!"' She was practically dancing round Hannah now. 'Does he have a phosphorescent map of the planets glued to his bedroom ceiling? Does he short-sheet your bed?'

Jazz broke off to rush into the local pharmacy, emerging to thrust into Hannah's hands what she called her 'one-night-stand kit' – a condom disguised as a lipstick, a toothbrush and pair of sunglasses for what she laughingly called 'The Morning Walk of Shame'.

The sky went dark and a light drizzle wet our faces. The rain melted away my newly acquired peace of mind. I was pleased that Hannah had found some consolatory happiness, but as far as fate was concerned, I was little more than a fist-magnet.

The next day I arrived late to school to find the staffroom taken over for an impromptu visit from two School Inspectors. They had, apparently, given in their report on our classwork. Mr Scroope was singing the praises of the teacher who had scored the top marks as I slunk into the back of the room.

'. . . a teacher interested in throwing off the shackles of conventional thinking and consistently coming up with big new ideas.' As he droned on, I made a cup of tea, avoiding the tan knobs in the sugar bowl from wet teaspoons and the used tea bags lying like dead mice along the draining board. I added a splash of milk which was, as usual, on the verge of curdling. I then drank my teak-coloured tea, with the string of the bag dangling from the cup. I was so engrossed in my tea-making task that it took me a few moments to realize that my Head's large lips were salivating in oleaginous platitudes about Perdita.

'Perdita?' I said in an anaemic murmur. 'Unconventional?' What was the man talking about?

'"Having a better sense of which ideas are break-through and which are incremental – and how to progress each of those appropriately",' he read from the Inspectors' notes. His jowls were made up of so many rolls of fat, he looked as though he was holding a stack of pancakes under his chin. 'She calls her strategy "Meeting Yesterday's Challenges Tomorrow".'

My head reared up and back like a rattlesnake surprised by a mirror. That was *my* title. I felt like the female lead in a horror movie whose car is about to run out of petrol in a dark, bleak place and she's going to have to walk for help.

'But they're *my* ideas!' I found myself shouting. 'You stole them! *She* stole them!' All eyes had swivelled in my direction. 'You made me write all that jargon in my reports just so that you could steal my ideas! You liar!'

'*Ms* O'Carroll! Perhaps we could discuss this later in my office?' Scroope's thatched eyebrows knotted menacingly. He spoke to the Inspectors in a whispered aside – 'She's going through some personal problems. Hubby ran off,' he confided, his voice sickly-sweet with fake compassion.

'But they're my ideas!' I said again to all and sundry. No one would meet my eye.

Perdita gave me a superior, predatory look which could have got her a part in a Dracula movie. 'I don't know what she's talking about,' the traitor simpered.

'Can't you just be gracious and wish Perdita the best?' insisted Scroope.

'What I *wish* is that she were in a plane which was about to make unexpected contact with the Atlantic Ocean.'

Mr Scroope's nose twitched. His face contorted into a gargoyle scowl. 'Well, thank you, Mrs Pendal, for generating and then implementing such break-through ideas. And thank you to our Inspectors for their favourable report,' he said oleaginously, bringing the meeting to a close. 'Mrs Pendal, would you like to escort our esteemed friends to the school gates?'

When the staffroom had cleared, Scroope turned to me and hissed his usual phrase. 'My office. Now.' I could only imagine that he was going to make me write out 100 times, *I must stop my compulsive, obsessive behaviour towards Perdita. I must stop my compulsive, obsessive behaviour towards Perdita.* I had completely underestimated her indomitable resolution to win. At my own cost.

'But they're *my* notes! She stole them,' I pleaded once more, as he closed the door behind us.

My boss's furry red brows collided on his forehead threateningly – the man really needed eyebrow mousse – but instead of yelling, he smirked. 'Falsely accusing a fellow staff member of plagiarism, humiliating the school in front of the Inspectors – I think we can safely say that this can be called your third strike. I am writing to the Board of Governors immediately.'

I wandered in a daze back to the staffroom and stood staring at the noticeboard with its Union flyers, yellowed with age, and collection of mildly humorous faux pas from children e.g. *Philistines are the inhabitants of the Philippines*. Three strikes and I was out. My reality cheque had just bounced. What would I do without teaching? I couldn't expect a reference. Roadsweeper and toilet cleaner were two of those excellent options that my careers adviser never mentioned. Teaching was my vocation. I reread a card given to me by

300

a pupil that day – *You're a cool teacher. You learned me real good* – and gave into my tears. Did a gypsy put a curse on me at birth, I wondered.

After school, I sought solace with Jazz, but she was also going through a Life in the Toilet stage. 'My husband is emotionally blackmailing me.' She spoke in a weary singsong as we struggled through the supermarket aisles, pushing trollies with club-wheels to do the weekly food shop. 'My son has gone all secretive and withdrawn, and I'm so broke I may have to break into my face-lift fund. I mean, look at this.' She held up her pale blue handbag. 'Things have got so bad I had to buy imitation Prada. And . . . I've broken up with Billy Boston.' She maintained their romantic demise was because he refused to have the tattoo *Sharyn* removed from his arm. 'He wanted me to change my name to Sharyn by deed poll, as it would hurt less than laser removal of the tattoo. Can you believe that?' She laughed with lunatic fervour.

Studz had vandalized whatever hope was left in the woman. Beaten and defeated, she sniffled into a tissue for a moment, then made a physical effort to shake off her maudlin anxieties. 'What we need is some fun,' she declared by the frozen food. 'I mean, at least one of us has found some happiness. And if she won't share it with us, we're just going to have to live vicariously.'

The person Jazz had in mind to spy on was Hannah. She had been so secretive about her lover that our curiosity was piqued. As ice-cream melted in the boot of my car, we sat outside Hannah's house, swigging from a bottle of cooking wine as we giggled like deranged schoolgirls.

'There! I see them!' Jazz squealed with excitement, when the lights in Hannah's bedroom came on. 'I'm so pleased she finally took my advice.'

We were laughing so much it took me a moment to realize that Jazz had started squeaking like a lost kitten.

'Jazz?'

I glanced over at her, bewildered. Her smile had become unhinged. The sort of smile that goes with braiding your hair and sitting in a corner humming.

'*What* is it?' I persisted.

She tried to answer but her mouth just fell open.

I looked in the direction of Hannah's bedroom but all I could see was the moon, pocked like a giant golf ball, looming over the house. Jazz flumped back into the passenger's seat in a fugue of shock, her eyes bare and round as light bulbs. She made a noise like a tyre going flat, but through the hiss I thought I heard the word 'Josh'.

'What?' My face burned in confusion.

'It's my son!'

I felt as if I'd wandered into a Greek Tragedy during the second act. 'Josh?'

And then I heard no more because the air was cleaved by my best friend's wailing.

CHAPTER 22

TOYBOYSRUS

Jazz was out of the car and pounding on Hannah's door before I could catch her. 'Open this door!' Her throat was on fire with misery. The window wheezed open above us. There was a general banging of doors, a scraping back of locks, and a few minutes later Hannah appeared, dishevelled and half-dressed. She stared at Jazz.

'Where is my son?' Jazz barged past Hannah.

'Why? Is it past his bedtime?' There was nothing weak or apologetic in Hannah's voice. 'He's run along home, actually. But thank you for suggesting I help Josh with his art assignment. He is a truly remarkable young man.'

'Yes. Yes, he is.' Jazz's voice was like acid and her look – well, it was a look which could have parted the Dead Sea.

Following Jazz into Hannah's state-of-the-art kitchen, I braced myself for the whole story. How could she possibly justify her actions? The person you go out with says a lot about you. Sleeping with your best friend's son says that you are a two-faced psychopath.

Hannah sashayed into the kitchen after us.

'Talking about art, we became so connected intellectually and emotionally, it was only natural that we share a sexual complicity.'

'Oh, spare us the details!' Jazz roared, in a voice that could have moved the earth out of its orbit.

Hannah uttered a little hiss of amusement. 'But *you're* the one who told me to take a toy boy. "The bitch is back", *you* said.' She swivelled onto a kitchen barstool and casually filed a nail. '"Kiss my tiara". "You have to be mean to be queen" . . .'

Jazz listened dumbfounded as her own words came back to haunt her. 'For God's sake, Hannah. He's seventeen!'

Hannah gave a brittle laugh. 'When *you* were molesting your tennis coach and I suggested that it was best, in general, not to shtup someone you could have given birth to, you said, and I quote, that was "ageist bullshit".' Her lips were moving like a pair of garden shears. And her remarks were suitably cutting.

Jazz was looking at her with the kind of expression you'd give an incontinent nudist who'd just relieved himself on your trousseau.

'I remember you said that sex with a younger man is the equivalent of jogging seventy-five miles – but sooo much more enjoyable! And you're so right. I mean – look at me! I'm glowing!'

Jazz gave a horrified moan. 'He's my *son*!' she croaked. 'If you were a mother you'd understand! Just as well you never had a baby, Hannah. Although no, wait – you could have farmed the collagen from the umbilical cord to puff up your lying lips.'

This time it was Hannah's turn to be cut by a sharp remark. But it was not hard to comprehend Jazz's wrath. The answer to, 'How do you keep your youth?' should not be: 'At my best friend's house in an upstairs bedroom.'

'Why don't you just crawl back to whatever sulphur-scented depths spawned you, you bitch. Do you have any idea how devastating this is for me?' Jazz said.

Hannah gave a sour smile. 'Well, I'm glad you now know what it's like to have your life devastated,' she said. 'Join the fucking club.' Her laughter crashed like a hailstorm all around us.

I looked at Hannah, aghast. This was all for *revenge*? It was a rationalization so convoluted I'd need Stephen Hawking to explain it. 'Have you no heart?' I asked. It seemed to me Hannah could qualify as an artificial heart donor, right at this moment.

'No heart and no decency!' Jazz spat. 'You're nothing but a calculating sexual predator.'

Hannah guffawed. 'Why do the words "pot", "kettle" and "black" spring to mind, I wonder?'

'But you deliberately sought out the most vulnerable of victims. Josh has just lost his family home. His parents are at war. His A levels are looming.' Jazz paced as she catalogued our friend's cruelties. 'You've acted with the most callous disregard to the damage you could cause him. Or me! Worse still, you have absolutely no remorse. I never ever want to see you again.' Her voice spiralled up into a shriek. 'Fuck off and die, do you hear me?'

Hannah tried to justify herself once more, but Jazz screeched over the top of her. 'Here, let me give you a twenty pence piece so you can go and ring someone who gives a fuck. If you come near my son once more, I will kill you.'

Kill was a little strong, I thought, but I wouldn't be surprised if Hannah were to lose a limb in a bizarre Moulinex accident.

In the handbook on ways to get rid of a girl-friend, the third most effective method would be to say, 'I'm going to miss you. I mean, hanging out with you makes me look so much slimmer!' The second most effective technique would be something along the lines of, 'Here's the pound I owe your husband for going down on me.' But the ultimate had to be to sleep with her son.

'Cassie,' Jazz turned to me. 'You must choose now. Me or *Her*.'

'Go on – take her side. You usually do,' crabbed Hannah, 'because you're so intimidated by her. This is the woman who sabotaged your marriage!'

I looked from one to the other, debating the wisdom of a response. I had to orchestrate a recon-ciliation. But how? To say my best girlfriends weren't getting on was putting it mildly. They had the same rapport as a gun-toting Islamic fundamentalist and an armed American GI. But I'd hesitated a moment too long because Jazz was exiting, slow and delib-erate, like a matador turning his back on the bull.

'Hannah! Apologize. You must run after her.'

Hannah just laughed mirthlessly.

By the time I'd blundered down onto the street, Jazz and her imitation Prada handbag had been eaten up by mist.

The menthol coldness of winter was upon us once more, but it was the coldness between we three that was truly arctic. The social frostbite felt more chilly and bitter than the nights. Mistrust, like a slow drift of snow, had banked up around us, making it icy and treacherous. Silence deepened in drifts.

I rang Jazz and Hannah constantly, to no avail. It was hard to believe that our twenty-five-year relationship was seeping away, almost mimicking the evenings, which were now dwindling into sepia grey, then darkness. How could something so delicately established over decades, be torn asunder so quickly? The centrifugal forces of loving friendship had held us in their grip, but suddenly gravity had evaporated and we were all flying off into space.

I thought of writing to Jazz, but what could I say? *Am so sorry your husband is a diseased philanderer, your house has been remortgaged and sold from under you, and your best friend is shagging your son.* But there just didn't seem to be a Hallmark card to cover that.

Lose a friend, gain a mother. Just when I thought things couldn't get any worse, my mother moved in. She said she had left my father because of the other 'she' in his life – the shed. Apparently he was always in there, mucking around with bolts and wires and computery things. 'On the keyboard of life, always keep one finger on the Escape key, dear,' she informed me. I emailed my father: *Shed some light, please?*

All week she catalogued my father's shortcomings. 'He's always timing things. "Oh, that walk took ten minutes and seventeen seconds". The man would time a guilt trip, Cassandra, if he could. Except of course he never goes on any!' she bawled.

My kids took to their beds. Jazz potty-trained her son early and had him into a bed by the age of two, while I had kept lowering my cot bases so the kids couldn't get out and wake me in the traditional toddler way – by pulling out my nostril hairs and singing 'Come on everyone get happy.' I'm a believer in kids taking long afternoon naps – but not when thay are at the age of puberty. This was *not* healthy.

Jamie had become so delinquent that I had to attend his parent-teacher evening under an assumed name. As for Jen, the only words my twelve-year-old daughter had addressed to me for the last six months were, 'I need money.' She was at that stage of locking herself in her bedroom and not coming out again until she leaves for University. Although the way her grades had been going since the summer, I think she was laying the foundations for a fabulous career in hamburger-flipping in some fast-food joint. And it was all my fault. I was a bad mother. My mother report card would read *Must Try Harder*.

Things had become so morbid, it was a wonder Vincent Price didn't drop in. Mum and I numbed our mutual heartache with alcohol – something I would normally have done with my girlfriends. But after the second bottle I started convincing myself that I was better off without Jazz and Hannah.

'I never liked either of those bossy-boots,' my mother confided, calling me to the dinner-table, just as she had done when I was a child. Oh, and just look at what I'd achieved and how I'd matured since then!

But shedding friends is harder than shedding pounds. There may be fifty ways to leave your lover, but leaving your mates is much more difficult.

'Sorry, guys, I don't want to play with you any more,' just doesn't cut it once you're out of the school playground. 'I think we should start seeing other people,' didn't really hit the spot either. Nor did, 'Look, I just don't want to see you any more.'

'You're better off without them, dear,' Mum concluded.

'Gggwwwhhhfffgh,' I replied.

'And you're better off without that lazy bugger of a husband of yours too, love.'

'FFFFFghwwwwaaach,' I added, before keeling over.

No orgasm, no husband, no mind and now – no friends. As soon as I sobered up, I vowed to leave my brain to medical science. Unlike me, it had obviously never been used.

CHAPTER 23

YOU ARE GOING TO ENJOY THIS MARRIAGE EVEN IF I HAVE TO DIVORCE YOU TO DO SO

Beginnings are easy. We know how to fall in love. Our bodies tell us what to do. We have all those pop songs, arias, poems, films and books which celebrate the euphoria. No, it's endings that are hard. What about the times when love no longer casts its spell? When joy has evaporated and we're filled instead with bile and blame?

'What if you crave passion, sex, friendship and children – all with the same partner? Can such miracles occur?' I asked the woman in the food-splotched bathrobe in the mirror, only to discover, to my horror, that it was me.

The realization that life hasn't quite turned out the way we thought it would hits us all at some time. It is prompted by many things. A lover leaving, the kids flying the nest . . . other people's gazebo extensions. For me, it was waking up alone in my marital bed with images of Bianca's spandex bikini thong between my husband's teeth, to find myself surrounded by wine bottles and chocolate

310

boxes, watching *I'm a Celebrity Get Me Out of Here*. You'd think reality TV shows would have helped to remind me that there are people out there who are even sadder than me. But without Rory or the company of my two best mates, I too could hear the jungle beasts growling and prowling as my little campfire flickered down to its embers.

Now that the friendship with Hannah and Jazz had evaporated, I wondered how many of our conversations had gone by, casually, taken for granted, unembraced? How I ached for one of those light-hearted chats about boot-leg jeans and body waxing. Girlfriends share secret lagoons of knowledge about each other's moods and dreams. One evening, unable to bear the empty skeletal coat hangers on Rory's side of the cupboards, I began to fill his space with my possessions, and found a card Jazz had given me at teacher's college.

Friends, you and me . . .
You brought another friend and then there were
   three.
We started our group. Our circle of friends.
And like a circle, there's no beginning or end.

On any normal day, I would have rung the cliché police, but tonight instead, found myself blubbering.

In the dentist's waiting room the next day, I picked up a mag and flicked to an article on health. It said that friendships between women not only

311

fill the emotional gaps in our marriages, but also reduce the risk of disease by lowering blood pressure, heart rate and cholesterol. The receptionist called my name but I kept on reading, riveted. I could have been in a hospital casualty ward cradling my severed arm in a Waitrose bag and still wouldn't have moved. It went on to say that not having a close friend was as detrimental to a woman's health as heavy smoking.

Oh great. With so little time left to live, why bother with fillings and flossings? I got up and left the surgery, unseen.

For the first time ever in my life, work was no salvation, although I tried to maintain an aura of zeal for the sake of my class. Luckily, there was a super-bug running rampant in London schools, so constant vomit-mopping kept me busy.

I had my coat on to go home one afternoon when Scroope called an impromptu staff meeting to announce that the promotion was going to Perdita. I sensed my mouth twitch into what I hoped was a smile, but was more like a rictus. Actually, the smile felt as though some multi-legged tropical insect was climbing across my chin.

Perdita was so gobsmacked with surprise that she nearly dropped her acceptance speech. 'Yesterday is history. Tomorrow is mystery. And today is a gift. That's why it's called "the present". Thank you for my present, Mr Scroope. I look forward to working as Deputy to such an inspirational Headmaster . . . No hard feelings,' Perdita effervesced as she passed me, her voice so sickly-sweet that I nearly slipped into a hyperglycaemic coma.

As the other staff members expressed their strong desire that Perdita made a success of her new job, I expressed *my* strong desire to anchor her with weights in a Jacuzzi with a school of piranhas.

Like a wayward schoolgirl I was once more summoned to Scroope's office. He explained that the Board of Governors, having seen my three written warnings, had left my fate in his hands. But as I had made my hostility to his new Deputy Head so apparent, it was clear to all that it would be best for the school if I saw this as a lifestyle down-scaling opportunity. When I looked at him blankly he tried speaking in English and suggested that I move on. I thought the same thing. But where should I move to? Emigration to Mars looked attractive at this point.

As Scroope droned on about my shortcomings, I looked out of the window through the drizzle at the brutish traffic. There was too much acrimony and way, way too much orange acrylic carpet in this school for me. The uninspired aspidistra in the Principal's office was dusty and wilting – and I knew just how it felt. As I watched the day dying through the wet window, I felt as though I was buckling from pressure – like trying to close a submarine hatch against a weight of water. As a primary school teacher, I had missed my calling.

I was much more suited to a job in a Philosophy Department. 'What is a grade? In fact, what is life? And is it really worth fucking living?'

An urgent, choking sob burst out of me and I was up, blundering from the office, down the corridor and out of the gate into the squelching world.

There is no doubt that the most satisfying sensation in the Universe is to bump into the woman your husband has left you for, in a bikini in a communal change room, while *you're* still dressed and *she's* naked, unwaxed and has gained 8 pounds. But needless to say, it never, ever happens this way. As I barrelled blindly on towards Camden, who did I run smack bang into? Rory and Bianca, of course. To say I wasn't looking my best was to put it mildly. I was gasping and wheezing, my nose was streaming and my eyes were swollen into slits from weeping.

As I stood there dripping in the rain, they remained in an oasis of warmth and calm, cocooned beneath their huge brolly. I thought about smiling hello, but it was just a waste of facial muscles.

'Oh . . . I've been meaning to call . . .' Rory stammered. His tone was one of pained geniality.

'Oh, don't worry. My life's been so busy, what with the sale at Asda and the dishwasher filter needing changing and all.'

I wanted to cling to my husband, like Robinson Crusoe clinging to his life-raft. Rory's eyes were bright and he swallowed hard several times. The muscles in his throat tensed and knotted, which made me feel that he too was fighting off an emotion he did not want witnessed.

Bianca gave me a chilly smile. 'Cassandra, that coat! I'm sure there's a homeless person in Romania who would just love it. Although, actually, on second viewing, I think even a homeless Romanian would send it back!' she chortled appreciatively at her own wit.

Bianca, of course, was looking delicate and expensive in furtrimmed cashmere. 'Well, your coat looks very pretty anyway,' I said, wondering if Rory had bought it for her.

'Oh, but it's such a burden you know, being pretty. Especially when you want people to take you seriously. I've always thought I'd gain more intellectual respect if I had a broken nose or a scar or something.'

'Really? Well, would you like me to smash your face in right now?' I offered.

Rory quickly stifled a laugh. Bianca, on the other hand, looked shocked and a little frightened before sighing condescendingly. 'You just make it clearer and clearer why your husband left you. Come along, Rory.'

Emotions scudded like weather across Rory's face. He hesitated – a pooch pulling on his leash. 'I'm taking the kids tonight, Cass. To the cinema. And they they're sleeping over. You didn't forget, did you?'

I had forgotten, in fact. With no job, no friends, no husband, Mum busy burning down Dad's shed, and now not even my children for company, I was adrift with no shore nor rescue in sight.

'Yeah, I must be going too,' I said. 'I'm sooo busy . . . I need to get home urgently to clean the neck of my tomato sauce bottle.'

And I turned on my heel to walk in the other direction. With my head bent against the rain, I must have looked like a dark question mark in the headlights of passing cars. And the question I was proposing was this – what the fuck had happened to my life?

I followed my feet, crisp packets scuttling and skittering in the windy gutters. It was 5 p.m. and already dark. I should have gone back to school for my books, but I just walked on, not caring about getting lost. It was an emotional map I needed. A life-compass.

There is a despondent grandeur to London's architecture, reminiscent of an old lady wearing a fur coat she's had since her thirties. I veered past the terraced houses of Primrose Hill and on into Regents Park. Trees thrashed in the wind. Towards Euston, the streets disintegrated into flimsy tower blocks which had spread like an architectural carcinoma after the Blitz.

On and on I walked. London in the winter is as grey as a parking garage; the monochrome colours matched my mood. The smell after rain was tart, and the air chilly. As I got closer to the

City, giant hypodermic buildings needled the sky. The beacon atop Canary Wharf resembled a push button on a toilet. One touch and London, with all its stench and chaos and rotting history, would just be flushed away. Cars clattered by, but down on the river, between Blackfriars Bridge and the Tower of London, it was dark and deserted.

I stood on the lip of the Thames, watching the wind whip the crests of the waves into cruel smiles. I don't know exactly how long I stood there on the riverbank, but Big Ben marked the hours with sepulchrally deep chimes. As the tide turned, the grey and white ripples became the colour of a gloomy tweed. Circumstances closed in around me like the sides of a coffin. I felt as if a great lid was being screwed down on me. Even though it was shadowy and murky beneath the bridges, so many long-hidden home truths were suddenly brought into the blinding light. I had undermined my own marriage. My fault. My fault. In the rear-view mirror of marriage guidance, every infringement, every flouted rule, every scrape, every emotional hit and run, is examined in minute detail, magnifying the problems. My fault. My fault. I had been unhappy, yes. But not as unhappy as I was now. Recklessly, I began to climb over the railing of the wharf on the East Thames path and teetered above the fast-flowing current. I was overcome with a desire to reinvent myself; to leave my clothes on a beach and fake suicide, emerging with a new identity as an hotel heiress say . . . or a beautiful, flame-haired sex therapist.

People can re-sit driving tests, so why can't we re-sit our lives when we fail? At that moment, the urge to kill myself off, like a character in a soap opera whose plots have got stale, was incredibly strong. I was shocked that such a thought could occur to me. There was no history of insanity in my family, except that my father did give up a job as a musician to become an accountant.

But what abruptly changed my mind about 'ending it all', was that just at that moment, I overbalanced. The eternity between losing my foothold and realizing that I was really going to fall to my watery death brought about a whole host of revelations, chief amongst these being that I no longer wanted to slowly sink, crippled by the terrible inertia of depression. It was such a relief to know for the first time in months that I was no longer in danger from this emotion. Anchored by my love for my children, negative feelings could no longer wash me out to sea.

But of course, the fucking river could.

As the scream ripped from my throat, I hit the cold with such force that it left me winded. I flailed out wildly, waiting for the surging water to pull me under . . . but there was no surging. In fact, there was no under. I groped about, plunging my hands into freezing . . . gloop. In the dark, I hadn't noticed how far out the tide had receded. Realizing that I had merely plopped onto my arse into the crud and mud, I laughed raucously. And once I started, I couldn't stop. The laughing and the frantic rush of the indifferent river out beyond me, seagulls gossiping casually overhead, helped put me back in my place.

Just because a relationship has ended doesn't mean it's a failure. The real failure is the marriage that has long worn out but which drags itself along in boredom and bitterness. Like two astronauts crammed into a space capsule, the loveless couple go hurtling through space together, starving each other of oxygen.

And so it was, on this bleak December night, sitting on the mudflats of the Thames with a bruised bottom, that I came to the conclusion that I didn't need my husband. In truth, I had always run the family single-handedly. Like most wives, I was a married single mum. Since the separation, the children had been cowed into obedience. Sympathy for me had calmed their behaviour and increased their consideration. And without Rory – well, in reality, it just meant that there was just one less child to look after.

To see the whole picture, sometimes you have to step out of the frame. I climbed back behind the railings. My hands were frozen, lips numb, coat porcupined in mud icicles as I hailed a taxi to take me home.

I had been a pushover for way, way too long. I was the type who would look both ways before crossing my arms. Obviously my sole purpose in life was to act as a warning to others. I couldn't blame Jazz, because the inequalities she'd pointed out in my marriage were real. And I had been guilty of a self-annihilating compliance. My friends, my family, the staff at school, my husband – they had all treated me like a slave. I did everything but peel them grapes and fan them with lotus leaves. Enough of my old life. I was reborn! I could now win the Shirley MacLaine Previous Life Achievement Award. As soon as I got home I would take drastic measures. I would sack Jazz, Hannah and Rory from my Friends and Family list with British Telecom. That would show them!

And then I would get a dog. Rory had been right about that, at least. Dogs are loyal, always happy to see you and are rarely stolen by another woman.

I felt the stirrings of a fledgling hope. I couldn't believe I'd stood on the precipice like that. But like getting dumped in big surf, sometimes you have to touch bottom in order to know which way is up.

CHAPTER 24

THE COMEUPPANCE

I awoke feeling big, bouncy and bumptious. (Take advantage while stocks last.) Not even my impending unemployment was enough to capsize my spirits. Scroope had decided to keep me on until Christmas, but he made me pay for his leniency by assigning me Late Duty every bloody day.

It was the last day of term, a wet Thursday afternoon and I was waiting in the bleak pre-fab building designated as the 'late room' with one child whose working mother had called an hour and a half ago to sob hysterically that she was stuck in traffic. Been there; been driven mad by that. Because I didn't want the kid to be in trouble or the mother to be blacklisted, I went to the office and signed out, called goodbye to my hideous Headmaster, loudly and firmly – then sneaked back down the hall to wait with the little boy, on the sly, in the quiet of the sick bay. Once he'd been dispatched home, out through a side gate and into the arms of his harassed parent, the atmosphere grew eerie. There was usually one caretaker holed up in the basement, smoking, but he too had left for Christmas. The school, all shut up and locked, seemed to be holding its breath.

Unnerved by the silence, and suppressing my sadness at having to leave my job, I snatched up my bag and tiptoed back past the Headmaster's office towards the staff car park. I was nearly out of the door, when I heard the strangest noise. The muffled thuds and moans emanating from the Head's office made me think he was definitely still in there and possibly having a heart attack. Except, of course, he didn't have a heart. With the stealth that comes from years of maternal spying, I squeezed open the door to Scroope's inner sanctum.

The look on my face must have registered more surprise than the congregation at Michael Jackson's wedding. Because there was my Headmaster with his trousers around his knees, spanking a bare-buttocked Perdita who was lying across his desk, skirt up, panties down. As the ruler swished across her porcelain buttocks she whimpered, 'I won't let other boys touch me again. Only you, sir.'

It was torture not to erupt into hysterical guffawing but I didn't want to alert them to my presence. Not until I had savoured the delicious piquancy of the moment – *and* videoed it for posterity on my mobile phone camera.

Their whacking and whimpering was so loud that I got a good minute of footage before

Scroope caught sight of me standing there, filming. He then looked like a hippopotamus having an epileptic fit. His Adams apple zoomed up and down his oesophagus like a mouse on amphetamines.

'Gee, I'm not sure this complies with Health and Safety regulations, are you, Mr Scroope?' I said loudly. 'Did you fill in the Risk Assessment form? Hmmm, let me think. What would fucking a member of staff on your desk rate? A medium, low or high-risk category? I would say high, wouldn't you? I mean, let's just think about the perceived risks and possible outcomes, shall we? Are you wearing a condom? No. Well, that would make it a high risk then. Oh. And what about a splinter or a paper cut – on a very private part of your anatomy. Not good Health and Safety is it, hmmm? Then there's the possible risk of me reporting you to the Board of Governors.' His ginger eyes, under fizzing brows, skittered around the room. 'Would you say that counts as a low, medium or high risk? I would say high, very high, you asshole. Unless I get reinstated. Possible outcomes if I don't? Let's see . . . accusations of corruption, public disgrace and humiliation – oh, and of course, divorce. Risk assessment of me calling your wife right now and forwarding her this video footage I've just taken on my mobile phone? Oh, high. Very, very, very, fucking high actually!'

'But . . . but . . .' Scroope gurgled in the quicksands

of moral justifications for a while before he went under. 'My marriage has been sexless for so long. But this has nothing to do with Perdie – with Mrs Pendal getting the promotion. It was a very hard decision.'

'Yeah. That's what it looks like in the video.'

Perdita was scrambling back into her panties. 'I didn't mean to borrow your ideas Cassandra. It's just I do suffer from this terrible inferiority complex, and—'

'Its not that you have an inferiority complex. You're just inferior, *Perdie*.'

'Have some compassion,' she begged. 'Some teacherly loyalty. Some sisterly solidarity.'

'Gee, I don't know,' I said, then parroted her response when she'd caught me sneaking into school after the Science Museum excursion. 'Duty before friendship.'

'What do you want?' Scroope asked bluntly.

It was then it came to my attention that I might not be as nice a person as I'd always thought I was. 'The promotion.'

'What?' Perdita's gasp was louder than her faked orgasm.

'Yes. I think this is just the excuse I need for you to promote me.' I mimicked his line to me. 'In fact, as you have made your hostility to your new Deputy Head i.e. *moi*, so apparent, it seems clear that it would be best for the school if perhaps you saw this as a lifestyle down-scaling opportunity and moved on, Mr Scroope,' I paraphrased.

'You little bitch,' Scroope spat. 'Get out of my school.'

'Okay then.' I shrugged. 'Perhaps we should just meet with the Board of Governors where you can discuss your um . . . extremely close working relationship with a member of staff whom you've just promoted?'

Scroope went pale. When he finally spoke, it was in a monotone. 'I am sixty-four. I suppose retirement is not out of the question.'

Perdita fired off a round of explosive expletives. Probably because she knew she'd have to change her sloganed herbal-tea mug, from *Best Teacher*, to *Scheming, Lying, Treacherous Amoral Teacher Who Does It 50 Times After Class With The Headmaster Who Makes Me Do It Till I Get It Right!* And all, as it turned out, for nothing.

I don't know if 'gloat' is the right word, but a definite feeling of warmth spread through my body.

'Oh, and by the way.' I paused at the door, 'Re. your rather obvious marital problems, Mr Scroope . . . Maybe therapy would rekindle a sense of wonder and mystery. I do have the number of an excellent marriage therapist – Bianca's her name. I'll email her details to you, shall I? Oh, and Happy Christmas to the both of you. Looks like they've all come at once!' It was an obvious pun, but oh, the pleasure it gave me.

As if Life couldn't get any better, the next cab off the Happiness rank involved Rory.

It was Christmas Eve. The kids were tucked up in bed and I was wrapping their presents under the tree, when the key turned in the lock and there he was, zigzagging towards me, weaving and tacking around the furniture, tilting dangerously to starboard.

'I'm soooo ssssorry,' he said blearily. You could have used his breath to clean my oven.

'Rory, did you drive here? You're completely smashed.'

'Naw, I walked. I was fiddling around with the camcorder today . . .'

I groaned and flinched, dreading that he might tell me *why*. Bianca had cast him in her sex video, I recalled. 'Yes?' I said.

'And anyway,' he hiccoughed, 'unbeknownst to me, Jenny video-ed the r-r-r-race.'

'The what?'

'The Mothers' Race. At her S-s-s-sports Day. It was bumpy and there was a lot of footage. Really. I mean, she shot half an hour of her foot. But Bianca did push you. I've replayed it twenty times. I'm so sorry I didn't believe you.'

When he bundled me up in his arms, I felt hidden, sheltered. From within the deep, crinkly folds of his cuddle I thought I heard him ask me to take him back.

'What?' I pulled away to look at him. It was a change of direction which could give a girl whiplash.

It was then my husband got down on a penitential

knee and made a cursory stab at reconciliation. 'Please take me back. I don't know what came over me. I must have been having a midlife crisis.'

'Um . . . How can you have a midlife crisis when you've never left puberty?'

'I feel so guilty. Believe me, if I were one of my own dogs, I'd have myself put down. It's the only humane thing to do. I should never have abandoned you for that woman.'

'Where *is* Bianca, by the way?' In a helicopter flying too low towards an electric cable, one could only hope.

'What I've realized is that Bianca . . . well, she's only in love with herself.'

'She'll have no competition there.'

Most love affairs, when stripped to their bare essentials, are as ridiculous as people stripped to their underwear. And my husband's was no exception.

'She needs a humility transplant.' He hiccoughed again.

'Well, *you* aren't qualified to be the donor, Rory, take it from me.'

Rory laughed. 'You see how clever you are?' His smile was like an embrace. My heart beat insubordinately. For a moment, it seemed that he really could metamorphose back into the man with whom I had fallen in love.

'I've changed, Cass, I really have.' He took me in his arms once more.

Looking up at his face, I studied him. Can men

change? I asked myself. Gear – yes. Tyres – yes. Underpants – occasionally. But their behaviour? Never. A new invention was required. The monogamous husband. Patent Pending.

'The only thing you've changed is that you've grown longer nose hair,' I told him.

For a moment he looked thrown, then rallied. 'Lemme guess. You're still carrying a little residual anger over the whole YOU SLEPT WITH ANOTHER WOMAN thing. If only you'd never taken me to those bloody classes, Cassie!'

'Hey, I did not make a fool of you, Rory. You did that all by yourself. We went to the classes because we were unhappy. You left me. And you know what I realized? That I don't need you. I was doing everything on my own anyway. Actually there's much less work to do without you. Women don't need husbands any more. If Jane Austen were alive today, she'd be writing about a Mr Bennet, arranging to marry off his four sad sons.'

Rory, whom I'd always thought would only ever cry if the local football stadium got washed away in a global-warming-related freak wave accident, sniffed back a tear.

'Just because I don't always express my feelings, doesn't mean they don't exist.'

I attempted a sympathetic smile, but it was too tiring. 'I'd like to feel sad for you, I really would, but I'm all depressed out. I just don't have any depression left in me.'

'Don't you . . . Don't you love me any more?'

It was a painful question. His mouth stiffened to meet the blow.

'I just don't need you any more.' It was breaking what was left of my heart, but for the first time in my life, I was independent. And the way I saw it, if I was standing on my own two feet, then he could never again walk all over me.

'But . . . but . . . I . . . can't survive without you.'

'Oh, you'll survive. You'll bivouac and build a campfire by rubbing two twigs together and slay an elk or whatever it is you men do.'

And then he enveloped me, hands everywhere. 'Take me back.' It was like being at the mercy of an octopus.

'Get off me, Rory. See? You haven't changed. You still think sex is the solution to everything.'

'But how else can I prove my love for you?'

'Gee, I dunno. In a court of law perhaps?' I suggested, showing him the door.

The next day he rang ten times asking if he could take the kids and me out for Christmas dinner. A guilt-edged invitation. But we were celebrating Christmas with my parents, who had reconciled and were about to use the fire insurance money for the shed and its contents to take a Mediterranean cruise. I texted Rory back. *Very sorry. Can't come. Lie follows by email.*

Was it a mean thing to do? I don't know. All I do know is that being abandoned by your husband for your therapist tends to recalibrate one's view of what constitutes good manners.

In a letter to the North Primrose Primary School parents which arrived around New Year's Day, the Chairman of Governors wrote: *It is with regret that I am writing to inform you of the resignation, with immediate effect, of Claude Scroope from the Headship of North Primrose Primary for personal reasons. We would like to thank him for his outstanding service . . .*

Oh, if only they knew just how out and standing his service had actually been.

It went on to say how well the school had performed in the national league tables last year.

That wasn't the only area in which he'd performed well, I thought, mischievously.

It concluded with *The Acting Head, and a position we hope to make permanent in the near future, is now Ms Cassandra O'Carroll.*

Was getting the Head position by blackmail an underhand thing to do? Probably. But life had taught me a lesson on maths, not covered in teacher's training college: when the odds are against you, get even.

PART V

CHAPTER 25

WHERE THERE'S A WILL, I WANNA BE IN IT

The telephone bell cleaves my cranium like an axe. I fumble for the receiver and croak into it.

It is Quincy Joy, Jasmine's solicitor. 'What day is it?' I say blearily. Through the window, grey clouds slosh across the January sky. In the web of tree branches, wisps of morning mist are snared here and there like hair.

'Monday. Jasmine's bail hearing's been scheduled for this afternoon.'

Bloody hell. Realize I've been scribbling this account on and off for a week. 'It's all written up for you.' Yawning, I gather the scattered pages from the floor beside the bed. 'The way I remember it.'

'Meet me at Holloway. I'll have to sign you in as my clerk. Bring your passport for ID.'

Now that I'm Acting Head, I make an implausible excuse to myself about why I won't be going into school today, totally believe it, and hurry to the prison.

★ ★ ★

333

When Quincy strides into the Stalinesque prison waiting rooms (actually, even Stalin would have found this architecture too brutal), I ask her right away how Jazz's case is looking. Her muddy eyes, deeply set in her serious face, darken. 'Not that good. The Prosecution have evidence from one Billy Boston that she attempted to hire him as a hitman to bump off her husband.' She stubs out her cigarette with a grind of her boot heel to comply with the No Smoking rule. 'He's on bail for welfare fraud, so the creep is no doubt offering a plea-bargain.' She swigs at a Starbucks double espresso.

'Reliable? Boston? First off, he's a convicted murderer and second, he's a playwright. Playwrights make a living out of lying!'

Quincy shrugs. 'What's a girl to do when there's someone in her life she would really rather were out of it? She chooses what might seem the most sensible route for any respectable middle-class woman: *she pays a man to do it.*' She pauses to cough up half a lung while moaning how badly she needs another cigarette. 'Most murderers are traced through a direct grievance, so a killing by someone unknown to the victim is more difficult to solve. A lover fits the bill nicely. This is the picture the Prosecution will paint. And they will not want her out on bail, interfering with their witness. Can you stump up twenty thousand pounds, in the slim chance that she does get bail? It's a guarantee that Jasmine turns up for trial.'

'Christ! *I* can't. I'm a single mother. My self-esteem

may be bouncing back, but, hey, so are my cheques. Still, I know someone who can . . .'

When we're admitted into the Holloway jail interview room to see Jazz, her voice is plaintive with defeat. 'They're gonna nail me, aren't they? I'm going down.'

It hasn't taken her long to pick up the criminal vernacular. The look in her eyes is reminiscent of the glassy orbs of the taxidermied creatures I've seen with Hannah on sale at Christies. The frightened sound in her voice doesn't match the media's soubriquet for her as 'The Merry Widow'. The papers are now running reports about how the wife of David Studlands, past President of the Royal College of Surgeons and distinguished World Health Organisation expert, has been arrested in London and charged with his murder.

'The prosecutor served me with his notice of additional evidence and he's building up quite a case against you, Jasmine,' Quincy elaborates, sitting side-saddle on the chair. 'So don't get your hopes up too high.'

'Case? What case? There is no case.'

'Apparently you told your hairdresser that there *is* an afterlife – after your husband dies. And did you or did you not often say that there are only two days when a husband is great fun to be around? The day you marry him . . . and the day you bury him?"

'Well, that's right. And "where there's a will, I want to be in it". Yes, yes, it's called wifely humour.

I was being facetious. Who are all these witnesses knifing me in the front?'

'Oh, don't worry. There's evidence about that too. Apparently your husband complained to friends that you attacked him with a carving knife.'

'Listen, I'm a chef,' Jazz responds. 'If I had wanted to kill David I would have administered drugs by stages and disguised the bitter taste in spicy foods, such as curry.'

Jazz's solicitor gags and her espresso snorts out of her nostrils. 'We'll just keep that little gem to ourselves, shall we? And did you or did you not tell Billy Boston that the good thing about having an ex-con as a lover was his advance weapons training?'

Jazz goes pale. 'Yes, but . . .'

'Boston maintains that you plotted with him to have your husband murdered, in order to cash in on his life insurance as your savings had dwindled, partly because of your profligate spending on toy boys.'

'No! Because David mortgaged our house without my knowing!'

'To do his good works in Africa. I don't think there'll be much of a sympathy vote there, Jasmine, somehow.'

'Sympathy? And will there be no sympathy for me, for trying to save my bloody marriage after everything he'd done to me? Good God! Do you have any idea what courage that took? Just before Christmas, David said that he wanted to put all his infidelities and betrayals behind us and get on with our life together. At first I didn't think I could work through the cycle of grief and anger. But eventually, I had to admit that there must have been reasons David had the affairs. Right? I mean obviously, the marriage wasn't giving him something he needed. I realised that how a couple resolves the trauma of infidelity depends on how much you loved each other in the beginning and how much you both value your shared past. David is the only man I have ever truly loved. He's the father of my only child, for God's sake. We needed to get Josh out of an unhealthy relationship he was having . . .' (she doesn't use Hannah's name, I note) '. . . so we planned a family holiday to Australia. And what I found was that my new emotional realism actually benefited our relationship. It really did. It helped restore my dignity and peace of mind. And David was genuinely contrite. He'd been under so much pressure. A business venture he was bank rolling in Africa was going wrong. I was resentful. Oh, all the terrible things we said to each other,' she shuddered. 'Well, we put it all behind us. We were so looking forward to a reinvigorated next thirty years. And now, if he's gone . . .' Her voice catches in her throat. 'How will I ever find a sense of purpose if David is dead? But I have to be strong to help Josh through this. My feelings are so raw. The pain will never go away. How can it? Every day it just gets harder, but we have to live in hope that David will walk through the door. If I fear the worst, then there's no hope left. And I do have this hope, in a tiny corner of my heart, that he's going to call and I'll hear him saying "Hi, darling. I'm in Darfur," on some medical mission he forgot to tell me about, or . . .' She drops her head into her hands.

Jasmine's solicitor puts a consoling arm around her client's shoulder. 'Look, you're not on trial yet. We just have to convince the judge that you won't flee the country, commit a similar offence or interfere with a witness.'

As Quincy prepares to leave, Jazz cadges a cigarette.

'The chaplain here suggested I give thanks for what I've got in life.' Despite the No Smoking rule, the match flares and Jazz puffs manically. 'But what have I got, Cassie? Imprisonment for something I didn't do, debts up the wazoo, a lesbian cellmate . . .' Quincy is sucking the liquid centre from a sweet with a wet slurping sound which makes Jasmine shudder. 'The whole country thinks of me as a murderess and I'm supposed to be burying my husband, a feat made more difficult by the fact that he may still be alive somewhere. Oh yes, I'm feeling fantastically fucking thankful at this point.'

In the hours I have left before the bail hearing this afternoon, I vow to do my best to help my oldest friend. And there is only one person I can think of to turn to . . .

★　★　★

The anticipation and dread I feel at seeing his indolent smile makes my heart race. We agree to meet in the Boom Boom bar. Walking from the tube cold gusts of air sweep like a searchlight back and forth across my face, and I interrogate myself about my real motive for being here.

When I tell Trueheart of Jasmine's plight, he erupts into an insolent laugh. 'So, lemme get this straight. You want me to testify that Billy Boston's lyin'? Grassing up a mate is a serious crime in my world, babe. So,' there's a halfsmile on his face, 'what exactly would be in it for me?'

As he unscrews the cap on his Coke bottle the muscles of his forearm twitch and fan out across his skin in a most unsettling way.

'You don't seem to be taking this conversation seriously,' I reprimand him. 'Her bail appeal hearing is this afternoon.'

'Oh, but I am,' he replies flippantly, before leaning over and, with cocky insouciance, unbuttoning the top of my blouse. Breezy and off-hand, he is full of overmedicated mischief. 'Real serious like.'

'Actually, I'm hopeless at sin. I'm much better at syntax. Maybe I could just tweak your dangling participle or something?'

'Think about it, babe,' he suggests as I leave for court.

And I do think about it, striding past St Paul's, towards the Old Bailey, heart galloping. What is holding me back? I am a single woman now. And Trueheart could audition for Denzel Washington's body double. Perhaps getting him into my bed would get Rory out of my head, and me into an orgasmic spasm?

In the area around Fleet Street and St Paul's Cathedral, the streets are full of mottled buildings of diseased appearance. The Old Bailey, with its clean, cold stone and imperious fluted columns is the ominous exception. Sleek sharks, otherwise known as reporters, circle outside, skittish, lunging, irascible. Solicitors and lawyers deal out business cards like a hand of poker. As a high-profile prisoner approaches under police escort, a fusillade of paparazzi shots explode.

Sick with nerves I wait in the crowded Old Bailey canteen and watch the older women, moulting magnificently from coats and craniums like ailing eagles. Slurping scalding tea and reapplying lipstick, I imagine they are the matriarchs of East End crime families. Then there are their younger counter-parts – interchangeable blondes, their short, flimsy frocks held together by face cream. They swear loudly and whine about not being able to smoke, their bare legs impervious to the cold.

Quincy taps me on the shoulder and I trudge, heart in mouth, into the ornate courtroom with its great blaze of chandeliers and lights and sit with her legal team, just as the charges are being read out.

'. . . The 1861 Offences Against the Person Act gives jurisdiction to the courts of this country to try an English subject for the murder abroad of another

English subject. We have other evidence obtained from the police of South Australia, my lord.'

The widow, her buttery hair swept up into a bun, looks frail and frightened in the dock. Although trying to remain dignified, Jazz's nerves betray her, and she licks her lips with her tongue like a cat. Jazz's solicitor has briefed a QC who asks eloquently for bail, the defendant meeting the criteria of having a place to reside plus the £20,000 surety.

The Prosecutor for the Crown objects forcibly. 'This woman intended to profit from her husband's death, my lord. She is *not* a woman who would mourn from his passing. On the contrary, she intended to celebrate it.' The prosecutor, rendered egg-bald by worry, is also no doubt bitter with the world about his acne scars, which give him a complexion like cottage cheese clawed with a fork; an obvious hindrance to any romantic aspirations. This can be the only explanation as to why he now goes on to paint a picture of Jazz as a gold-digger, caught up in the web of the criminal underworld.

'There is no doubt that a crime has been committed. The happy family holiday was a sham. For months Jasmine Jardine had been in the throes of an acrimonious separation from her husband, battling over assets and custody of their son.' He then accuses her of setting up the contract murder of her husband, to get the £2 million insurance payout, by luring her lover, Billy Boston, who was also in Australia at the time as the guest of a literary festival, into murdering her husband and throwing his body into the sea. 'When Billy Boston declined, she obviously sought other means. This highly manipulative woman had two reasons for wanting David Studlands dead – money and sexual freedom.'

Uh-oh, I think, gnawing my nails. And sure enough the loquacious prosecutor now reveals that Jazz has cheated on her husband with over a dozen men in the past year. 'Shady men; men who could no doubt offer her ample escape routes out of the country. Boasting that she would soon be a rich widow, she embarked on a series of affairs, while her husband was working for the poor of Africa.'

The judge throws in a disparaging harrumph at this point and glares over his spectacles at the Scarlet Woman. I want to call out that it's actually Jazz who nearly died of an overdose of wedlock and that her husband had been exploiting the poor, but as I'm not even supposed to be here, bite my tongue.

'My lord.' Jazz's lawyer stands and adopts the obsequious pose of a royal footman. 'This is a missing person's case. Police in Australia have launched an enquiry to try to find Doctor Studlands. *Crimestoppers* are now offering a substantial reward. There is no evidence of any crime, only the word of a convicted felon.'

Jazz whimpers and mops at her eyes with a hanky.

The prosecutor, oozing sarcasm, reminds the judge that no one is ever more apparently grief-stricken than the widow. 'So grief stricken that within hours of his disappearance she was asking about his two million pound life insurance policy and pension death-benefits payouts.'

'May I speak?' Jazz asks, though she doesn't wait for a reply from the Bench. 'The grief that my husband might have drowned had to be faced so that I could help my son. Josh has to get on with the rest of his life—'

'Can I remind you of the need to put your defence at the right time?' The judge tries to silence her, his heavy, rounded vowels raining down on her like blows. 'And through your counsel,' he reprimands. But Jazz ignores him. This is a woman who has the courage of her convictions, i.e. that she doesn't want one.

'Although I have to learn to accept the unacceptable – the possible death of my soulmate – I will *not* allow grief to blight the life of my boy. If you keep me in jail, I can't comfort my child.'

'Please be quiet!' The judge makes a noise like a sea lion in labour and I start to seriously worry about how Jazz will cope with stamping due dates in the prison library for the rest of her natural life. She'd thrown herself on the mercy of the court and gone Splat.

'There is a real concern that the defendant will interfere with the witness, who is out on bail,' the prosecutor continues. 'We have evidence that she once tried to kill her husband by substituting the wrong malaria tablets, thus exposing him to the parasite *plasmodium falciparum*. She also once mis-sized his bulletproof vest. More evidence of her ruthlessness.'

Once again, my fine legal brain goes 'Whoops.'

A sob chokes Jazz's throat. But the only thing that would move *this* judge are his bowels. He is peering over at Jazz in a cold way, as though she's nothing more than a specimen beneath a microscope. Fright shivers through me. I have now used up my nails, and am chewing down to my elbows. But just when it seems that her future is teetering, like a tightrope walker, a court usher bustles up to the prosecutor with a faxed page on official notepaper. Speed-reading, his face elongates with amazement and his cottage-cream complexion curdles.

'My lord, word has just come from the South Australian police that the torso of David Studlands has been discovered in the belly of a Great White Shark. It says here that the Fisheries Office have been hunting Great Whites because of an upsurge in attacks,' he reads aloud. 'The man-eater containing the torso which has now been identified as Doctor David Studlands, was as wide as a car and twenty-three feet long. It is impossible to say what triggered the attack as it was not whale migration season. The victim was in the water at dusk, the most dangerous time. Sharks can also detect the most minute amount of blood and a used tampon has been found in the back pocket of the victim's swimming shorts.'

There is a cry, and I look across to see Jasmine fall down in a dead faint.

★　　★　　★

There are many good things about being female. One is that you are escorted off sinking ships first. Another is that you don't have to readjust your genitalia in public. And the third is that you can scare male bosses, policemen or aged judges with mysterious, gynaecological disorders or the mere mention of the word 'tampon'.

The judge's curiosity overrides his embarrassment and he breaks with protocol to ask Jazz, who is crying quietly in the dock after a half-hour recess to cope with the shock of the news of her husband's death, for an explanation regarding the 'feminine hygiene product'.

'It's proof, that's what it is. Proof of just how well David and I had been getting on,' Jazz whimpers. 'We were frolicking around in the shallow water by the rocks. David wanted to have sex. I had my period. And, well, I didn't want to leave the tampon in the ocean. I mean, it could have been picked up by a wave and hit some poor swimmer in the face. So David gallantly offered to put it in the back pocket of his shorts. That's how intimate and loving we were, my lord. Afterwards, I was tired and wanted to swim back. David said he'd join me later for a sunset cocktail, but while I was showering, I suspect he snorkelled out beyond the headland where we'd been warned not to venture. He was like that – so fearless. A true hero. And well . . . you know the rest.'

The entire courtroom is staring at her now. I can't believe that Extreme sports enthusiasts, otherwise known as 'organ donors', haven't taken up 'Used

Tampon In Pocket Whilst Swimming in Shark Infested Waters' as the ultimate risk-taking thrill.

'We're English,' Jazz suddenly cries out. 'We didn't *know* that sharks feed at dusk. We also didn't know that they can detect the most minute amount of blood.'

She breaks down again. Tissues are produced and a glass of water fetched.

I glance anxiously at Jazz's lawyer. I am not sure if this latest revelation has helped her case or not. Jazz has only been arrested for attempted murder, thanks to the evidence of Billy Boston. Now there's a body, has this increased or decreased her chances of freedom?

The kerfuffle behind me is Quincy Joy, striding back through the courtroom door. I watch her whisper into Jazz's barrister's ear. He rises magisterially.

'My lord, Ms Jardine's solicitor has been approached by the witness who wants to withdraw and has been advised to go to the police to verify this. As the Crown's reliable witness has proved unreliable and withdrawn his statement and the remaining evidence being hearsay and speculation, I'm sure you will agree that the Crown Prosecution must drop all charges.'

Jazz looks in my direction. I gaze back. All I can think is that Trueheart must have decided that he does need his dangling participle tweaked after all.

★   ★   ★

346

An hour passes as I wait by the old cell door for the police and the prison to confirm that Jazz is not in custody on any other charges. When her release forms are finally signed, she appears. I wonder how many times a prison officer has flung open this door for two women to collapse into each other's arms, laughing and crying simultaneously. We are both awash with relief.

'Thanks for offering to put up the bail money, Cassie,' Jazz snivels. 'You truly are a great friend.'

'Actually, it wasn't me. I'm skint as usual . . . It was Hannah.'

Jazz looks dumbfounded for a moment, before slipping back into her usual abrasive banter. 'Actually if I'd known *that* I would have preferred to stay in prison. I mean, look at me, sweetie. I've lost a stone in weight, I've detoxed from alcohol and taken up reading again. A short stay in a low security prison could be the new ashram.'

On the way out of the Old Bailey to a bar on Fleet Street for a celebratory drink, Quincy takes my arm. 'I believe you owe your old man a kind word.'

'Who – Rory?'

'Yes. I *accidentally* let him know Billy Boston's bail address. And *apparently* he paid him a little visit – along with a Rottweiler, a Doberman, a Great Dane, a jar of venomous spiders and a bag full of pythons.'

'Rory did that?'

I am flummoxed. During this adventure in the Old Bailey, a place of notorious corruption and vice,

I have met two police officers who were courteous, and Jazz has told me her barrister had said menacingly that he was called Graham and how anxious he was to keep down her legal costs. So, perhaps my preconceptions were wrong about other things too – like whether or not a low-down rotten mongrel husband could tranform into a Knight in Shining Armani?

But there's no time to dwell on this conundrum. After a few celebratory glasses of champagne, it is suddenly 8 p.m. I have to let the babysitter go, clean up the kitchen, defrost tomorrow's meal, check homework, get the kids to bed, pay bills, do various household DIY and – oh God! Try to find a plumber. It would be easier to find my orgasm again than to find a plumber on a freezing January evening. My central heating is one of those models that has been pre-programmed by the factory to break down the minute the temperature reaches winter levels. And apparently, the repairman I booked couldn't find my house – even though he must have scoured the street for literally a nanosecond before zooming off home in his heated white van to his roaring fire after leaving me a note that he could make it back to me by, oh, say *January next year*.

Rory has always taken care of the plumbing before. Oh well, at least in the last year he's brought religion into my life. I now really do know what it's like to be in hell.

CHAPTER 26

THE HOUSEHUSBAND

Apart from the discovery of a Condoleezza Rice/George Bush sex video, and for it to be authenticated, the most cheering thing that could happen to an exhausted single mother is coming home to find her house miraculously painted and the garden weeded. At first, I allow the taxi to drive right past my house. It's so neat I don't recognize it. The lawn is shorn, the hedges trimmed, the bins out of sight, the flaky front door painted pretty pink. Hell, the ficus tree's even been re-potted. When I dazedly let myself inside, the warmth of the hall embraces me – as do the aromas emanating from the kitchen. God! Is that roast chicken and apple pie I detect?

'Darling.' And there's Rory, in an apron.

'Are you actually *baking*?' My pulse quickens.

'The homework's done and I've put out their school uniforms. I've rotated your tyres, read, then filed all the warranties, bled the radiators, fixed the central heating, de-leafed the gutters, assembled the Ikea flatpack furniture, replaced the dud light bulbs and closed down the surgery. I've also rented some rooms on Kilburn High Street for the practice so you no longer have to put up with all my smelly animals. I thought we could use the extra space for the family – knock the walls through and give the kids a den and you a study. I mean, now that you're an Acting Head Teacher. I'm so proud of you.' And he grins, his eyes crinkling with kindness. 'Your first job as Head is to make me write out one hundred lines *I must worship my wife and wash up occasionally.*'

I stare at my husband in astonishment. What on earth was I going to do with my lips now that I couldn't thin them whenever I looked in his direction?

'You see?' he went on. 'Men *can* change.'

'Ohmygod. What's that noise?' I reply. 'Oh, I know. It's the sound of millions of women laughing themselves to death.' I narrow my eyes. 'How long do you think this phenomenal change will last, Rore? Don't you think I've figured you out by now?'

'Well, there's only one way to handle a woman, although nobody has bloody well worked out what *that* is yet! But I *will* clean up more and listen more, and I have now got directions to the G spot, and a lovely little spot it is too! So lovely that I actually intend to spend a lot more time there. And I love you loads. So it's a start, right?'

Words burble out of him as though he's an auctioneer. And what he's selling is himself.

'Rory, the thing is, I'm over you.'

'Over me? Christ, what am I? The *flu?*'

350

I shrug off my coat and amazingly he takes it from me and hangs it up. He then steers me gently into the kitchen, which is, by the way, spotless, and sits me down at a table, prettily laid with polished silverware on a spotless cloth. Where have we moved to? Stepford? 'Did you really go round and terrorize the prison playwright into withdrawing his statement?' I ask.

'Yeah. It's amazing what people will do when they have a loaded Doberman pointed at them. I didn't do it for Jasmine, though. I did it to prove how much I love you. Please,' he begs remorsefully. 'Please take me back.' If his voice had legs it would be on its knees. 'Forgive me, Cass.'

I shake my head in tight, quick, determined little movements.

'Is it because of my air guitar? Or is there some other little thing?' he asks nervously, serving up my dinner.

'Oh no, not much – just that when the babies were born, okay I stayed home, but then when I went back to work fulltime, you just expected me to continue doing all the washing, cleaning, cooking. You left it to me to organize the kids and get up with them at night. And I started to resent it. My personality changed. I felt I couldn't be myself. I lost interest in sex – Jesus, my pussy's been drier than Gandhi's left flip-flop. But did you notice? No. Which is why I suggested therapy. And we both know how that bloody well worked out . . . But apart from those little, teeny, tiny

351

things, I'm fine. I really, really fucking am!' I shovel a forkful of food into my twitching mouth – food which is tonsil-ticklingly good, I note.

Rory winces. 'Listen, what I've learned is that the only rule for achieving a good marriage is to talk through any problems with sufficient honesty to be able to agree that *I'm always wrong*,' he adds playfully.

Is this my *husband* talking? He must have taken a course at Say The Right Thing School. I stare at him suspiciously.

'Cassie.' He sits down opposite me. 'I know you want me to express my deep innermost emotions and share my feelings. And I would, believe me, only I'm a guy. I don't think I *have* any deep innermost feelings . . . Except for you, Cass.'

I look at him the way a turkey looks at a farmer the day before Thanksgiving.

'What are you thinking?' he asks.

What I'm thinking is that this dinner is delicious. 'That my heart has grown scar tissue because of you, from hurt feelings.'

'Mea culpa,' he says contritely. 'But couldn't there be a Statute of Limitations on adulterous guilt? I can't go on without you, Cassie.' He crosses his eyes and pretends to strangle himself. 'You can't leave me. Not now I know the right temperature to wash coloureds.'

I must be smiling at him because he lights up. 'I think she's warming up to me,' he says to the heavens. 'I mean, she's only kneed me in the groin twice during this conversation!' And then he zaps me with that smile. It's a smile which renders him instantly likeable. I get up quickly and pretend to put something in the bin, just to remove myself from his Charm Range, and am dumb-founded to note that the empty milk carton has been thrown away and not just put back in the fridge. When I open the freezer for the vodka, I see that the ice-cube trays have been refilled. He smiles at me again, so I remove myself to the loo – only to find it scented and soaped. Not only have the tiles been scoured with a grout brush, but the toilet roll has been replaced on the spindle. Will miracles never cease? I have the feeling that even if I were parallel parking, Rory would sit quietly and say nothing!

'I know I'm insensitive, Cass,' he says when I return to the table open-mouthed. 'Christ. My best mate's family could be wiped out by a chainsaw-wielding Triad member and I wouldn't know because I'll have been far too concerned with debating last night's footie score. I'm not good at expressing my feelings, not verbally. But there are other ways.' And then he pulls me into one of his blanketing hugs. He smells of minty teeth, like a child, and newly ironed warmth. His hand on my hip is familiar and comforting. He is like a favourite, faded pair of jeans which I can slip into without thinking.

'I do love you, Cass. If only I were better with words. I know it sounds cheesy, but I'm sorry, so desperately sorry for hurting you. And the kids. I tired them out today with house cleaning.'

And then he leads me by the hand, up the stairs and into the children's bedrooms, which are tidied to pristine perfection – even the doorknobs have been polished – to gaze at our loved ones tucked up in bed, dreams flitting across their faces soft as moonlight. As I move back towards the stairs, he reaches for my hand and squeezes it. I lean across and kiss his mouth. It's impossible to say which of us is more astounded by this act. And then he looks at me as though I'm crème brûlèe and he's the spoon.

'I want you,' Rory says, and I can feel his voice in the pit of my stomach like some Mills & Boon heroine. Feelings long blunted, erupt hot. My salivary glands shift into overdrive. And then he kisses me, with everything he feels. The tiny wedge of beard he's grown tickles me enticingly, making the nerves in my neck jump wildly. As his hand slides up under my skirt, he nuzzles words into my ear, words like adoration, devotion. He also seems to have developed a new dedication to the C words. Commitment is mentioned. As is Compromise. Followed by Communication. Then Cleaning.

'Cleaning?' I marvel, but as I breathe in, I inhale the piney smell of skirting boards which no longer have topsoil, and feel heady with delight. Rory kisses me with increasing warmth, savouring my neck and throat until I'm slippery as a fish, the seaweed tendrils of my pubic hair coiling moistly around his fingers. He tugs at my panties and I have a ludicrous pang of embarrassment about him seeing me naked. He's seen me naked so many times – hell, I've pooed on the man in childbirth! – but it feels awkward suddenly somehow. But then he brushes his fingertips across my clitoris and, 'Ohmygod,' I'm gasping 'Yes! Yes!' And I'm clawing at his jeans buttons, Versace, I notice and not ones I've bought him either – but they could be polkadotted hot pants for all I care at this particular moment. My husband then eases me open with steady, strong strokes, deeper and deeper with his fingers and, kneeling before me, his tongue. The tension twists tighter inside me as the rhythm builds along with the pleasure. My fingers are in his hair. I feel the surge in my blood and I'm flooded with heat and starting to shudder.

And I can feel an orgasm taxi-ing onto the runway, into holding position and preparing for takeoff. My ears are popping, obviously due to a change in latitude, because he's lying me down on the oh-so-freshly vacuumed carpet, parting my knees with his body and pressing into me. I radio air-traffic control. Air-traffic control itemizes its checklist.

He's more focused on your pleasure than his? Check.

He's shown emotional intimacy? Check.

He's cleaned the house? Check.

He's made gravy? Check.

He's made you feel cherished, loved, respected,

adored? Check. Check. Check. You are now cleared for takeoff.

Booster Thrust Engines on. Hormonal Houston, we have lift-off!

It's time to call Lost and Found. Located, one orgasm. One bonemarrow-melting, heartstopping, knock-out, knock-kneed ohmygodgasm. The *Marie Celeste* is salvaged. Amelia Earhart – discovered at last, alive and well. The Bermuda Triangle, mapped. The Loch-Ness Monster, netted. The Yeti, tamed. The square root of the hypotenuse . . . Oh, for God's sake. Who cares about maths at a time like this?!

The inner quake that has so eluded me, takes hold. Until there's nothing but obliterating sensation.

'Luckily you're a woman who doesn't need a lot of foreplay,' Rory says with cheery rascality.

I squeeze open one blurry eye, too consumed with the incandescent aftershocks to get my breath back.

'It's a joke. Okay, too early to joke, but kitten – wahey!' he grins darkly. Rory then picks me up off the floor like a marauding Viking and carries me, wearing nothing but my boots, over his shoulder to our bedroom. The room is sparkling clean, and rioting with flowers. He tips me onto sheets which are lemon-scented from fresh laundering and crisp as snow and, oh-I-have-died-and-gone-to-heaven, *ironed*.

'Wahey!' I reply.

And we're entwined once more, reverberating. And, well, I didn't just find my orgasm again. Hell, I found two. I had waited so long and yearned so much, it made Krakatoa look like a slight tremor. Sex in a marriage? Well, it's like when it slips your mind that you've put your windscreen wipers onto intermittent. You've forgotten about it and then – WHOOSH!

Lying there in my picture-postcard-perfect house in my dazzlingly immaculate bed, with my New and Improved Husband, basking in the sweet and sour scent of our bodies, I stretch as contentedly as a cat – the cats I no longer have to put up with.

'So I can come home? You wanted me to make some changes, some of which I've agreed to – but all of which I'll do,' Rory promises. He starts to make love to me again, then stops abruptly. 'Oh wait. Let me wash the dishes first.'

Be still, my beating heart! While he's downstairs, the phone rings and the answermachine picks up. I can hear Bianca screaming down the phone. Rory doesn't answer and I feel even more deeply satisfied. I notice he's put a basketball hoop above the laundry basket to encourage his aim, and laugh. (It was something I must teach my son – do half the housework and your wife's spirits will know nothing of Sir Isaac Newton and his absurd gravitational theories.) Ten minutes later, he's back, taking me in his arms, all the mess of my life purged, the past purified.

'Yes. You can come home.' Peace of mind softens his face, until I postscript, 'I, however, am leaving for a while.'

'What?' He jerks up onto one elbow. 'Why?'

'Well, the Board rang at the weekend to officially offer me Scroope's old job. However, the appointment doesn't come into effect until after Easter. So, before then, I'm taking a little sabbatical. I have some urgent sitting-around-chatting-with-my-girlfriends-while-you-look-after-the-kids to do. The way I see it, you owe me at least three and a half years of saying "Have you cleaned your teeth?" You owe me at least *five* years of wiping up after them at mealtimes. Six *months* of queuing for rides at funfairs, *years* of being rained on at sports galas and a *decade* of sitting around the local pool bored to death watching them not win the hopping-across-the-shallow-end-on-one-foot-unaided events.'

'Oh. Right.' Rory nods sheepishly. 'But when you come back? We will be together again, won't we?'

'Maybe,' I say warily. 'Let's just see how you go.'

And he takes that as his cue to go again, touching me in all the places I love to be touched, as he looks into my eyes and tells me he loves me. And I gaze back, living in each kiss. Sliding up against his muscled body I try to tell him I love him too, but my heart seems to be in my throat.

Cheesy? Hell, it's the whole Stilton.

CHAPTER 27

HOW TO KILL YOUR HUSBAND –
(AND OTHER HANDY
HOUSEHOLD HINTS)

The English think optimism is an eye disease. But me? I'm a sunny-side-of-the-streeter. I always have a secret hope that Juliet's snooze alarm will wake her up in time to stop Romeo from quaffing the poison potion. That Desdemona will tell Othello to stop the paranoia and book in for some anger management. That Hamlet will get some grief counselling and marry Ophelia. So, when it came to Jazz and Hannah, I had high hopes of salvaging our friendship.

Friends define us far more than our partners or family. Lovers and husbands come and go, children fly the nest, but girlfriends, in all their bickering, ribbing, chortling glory, are the back-bone to your life.

It was this realization, Hannah's offer of bail money and her timely holiday rental of a Caribbean yacht complete with crew, which convinced Jazz to put the Freudian hiccough of her son's seduction behind her. We'd been in the bar near the Old Bailey, celebrating Jazz's freedom, when Hannah had phoned from the Turks and Caicos Islands to extend her exotic invitation. 'So, you'll come and join me, dah-ling, to go island-hopping?'

'Well, actually I have to go pluck a few stray nipple hairs. Of *course* I'll come, you idiot. Are you kidding me?'

'I wouldn't piss on her if she were on fire,' Jazz had grumbled when I passed on Hannah's invite, but I knew she was already planning her wax. Josh, weary of press attention and coming to terms with the loss of his indifferent dad, had opted to go backpacking with some older friends on their gap year. He would do his A levels later at a college. So, there really was nothing to hold Jasmine back.

Which is why, two weeks after Jazz's release, I have my lips locked around the first of many cocktails as aqueous sunlight ripples over the deck of Hannah's gleaming white yacht. This life would make pigs in clover look maltreated.

Hannah, the human swizzle-stick, comes on deck, looking decidedly plump in white culottes and T-shirt.

'Have I put on weight?' she asks.

'No, love,' I say, while whispering to Jazz, 'Weight?! Jesus Christ. Military planes might mistake her for an aircraft-carrier and land on her abdomen.'

There are other changes too. She's wearing no

make-up, her skin is brown as a violin and nothing's very well shaved.

'I'm pregnant,' she says.

If the boat's sails were hoisted, the united gasp Jazz and I make would have propelled us to St Kitts. But the yacht stays anchored with the other big boats in port, snuffling up to their moorings.

'Dear God.' Jazz sits down hard on the deck. 'Please don't tell me you're carrying my grandchild?'

'No! I'm sorry about Josh. It lasted all of a week. I think I must have been having some kind of a breakdown. But not any more! I'm nearly three months gone. At forty-four. Amazing, isn't it?'

'Do you think it's wise to have a baby at your age? You might put it down somewhere and forget where you left it,' Jazz, still smarting, comments bitchily. As we cast off upon the sun-sequinned sea, in an act of revenge, she then regales Hannah with every hideous birthing story she can remember. 'I bet those eyes are starting to water, eh? Beginning to regret all that nookie with your cabin boy now, right?'

Hannah, lounging back in her deckchair, interrupts to explain that she bought the sperm and then had her egg fertilized, outside the womb. 'Don't look so surprised,' she tells us. 'You must have been to more than one baby shower that had two mothers and a sperm donor or a single mum and a turkey baster.'

'At least you're programmed to the baby's schedule – up all night drinking,' I laugh, but to be honest, I can't quite picture Hannah with the carcasses of plastic action figures in her canopied, mahogany bed.

As we slip past coves, lagoons and luminescent, powdery white beaches, Jazz stretches out on a pink towel in a peach bikini. 'I don't get it. For years you've lectured us on the fact that raising kids is tedious beyond belief.'

'So is writing a two-hundred-page marketing report on art-price fluctuations, already. But a marketing report doesn't kiss and cuddle and come to visit you in the nursing home when you smell faintly of pee, now, does it?'

The midday sun may be pitiless but I look at my friend with sympathy and affection. Even Jazz eventually softens.

'I'm happy for you, *I suppose*,' she concedes. 'Now just go and give birth in shame and degradation like God intended. And make sure it's a boy so I can seduce him while I still have the use of my legs.'

'But the money, Hannah,' I ask, gesturing around. 'Where is it all coming from? I mean, with the palimony for Pascal and . . .'

Hannah's grey eyes go a shade darker and narrow like a cardsharp's. 'Cone of silence, you two?' she demands and we nod, affirming our discretion. 'Well, Pascal wanted half of everything. And, despite how he's betrayed me, I was willing

362

to be generous. I sold our house to pay him off. But when that shmuck insisted I cash in my beloved art collection as well so he could get half the dosh . . . I couldn't let him get away with it. So . . . I had them copied.'

'Forgeries?' I ask, painting on a thick paste of sunscreen.

'*Expert* forgeries. Well, as you can imagine, I have made quite a few contacts in the art underworld over the years, dah-ling.'

Once again, Jazz and I gasp with such force that this time, as the sails are up, the boat does momentarily change course for Columbia.

'I gave Pascal the fakes. That putz, the great artist, didn't even realize they were shlock. Then I secretly sold the real canvases on the black market.' Hannah plumps up the deck cushions behind her back. 'Needless to say, dah-lings, I can't go back home for quite a while. These islands are a pretty agreeable place for a tax haven, don't you think.'

'You can have your Turks and Caicos and eat it too,' I suggest, as the alcohol kicks in.

'I can't go back either,' agrees Jazz, lighting up her tenth cigarette of the day.

'Oh Jasmine.' Hannah waves away the cigarette smoke, but for once doesn't complain. 'You have been through the most awful ordeal, dah-ling. I can't imagine being put in prison when all the time you're innocent. At least your conscience was clear.'

Jazz exhales smoke down her nostrils, like a dragon. 'A clear conscience just means a really bad memory, sweetie.'

The sunlight on the water dazzles, launching quasars at her jade-green eyes so I can't quite read them. Still, sitting downwind I'm more concerned with the fact that I'm choking on her cigarette smoke. 'Why are you still smoking those vile things? You can tell Hannah about the HRT patch, darl. Cone of silence?' I ask, and Hannah agrees. 'Jazz has been wearing this HRT patch since last January. She only took up smoking so people would think it was a nicotine patch, 'cause she didn't want anyone to know she was going through the menopause.'

'You're menopausal?' Hannah is amazed. 'At least it cuts down on winter heating bills, dah-ling.'

'I think it was brought on by stress. Ironically though, all that time I was pretending to smoke, I actually did get addicted to nicotine. Now I really *am* wearing a Nicorette patch.' Jazz laughs, revealing the small square Band Aid on the underside of her arm.

I laugh too, but then add, 'So where's your HRT patch? On your ass?'

'Oh, HRT didn't suit me, sweetie. I started putting on weight so I gave it up. Haven't had a period since June. It's quite liberating actually!'

'But . . . what about the blood-soaked tampon in the back pocket of David's bathers?' I ask, bewildered.

It is now Jasmine's turn to demand the cone of silence. When we nod our agreement, she explains, 'Well, I didn't say it was *my* blood. Losing a husband can be very hard. And in my case it was almost impossible! You have no idea how many filet steaks I had to buy on that Oz trip. I found that steaks contain the most blood for soaking up into tampons. I was buying steaks and soaking tampons for the entire goddamn trip. Broome, The Barrier Reef, Cottesloe Beach in Perth – loads of people have been eaten by sharks there, the southern end of Bondi which has a famously treacherous rip nicknamed "the backpacker's express". I would just paddle on the shore, you understand . . . Then at Cape Catastrophe, South Australia, a shark finally took the bait.'

The shimmering sea seems to shiver at her revelation. Even the waves appear to recoil from the bow in revulsion. The air is laced with currents; currents as treacherous as the sea, as treacherous as Jasmine Jardine. The ocean's hypnotic boil, the reek of salt, brine and rotting seaweed, overwhelms me for a minute and I rush to the railings to be sick. Feel as though I'm underwater. Can't breathe. Hang my head over the side, silently heaving. Eventually collapse against the cold steel, my watery eye on the horizon. There is one last headland before we hit the open sea. It juts out into the bay like a bent thumb, as though it wants to hitch-hike to some other continent; some place where desperate housewives do not kill their husbands.

I try to see Hannah's expression, but it's hidden from me by her hatbrim.

Hannah's captain steers our boat through the straits and into calmer waters. A meal comes and goes on deck as Jazz talks us through what happened on that beach all those months ago. She talks until the sun sinks in a positively murderous display of bruised purple and violent reds. She talks about how she married on an impulse, an event that should be included in the Elite SAS survival course. She talks about how her husband changed; how he became self-obsessed and ruthless, craving prestige and then power. She talks about how she began to fear for her life, maintaining that she only acted out of self defence. 'I didn't kill him. I just increased the risk factor in his risky life.'

But it seems to me Jazz has excised him as cleanly and completely as the tumour she thought he'd given her. I poke at my sashimi with the tip of one chopstick, lifting the slices of raw fish as if they are evidence at a crime scene. Hannah plays with her food too, culling the prawns from the rice and lining them up on the table like little pink commas. Later on, moored in a bay under the stars, as the tide burbles beneath the boat, we are still trying to come to terms with Jazz's deception.

'Come on, girls. A good girlfriend bails you out of jail. A *great* girlfriend will be running away from the police with you, squealing, "Good God! That was bloody close!"'

I look at her in the gloaming. Her smile is so luminous that even on this moonless night, ships would detour around her, fearing for rocks. She is a wild, fishlike creature of moist, perfumed heat. Jazz talks on for most of the night, pouring her heart out.

'Ironic, isn't it, that such a misogynist male was killed by a tampon. A point no doubt lost on the coroner, dah-ling,' Hannah finally announces, pre-dawn. 'In some ways it's an update of *Madame Bovary*: unhappy wife is unfaithful, but *he* dies and she gets away with it – don't you think, Cassie?'

What I think is that it's pretty safe to say that after twenty-five years of worshipping Jasmine Jardine, she is now officially no longer my role model. I'm also thinking about turning her in. But what good would it do? A twelve-week trial before a dozen people not smart enough to get out of jury service, chosen to deliberate over who can afford the best lawyer?

At 5 a.m. Hannah fetches champagne to proffer a toast to the three of us, as we deserve some kind of Lifetime Achievement Award for enduring all our cat fights, all that infidelity, paying all that palimony, suffering through a divorce, a death and, in my case, dodgy DIY and living to tell the tale. She then suggests that we form a kind of coven and throw our wedding rings into the sea so that we can start again. At dawn we lean on the railings at the prow of the ship, the murderess, the forger and me, Head Teacher and Blackmailer.

'On the count of three. One, two, three . . .'

I see my wedding ring fall and then the sea's foaming lips close over it. I do still want Rory, but Under New Management.

'What are you going to do now?' Hannah asks Jazz, as we sit down companionably to revive ourselves with hot coffee and croissants.

'I'm going back to work,' says Jazz, the Domestic Goddess, basking like a lioness in the early morning sun.

'As a chef?'

'Yes, but in my own restaurant.'

'You can say you came into some money through a lucky stroke – your husband's,' I quip pointedly.

'Maybe in Australia. They're used to criminals there,' Jazz retorts.

'Oh really?' I sniff. 'Actually my grandma didn't want my family to move to England because she said that's where all those dreadful convicts came from!'

'And no more men. I'm just going to buy a super deluxe, top of the range vibrator, which can do everything imaginable.'

'Like changing nappies?' asks Hannah hopefully. 'It's all booties and bottles for me from now on,' announces the shoulder-padded careerwoman. 'One thing's for sure, I'm not giving advice any more. Except never to sit in the front row of a Briss . . . Jewish male circumcision,' she decodes for her shiksa friends.

'From now on my only advice is never to give

368

advice,' a reformed Jazz adds. 'And what about you, Cassie?'

And what about me? I look at my oldest friends and dwell on the seismic changes which have taken hold of us this year. It's been such a marital saga. Something old – a stale marriage. Something new – a toy boy. Something borrowed – sleeping with your best friend's son. Something blue – finding my orgasm. And what I've realized through it all, is that marriage is happiness and joy – followed by children, chaos, disappointments, terror, tenderness, surprises, betrayals and more chaos. You muddle on for another decade or so then you come to your children's children, meaning more chaos, disappointments, terror, surprises, betrayals and yet more chaos. And then, in the end, happiness and joy that you survived all that chaos, children, disappointment, terror, tenderness, surprises, betrayals and endless chaos.

I've also realized that love comes in spurts. A little, then a lot. It's not a permanent wave of happiness. Permanent waves only happen to hair – and even then you have to get them redone every six months. Love is an hors d'oeuvre, a caviar-encrusted canapé, *not* a staple diet. I need the meat and potatoes of family, kids, new tiles for the kitchen, whining about income tax, the stodgy, day-to-day fare of domestic life. They're the emotional carbohydrates which I crave . . . with, just, the occasional fabulously, fattening sticky pud.

Hannah and Jazz are bantering in the background. I'd like to join in, but how can I stay friends with a murderess? Well, not that Jazz actually murdered Studz. Sure, she'd loaded the gun. But it was fate which had pulled the trigger . . . Maybe one day, I'll bring it up in therapy . . . Yeah, *right*.

And so we sail into the sunrise, buoyed up by this friendly fug of banter and bonhomie, sputtering and swaying and shrieking with laughter, though it'd be impossible to explain what we found so funny. Okay, it's not a perfect friendship. Now that I realize I'm harbouring two felons, it's rather spectacularly flawed, actually. But hey, what isn't?

Life is not black and white. It's kind of grey – like the water in the washing machine – the washing that I hope Rory is still doing diligently. And then I think about my husband. Warm rays of morning sun reach my upturned face like kisses. The air is thick with the savoury tang of the sea. The briny effervescence makes me think of him, naked. A slanting tongue of sunlight warms my lap and my pulse gives a little surge of lust. And as the day begins to thicken into gold, I think that pretty soon, as soon as Rory has become good at Doing Sensitive Things With Snow Peas and has mastered the ironing – oh, the helium-filled happiness of being made love to by a man who adores you – *and who has just hoovered your entire house* – I might just go home for an orgasm.

ACKNOWLEDGEMENTS

This novel was completed with only a few minor injuries from girlfriends' husbands. Needless to say, any likeness between any of the author's girlfriends' husbands and the husbands in this book is purely coincidental.

Thanks to my good friend and editor Suzanne Baboneau, my publisher, Ian Chapman and to the Ed-ocet missile of agents, Ed Victor. Thanks also to my first draft endurers, my sisters Liz and Jenny, Victoria Hislop, Michael Brian and Grainne Fox.

Naomi Felber and Mimi Greenburg were kind enough to help their shiksa friend with Yiddishisms. Angie Mitchell and Siobhan McGrath ran a red pen through the manuscript for verisimilitude about the work of primary school teaching, as did Jeannie Mackie, Jane Belson and Mark Stephens for the family and criminal law, and Sarah Liddon for veterinary facts. In other words, if anything's wrong you know who to blame!

Thanks also to Tabitha Peebles for all that typing and to my brothers-in-law, Craig Doyle and Tim Robertson for various last minute dashes to copiers and couriers. My heartfelt thanks to Pam

Carter for appointing me the Savoy Hotel's Writer in Residence, where I became seriously suite-wise and began this book.

And to Julius and Georgie, as ever.

The author would also like to thank her lawyer husband, whom she would never kill, as he is the only one smart enough to get her off.